VERY MERRY BOOK ONE

LYRA PARISH

Praise for A Very Merry Mistake

"If you love Hallmark Christmas movies, you will love this book!"
-Resa, Early Reviewer

"Oh my goodness, once I started reading, I couldn't put this story down. "A Very Merry Mistake" is a fun, flirty, and sweet Christmas strangers-to-friends-to-lovers romance set in the perfect Christmas town."
-Trish, Early Reviewer

"This book had me hooked from the first page. This book will definitely be on my list of favorite holiday romance books. It had me feeling all the emotions. It made me smile, laugh, and get teary-eyed (sad and happy tears)."
-Heather, Early Reviewer

"The SMUT!!! Ohh the Smut made me feel things I haven't felt before."
-Katherine, Early Reviewer

"If you love Christmas like I do, you will want to read this entertaining, feel-good, magical read."
-Jackie, Early Reviewer

"A Very Merry Mistake is everything I look for in a romance book. The story was well written, entertaining and I quickly became invested in Claire and Jake's story."
-Erin, Early Reviewer

"This is one of those feel-good, very realistic, festive books that is centered around Christmas and New Years. I just really love this book and can't say enough good things. This is a must-read 5+ stars, that I will be reading again."
-Arieste, Early Reviewer

"The characters are unique and loveable, their conflicts and issues are relatable, and I LOVED that it was finally a rich girl and regular guy."
-Miriam, Early Reviewer

Copyright © 2023 Lyra Parish
www.lyraparish.com

A Very Merry Mistake
Very Merry, #1

Cover Designer: Black Widow Designs
Illustrator: Qamber Designs
Editor: Librum Artis Editorial Services
Proofreader: Fairy Proofmother Proofing
Proofreader: Charley Henly

BLURB

A sexy cinnamon-roll lumberjack offers me a ride into town, a stay at his cozy cabin, and eventually his bed. All things I can't refuse.

After several flirty glances and heated mistletoe kisses, we create rules: no strings attached and no falling in love. Agreeing to the impossible might be my biggest mistake yet.

I visited the small town for one reason only: to prove a point to my father.

Now I've got a fake boyfriend.
A secret to keep hidden.
And a choice to make that will determine more than just my future.

A Very Merry Mistake is a standalone with a sweet-as-gingerbread happily ever after. This small-town contemporary romance has a dash of grumpy/sunshine, forced proximity, secret identity, found family, and tons of Southern goodness. Fade to black is NOT included!

This book is dedicated to those who love a cinnamon-roll hero who appreciates a good girl.

HAVE I KNOWN YOU 20 SECONDS
OR 20 YEARS?

—TAYLOR SWIFT, LOVER

CHAPTER 1

CLAIRE

"No, please, no!" I mutter as I press the gas pedal of the gigantic truck to the floorboard, hoping it will pick up speed. Instead, it sputters before losing momentum. The steering wheel locks and it takes all the strength I have to guide the behemoth off the country road and onto the shoulder before coming to a stop.

The engine is no longer running. I'm *officially* stranded.

Renting something nearly the size of a bus—that I practically need a ladder to get inside—wasn't my idea. It was the only option the rental company had, so it was more of a take-it-or-leave-it situation. Considering there's an Arctic cold front moving across the state, I took it.

Against my better judgment, I signed the agreement and continued on my merry way to the Christmas town in middle-of-nowhere Texas.

I told myself I'd at least fit in with the Southerners, even if I'd never be able to park it. Call it determination, but I refused to allow one mishap to deter me from visiting Merryville.

But *this?* This shit is next level.

I push the button to see if the engine will start again, and I'm reminded why I don't drive. Something like this always happens when I get behind the wheel. It's why I enjoy New York and Paris, where walking is common. More proof that this secret trip is out of my comfort zone.

As I lean against the smooth leather headrest, I notice the temperature displayed on the dashboard—forty-two degrees.

I can't say I've ever visited Texas in December or that I ever want to again.

When I turn on the radio, a weather warning plays and it's on every station. *Deadly, freezing temperatures. Ice on roads. Do not travel. Stay indoors.*

Waiting here, hoping someone will pass me, could be dangerous. I haven't seen another car on the road in hours. Right now, I need to take action and schedule a tow truck.

I reach for my oversized Louis Vuitton that's on the passenger seat. I dig around in the bottom and fish out my phone. The thing dies as soon as I unlock it. And, of course, there is no built-in GPS in this stupid truck, so I'm not even sure where I am. There's only a tiny screen that shows the radio station and time.

When the weather warnings repeat, I turn it off. I've never been stranded like this, but I've never traveled to a remote location alone, either. I hope this isn't a sign of how the rest of this trip will go.

For the next five weeks, I must learn everything I can about Merryville, though I've memorized the key facts.

The famous Texas town celebrates Christmas three hundred and sixty-five days of the year.

It's a tourist attraction, a place the influencers visit for their Christmas-in-July photos.

. . .

2

Merryville also celebrates other holidays, but Santa is always in attendance.

A strong wind rocks the truck, returning me to my shitty reality.

Concentrate, Claire.

I search for my charger, dumping everything onto the seat —just a pack of gum, several pairs of designer sunglasses, and my wallet. No cord.

If it weren't for bad luck, I'd have none.

That's been my entire year, though. Why would it be any different in December? At this point, it's expected.

I squeeze my eyes tight. The only option I have is to walk to the inn, where I have a reservation for the next five weeks. I'm hesitant because the boots I'm wearing are fashionable but not remotely practical.

I've seen no one on this country road while contemplating my next move. It's almost as if I'm heading to a ghost town with zero people going in or out.

The straight road in front of and behind me seems endless.

When a few drops of rain thump against the hood, this situation quickly becomes a living nightmare. I try to push the intruding thoughts away.

The arctic cold front is supposed to carry an awful combination of rain, sleet, ice, and potential snow. In some places, possible flooding. I did my research before I flew out this morning, but I thought I'd beat it here.

As the minutes keep ticking, I pump myself up to trek to Merryville, but I'm unsure how far away it is. The last sign I saw stated fifteen miles, but that felt like fifteen miles ago. So I have to be close. The sun is setting soon, and I need to make a decision.

Is my father's assessment of me correct? Maybe I don't have what it takes.

I groan, knowing I grabbed that damn charger before leaving my penthouse this morning. Things don't just disappear. I turn on my flashers and get out of the truck. The wind nearly knocks me over as I search for the release of the tailgate. When I find a handle, I lift it, then climb into the bed.

A shiver runs over my body, and it takes all my strength to drag my suitcase to the edge and unzip it. I rummage in my perfectly organized packing cubes but come up empty-handed. No charger in there, either.

I curse under my breath. If I'm walking, I need to leave now. So I grab my shit and let the burning anger inside push me forward. There's no point in waiting any longer. The road is slick from rain and will be covered in ice as it grows colder.

As I wheel my suitcase behind me, I think about my past, present, and future. I've spent the last thirty-five years trying to prove my place in this world, and I don't want to spend the next thirty doing the same. I want to be successful and respected for *what* I've accomplished. Not for *who* I am.

Merryville is supposed to be my escape for the holidays.

I'm surrounded by wide open skies and land that goes on for as far as the eye can see. It's rugged, the type of place someone goes to disappear.

The quiet is disorienting, considering I'm used to the hustle and bustle of large cities, and if it wasn't for the loose gravel of the road crunching beneath my feet, my ears would be buzzing. I try to pick up my pace, but it's pointless when pulling seventy pounds on plastic wheels against worn concrete.

I feel an overwhelming surge of panic bubble, and it causes my heart to race. I can't do this right now. Not here.

So I try to pull my mind away.

I think about some useless facts I've picked up over the years.

4

When I was a little girl, I'd get panic attacks in public places. Anytime I spiraled, my mom would hold me in her arms and tell me random things to calm my mind.

Scotland's national animal is a unicorn.

The voice artists who played Mickey Mouse and Minnie Mouse got married in real life.

Australia is wider than the moon.

Before the invention of toilet paper, Americans used corn cobs.

The wind gusts make me wish I'd packed a pair of gloves. Then, behind me, I hear the roar of an engine. A spark of hope erupts inside me, but I keep my gaze forward. I find it difficult to ask for help from anyone and have learned to problem-solve alone.

When the faded red antique on wheels passes me, I almost wish I'd stuck out my thumb, but I'm too proud. It might be a flaw that turns fatal if I freeze to death out here.

I watch the taillights nearly fade into the distance, unsure of how I should feel.

As I come to terms with that being my last hope for rescue, I catch the flash of light and realize the vehicle has made a U-turn, and now the headlights are pointing directly at me. When the truck nears, it slows to a crawl, and the engine sputters, then backfires.

I pretend not to notice, keeping my focus forward as the fogged window of the driver's side lowers.

CHAPTER 2

JAKE

"Hey." I nearly hang out the window to grab the attention of the gorgeous woman wheeling her gigantic suitcase down the country road. The curled ends of her brown hair bounce as she struts like she's on a runway. It's painfully obvious she's not from around here, especially considering the swanky winter clothes she's wearing that are more suited for a photo shoot at a ski lodge than the middle of nowhere in Texas.

While she's pretty, it's not the reason I turned around. If it was me, I'd hope a random stranger would grant me an act of kindness and offer me a ride. I've learned that in life, you get what you give. So I'd rather put more good in the world than not.

Many influencers visit Merryville for their year-round photo ops with one of the most believable Santas in North America, who also happens to be my dad. She's pretty enough to be one.

The truck's engine is loud, so I put my fingers in my mouth and let out an ear-piercing whistle, the same one my mama used to round up all the kids after dark.

"I don't talk to strangers." She doesn't even turn her head

to acknowledge my existence as she hypocritically answers. I should leave her be since she's so damn determined to keep walking, but my conscience won't allow that. I've watched the radar closely since yesterday and understand what's heading straight for Merryville.

Time is of the essence.

If it gets back to my family that I left a woman alone this far outside of town, I'd never hear the end of it. *Sure, Ma, I stopped, but she essentially told me to fuck off. So I did.*

I'd never hear the end of it.

Everyone within a hundred-mile radius is preparing for the impending weather we've been warned about since last week. I'm the only idiot on the road right now because I had to make a tree delivery that couldn't wait.

"Ma'am, I'm sorry, but I can't leave you out here like this," I insist, watching her, expecting some sort of reaction but getting none.

I can only imagine the drama if she shows up to the inn soaked and half-frozen. Or worse, never makes it there. My reputation, which I've been working hard to repair since I was publicly humiliated a few years ago, will be ruined once again.

I can't allow that.

But I'm also wondering, *Why me?*

Why did I have to be the one to find her out here alone?

"So you're headin' to Merryville? It's a pleasant time of year to visit."

I put the truck in reverse to keep up with her, which isn't difficult since she's walking like a slowpoke.

"Not sure if you're aware or not, but there's a bitch of a storm rollin' in right at this very moment. Unless you enjoy a firsthand kind of experience, I'd strongly advise you to let me give you a ride into town."

No comment.

Considering I'm the outdoorsy type, and she's obviously not, maybe I need to explain.

"Ever heard of frostbite?" I ask. I'm almost at a loss for words, but I don't give up yet. "Will make your nipples *and* toes fall off."

I'm pretty sure I hear her groan.

The temperatures are dropping, and I know she's cold. Her cheeks and nose are bright red. She'll have wind burn on her face from the frigid blasts continuously slamming against her. It doesn't take much in these elements. Also, she has no water, so dehydration is a possibility, too.

The search-and-rescue part of my brain goes into overdrive.

Each time she lets out a warm breath, it mixes with the cold air and immediately evaporates. The wind violently blows and whips her hair around. Luckily, she's wearing a hat, which will help regulate her body temperature, but her hands are bare, so it's a lost cause.

I look up at the clouds—it's sprinkling, but a downpour is coming—then I stare at her.

This woman may seem like she's got her shit under control, but I can see right through it.

This is pure desperation.

No one in their right mind would walk that far in those clothes in these temperatures without it.

I chuckle as she keeps her steady pace.

She glares at me like she's ready to kick someone's ass, that someone being me. But I'm undaunted.

"I'm Jake Jolly. My friends call me JJ. What's your name?"

She lets out a harrumph.

"Guess I'll just have to call you Stubborn Susan, then. Fine with me. I don't need to know your name. I don't need to know nothin' about you, but I can't leave ya out here like this."

I keep my tone friendly and light. I've heard over the years that you get more bees with honey than vinegar.

8

Her head whips around, and her blue eyes pierce straight through me. "I'm *not* stubborn."

I furrow my brows. I'm not sure if she's trying to convince me or herself. Regardless, I don't believe a word of it.

"Hate to break it to you, darlin', but your actions are speakin' much louder than your words right about now."

I glance at the clock on the display and then turn my attention back to her.

"Trust me, I have other places I'd rather be, too," I mutter. I wanted to get home before the rain started, but I've now wasted too much time. I'm pretty much fucked.

"Since you're marchin' to Merryville, hop in, because I'm also headin' there now." I tap the side of my truck, hoping she'll read the Jolly's Christmas Tree Farm logo and notice the town's name in a block print across the bottom. I'm not some weirdo trying to pick up a random woman from the side of the road.

"Thought you should also know there ain't nobody else out right now. I'm your last resort, so come on." I pat the metal of the door again.

"Or what? Will you throw me over your shoulder and force me?"

All I can do is laugh. She's feisty. Gotta give her that. Merryville is always full of tourists around this time, but I don't think I've met one as stubborn as her.

Logic can't win. That much is obvious.

I clear my throat, hoping to snag her gaze, even if only for a split second. I'm growing desperate. The dark clouds are rolling in, and I'm obviously taking this more seriously than she is.

"Ma'am. I don't think you realize you're 'bout ten miles outside the city limits."

She glares at me, confidence oozing off her. "Ten miles? I'm certain it's closer than that."

I raise my brows. "Okay, I might be off by a mile, but why

9

would I lie about that? It's a long walk in the cold. If you stay at the current pace you're hikin', you'll arrive in three hours."

She tries to walk faster, but her fancy, heeled boots slip on the rutted pavement, and she slows down again.

"So, would ya like a ride or not?"

She looks at me, narrowing her eyes like she's trying to read my mind. "You could be a murderer."

I'm so startled a laugh flies out before I can stop it. "Come on now, Susan. I wouldn't harm a fly."

"Stop calling me that. And also, that's what someone who buries bodies in their backyard would say to build trust. You wouldn't want to accidentally give away your true identity to the single woman who broke down on the side of the road, would you? I *won't* be a statistic."

"Darlin', you look like the type of woman that if you went missin', someone would be quickly searchin' for your whereabouts. I don't need that kind of trouble in my life, and I much prefer stayin' off the radar. Attention ain't my thang. Anyway, you got a raincoat in that big ol' suitcase of yours? 'Cause you're gonna need it when it starts pourin' in 'bout twenty minutes."

She stops walking and places her hand on her hip. "Is that all?"

"I guess so. You seem real damn determined, so I'll just leave you to it. Good luck. See ya 'round town. Oh, and if no one has told you yet, Merry Christmas."

I place the truck in drive and creep forward, then make a U-turn to head back to town. As I pass her the second time, I shake my head. But when my gaze flicks to the rearview mirror one last time, I see her standing in the road, waving her arms in the air.

I sigh and put the truck in park.

Stubborn Susan prances toward the truck and cracks open the passenger door.

I lift my brows at her, unamused.

"Okay, okay. I would greatly appreciate a ride to Merryville if it's not an inconvenience."

My mouth slightly parts. "It's not a problem at all. But it would've been nice if you'd have just said that ten minutes ago."

"Apologies." She rushes back to her suitcase.

As she struggles to lift it, I get out and help her, rolling it back to the truck and dropping down the gate so I can throw her bag into the back.

"Oh my God." She stares at the wooden handles and blades in the truck's bed. "Are you an axe murderer?"

I snort. "If you had to compare me to anything, I'd say I'm more like a lumberjack, but only durin' the winter months, when it's wood-choppin' and Christmas tree-shoppin' season."

She studies me as if she's memorizing my features. Her gaze moves down to my lips, then back up again, as I open the door for her.

Once we're traveling down the road, she speaks. "I suppose this isn't the worst thing that could've happened."

I don't know who she's trying to convince, but I notice she's shivering, so I reach over and turn on the heat. She places her hands over the vent and warms them. I'd bet anything her fingers are like icicles.

"Thank you so much." I can hear the sincerity in her tone.

"You're welcome very much. See, that wasn't so hard, was it?"

She playfully rolls her eyes. "A girl can *never* be too careful."

"You're right. But also, don't you have a cell phone?" I glance over at her. Everyone has one these days. My three-year-old nephew has one and knows how to use it, too.

"I do. It's dead. No charger."

I reach for the cord I have. "Will this work?"

She digs in her oversized purse. "Yeah, actually, it will."

When she plugs it in, it doesn't power on.

"Will probably take some time, depending on how drained it is."

"Yeah." She shoves it back into her bag. "Oh, I'm Claire."

I wait a moment for her to continue, but she doesn't. "So just Claire? Like Beyoncé?"

I see a hint of blush hit her cheeks.

"Claire. *Chester.*"

I keep my focus on the road. "Do your friends call you CeCe for short?"

"No, they don't."

"Do you have any nicknames?"

She shakes her head. "I thought you were going to ask if I had any friends."

This makes me chuckle. "Since you brought it up, do you?"

"A few. But none have given me any nicknames. Not ones they'd say to my face, at least."

"Then this seems like the perfect opportunity."

"I'd prefer Claire."

"Okay, *CeCe.*"

She shrugs. "Whatever. I can't guarantee I'll answer if I see you in town, though."

"You're good at ignorin' people when they talk to you. Guess that's me sayin' I'm already used to it?"

I see her grin in the window's reflection when she turns her head.

"So where ya from?" I can't seem to place her accent. If I had to guess, I'd say California.

She swallows. "All over."

"Ah. Was your dad in the military? I had a friend who moved around to different bases. It seemed like he was in a new state every year."

"No, he wasn't."

"Oh," I say, struggling to find a new topic for discussion.

Maybe I'm talking too much. My nerves get the best of me when I'm near a beautiful woman. "I was born and raised in Texas. Have lived in Merryville my whole life."

"Really? I would have *never* guessed."

I smirk. "Am I detectin' a little bit of sarcasm?"

That makes her perfectly plump lips turn up into a smile she can't hide. I like to see it.

"Apologies. I'm being rude, aren't I?"

"Kinda, but I'm not takin' it personally. I know it's not me, but a reflection of you and the day you've had. You've been travelin' and were down on your luck. That's enough to make anyone a grump."

She nods. "Seems I left my manners in New York."

"No problem, darlin'. It happens."

We ride in silence for a few moments. "So…you're a city girl. That explains a lot," I say with a wink.

"I'm going to let that comment slide," she tells me as we pass the large *WELCOME TO MERRYVILLE* mural that was painted a few years ago on the old coffee bean roasting plant. It's an artist's rendition of the downtown area with Santa flying overhead. White powder covers the buildings and sidewalks, but it's not a good representation because snow doesn't happen that often. If we get a flurry, it barely sticks. Mostly, we're hit by ice, and it shuts the whole town down.

"So where are ya headin'?"

"Can you take me to Main Street Inn? I have a reservation."

"Sure thing." I stop at the four-way intersection. A few people cross the road quickly, but no one else is around. On any other evening, the sidewalks are packed. Most are indoors, preparing for a loss of power.

When we arrive at the inn, Claire unplugs her phone and tucks it in her pocket. I get out and follow her.

She looks at me over her shoulder. "Oh, you don't have to come with me."

"The owners are family friends. I've been meaning to stop by and say hi." I catch up to her fast pace and fall in line beside her.

She steps up on the sidewalk, and I open the door for her. The smell of freshly baked cookies and wood burning in the fireplace reminds me of home. A large tree with colorful twinkling lights is in the corner, and holiday music plays quietly in the background.

Claire approaches the front counter that has an old cash register, stacks of paper, and a laptop on it. There's a bell, which she lightly taps.

Heidi, the innkeeper's daughter, emerges from the back room, where it sounds like she's watching a trashy reality show on the television.

Heidi immediately greets Claire with a wide grin. She pushes her blonde hair back out of her eyes, and I notice her sleeves are rolled to her elbows. It is hot in here.

I give her a hello, and she looks between the two of us.

"Howdy," Heidi says. "How can I help you?"

Claire pulls her wallet from her huge purse. "I have a reservation for Claire Chester."

As Claire slides her ID and credit card forward, Heidi types away on the keyboard.

"Is it possible it's under another name?"

Claire shakes her head. "No."

After a few more mouse clicks, Heidi speaks up. "I'm sorry. I'm having trouble finding it. Can you tell me the dates you were supposed to be staying?"

Claire grows frustrated. "December first, which is today, through January seventh."

Heidi searches again, her kind expression fixed in place. Sometimes, tourists can be the worst people on earth, even at one of the happiest places on the planet.

Claire takes in a few deep breaths. I can only imagine

what's going through her mind as Heidi tells her she can't find her reservation, especially after the day she's had.

"This has to be a mistake," Claire insists.

Heidi shakes her head. "I'm sorry, but I'm not findin' anything for those dates or your name. Are you sure it was Main Street Inn for Merryville? There are a few all over the country named that."

"It was here. I thought I had a confirmation number." Claire unlocks her phone and then huffs. "It died. Of course it did." She smiles sweetly at Heidi. "Do you have any spare rooms? Price doesn't matter. I'll pay whatever you'd like."

Heidi shakes her head. "I'm so sorry, but we don't. We're fully booked. Winter is our busiest season, and the rooms are reserved a year in advance with very few cancellations. I wish there was something more I could do."

"This is insane," Claire groans. "Do you know of any rentals in the area?"

"Gonna be hard to find something available. If you'd like me to contact the motel in the next town over, I'll gladly do that."

"Sure," Claire says.

Heidi picks up the phone and dials the number. When she ends the call, she gives Claire a sad look. "I'm sorry. They're booked, too."

"Okay, thanks so much for checking. Do you have a waiting list?"

Heidi pulls a notebook from under the counter and flips through several sheets of names.

"Claire Chester, correct?"

"Yes, that's right."

Heidi scribbles it at the bottom, and Claire gives her a contact number.

The writing is on the wall. There is nowhere for her to go.

Claire offers another thank-you, followed by a polite smile, before moving toward the exit.

"I'm sorry," Heidi tells me. "I would let her stay if I could."

"I know. Don't worry about it. Shit happens. Hope you've been well."

"I've been makin' it," she says.

"Good to hear." I pat the counter, then leave.

Claire is standing on the empty sidewalk with her arms crossed over her chest. I see her wipe a tear from her cheek, but I don't bring attention to it.

"What am I going to do now?" She turns and looks at me. "I have no vehicle. No room. Coming here was a mistake."

I breathe in deeply, the cool air burning my lungs. "You can stay at my place until you can figure it out. I've got a couch."

"I can't do that."

"Okay, *Susan*." I meet her eyes. "What other options do you have?"

She doesn't answer.

"You could sleep on the sidewalk as the storm rolls in. You could hang out in the café for the night, but after a few hours, get ready to start answerin' questions or washin' dishes. There are no hotels nearby. The inn is booked. And you have no transportation. Even with all that, you're so proud you won't accept my couch?"

"I'd be an inconvenience. What would you say to your girlfriend? 'Hi, honey. I picked up a random woman walking into town with no place to stay.' Sounds sus, don't you think?"

Laughter escapes me. "There is no girlfriend. The only woman in my life is my cat, Tinsel. She will probably hate you, but she hates most everyone. Having to deal with an elderly cat who snubs and hisses at you is better than your other options."

She focuses on me with her head tilted. "You seem like more of a dog person. Golden retriever owner."

"Nah. Love my kitty. But I'm noticing a pattern. I have a

knack for picking things up off the side of the road. She was a rescue, too."

"I'm not a charity case," Claire snaps.

The sprinkles begin coming down in greater concentration, and I sigh.

"I won't beg you, but the offer is on the table. Let me know where you'd like me to take you if it's a no. Or if you'd rather figure it out on your own. Doesn't matter to me, but we need to get goin'."

She closes her eyes and breathes in deeply.

This woman is so stubborn I'm almost convinced she will march straight to the café with her suitcase as I wait for her to answer.

CHAPTER 3

CLAIRE

I'm shivering.

I don't know if it's because I'm cold or if the stress I've been through over the last twenty-four hours has finally caught up with me. I've lost control of the situation and am at the mercy of a man I just met.

No vehicle. No place to stay. This is the worst-case scenario.

Traveling here was awful, and now that I'm in town, I'm contemplating asking Jake to drive me back to the airport so I can go home. But I'm sure they canceled all flights leaving Texas, anyway. That definitely appeared to be the case when I was in the terminal earlier.

I can pay him any amount of money to cover his time, but I've already wasted enough of that today.

He's a saint. I wouldn't have been as patient with me.

If this storm passes quickly, I'll ask him tomorrow. Or if I could get my rental repaired, I could take my chances and drive across the country to New York. However, that sounds like a disaster waiting to happen.

This morning, I was determined and refused to let anything stop me. But now, so much has gone wrong that I'm second-guessing everything.

Why am I here again? *To prove a point.*
Is it worth it? *Eh. Still to be determined.*

This trip was supposed to be stress-free. For months, I visualized how I'd spend my time in the small Christmas town. I'd reserved the largest room in the historic Main Street Inn. Everything I needed was within walking distance, including a twenty-four-hour café and a quaint little coffee shop. I'd people-watch, make friends with the locals, try new foods, and even visit the antique stores. It was supposed to be an unforgettable experience. I'd looked forward to this all year as I researched the town's history.

Jake clears his throat, grabbing my attention. "Well?"

"I'm sorry," I say, aware I don't have many options. Jake waits for me to answer him as icy rain falls from the sky, leaving dark slashes on the pavement.

This day keeps getting better.

"I won't beg you," Jake finally tells me. "But we should probably get in the truck before this turns into hail."

"It's already hell," I mutter as he continues forward, leaving me where I stand.

Thunder rolls overhead, and with the way my luck has been, getting struck by lightning is a definite possibility. So I brace myself and follow behind him, trying to keep my balance on the wet cement. Unfortunately, the bottoms of my boots are slick, so I look as if I'm ice-skating, trying to keep my balance. I concentrate on not busting my ass, even if it would be icing on the shit cake of a day I've been served.

Jake glances over his shoulder and smiles when he sees me behind him. Instead of going straight to the driver's side, he opens my door so I can slide into place. "Thank you," I say breathlessly as my body trembles.

"No problem." He pushes the door shut and makes his way around the front.

I'm nearly out of breath when I buckle, and I promise myself that when I return to the city, I'll start jogging again.

The engine rumbles as the heat blasts in my face, and I try to relax.

"So…" He turns and looks at me. "Have ya made up your mind on what you'll do?"

I nod. "Yes. I'll take your offer, but I don't want to inconvenience you during the holiday season. So I'd like to go home at the first opportunity available. Staying here just wasn't meant to be."

"I understand." He backs out of the parking space and heads north. Merryville is all but abandoned at this point, with the storefronts closed and windows dark.

"Are there any mechanics in town?" I ask as we continue forward. I try to scan my memory and am sure there is one, but I don't recall any information about it.

"My best friend Hank and his family own a shop a few blocks up the way. You got the keys with you?"

I nod.

"Great. We can stop by and see if they're still there. I'm sure he'll be happy to take a look at it after the storm passes. We'd better hurry, though. It's almost closin' time for them."

I glance at the clock on the dashboard, and it's twenty minutes until six. A little spark of hope ignites inside of me. Maybe this is the end of my bad-luck streak.

"He's the best around," Jake explains, making small talk as I reach into my purse and dig the key fob from the bottom. We drive to the edge of town, passing a candy store, a soda shop, an old movie theater, and several antique stores. Each one has closed signs on their doors.

When Jake pulls into the large gravel parking lot, I can't help but notice the row of vehicles behind the tall chain-link fence, and I hope I won't have to wait weeks for a repair.

As if Jake can read my mind, he immediately speaks up. "Many of those cars aren't a priority. Also, Hank owes me a few favors, so I'll make sure you get taken care of quickly."

"Thanks," I say, happy to see the lights are on inside. Even though this man shouldn't be wasting his favors on me, I appreciate the sentiment, especially if it helps me get out of here.

"You wanna come in?" Jake asks as he parks.

"Would it be okay to stay here? I'd love to charge my phone." But I'm also cold and feel frozen from the inside out.

"Sure thing. I'll be right back." He hands me the cord, and I plug it into the bottom of my phone as he gets out of the truck. I watch him walk across the parking lot, waiting for the logo to appear on the screen. It takes a few moments before it sluggishly powers up. As soon as I unlock it, notifications flood me.

Emails, text messages, and meeting reminders…oh my.

They don't stop coming, which is why my phone died.

My sister is the only person I want to talk to right now. She's the only person who knows where I am, and I need to check in sooner rather than later. So I take the opportunity to call her before Jake returns. Too much has happened since we chatted this morning before my flight.

"Oh my God! I've been worried about you. I was going to file a missing person report in the morning if I hadn't heard from you by then."

"By morning? That's too long. If you don't hear from me within twelve hours—"

"Don't tell me that unless you mean it," she warns. "You know I will."

"I know."

Emma's three years younger but always worries about me. I'm not sure anyone else does. My father hasn't noticed I've left the state. He's too busy. He's *always* too busy—and has been since my mother passed away when I was eleven.

"Are you okay? You sound tense," she says.

"Sorta. It's been a very strange day, and a major storm is

rolling in as we speak." I look up at the sky, happy Jake was so persistent. I'd still be walking.

"Come home, Claire. You can do this another time. I think you've gotten the hint that visiting was a bad idea."

"I can't, at least not yet. I wanted to experience Merryville during Christmas. Now I'm not sure that's going to be possible."

"You do realize it's Christmas there every single day out of the year, don't you?"

I roll my eyes. "Of course I do, but everyone online said it's different in December."

"Different doesn't always mean better."

"Well aware." The rain pounds on the roof, and it's so loud I can barely hear Emma.

When the line goes silent, I'm concerned I've dropped her call, but then her microwave beeps. I guess it's time for dinner. It's been such a whirlwind I hadn't noticed.

"Have you heard from Dale?" I hear the clinking of a spoon stirring something.

At the mention of his name, I suck in a deep breath. I've mastered not thinking about him and forgetting he exists until he's mentioned. Dale is my ex, if I can even call him that. He broke my heart, and I never want to hear his name again for the rest of my life.

Fuck Dale. He's the reason I currently have trust issues.

"He texted me right after my plane landed. I haven't replied."

"Good," she says. "Don't."

"I've learned that no response is the best reply, and silence speaks louder than my words. Especially after everything he put me through. I just can't do it anymore. I'm tired of men who use me and relationships that don't last. I want to focus on myself and figure out what I want in life without the pointless drama."

"That's the spirit. I hope you can find some peace while you're away."

"Me too, but I'm not holding my breath."

"You never know. So how's the inn? Just like the website you sent me?"

This was a question I was hoping she wouldn't ask. My sister is well traveled and loves living out of a suitcase. I already know how she will react when I tell her what happened. I'm almost expecting it.

"Not quite. There was a mix-up with my reservation, and they had no spare rooms." I linger for a moment, debating on how much I should confess. "So I'm staying with this guy who picked me up when I was stranded on the side of the road."

"What?" Her voice rises an entire octave. It's the response I'd give her if the roles were reversed. But saying it out loud makes it sound worse than it is. "How does that happen?"

"I'm not sure. I haven't researched it yet because I called you first."

"That's not the part that's concerning me, Claire. Reservations get messed up all the time. I've dealt with it more than I'd like to admit. I'm talking about the part where you said you're staying with some man! Have you lost it? You don't know him."

"If it makes you feel any better, he seems like a genuinely nice guy."

"Yeah, you don't seem to have the best judgment regarding men. Sorry, but no. Also, most serial-killer psychopaths are *nice guys*. They're very charming. Happy-go-lucky. Cunning. Attractive."

"You've watched too many docuseries," I argue, but I thought the same thing when Jake picked me up.

"Ted Bundy is a perfect example. Claire, you can't go home with a stranger. Please. I will enact the 'my sister is in danger' rule."

23

I sigh. That's the name of our agreement, something I suggested be put into place since she travels often. We've promised to keep each other in the loop with what we're doing, even when we don't tell anyone else, but if something happens, all bets are off, and we'll do whatever we can to protect one another.

Some places she's visited have made me nervous, though she's always been fine. The rule goes both ways, though. I won't tell anyone where she is unless she's in trouble or needs help.

"Please don't do that. I don't have a choice. Not right now, at least. It's dark, and I don't have transportation. All flights in and out are canceled. There are no other hotels or rental cabins available. The woman at the inn called around for me."

"Do they know who you are?"

"No, of course not. The less anyone knows, the better. That way, I can fade away after this is finalized and never visit Merryville again."

"That sounds cold. When did my sister become the Grinch?"

I can only imagine the horrified expression on her face.

"I'm not a Grinch. I have to do this, Emma. Also, please don't worry about me. I have my phone, as long as I can keep it charged. I'm staying at Jake Jolly's house if anything happens to me."

She nearly gasps. "Jake Jolly?"

"Yes, but his friends call him JJ. He's like a Christmas angel. Him picking me up could be a sign I'm on the right path after everything that's happened."

"If you say so." She almost sounds disappointed. "Well, tell me what this Jake Jolly looks like."

"I don't know how to describe him properly," I admit. "Tall. Green eyes. Muscular. Carries axes in the back of his truck. He's a lumberjack."

"What actor would he be related to?"

"Chris Hemsworth," I say without missing a beat. "But

Chris with scruff along his perfect jawline. Long lashes. Incredible smile. Smooth-as-chocolate voice with a strong Southern accent. And he has huge hands. Men like him only exist in fairy tales."

"Uh. And you're staying at his house?"

"Apparently. I'm not sure for how long, though. It depends on how I feel tomorrow. You know how I get when my plans are disrupted."

"I do. That all-or-nothing mentality will be your demise. But anyway, is he single?" I can tell she's smiling.

"He says he is, but men lie."

"You should take a picture of him when you can and send it to me."

I chuckle. "We'll see. I just want to make it through the night. My brain is mush, and I'm exhausted. The flight was awful. The luxury vehicle I reserved was rented to someone else. Then, when I showed up at the inn, the woman couldn't find my reservation, which was embarrassing. It took everything in me to keep from having a panic attack."

"When did you make your reservation?"

I think about her question for a moment. Then I remember asking my father's assistant to take care of it.

"I had Gwyneth book it for me in January."

"That was your first mistake," Emma says.

"You're right." I open the app on my phone and search for the confirmation email she sent me. I immediately notice it was for an inn located in a different state. While I want to type her a strongly worded email, I should've paid more attention —but I was enamored with Dale at the time.

Everyone knows my dad's secretary isn't intelligent. The only reason she has a job is because she's a side chick.

I've been so preoccupied with my drama that I didn't double-check everything was in place. I gave her the benefit of the doubt. This is what I get for having faith that someone else will do their job correctly.

I close my app without doing anything that would alert someone to my absence. I'm sure Gwyneth forgot she booked this trip. At least this mishap will cover my tracks if my father snoops.

I change the subject and ask a question that's on my mind. "When Dad retires, do you think I'll be the one to take over?"

I know I'm putting Emma on the spot, something I don't do often. We handle each other with care, but I also respect her opinion because she's the only person who won't bullshit me and tell me what I want to hear.

She sighs. "Oh, Claire. Should we talk about this right now? Aren't you already having a bad enough day?"

"Yes, but—"

"It doesn't matter what I say or think, okay? You're smart. You're beautiful. And you don't need unnecessary stress. You're in Merryville, so go be merry."

I squeeze my eyes shut. "I guess I'm a glutton for punishment. I'm feeling...lost. Alone. And my bladder is so full I might pee myself. God, it just hit me."

"You're not supposed to hold it. You better go to the bathroom before you add a UTI to your very bad day."

I look out the window, cringing at the thought of leaving the cozy truck but not knowing how long we will be here or how far away Jake lives. How long can I hold it? Two minutes? Five minutes? Ten? Absolutely not.

"You're right. We'll talk later?"

"Absolutely," she says. "I need an update every twelve hours. And try to have a better night, okay?"

"Okay. I need to go."

"Promise me."

I immediately groan. "I promise. Bye."

She laughs. "Bye!"

I end the call, leaving my phone in the truck, and bolt toward the entrance. The rain pounds down on me, and I silently scream as the wind cuts right through my fashionable yet useless jacket, but I keep jogging. If I don't, I will embarrass myself more than I already have.

As I hit the entryway, I reach out to turn the knob, and as it opens, I trip.

All that's missing are the sound effects as I fly forward like a cartoon character.

CHAPTER 4

JAKE

"Look what the cat dragged in," Hank says, leaning against the counter as he scrolls on his phone.

I shake my head as I walk past the sitting area, where a remodeling show is playing on the old-fashioned tube TV. I stop at the soda machine, put in a few quarters, and grab me a canned cola.

"You workin' hard? 'Cause it looks like you're hardly workin'." I take a sip.

"Pftt. In this weather? I'm waiting for the minutes to pass so I can leave. You know how Dad feels about closing the shop early; it's against his religion. I let Charlie leave a few hours ago so he could grab some groceries since everyone's predicting the storm is gonna be pretty bad."

I lift a brow. "Oh, you're still takin' customers, then?"

He points up at the clock that's hung on the wall. I'm pretty sure it's five minutes fast, but I don't mention it. He probably changed it himself. "I still have fifteen minutes, then I'm hoping and praying for it to sleet and ice over so I can have a few days off. I would kill for a vacation right now."

"Vacation? You mean you actually lift a finger while you're here?"

"I can lift this one." He shoots me the bird and sets down his phone. "Speakin' of people who can fuck off; I saw Lacy yesterday in the grocery store."

I glare at him, my mood instantly souring. It's been years since we ended things, and I avoid that woman like the plague, but she still lives in Merryville. So we do have the occasional run-in. Usually it's me running in the opposite direction from her, though. "Don't mention her name around me. You know she's like Beetlejuice. Say it three times and she appears."

Lacy is my ex, the Wicked Witch of the South, who nearly ruined my life after a very messy breakup.

"She was fake nice and using that voice of hers that I can't stand. The high-pitched, nasally one, like she's talkin' to a five-year-old. I was thinkin' how you really dodged a bullet with that one. Woof. Her personality makes her ugly."

"I know. Don't know what was going through my mind," I say.

"It wasn't your mind that was thinkin'. It was your dick."

"True. Can say this, though: every day I wake up and she's not sleeping next to me, I say a silent prayer of thanks that I didn't marry the devil."

He slaps his hand on the counter and laughs. "True. Glad Satan ain't waitin' up for ya. But anyway, I know you didn't come here to shoot the shit. What's up?"

Before I can say a word, the door slams open, bouncing off the wall, sending the jingle-bell wreath sailing. Claire flies into the room, arms out like she's Superman, hits the floor, and shoots across the recently-waxed tiles, slamming into a small table in the corner with a miniature Christmas tree, which topples over and lands next to her head.

"Holy shit!" barks Hank.

I have to stifle a laugh, as I know she won't appreciate the humor. I cross the room in four steps and squat down beside her. "Claire, are you okay?"

"Please tell me this is a bad dream!" she moans, not meeting my gaze.

Hank rushes over. "Ma'am, are you all right?"

"Please wake up," she whispers to herself, eyes squeezed shut.

I place my hand on her shoulder. "Claire? CeCe?"

Her eyes fly open, and she glares at me. I knew her newfound nickname would grab her attention.

"So I really am awake. Lovely," she grumbles as Hank offers his hand and we help her up. "I'm fine. I'm fine."

She pulls her beanie off her head and puts her dark-auburn hair back in place before repositioning it. "Could you please direct me to the ladies' room?"

Hank points over her shoulder down the small hallway. "It's a shared bathroom."

She gives him a smile, turns on her boots, and walks away. I hear the door click closed, and Hank stares at me.

"How do you know her? She some mail-order bride?"

I roll my eyes. "Shut up."

"You said over drinks you were thinkin' about it."

"I was kiddin'," I whisper-hiss. I imagine Claire will be in there for a little while, considering she looked as if she'd hitch a ride out of here with aliens if they showed up with a working vehicle. "I picked her up off the side of the road."

His mouth falls open. "How is that better?"

"What?" Then I realize what he's suggesting. "No. Not like that. She's not a *prostitute* if that's what you're insinuating."

"You're sure?" He looks at me, concerned. "You're gullible as fuck."

"No, I'm not."

"With a last name like Jolly, how could you not be? If someone is lyin' through their teeth, you'd believe them."

I shrug. "Innocent until proven guilty."

Then I think about what Hank is suggesting. "It wouldn't matter if she is or isn't."

"Are you taking her back to your place?"

I meet his eyes. "Yes."

"Oh God. She's going to take you for everything ya got! I've read stories about this type of scam on the internet. Let me guess, she was walking into town and has no place to stay." He glares at me.

My mouth falls open. "Fuck."

"Please tell me that's not what happened." Hank waits for my reaction, and all I can do is purse my lips as I breathe in deeply. I avoid his eyes and shove my hands into my pockets.

"Jake. You can't take her home with you!"

I point at him. "Shut the hell up! You're bein' too damn loud!"

"What are you gonna do?" he asks in an elevated whisper instead, but it's not any quieter.

"I don't know. The storm is rolling in, and she has nowhere else to go."

He shakes his head. "Nice knowin' ya. I'll make sure when you go missing that I tell your parents a pretty brown-headed girl was walking into town and had no place to stay, so my dumbass best friend picked her up and brought her home with him!"

Claire clears her throat behind us, and I shoot him my best I-hate-you look, then turn to greet her with a smile. "You good?"

"I'm fine. Are we almost done here?" She glances at Hank, then back at me. I don't answer because the stupid thoughts my best friend put into my head are still floating around.

Claire's gaze returns to Hank. "Did Jake give you the keys?"

"To what?" Hank asks.

"Oh yeah." I dig into my pocket and pull out the fob. "You think you can tow this truck in and let us know what's going on with it? It's about nine miles outside city limits on the shoulder."

There's only five minutes left before he can officially leave for the night. Hank glances back at the clock.

"There's no rush," Claire states. "You can take care of it after the storm clears."

Hank gives me a look with an arched brow.

Claire notices. "Did I say something wrong?"

"No, no. He's just being dramatic. It's nothing to worry about." I take a big swig of my cola. "It's going to be fine."

He needs to understand it's too late for me to pull out of this now.

I'm committed to this woman until she leaves. I'm all she has.

Hank nods. "Okay. Whatever you say. I'll get to this as soon as we open again. It could be a few days if the storm is as they expect."

This news seems to deflate her. "A few days?" she asks.

Or is she acting?

Hank has me questioning her motives.

"Yeah. But I've been told it could shut us down for up to a week." Hank glances at me and then at Claire.

"I was hoping I could get back to the airport as soon as possible. Let's say you can't fix my vehicle before I can book a flight. Could I pay you to tow it to the rental center?"

Hank tilts his head at her. "That would be quite expensive."

"Money doesn't matter," Claire tells him with the confidence of a royal heir. And I find it sexy as hell. The woman who wanted to crawl into the grave after tripping on the raised lip of the door has vanished.

"It could be close to two thousand dollars," he warns.

"Then I'll double it," she states.

Hank is just as confused as me. "I know you're not from around here, ma'am, but that's not how bargainin' works."

She smiles, and her eyebrow perks up. "Oh, I'm aware. I'd like to make the inconvenience worth your time. Plus, maybe it will help you forget my grand entrance. Please just keep me updated on the progress. If Merryville doesn't work out for me this season, I'd rather be in New York, where I'm not a burden to anyone. Never mind on the last part. I've realized what I've said. Seems I'm a burden wherever I go, but at least I'd be home." There's more behind those words than I think she meant to reveal.

Hank notices, too, but he manages to keep his mouth shut for once. "Sure. Want to leave me your number?"

"I don't have any business cards on me, but if you have a pen and paper…"

Hank pulls a yellow, lined notepad with different prices scribbled on the side and picks up a dull pencil with grease stains and teeth marks on it. He hands it to Claire, and she looks down at it, then back at him, and her lip curls ever so slightly.

He snatches a pen off the top of the counter. "Sorry 'bout that. We're all mechanics here. Not afraid to get our hands dirty."

I narrow my eyes at his ridiculous attempt to flirt with the woman he just accused of being a mail-order bride, a prostitute, and a serial killer.

"Yeah," she says, completely unamused, not giving him a second glance as she jots down her information. Then she turns to me.

"Ready?" I ask with a side smile.

"I am now," Claire says as she walks past me.

I look at Hank over my shoulder, and he laughs.

"Keep me posted," I tell him, referring to the truck.

"JJ. Hold up." Hank runs toward me and places his hand on my shoulder. "Remember, back in the day, when you told me that you could make anyone fall in love with you, and if you couldn't, you'd give me your motorcycle?"

33

I glare at him. "You remember that?"

"Of course I do. And you said I could cash it in at *any* point until you were in a serious relationship or married. I thought I'd lost my opportunity."

I groan, shaking my head.

"My friend, the day has come to fruition. I choose her." He looks out the window at Claire, who's waiting patiently under the covered porch.

"Oh, come on. We were young and stupid. A lot has happened since then."

"You goin' back on your word?" He raises his brow.

We made that stupid bet when I was *fifteen* while my pops and I were rebuilding an old Harley. It took us four summers to restore it back to its original state, and it's sitting in my shop right now. I was cocky as fuck and said a lot of stupid shit back then. But to a Texan, our word is our life; if we don't have that, we have nothing.

I swallow hard, knowing I'm not up for the challenge. "You're a dick. You know I'm rusty and out of practice."

"I'm just a man of opportunity."

I roll my eyes. "Thanks for kickin' me when I'm down. Mama always told me that my teenage cockiness would get me in trouble. I guess trouble finally found me."

"You keep me posted," he says with a friendly wave and a chuckle. I want to flip him off, but I fight back the urge and slip outside once more.

The cold wind immediately slams against me as the rain falls in sheets from above. I glance over at Claire, who's looking up at the sky, and I'm pissed that Hank remembered that dumb-as-fuck bet. Claire is the type of woman who deserves better than that. I just met her and know that as fact.

So I make a decision to just see what happens. When love is forced, it never works out. I learned that the hard way.

I move closer.

"I don't have an umbrella," I say in apology as she lifts the fur-trimmed hood on her jacket.

"It's fine. Shall we just go for it?"

I squint at the truck. The windshield wipers are still going, and the lights are on. Then I hear it idling. "You didn't turn off the engine and take the keys?" I glance at her.

"No. Isn't Merryville safe?" she asks.

I nod. "I guess you have a point. Don't remember anyone getting their vehicles stolen. Well, at least for not as long as I've been alive."

"Forty years?" she questions, her breath coming out in smoke.

"I'm not forty yet. I'm the ripe old age of thirty-six."

She snickers.

"And what about you, Grandma?"

"I turned thirty-five on Thanksgiving."

"No way. You're a Thanksgiving baby?"

She rolls her eyes. "Gobble, gobble. My birthday doesn't always fall on the holiday, just sometimes, and when I was born, obviously. It's probably why the turkey jokes have followed me around my entire life. Go ahead, laugh. I know you want to."

"I don't, CeCe. I think it's adorable. Why don't you stay here under the covering and I'll come and pick you up?"

She gives me a look. "Are you sure?"

I finally laugh. "You and those boots are not friends today. Stay here. I'll be right back."

I run across the parking lot, and the rain pelts against me, but luckily, most bounce off my coat. It's so hot inside the truck that the windows are fogged. I try to wipe the windshield so I can see. This old thing doesn't have a defrost setting.

Slowly, I back out of the parking space and crawl my way to Claire. Reaching over, I open the door for her, and she heaves herself inside, shutting the door behind her.

She breathes out. "Thank you. That was kind."

I give her a smile, and I see one touch her lips. "It's called manners, ma'am. Sorry you haven't been around a bunch of people who have them."

She nods so slightly that I wonder if she meant to.

"Now make sure you're buckled," I tell her, reaching around her front and pulling it over her before snapping her in. I think I see her breath hitch as I meet her gaze. "Can't have you riskin' anything else today."

She double-checks the belt. "You're right."

I put my blinker on to drive back into town. The rain is falling so heavily I can barely see a foot in front of me.

"You hungry?" I randomly ask, knowing if we bide our time, we might be able to find a break in the storm so it's less dangerous to be on the road.

"Actually, I'm starving, but I didn't want to say anything."

"I love to eat, and I love to cook. You ever tried chicken fried chicken?"

"No. I don't eat a lot of carbs."

"Ahh. You're one of those. Might have to ditch that philosophy while you're here." I chuckle.

She sighs. "I had planned to eat my way through the café's menu since it was within walking distance of the inn."

"You still can." I park a few feet from the door of the building, and my stomach growls loud enough for her to hear it.

"Let's take this conversation inside," she suggests.

I give her a nod, not remembering the last time I ate. I skipped lunch and had a cola at Hanks. So it must've been that shitty granola bar I grabbed off my grandmother's counter this morning when I brought her newspaper inside.

Damn. I really lost track of time today.

When we walk inside, the hearty smell of bacon on the grill makes my mouth water. There is only one other person eating.

Glenda greets us at the entrance and grabs two menus.

She smiles at Claire, then waggles her brows at me. I playfully roll my eyes as she leads us to a booth that overlooks the parking lot. We both slide in as the menus are placed in front of us. Claire opens one, but I focus on her since I've got it memorized. I've only been eating at this place for as long as I can remember.

"Whatchu two kids havin' to drink?" Glenda asks, smacking her gum. She's an older woman who draws a mole on her face. Over the years, it's definitely changed locations. The woman has a heart of gold and would always bring me and my brother extra syrup with our pancakes when we were kids. We would literally drink the stuff, it was so yummy, but most homemade things are.

"I'll take a coffee," I say. "Cream and sugar."

She points at the table. "Sugar is there."

"Yes, ma'am," I say as Claire orders the same.

A few moments later, Glenda places two mugs on the table. Then, she sets down a miniature pitcher of cold cream that came from the fridge.

"Need a minute?" She gives us a warm smile.

"Yeah, please," Claire says.

As Glenda walks away, she shoots me a wink. This is exactly how rumors get started.

Claire reads the text on the outside of the mug. It's in a funky font that matches Glenda's personality. "Glenda's Café. 'Cause there's no place like home." She smiles. "Cute marketing."

Then she goes back to reading.

Claire eventually notices I'm staring. "What?"

I shake my head. "Nothin'. You just look like you can't make up your mind."

"This menu has three hundred items on it. I'm used to having four or five options. It's like a buffet on paper."

"There's not a bad choice. It's why the menu hasn't changed since the day the place opened in 1977. Dorothy, her daughter, will take ownership when Glenda finally retires."

She holds up her hand. "No."

I give her a look.

"She named her daughter Dorothy?" Claire's brows furrow. "I'm not that gullible."

A chuckle escapes me. "I'm not making it up."

"So Dorothy will inherit this place?"

"Yep. That's how it usually works around here. Generational wealth is passed down. People tend to appreciate and trust those who have kept things in the family. I guess it's a small-town thing."

The same expression I saw on her face earlier returns, but for just a split second. "Sounds like it."

I pour the cool cream into my mug and add two spoonfuls of sugar before lifting it to my lips and sipping. It's warm and immediately brings my body temperature up as I hold it in my cold palms.

Claire blows on the top of hers before taking a tiny sip.

"No cream? No sugar? Are *you* the axe murderer?"

She smirks. "I'm all business."

"Apparently. Also, Glenda has a little dog, too."

"Please, no." She grins wide.

"Can you guess his name?" I take another sip of my drink.

"I'm literally dying. But honestly, it's so damn adorable."

"It really is. It's a whole theme. I guess the *Wizard of Oz* was popular when she was young, so she dug into it. If you can't change the hand you're given, you learn to go with the flow. Her husband literally looks like the Cowardly Lion with his long beard and hair."

"I love it," she says with a delighted grin. "It's clever."

"It really is."

Moments later, Glenda returns with a coffee carafe and refills my mug as she takes our order. She doesn't need a notepad. The woman can remember phone numbers from forty years ago.

"I'm gonna have a bacon cheeseburger with mayo, lettuce—"

"Onions on Texas toast. Got it." She glances at Claire.

"I can't make up my mind," she finally tells Glenda. "Can you surprise me?"

"Any allergies?"

"Only to shitty men," Claire mumbles, and Glenda nods.

"So, are you a savory or sweet gal?" Glenda asks.

"Both?" Claire shrugs.

"I've got you, sweetie. I know just the thing."

"Can I keep this menu? I want to finish reading it," Claire asks, a hint of blush on her cheeks.

"Absolutely," Glenda tells her before walking away.

That's when Claire notices the ruby-red slippers on Glenda's feet. "She's life goals."

I chuckle, watching her.

Claire eventually flips over the menu and runs her finger down the list of desserts. "Raspberry chocolate cake?"

"It's a house favorite. We should get some slices to go."

"I'd like that," she tells me.

"You ever had it before?"

She shakes her head.

"Might be experiencing a lot of firsts together in the next few days with this storm," I say.

"In a strange way, I'm looking forward to it," she admits.

CHAPTER 5

CLAIRE

I study his green eyes and hate how attractive he is. He's too gentle and too handsome. He's the type of man you wish you could find—the kind that once you have him, you never let him go.

However, my sister is right. When it comes to men, my judgment is awful. Maybe this is a persona, an act to hook, line, and sinker me. But Jake has nothing to gain. He has no idea who I am or why I'm here. He hasn't asked me once, either.

Jake Jolly is a nice guy who's doing nice things. That's it.

My fear of being used is a trauma response caused by my past relationships. Being able to recognize it is actual progress. I'm proud of myself for even noticing. Questioning someone's motives before giving them any details about me is a win, and I'll take it.

I pause after taking a drink of coffee. "Can I ask you a question?"

"Shoot," he tells me, and I give him a look. "It means to go ahead."

"Ahh. Added to my Texan lexicon. Anyway, why are you being so nice to me?"

His brows furrow. "What do you mean?"

"I'm not used to people being kind for no reason. So I'm curious as to why. Most don't do things out of the *goodness of their hearts*." I add a failed attempt of a Southern twang to the last words.

At first, I think he's offended, but then a bark of a laugh escapes him. "You're adorable, but also, that makes me feel kinda sad for you. I don't like knowin' you're so used to bein' treated poorly that when someone is kind, you think they need a reason."

"I'm somewhat sad for me, too," I admit.

"There ain't no reason other than this is the way folks are around here. Why be a dick? What's the point? Takes so much energy, and I dunno about you, but I don't want to be the reason someone has a shitty day. It's Christmas year-round here. We're giving, caring, and most of all, merry people."

"So being kind is a part of your culture."

"Yes, ma'am. You're right about that."

I think about the things I've read about Merryville. All of them raved about how incredible the town was. Many reviews mentioned visiting in December. Merryville is kinda like Disney; it's one of the happiest places on earth. If I were to make an addition to that, I'd say it has some of the happiest people, too.

Just as I open my mouth to ask Jake another question, Glenda slides three plates in front of us. Jake's burger looks like it was plucked from a television ad, with a perfect presentation of the seasoned fries and pickle. My scrambled egg biscuit and a gigantic stack of red-and-green pancakes are Instagram-worthy. I smile, and she winks. Then I pull out my phone and take one photo of the pancakes, framing it so the stack looks bigger than it is. Melted butter drips off the side, and my stomach growls with anticipation.

When I cut a small triangle from them and pop the warm, sugary bread into my mouth, I moan. It's so buttery, with the right amount of sweetness. As Jake bites into his burger, I snag one of his fries.

"Have as many as you'd like," he offers, so I take another.

"Want some of my pancakes?" I ask.

I didn't expect him to do it, but he takes the utensil from my fingers, cuts a sliver, and then pops it in his mouth. He hands me back my fork.

"Mm. Forgot how good those were."

"If I lived here, I might eat these every day."

He laughs. "Nah, you'd work yourself down the menu. The banana puddin' is great."

As we hold a playful conversation, today doesn't seem so bad. Being here with Jake is much better than sitting in an old inn. When I'm around him, he steals my attention and thoughts away. It's just me and him in the moment, having dinner, talking about nothing. I'm not used to this.

"So whatcha think? You can be truthful." Jake squishes his burger flat and takes another bite.

"It's really good," I tell him, covering my mouth, trying to remember my manners. "Best pancakes I think I've ever had. Might have to post this place on social media."

"Welcome to the South. The secret ingredient is butter. But don't tell nobody."

This makes me snicker. "I believe it. But I'm not complaining."

"You kids okay over there?" Glenda asks from behind the counter.

I nod, and so does Jake.

"Yes, ma'am. We're doin' real good."

I've met plenty of people who stumble to kiss the ground I walk on, but that's because they have to or want something from me. There was nothing genuine about it. So to experience being treated this way without reason is boggling my mind.

"Honestly, the food is why I don't think I could ever move away from Merryville."

"Never?" I ask, finding it hard to believe someone his age is already so…settled.

"Nope. Wouldn't even consider it." There is no hesitation or second-guessing in his answer. "I've got everything I need here. Occasionally, I travel. Go on week-long hiking trips in the summer. Fish in the Rockies. Life here is slow, easy, and predictable. Until people like you show up."

I pretend to act offended. "What's that supposed to mean?"

He sits back, a smirk playing on his perfectly plump lips, and picks up his coffee. Jake eyes me over the rim before taking a sip. "City folk. Those who come here searchin' for something."

His words cut deep, and I'm not sure why because there is truth behind them. Truths he doesn't know about. "And what are they searching for, exactly?"

He continues. "For what they're missing in life. Love. Adventure. Holiday magic. Acceptance. But ultimately, I think the lost ones are lookin' for a place to feel at home. And see, that's the thing about Merryville. We're one big family. The whole town is family run and owned. All small businesses. I think it says a lot about who we are and our culture here. It really brings to heart the small-town feel. It's why it's a national treasure, a place to be protected."

"Did you know Merryville is the number-one-grossing holiday small town in America?"

He nods. "Don't use big words like gross and sums and all of that fancy business talk. Most of the people here do well. But it's not like that for everyone."

I study his face, just like I studied every fact about this town. Facts that seem to repeat in my mind. There are several books written about this place because it's iconic.

·   ·   ·

Merryville was established in 1812 after Harry and Anita Merry decided they wanted to share their vision of Christmas with the world.

Three families founded the town. The Merrys. The Jollys. The Mistletoes. It became a haven for those with Christmas last names. The Gingerbreads and the Sleighs joined them six months later. Within the first decade, more people flocked to Merryville. The only ones who stuck around seemed to have a last name associated with the holiday. Some call it the Christmas spirit and it's why the town can't be replicated. There have been copycats, but only a few have survived.

Merryville's small businesses' gross income competes with larger cities like Amarillo due to the extreme tourism year-round. The residents are earning big-town money while keeping their small-town charm.

"Are you okay?" he asks.

I shake my head. "Sorry. I've got a lot on my mind. The day has felt like a blur, honestly. Just tired."

"Totally understand. I'll ask for the ticket so we can start headin' back to my place. Looks like we might see a break in the weather in about ten minutes."

"Great. Quick question…"

"Yeah?" He pulls his wallet from his back pocket.

"What's Glenda's last name?"

"The owner?" He glances at her before looking at me. "Elf."

Of course it is. When Glenda walks over, Jake hands her his card.

"I'll pay," I tell him. "You're doing me a favor. Please, I insist."

Glenda doesn't even wait for my protests and walks away.

"A gentleman never lets a lady pay for a meal. It's just not somethin' we're accustomed to here in the South."

I nod, begrudgingly accepting this part of the Texas culture. The "yes ma'ams" and "no ma'ams" are included. Next time, instead of asking questions, I'll remind myself they're all just Southern. I think their hospitality and manners are giving me culture shock. The people I've surrounded myself with act as if they're the only ones in the room because they're selfish. And they talk so much because they love the sound of their own voices.

I've never fit in anywhere. Not in the city. And surely not here.

I take another gulp of my coffee.

"No rush," he tells me. "We'll leave when you're ready."

"Thank you," I say, letting out a breath. I don't like anyone waiting for me, mainly because I usually don't have time to wait on others. It's the go-go-go mentality that's been ingrained into me since I was a teenager. So when it's time to slow down, I'm not sure how to act or what to do.

When he asks Glenda for a refill of coffee, I know he means it. Jake is used to living the slow-and-easy life with a *we'll get there when we get there* mentality. In New York and Paris, life moves fast, and the cities never sleep. Neither do the CEOs.

Jake pours two more spoonfuls of sugar and cream inside his mug and notices I'm staring. Men like him don't exist. And when I look at him, I still can't help but wonder if I'm dreaming.

"You know, it's not polite to stare," he drawls with a tilted brow, though I notice he hasn't been able to take his eyes off me since we sat down. I'm not complaining. I don't mind holding his attention because he intrigues me.

I smile. "Sorry. Couldn't help it with the view."

Jake grins and winks. "Thank ya, ma'am."

I laugh. "Typical Texan. Maybe that should be your nickname."

"I am a man who loves a good nickname, but it's too close to JJ."

I breathe in. "I think I'll call you Mr. Nice, then."

He pops a brow. "And would that make you Mrs. Naughty?"

The growl in his voice—and the way he chews on the corner of his lip before he gives me a wide, perfect smile paired with a smoldering gaze—has me ready to internally combust with just one damn look. Am I that desperate for someone to be nice to me that I already find this man attractive?

I swallow hard and clear my throat. My cheeks are burning.

"You're blushing," he murmurs. "Didn't realize that's all it would take."

"Well played. I've got to give it to you for catching me off guard. That doesn't happen often," I admit. I'm usually more on my *A* game than this. Maybe it's the green in his eyes and the confidence that rolls off him that makes him so attractive. Or maybe it's the Southern drawl, protectiveness, and manners. Either way, I have to keep my focus while I'm here. There is no room for mistakes or distractions.

I finish my pancakes, and Glenda refills my coffee. We sit for five more minutes before we're both satisfied and ready to go. Don't remember the last time I've not been rushed by either myself or outside sources.

All of this is out of my control—the truck, the inn, the godforsaken weather—and maybe I should take a page out of Jake's book and try to enjoy the time I have here.

It's not the experience I planned, but it's the one I'm having.

At least until returning home becomes an option.

CHAPTER 6

JAKE

B y the time we leave, the sun has set and it's sprinkling. It's the break in the storm I was hoping we'd get.

We travel five miles outside of town, and soon, I turn into the farm. Claire leans forward, looking up at the sign that greets everyone who's crossed the property line since the day my great-great-grandfather started Jolly Christmas Tree Farm. Over the years, the wood has rotted and been replaced, and the green background and logo have been touched up and eventually repainted. Right now, the sign has chips, and the words are faded. It's seen better days, but I guess the farm has, too.

"Oh, this is the Christmas tree farm," Claire says. "It's been in business quite a long time."

I chuckle, and glance over at her. "Yeah, it has. I just hope it can stay that way."

I didn't mean for those words to topple out, but thankfully, she doesn't ask any questions. We bump along the road for a few moments in silence.

"What does that mean, exactly?"

So much for not asking questions.

She's not being rude, but I can see a twinkle of curiosity in her eye.

So I tell her. "When my grandfather got sick and eventually passed away, my grandma tried to keep up with finances. The hospital bills were out of control, and she did what she could to keep afloat. She emptied their savings to keep my grandfather alive just a little longer. The time they got together was priceless, but it left the farm in crisis, one we haven't been able to recover from yet."

"I'm…sorry," Claire says. I don't think she expected me to go into detail, but why hold anything back? She won't be here long enough for it to matter. I've seen thousands of her type over the years; they come in flocks, but they always go. Women like her never stay.

"It's nothing to worry about," I tell her. "It will work out."

She nods. "I'm happy to hear that. I hope you're right."

I hope I am, too.

"It will." I smile as we approach the cabin I designed myself.

"Wow," Claire says, getting out of the truck. She stares at it with amazement. "This is gorgeous."

I look at her and grin, shoving my hands in my pockets, taking a moment to admire her. "Thanks."

I want to get to know her better, learn all of her secrets and hear about the things she loves. Based on how she speaks and presents herself, it's obvious that she's someone. The only question I need to answer is…who? Who is Claire Chester from New York? She seems familiar, but I think that's how I feel about women with blue eyes, cute button noses, and pouty lips. Everyone has a type, and she's mine.

I grab her suitcase, which feels like it's full of bricks, and haul it up over the edge of the truck. She pulls her purse from the cab and falls in line beside me. As we walk up the porch, I see Tinsel in the window. She looks at me and meows, but when she spots Claire, the fur on her spine rises and she hisses.

"Oh no."

I chuckle as I punch 1-2-2-5 into my keyless entry to unlock the door. "She'll warm up to you if you're around long enough."

"So she does that to everyone?" Claire asks as I stand behind her, slide her jacket off her body, and hang it on the rack.

"Pretty much," I admit. "She only likes me and one other person."

She removes her hat as I put my gear next to hers. With her mouth slightly open, she takes in the large cathedral ceilings, gigantic windows, and natural wood walls that are painted to preserve the look. To see her obviously impressed as she glances around makes me feel like a rock star because I designed every aspect of this place myself.

It's my dream home.

The windows allow natural light inside during the day. I remove my boots, and she follows suit before stepping forward. She walks past the oversized chair and couch, studying the framed pictures I have on the mantel I carved. Her fingers slide across the smooth wood from trees I handpicked and sanded down. This place was a labor of love.

Knowing the temperatures are dropping, I move to the fireplace to start a fire with the extra wood I have stacked next to it. The windows are incredible, but in the winter, it's draftier than I'd like. The dry logs immediately catch, and I step back, watching the flames lick up the side. Claire sighs and relaxes, soaking up the heat.

"That feels good," she mutters, and it's almost a whisper in the wind.

Moments later, Tinsel trots past me, and the bell on her collar jingles.

"Hey, sweet girl," I say, moving toward her to pet her head, but when I bend down, she darts away. "Oh, don't play hard to get. You know you missed me."

I reach for her again, and she gallops away. As I stand upright, I shake my head and turn to see Claire watching me with a wry smile. "You talk to all the ladies in your life like that?"

I snicker. "I don't date sweet girls. It's why I'm always single. I tend to gravitate toward the bad ones with something to prove."

She swallows hard, but I see something flicker behind her eyes.

"What? You've got something to prove?"

She clears her throat. "I do, actually. But isn't that life? We're all on this planet trying to prove something to someone. If we're good enough, smart enough, rich enough, pretty enough, popular enough, loved enough... I could keep going."

I tilt my head and meet her eyes, really seeing her. "Actually, you're right. I never thought of it that way."

"Perspective." It's all she says, and I get it.

She's lived a different life than I have. That's obvious. She's New York, and I'm Texas, universal opposites in every way.

"Will you show me around?"

"Of course. Sorry about that. Right this way," I say, leading her into the kitchen she could see from the living room since it's an open-concept design. She walks around the island in the center of the space that I wanted for when I throw parties, something that hasn't happened in far too long. That's something I might have to change in the new year.

"May I?" she asks, reaching for the pantry door and sliding it open. When she flicks on the light, she gasps. "The organization. This is incredible."

I show her the laundry room and then lead her across to the other side of the house. "This is the bathroom. Shower. Tub. Toilet. Towels," I say, opening the closet.

Then I open another door that leads to my bedroom. A

large, hand-carved, four-poster bed is in the middle of the room, along with several rugs, because the hardwood can be cold in the winter. Her eyes trail over it, over the windows, the large dresser, and the television. "Another fireplace?"

I shrug. "Why not? Can one really have too many?"

"Point taken," she says.

"You can have my room if you'd like," I offer. "I know you've had a long day, and I don't think I'd feel right about you bein' on the couch."

"I can't do that." She shakes her head. "I'm tired enough that I won't care where I am once I'm asleep. As long as I can shower, I think I'll be able to handle it for a night."

"You're sure?" If there is one thing I've learned about Claire in this short amount of time, she's stubborn, and when she puts her mind to something, I don't think she's easily swayed. I might not always be the best judge of character, but I've witnessed that much myself.

"I'm sure. You've done enough already," she says.

"Let me draw you a bath. The tub is great after a long day. Just a warning, you might not want to get out."

"That actually sounds divine," she admits. "I'll get my clothes and toiletries from my suitcase."

Claire walks away, but the hint of her sweet perfume still lingers. While Claire is in the living room, Tinsel presses two paws against my door and cracks it wider before prancing inside with a meow.

"Yes, Your Majesty?" She walks past me, leaning her body against my leg, her tail trailing against my pants. I turn around to look at her. "Are you still mad?"

Tinsel jumps up on the ottoman and then hops onto the bed. She's ten, an elder kitty at this point, and sometimes she's lazy. With a thud, she plops on her side and starts kneading imaginary biscuits in the air with her paws. I pet her belly, feeling her purrs. When I give her too much, she swats at me but then leans into my touch. "Don't be upset. She had nowhere to go."

I give her one last belly rub before walking to the bathroom. I sit on the edge of the tub, getting the temperature of the water just right, then set two towels on the counter. Claire walks in with a bag full of items.

"Take your time," I tell her, standing from the edge.

She glances at the deep tub. "Thanks. I just might."

When I go to walk away, Claire reaches out and stops me. Her soft hand is on my arm as she peers up into my eyes.

"Thanks, Jake. You didn't have to help me, and I appreciate you being persistent. I'd still be walking."

"You're welcome, CeCe. I don't think I would've let that happen."

"So you would've swung me over your shoulder and forced me to get in the truck?"

I laugh. "You better believe it."

CHAPTER 7

CLAIRE

The door closes behind him, and I pull my phone from my pocket. There's a text from the man that shall not be named.

DALE

> Please don't ignore me. We can talk this through.

I close out of the app, lock my phone, and then undress as the water fills the tub. As I run my fingers under the stream, I remember I brought a travel bubble bath with me that came as a bonus gift with my perfume.

The inn had shared bathrooms, so I was prepared to deal with that and packed a bag with my favorite items that I knew I'd never find on the shelves in Merryville. Not when everything here is locally made except for the items in the grocery store. If they could manage their food distribution in bulk, I'm sure they would. *Keeping it local* should become their slogan.

I unscrew the golden lid and pour some into the water. Instantly, it foams, and the sweet smell fills the room. I smile, setting it on the counter. My phone vibrates, then dings with another message, and I glance at it.

DALE

I heard you left town. Where are you?

"None of your damn business," I mutter, powering down my device to end the temptation to tell him to go fuck himself again. Or his wife. Whichever is more convenient.

I grab a spare ponytail holder, twist my hair into a high bun since it's not a wash day, and slip into the tub. A moan escapes me as my tense muscles relax. The temperature of the water is exactly how I like it. Not too hot or cold, just perfection.

That's when I notice there's a TV hanging on the stone wall. To my left is a bamboo shelf with a remote on it. I laugh when I turn it on and see the Country Music Television channel. The volume is low, and I imagine Jake listening to music as he bathes. Typical Texan.

I sink deeper in the tub, letting Reba McIntire sing "Does He Love You." It makes me think about Dale, and I grab the remote to turn it off, needing to focus on something else.

Merryville is one of the few towns that has successfully kept holiday traditions for over two centuries, which started with the lighting of the town tree on December 21 to celebrate the winter solstice. Afterward, they have a bonfire and a town dance. Everyone attends.

. . .

Merryville has its own anthem that was written by the founders of the town.

I reposition myself when my hairline touches the water and rest my arms on the edges of the porcelain tub. Steam rises around me, the bubbles floating around my body, and I take in several deep breaths, trying to calm my heart. I don't know what I'm doing in this stranger's house, but I'm at peace. I'm not worried about anything.

What if I don't leave as soon as possible and stay here with Jake? That thought takes me by surprise, but there's something calming about him. I'm drawn to him. And it's obvious we're both lonely and broken.

Is it possible that the right man has fallen into my lap?

No. I laugh, remembering my terrible judgment.

Hopefully, taking this risk doesn't come back to bite me in the ass.

When my skin prunes and the heat of the water fades, I decide it's time to get out and dry off. Reaching forward, I pull the stopper from the drain, and soapy water whooshes past my body. Steadying myself, I step out and grab one of the fluffy towels he left on the counter. I wrap one around my body as I go through my nightly routine. Inside my bag are my skin creams and body lotions. After I brush my teeth, I slide into my silk pajamas.

The pads of my feet touch the cool wooden floor as I go to the living room with my bag over my shoulder. Jake is sitting on the couch, drinking a glass of whiskey. His cat is right next to him with her paws on his lap. He looks over his shoulder at me with a twinkle in his eye. "How was it?"

"Perfect," I say with a smile, moving to the oversized armchair. His cat glares at me briefly, then returns her head to his lap.

Understood.

I know that look from anywhere. It's the stay-away-from-my-man glare.

He puts his large hand on her back and pets her smoky-gray fur. "No cattitude allowed."

He adjusts his body, moving her to the side of him as he stands. Tinsel growls, then hops on the floor and lies on the rug.

"I grabbed some spare blankets for you. That's a quilt my mawmaw made."

I glance at the carefully cut and sewn squares, a collage of different red-and-white Christmas-themed patterns. A yawn escapes me, and he notices. Most would just ignore the gesture because the people I'm surrounded by at home are high on caffeine, trying to ignore their own exhaustion.

Jake grabs a sheet and places it on the cushions, tucking it into the couch, then spreads the beautiful quilt on top before placing a pillow that came from his bedroom at the end.

"Your bed awaits you, milady," he states, presenting it to me.

I try to hold back a smile as I take a few steps toward it and slide inside. When I glance over, I see Tinsel staring. Her tail flicks a few times, but her stony gaze doesn't falter.

"Does she look at everyone like that? Like she wants to murder them?"

"My sweet girl would never," he says as he looks at her with a fond smile, and she blinks slowly, that tail still whipping around like she's agitated. Then he brings his attention back to me. "Need me to leave a light on? Or close the curtains?"

I have the perfect view of the moonlit land surrounding his sanctuary in the woods. "No. I don't need any special treatment. You've done enough already."

"If you change your mind, you know where my room is. I'll be in there. Okay?"

"Thanks. Good night, Jake."

"Night, CeCe."

I smile, sinking deeper into the cushions. "Your couch is much better than the sidewalk."

"I'm not sure how high a compliment that is, but it's yours for as long as you need it. Even if that means five weeks."

"I couldn't impose." I yawn, not able to hold back a smile. We've just met, but I feel like I've known this man for years.

"Never say never." The overhead light turns off, and the flame from the fire casts a warm glow in the room.

I hear Jake's door open, followed by the sound of Tinsel's collar jingling as she trots down the hall. The soft click of it closing is the last thing I remember as I drift off to sleep.

When I wake, I'm not sure what time it is, but it's still dark outside. I blink a few times and realize I'm parched. After traveling all day and dealing with the catastrophe I call life, I know I'm not hydrated.

The logs in the fire are glowing red, and there is a tiny flicker of a flame, but it's mostly out.

As I sit up to go to the kitchen for some water, I see movement outside. Immediately, my heart races as a long shadow dances across the ground. I'm scared, so scared that I rush to Jake's room. When I open the door, I see him sprawled across the bed with Tinsel curled up against his shirtless torso.

There's a lit Christmas tree in the corner and then I notice his bed. Red sheets with a white comforter.

"Jake," I whisper. He doesn't respond. "Jake." I use my full voice but don't want to startle him, so I focus on controlling my volume even though my anxiety is creeping up.

His eyes bolt open. "What's wrong?"

"I think I saw someone outside," I admit.

He slips out from under the blankets and puts on a pair of black-framed glasses that complement his strong jawline.

Nerdy but confident men are my weakness. He moves toward me, muscles cascading down his hard body as his joggers ride low on his hips. I can't find my words.

Gently, Jake rests his hands on my shoulders while studying me.

The moonlight shines enough for me to see his full expression.

He smells like cedar and mint and man.

I look up at his scruffy jaw and study his lips before finally meeting his green eyes that are full of...something.

Is that *worry*?

"You're shakin' like a leaf. Are you all right?" I hear the calm sincerity in his tone and feel guilty all over again for being in his home.

I nod, trying to catch my breath, not wanting the panic to take over. Part of me wants to shake him and tell him to never let strangers into his home. I could've been anyone, a complete psycho. The only people who know I'm with him are Glenda and Hank. Neither knows *me*, though.

Jake is too kind for his own good. Though he honestly doesn't need any protection with the muscles he has. I'm sure he's more than capable of handling himself.

Can't remember the last time a man was interested in what I had to say at dinner or even offered to pay or open the door for me...

"CeCe?"

I try to speak, but he's stolen my breath as his thumb brushes against my cheek.

"I'm okay," I whisper, but my legs are shaking. How can I feel like I've known him a lifetime when we've only just met?

"Stay here with Tinsel. I'll be right back." He removes his hold on me without hesitation and goes to his closet. He opens a safe in the back of it and pulls out a gun.

I place my hand over my mouth, wondering what he plans to do with the weapon he's brandishing. I've never seen a gun in person or been in a house with one, and I'm having another one of those culture-shock moments. It causes my anxiety to spike again.

"Wh-wh-where are you going?" I whisper as he crosses the room toward the door. He can't go out there, and…and… there's only one thing a gun is designed to do.

He turns around and meets my gaze. "Where did you see them?"

I hesitate. All of this is happening too fast. "In…in the backyard. Moving from east to west."

He makes his way through the house. Tinsel lifts her head to see where he's going but decides it's not important and snuggles back into the warm spot Jake abandoned. In my next life, I think I might want to be a cat, living a life of luxury with a sexy man who treats me better than some humans treat me now. I've never been jealous of a feline, but I think I might start.

When I hear the sliding door open and close, I stupidly decide to tiptoe down the hallway and peek around the corner. I have a clear view of the outside and see him shirtless, with joggers and boots. He's shivering as he shines a bright flashlight. Then, moments later, he bursts into laughter as he lowers the weapon. He comes inside wearing that boyish grin of his.

"It was a buck."

"A *what*? It looked like a big, scary man."

"A deer. He had a huge rack. Antlers up to here." He holds one arm up, giving me a visual.

The icy breeze fills the space, and a chill runs over me as Jake shuts the sliding patio door. His nipples are rock hard, and goose bumps trail over his skin. Spray him with oil, and he could be an underwear model with those abs of steel. I lick my lips when I scan over his V and the dark, happy trail that leads to the package he's carrying inside those pants.

My face heats, and I keep my eyes focused on his, not allowing my gaze to wander again. Those glasses paired with this body... Did Clark Kent take me home with him? The dark, messy hair on top of his head doesn't help at all.

"Do you want to sleep in my bed?" His voice is low and gruff as he removes the boots from his feet.

"And where will you go?" I swallow hard, wishing I had that glass of water I wanted earlier.

"Next to you."

I suck in a sharp breath. "But..."

"I'll protect you if a big, scary man is outside. Or a deer."

I lift a brow. "Tempting. What if I said I like to snuggle and I can't control where my hands go?"

"Tell me, is that a promise, darlin'?"

My heart fucking flutters.

Why? How? I'm too tired. That's what this is. And Jake is too damn sexy for his own good. I rub my hand on the back of my neck, trying to massage the muscles. "Ugh. I'm stiff."

He chuckles. "I'll keep that joke to myself. But I could help. I've been told I've got magic fingers."

The butterflies return as I think about everything that can possibly mean. "It's okay. I woke you. You should probably get back to sleep."

He nods and leads the way to his bedroom. Before walking inside, he turns and looks at me over his shoulder. "You comin'? I mean, if your boyfriend would be upset, I understand your reasonin'."

"No boyfriend," I confirm. My voice isn't much louder than a whisper, but he hears me.

As Jake stares at me, I know I have a choice to make. I can return to the couch, where my mind will wander alone, or I can follow Jake. I hear my internal monologue, which wants to take chances, and it urges me to step out of the perfect box I keep myself tucked away in.

When I step toward him, a smirk plays on his lips.

I pass him, inhaling his scent again, and stand next to the side of the bed that's still made.

"Once I'm asleep, I don't move much. So you'll have most of the space to yourself. I hang out near the edge with Tinsel." He returns the gun to the safe and then adds more logs to the fire.

"Okay." Though I wouldn't mind him being close. And right now, he looks like he could use the warmth.

The burning wood pops and his cat is where she was when I left. Jake removes the black-framed glasses from his face and sets them on the dresser before crawling around her. He successfully leaves her undisturbed. Once he's settled, he looks over at me and pats the empty side of the mattress. I lift the fluffy white comforter and slide into red silk sheets that feel cool against my body.

"Good night, CeCe," he says, then he rolls on his side, with his back facing me.

For a few minutes, I stare at the tall ceilings in his room, noticing how the beams cast shadows from the moonlight. My eyes grow heavy as I replay everything that happened today. Just as I fall asleep, laughter escapes me, and I wake myself. I feel the mattress move, and I glance over at him.

"What's funny?" he asks. His voice is velvety smooth.

I close my eyes, hoping I can quickly drift off. "Nothing. Today has been one of the weirdest days of my life."

"Welcome to Merryville." I can hear the smile in his words.

"And what a welcome it's been," I say, sucking in a deep breath and relaxing into the soft bed and pillow. I feel like I'm lying on clouds, knowing I made the right decision to follow him. It's a thousand times more comfortable than his couch.

As I drift off, I won't be surprised if I dream about ghosts of Christmas past and sugarplums—or Jake's lips and hands on my body.

The early morning sunrise wakes me. My arm is wrapped over Jake, and my chest is pressed against his bare back. Even though he didn't move an inch, I found my way across the mattress to him. He's warm. He's comfortable.

We're spooning, and he's holding me hostage because my arm is under him. He thought I was joking last night when I warned him. Well, I wasn't. I've always been a snuggler; I just don't have anyone to snuggle. While he shouldn't be surprised, I *somewhat* am.

I squeeze my eyes shut and slowly try to pull my arm out from under his without waking him. Just when I think I've escaped his warmth, he speaks up.

"Mornin'."

The gravel of his tone. The twang in his words. I'm doomed.

"Good morning," I say in a whisper, frozen for a brief moment.

"I didn't know you talked in your sleep," he mutters as I slide out from his smooth sheets and find my way into the bathroom, wishing I would disappear.

Mortified. It's the only thing that can describe how I feel.

No telling what I've said.

There's been so much on my mind.

And last night, before I went to bed, I was thinking about him and this town and my messy life. I can't even look myself in the mirror as I pass it.

Sleep talking is how my sister discovered I was dating someone I shouldn't have been with.

We'd gone to an art show in Scotland so she could post photos on social media. That night, I'd gotten too tipsy, and when we returned to the castle we'd rented, I fell asleep on the sofa. Spilled all of my secrets. Had a whole conversation about it, apparently.

Something I should've thought of last night before crawling into that gorgeous man's bed.

CHAPTER 8

JAKE

I reach out, feeling the warmth where Claire was. She did indeed talk in her sleep, but it was adorable. Tinsel's collar jingles as she stretches and lets out a lazy meow. A few moments later, she stands and jumps off the bed, prancing out of the room.

Claire is in the only bathroom in the house, so I decide to take care of Tinsel while I wait my turn. Thankfully, I remembered to put my glasses back on the nightstand last night. I'm blind as a bat. Without them, everything is blurry. When I'm staying inside for the day, I usually wear glasses, but when I'm out in the field, it's contacts. I've broken too many frames over the years and have learned my lesson.

Tinsel leads the way to the kitchen, and I stop and look out the windows into the backyard. Giant icicles hang from the edge of the house, and the grass is coated with ice. Everything outside has a layer of frost that reflects like glitter.

A meow brings me back to my task at hand.

I place a can of the senior cat food in Tinsel's bowl. She sniffs it, then blinks up at me with another meow. Shaking my head, I grab a few of her favorite treats and set them at her feet like she's a queen. She examines them, and she strolls away without touching any of them.

"Sometimes I think you do that to remind me who's in control," I tell her as I hear the bathroom door swing open. Claire rounds the corner and our arms brush against one another. I look over my shoulder at her, but she keeps walking.

I wonder if she just felt that jolt of electricity, too?

As I'm in the bathroom going through the morning motions, I can hear the zipper of her luggage and a thump in the living room. I'd bet my best axe she's digging through that giant suitcase that's probably packed with impractical shoes and clothes.

This woman isn't like anyone I've ever met before, and I find myself longing to learn random things about her. The things that make her tick. Her dreams and aspirations, her fears, and even her favorite color. She hasn't offered much about herself, and based on the conversation she had with Hank yesterday, she wants to leave Texas. But I don't know if I'm ready for her to go yet.

After I brush my teeth and throw on jeans and a long-sleeved flannel, I meet her in the kitchen.

"Are you hungry?"

She smiles. "What about coffee first?"

"Espresso good for you?"

"As long as it's not crappy espresso."

"I'll let you be the judge of that," I say and refill the reservoir of the maker with filtered water.

"I'm a bit of a snob, so you've been warned," she tells me.

"I love a good challenge," I murmur as I allow the machine to heat before it starts auto-grinding the beans. It was expensive, but after my last breakup, where I set clear boundaries and decided I wouldn't be a human doormat, I treated myself. Lacy convinced me that coffee was bad for me, so I gave it up for years. Once we ended things permanently, this shiny new machine was delivered and has been on my counter ever since.

"You must really enjoy your coffee if you've invested in something like that."

"I appreciate all the options and how easy it is to brew a few shots or a mug. On my days off, one of my rituals is to watch the sunrise in the mornin' with a hot cup. In winter and spring, a herd of deer graze in the open. I usually watch them until they decide they've had enough and leave."

She laughs. "It's almost as if you're living in a Disney movie."

This makes me chuckle. "Never thought of it like that. But I guess you're kinda right. I've seen rabbits, deer, birds, a fox, and even a few field mice."

"Really? All at once?"

The beans finish grinding, and the espresso drips. "Nah, different times, different seasons."

"Do you have armadillos here?"

"Sometimes. Haven't seen them often, though. Not in this part of the state."

"They seem cute," she says as I slide the double espresso across the bar top toward her. She picks it up and smells it, studying the crema that formed on top. As if she's a connoisseur, she takes a tiny sip. The smile that meets her lips is contagious.

"What brand of beans?" She inhales again.

I pull the gold-and-red plastic bag from the cabinet and hand it to her. After she studies the label, she returns her attention to me. "It's local?"

"Yeah. They've been roastin' their own beans for decades. Their coffee shop and warehouse are at the edge of town. Can't miss it if you're lookin' for it."

She seems as if she's searching through her memories. "Oh, I think I saw it. They have the Welcome to Merryville mural painted on the side of their building."

"Yeah, they do. The Santa scene. It used to be different, though. That one was revealed a few years ago during…"

"The celebration of Christmas in July," we say in unison.

I look at her. "You know a lot about Merryville."

She takes another drink, and if I didn't know better, I'd say she's trying to avoid the conversation, but then she answers.

"I have this thing where I memorize weird facts about places, the most random things that people don't even care to read in the first place. A lot of the Merryville facts are ingrained in my memory. I've been intrigued by this place since I was a kid."

"Really? Did you love Christmas?"

"I used to. Until my mother passed away."

My face softens, and I reach forward and touch her hand. She doesn't pull away.

"I'm sorry."

"Nah, it's fine. It was over twenty years ago."

"So what?" I tell her. "A person just doesn't get over it because time has passed, especially losing someone so close to you at a young age. It must've been hard."

"It was, and you're right. I'm so used to dismissing what I went through that now it's a habit. My dad is the let's-hurry-up-and-move-on type. He's been married three times since then."

"Three times?"

She nods. "He can't seem to find the one. I think he's searching for the wrong things in women, but who am I to judge? Not the best person when it comes to relationships." She stares into the bottom of her cup. "I'm more like my father than I like to admit at times."

"Kids mimic things. You're an adult now. You have choices. Decisions. If you don't want to be like him, you're free to do whatever it is that you want."

She laughs, but it comes out almost sarcastic.

I lift a brow because it's obvious that she's not convinced. "It's true. Once you stop trying to prove yourself to other people and put yourself first, you'll be a lot happier in life. I learned that the hard way."

I stir cool milk with the hot liquid, then shoot it back in one big gulp. Just as I'm getting ready to brew another one, the lights shut off. The motor in the fridge quiets and everything is still.

"Please tell me you have a generator?" She grabs the cup between her hands, concern on her face.

"Yeah," I tell her. "But it only runs the fridge." On cue, the motor clicks back on. I go to my bedroom and grab my phone so I can do a quick internet search on the power outage situation. It looks like the entire town is dealing with this at the moment.

"What?" she asks. "I don't like that expression."

"Could be longer than a week."

"I thought your friend said *days*." Her voice goes up an octave toward the end.

"Hey. Look at me," I say. "Come on, CeCe."

It takes her a few seconds, but she does. "Those glasses."

"Your kryptonite?"

"Yes," she whispers, moving her gaze away.

A fire ignites inside of me; the attraction is undeniable. I place my hand under her chin and force her attention back on me before she puts up her wall. "I've got plenty of food and water. Unlimited firewood. And a gas stove. Moonshine. And board games. Just think of it like a mini winter adventure."

She doesn't look convinced. "I've never not had electricity."

This makes me laugh. "Outages happen often around here durin' this time of year. If there's a lot of ice, it will snap power lines. High winds will knock over poles. It's just a part of country livin' that you learn to deal with."

"Or you get a generator that will run your entire place, so you don't have to worry about it."

"It's on my list of things to buy. Maybe one day, but for now, we'll rough it."

"I don't like the sound of that." She sighs.

"At least you'll have a fun story to tell your friends."

This makes her roll her eyes. "Corny."

"Maybe so, but you're safe. I'm not gonna let anything happen to you."

"Thank you. You're a gentleman."

I start preparing us for what's to come as Claire finishes her espresso at the island. First, I work on the fireplaces, and as soon as the wood catches, it lights the room. I'm thankful I brought extra wood inside last week when it was clear we'd be experiencing severe weather. It will be important to keep the house as warm as possible because the forecast predicts we'll hit the lower teens by tonight. I close the thick curtains, knowing the fabric will keep most of the cold out of the house.

"I need to get some supplies from outside. I'll be back."

I put on my boots and head to my workshop, where I do my woodworking projects throughout the year. Inside are a few lamps and an oversized battery tank I bought over the summer for my camping trips. I've kept it charged, but the cold can affect its efficiency, so it's better it comes inside with me anyway.

With hands full, I glance over at the motorcycle that's covered in the corner of my shop, then shake my head. Hank is an asshole.

When I return to the cabin, I take off my boots. My shadow dances on the wall as I walk across the living room to the kitchen. Claire is on the stool where I left her. I turn on a lamp and hand it over.

It lights her face, and I smile as I hold up the battery that's shaped like a small ice chest. "This is if you need to charge your phone."

"Shit," she hisses. "I need to text my sister so she doesn't worry. At least she knows where I am."

"Oh, really? You told her about me?"

Her mouth twitches. "I did."

"And did she tell you that you'd lost your mind for coming home with me?"

Claire crosses her legs and tucks a loose strand of hair behind her ear. This woman is a flirt as she bats her long lashes at me. "Actually, yes. And she'll really lose it when I explain I slept in your bed."

"She's going to call the authorities. Going home with a stranger. Sleeping in his bed with him."

"Moving in with him for a month." She shrugs.

"Are you?" I ask, hoping she's not kidding. "Because the offer is one hundred percent on the table."

"I'm considering it."

I lift my brows. "Wait, you're serious?"

"As long as you don't mind."

I can't hold back my wide smile. "I think it would be fun."

"There's only one problem, though. I don't like owing anyone anything. So I insist on paying you something."

I shake my head. "That's not happenin'."

A smile touches her lips. "I'll do whatever I want, Jake Jolly."

"I have no doubt about that. So how long are you stayin'?"

Claire puts her mug in the sink. "My flight is scheduled for January seventh. But I can always leave early."

"So five weeks," I confirm. "That means you'll get to experience Merryville like a local. There are lots of events throughout the holidays."

"I haven't celebrated Christmas in a very long time. If I'll ruin your plans, I can leave ear—"

"CeCe. This is typically one of the loneliest times of the

year for me and has been for a while now. It'll be nice having some company," I assure her. "It will be our winter adventure."

She laughs and shakes her head. "If I have too much fun, I might not want to leave."

"You never know what could happen," I say.

"You're right about that."

CHAPTER 9

CLAIRE

J ake continues preparing the house as I grab my phone. I turn it on and text my sister to let her know we're without power. I also explain that I'll be conserving my battery and will check in with her as soon as possible. Once the text shows delivered, I scroll through my other notifications.

DALE

I miss you.

Reading that text makes me want to throw up in my mouth. So I hold the side button and turn it off. I'll use this time to unplug from the outside world, something I haven't done in far too long.

As I shove my phone into my purse, I notice the floor-to-ceiling bookshelves built into the wall next to the fireplace. I grab the lantern and make my way across the room, lifting it higher as I peruse the titles.

Some of the books look like they belong in an old library.

The warmth of the yellow bulb makes the gold lettering nearly glow.

"They're classics." Jake startles me; I was so entranced I didn't notice him behind me.

"Many are over a hundred years old. They were my great-grandfather's."

"Do you enjoy reading?" I ask.

My eyes scan over the spines, and toward the end are more recent works, but still, they're all in hardcover. Have to appreciate a well-read man. "I do. I read a book per week these days."

"Really?" I ask, impressed. "And who's your favorite author?"

He chuckles. "That's like asking a parent who their favorite kid is. Depends on the day. Depends on the mood. Depends on the genre."

"I understand that more than you could know." I move to his modern-day shelf. "Thrillers. World history. String theory. And even a few romances." I spot one and pull it from the shelf. "You read this?"

He smirks, and I notice a cute little dimple in his cheek. Has it always been there?

"You're telling me you haven't?"

"Are you shaming me?" I nearly laugh.

"Every week, I download and read the number-one bestselling novel. If I enjoy it, I buy it in hardcover."

"Really?"

"Yeah, and this one is great. Funny. Sad, too. But as expected, the hero and heroine get their happily ever after."

I give him a smug look. "It's just not realistic."

"Maybe not, but it's fun to imagine it is. Two people falling in love. I understand why so many are obsessed with the genre. You should give the book a try, though."

"Nah."

"I bet it makes you cry."

I narrow my eyes. "Doubt it. Can't remember the last time I cried about anything."

That's not entirely true, but I keep my awful breakup to myself.

"Take the challenge, then. Read the book, every word, from front to back. No one has ever made it through without getting emotional. And if you do, you're dead inside."

"Did it get to you?" I wish I hadn't powered my phone off so I could search for spoilers. But I'm a good sport.

"It was sad as fuck. I'm not ashamed to admit that. But I guess you can't handle it."

I frown. He holds out his hand, waiting for me to give him the book, but I keep a firm grip on it.

"I'm going to read it for no other reason than to prove you wrong."

He chews on his bottom lip. "Great. Stubborn Susan is at it again. Just remember, those who try to be tough are the ones who have the furthest to fall. Wishin' ya all the luck, though."

"Pfft."

He lifts a brow. "Before I forget, there is one rule to the game: you aren't allowed to read the synopsis on the inside cover. You have to go in completely and utterly blind. So hand over the dust jacket. Can't have you be tempted to cheat."

My curiosity nearly gets the best of me, but I unwrap it and give it to him. Jake places the sleeve on the shelf where the book originally was.

Now that it's bare, I look down at the dark-brown leather cover that has a single rose on it, then read the embossed one-word title that's printed in red—*YOURS*.

I'm not sure what could be in the pages that pull at everyone's emotional heartstrings, but then again, I'm not like everyone.

I've been raised to be tough as nails.

Fearless.

To be a mold of my father, even if he looks at me like I'm

a disappointment. For years, he's told me he should've had a son. Instead, he has two daughters, and my sister isn't interested in the family business. She's too busy living her own adventurous life.

I'm it.

I'm all my father has, and he's convinced I'm unsuitable for the job.

As I move to the couch and sit, Jake follows me. "You hungry? We never ate."

"Oh, you're right. I typically skip breakfast, but I could eat something. Want me to help?"

Jake lifts his brow. "What's your favorite dish?"

"A teacup. Gold rimmed."

He snickers. "You eat teacups?"

"Oh, clearly, I haven't had enough caffeine today." I shake my head, feeling stupid. "Um. Tuna. I don't cook much. Or ever."

"We've got five weeks to change that," he tells me, waving me over. I grab my lantern and set it on the island. He opens the fridge and takes out the ingredients before shutting the door. "You said you don't eat tons of carbs, right?"

"Yeah. You remembered."

"Of course," he says over his shoulder. "Come closer. You can't learn from there. I like to use the hands-on approach."

I gulp and wish his hands were on me, but I quickly push those thoughts away. I stand close to him, and our arms brush together.

He glances over at me. "I'm gonna teach you how to make scrambled eggs. There's a trick to it. Low heat, lots of butter, and you have to remove it from the flame at the perfect time."

He gives me the spatula and lifts the skillet to ensure the fire is where he wants it. After setting the pan down, he slaps a big slab of butter inside.

I nod, watching it turn into a puddle in the pan.

"When it bubbles in the middle, that's how we know it's ready for the eggs."

Jake cracks four eggs into a bowl with one hand. Then he tosses the shells in the garbage. "Want to mix it?"

"Sure." He gives me a fork, and I stir the yolk with the whites.

"Now pour it in," he instructs.

As I do, it coats the bottom, and he turns off the heat. Then he hands me the spatula.

"Almost there. Don't let it stick on the bottom."

I do as he says, following his instructions. The eggs are fluffy as I mix them.

"Oh, almost forgot." He pulls two slices of American cheese from the fridge and rips them into fours before setting them on top.

"Mix that in. It's gonna taste so damn good."

The cheese doesn't completely melt, so Jake turns the burner back on, giving it just a little more heat. Within a minute, it's melted and mixed together. He pulls two paper plates from the cabinet, and I look down at them.

"I'm not doin' dishes, are you?"

I shake my head. "No thanks."

Carefully, I grab the handle and divide the eggs into equal parts. I clear the pan and then set it on the stove.

"Would you like some Texas toast?" he asks.

I give him a puzzled look. "Is it oversized?"

"Huh?" He pulls the loaf from the bread box on his counter.

"You know, because everything is bigger here?"

A roar of laughter escapes him. "It's the same size as a regular slice of bread, just thicker."

I look at it. "Sure, I'll have one."

"Great." He heats the skillet again, and when it's sizzling hot, he tosses two pieces of bread into the bottom. After thirty seconds, with his bare hands, he flips the toast. It looks perfectly cooked and smells so delicious. Once it's finished, he puts them on our plates before grabbing us two forks.

"Let's eat," he says, turning and finding the stool closest to him. I walk around to the other side of the breakfast nook and sit. Following Jake's lead, I scoop the cheesy scrambled eggs onto the slice of bread and fold it in half. Then I take a large bite. I can't help the moan that escapes me. It might be the best egg sandwich I've ever eaten in my life.

Jake notices and gives me a grin. "Good, huh?"

"Excellent. I think this may be my new favorite meal."

"If you're staying until the first week of January, I've got a repertoire of easy recipes I can teach you. They take little to no skills and taste good."

"I'd love that," I admit truthfully. "I've thought about taking a few cooking courses, but time is always my issue. My schedule is hectic, and it never worked out."

He takes another bite. "I understand that. Most of the stuff I learned from my mama. Other things, YouTube. I swear a person can learn to do anything they put their mind to by watching tutorials."

"That's true," I say. "One time, I learned how to tie a very specific sailing knot by watching a video."

"Sailing? Like on a boat?"

A few clumps of egg fall out of the back end of my sandwich, and I scoop them up with my fork. "Yeah. I've done a few trips. Not my favorite, though. I get horrible seasickness, something meds can't really cure. Long story short, I avoid the ocean and boats now. I much prefer having my feet on the ground anyway."

"That sucks," he says. "Did you enjoy sailing?"

I think back to all the times I've gone on the boat and the company surrounding me and answer truthfully. "No. Hated it, even without motion sickness. I feel like the only people I've met who actually enjoyed sailing are assholes. Not the company I like to keep."

But somehow, it's the company that's always surrounding me. I keep that part to myself.

"That makes a lot of sense." He chuckles. "Most people I've seen on TV who enjoy it are dicks, too. I actually hate flying."

My eyes widen. "Really? Why?"

"Heights. They freak me the fuck out. I like my feet planted on the ground."

Jake stands and grabs two bottles of water from the fridge and hands me one. I take two big swallows, the cold water quenching my thirst and cooling me down all at the same time. I'm not sure what it is, maybe the excellent food and conversation, but I'm hot from the inside out.

"Have you ever been to the top of an extremely high building?"

Jake shakes his head. "No. Not something I plan on doin', either."

"Don't blame you. I've been to the top of the Empire State Building a few times. It's extremely disorienting, but the view of the city is beautiful. Three-sixty view of everything."

"Nothing I can't Google and enjoy more since I'm not worried about plunging to my death."

I chuckle.

"What?" He lifts a brow.

"Just thinking about all the things I know about it. For instance, on a windy day, the building can sway up to three feet."

He blanches. "No way. That's now been added to my never-ever, not-even-once list."

"I don't think you can really feel it, though. Some experts believe that during an earthquake, a modern-day skyscraper is one of the best places to be."

"Don't want to find out." With a lifted brow, he pops the last bite of his sandwich in his mouth. I finish my food, too. He places our forks in the sink and throws our plates in the trash. I stand and stretch before making my way to the couch.

"I wonder if your friend picked up my truck yet."

"Probably not. Don't imagine he'll even go out there to tow it until after some ice has melted. Speaking of," he says, pulling his phone from his pocket, "let me look at the weather again."

Jake sits beside me, and moments later, Tinsel hops up between us. She glares at me before placing her paws on Jake's thigh and getting comfortable. Her long, bushy tail flicks against my arm, and it tickles. As he scrolls, I pick up the book.

"Oh, hold on, I have a reading light you can use to make it easier." He walks over to his bookshelf and grabs it, then hands it to me.

When he finally returns, Tinsel is curled up in his seat. He lifts her and she hisses before prancing away. "The chair thief did not succeed," he says, shaking his head.

"Your cat is a diva," I tell him, clipping the light onto the back cover and flicking it on. It's bright and lights the pages perfectly.

"Yeah, she is. But gotta love her. She wouldn't save me from an intruder or get help if I had an emergency, but I know she enjoys my company, even if it's on her own terms. What about you? Do you have any animals?"

"I don't," I say. "I'm hardly ever home."

"You could always get one of those small dogs that'd fit in your big-ass purse," he says.

"The responsibility is too much. I like worrying about myself and that's it. Animals can complicate plans just as easily as kids. It's why I have neither. I'll get an animal when I settle down. Though with how things have been going, that might not be anytime soon."

"Ya never know. I've always heard a person finds love when least expectin' it. When you stop lookin'."

I glance at him. "Yeah? What about you?"

"Oh, I'm on the market but not actively searchin' for a partner. I've decided that going forward, the relationship has to progress naturally. It will happen when it happens. I won't change who I am for anyone. Take it or leave it."

"A great philosophy." I go back to the book, and the two of us sit in silence. I try to reposition myself to get comfortable, and Jake lifts my legs and places my feet on his lap, allowing me to stretch as he scrolls on his phone. I give him a grin, then dive back in.

"Your toes are festive," he finally says, locking his phone.

I close the book, set it down on the coffee table, and push myself up on my elbows to look at them. "Ah, yes. It was my tech's idea to do them red and green. I usually just go for red. She told me to live a little."

He grabs my foot, studying my toes, and I jerk away.

"Are you ticklish?"

I tuck my lips into my mouth and shake my head no.

"You're a bad liar," he says. "Just in case you didn't know."

I roll my eyes. "No one knows how ticklish I am other than my sister."

"Your secret is safe with me unless I have to retaliate. Then you're getting the tickle monster." He wiggles his fingers and I squeal, bringing my knees up to my chest and tucking them in.

"I'd go down kicking and screaming."

His phone buzzes, pulling his attention away. "Hank," he says, then answers. "What's up?"

I can hear his best friend chatting on the other end of the line, but I can't tell exactly what he's saying. Moments later, Jake ends the call. "He hasn't gotten your truck yet."

"I wouldn't want him going out in this. I'd feel terrible if something happened."

"Yeah, gets dangerous out there with the icy conditions."

He changes the subject as a smirk plays on his lips. "So, what did your sister say about your escapades?"

"I didn't wait for her response. Yesterday, she begged me to come home and forget about the trip."

"You were sayin' the same thing, though. Why the change of heart?"

I smirk and lick my lips. "The magic of Merryville, of course."

He bursts out into laughter. "Ahh. Be careful. People come here and never leave once they discover it."

CHAPTER 10

JAKE

The following day, I wake up to Claire sleeping soundly beside me. Her brown hair is spread across the pillow, and she looks like a princess. A smile touches my lips as I climb out of bed, trying my best not to disturb her.

I add a few more logs to the fire, then take a quick bathroom break before going to the living room.

Tinsel's sleeping on the back of the couch, and I stop to pet her. "Good mornin', baby girl," I croon, giving her a kiss on her head. "Ya hungry?"

Once I've said the magic word, her pupils dilate, and she stands and stretches. It doesn't take much to get her up, just one of the few words she knows—hungry, food, naptime, treats. One of them always does the trick. Tinsel's collar jingles all the way to the kitchen as she trots to her bowl. Before following her, I rearrange the half-burned wood and add more to the pile until it catches. The flames lick up the side of the dry logs, causing the fire to pop and crackle.

I hold out my hands, warming my fingers, hoping the temperature rises quickly. The mornings are usually the coldest, thanks to the large, double-paned windows overlooking the rolling hills. The curtains help, but only so much.

After Tinsel is fed, I put a pot of water on the stove to boil for French press coffee. I grab the carafe from the back of my pantry and rinse it out before pouring ground beans in the bottom. This isn't my favorite way to prepare coffee because it sucks to clean, but there aren't many options. The bonus is it tastes great, not like the shitty instant crap I drink when I'm backcountry hiking.

When the water begins to bubble, I pour it over the grounds and put the lid on top, allowing it to steep for the next ten minutes.

As I wait for it, the chill in the room vanishes.

Just as I'm pressing the coffee, my phone buzzes on the counter. The giant battery bank I bought for times like this still has ninety-eight percent left. At this rate, I'll be able to use it for the next month and a half.

I walk over and answer, realizing it's just past eight. I slept in.

It's my mom. "Hey, sweetie, how's it goin'?"

I hear water running in the bathroom, which means Claire is awake, too.

"It's goin' fine. Y'all good over there?"

"Actually, I was wondering if you could come over and help your dad bring some more firewood into the house. He pulled his back earlier this mornin' when he carried a load in."

"It must've been too heavy," I say.

"You know how he is. Santa thinks he's Superman and doesn't listen to anyone."

I snicker. "I'll be right over. Give me about thirty?"

"Thanks, I'll have breakfast for ya."

"Got enough for another person?"

"Sure, tell Hank he can join us. Oh, your brother is calling. See ya soon."

I don't have time to correct her before she ends the call. I run my fingers through my hair. This is going to be interesting.

Tinsel lifts her head and looks at me. "It's gonna be fine."

Her tail flicks, and she goes back to her food bowl.

Claire comes from the bathroom, her hair in a messy ponytail on top of her head. I try not to stare at how damn beautiful she is without even trying. Flawless, glowy skin and bright-blue eyes. She's still wearing her silk pajamas, and they hug her body. I grab two mugs from the cabinet and set them on the counter, then pour her a cup and one for myself.

She immediately picks up her pace and grabs it with both hands, inhaling the sweet scents. "Chocolate notes."

"I almost forgot you were a coffee connoisseur."

She grins, blowing on the top. I do the same.

"You want to meet my parents?"

Her mouth slightly parts. "Really?"

"Why not? You're gonna be joinin' me for Christmas dinner there anyway."

"Am I?" She looks even more puzzled. "I don't recall having that on my schedule."

"Did you think I would let you stay here all alone on Christmas Day?"

She opens her mouth and then closes it. "I would be fine. It's just like every other day. And don't you dare call me *Stubborn Susan!*"

I laugh. "I would never let you spend a holiday cooped up here with Tinsel when I'm at my parents' eating a big, home-cooked turkey dinner. There will be plenty of desserts, too. Afterward, we always play a long game of Monopoly with spiked eggnog. But it might be less awkward if you meet them now as opposed to me bringin' a pretty woman with me to a big celebration and them gettin' the wrong idea about us."

"And what idea would that be, exactly?"

I give her a pointed look. She's not this dense; I know better.

She lifts her brow. "Would it be the worst thing that could happen?"

I shake my head, taking two steps forward and removing the space between us. "You bein' my girlfriend? They'd honestly be giddy if I brought someone home. I'm already gonna get the third degree, and even then, after I explain what happened, they probably won't believe the truth. But I'd rather just rip the Band-Aid off now if you'll be stayin' here for a few weeks. Otherwise, the rumors will start flyin'."

"Yes," she says.

"Huh?"

"Yes, I'll go with you to your parents'." She gives me a mischievous grin. "When?"

"In about five minutes."

Her eyes widen. "That's barely enough time to get dressed."

"It doesn't matter what you wear. Fashion won't impress them. That said, they're old-fashioned, so be on your best behavior."

She lifts a brow. "I know how to be polite."

"I have no doubt about that," I assure her as she rushes toward the bedroom, and I follow. When I enter, clothes are thrown on the bed like she's pairing outfits together. She looks stressed. I meet her gaze.

"What's up?"

She pulls her hair down from her ponytail. "First impressions are important. They're everything."

"Are they? I mean, the first time I met you…"

She holds up her hand. "That was different. I had no preparation."

"Whatever you say." I shoot her a wink, then go into my closet and grab a hoodie, tugging it over my body along with some jeans.

When I walk into my room, she's wearing a blue, fuzzy sweater that matches her eyes and some black slacks, along with those boots again.

"Wow, you look…amazin'."

"Really?" She doesn't sound convinced. "You're sure it's not too much?"

I shake my head. "Nah. My parents are gonna love you. They've never met a stranger and never disliked a single human."

She sucks in a breath. "Okay. Awesome. I'm nervous. Totally out of my comfort zone."

"It's fine. My mama will do most of the talkin' anyway. We won't be there very long, but I thought it might be nice to get outta the house."

"Yeah, I think so."

She walks out of my bedroom, and I place my hand on her shoulder and squeeze. "It's gonna be fine."

"I hope you're right."

As I move toward the door, Tinsel jingles toward me with several meows. She trots past me and runs straight to the kitchen. "Just one second. I forgot to give her treats earlier. She'll be pissed at me for the rest of the day if I leave without giving her some," I explain as Claire puts on her coat.

I pour a few treats onto her food mat, and she eats one, then looks up at me with her big golden eyes. If I didn't know better, I'd think she could count. I sigh. "Just a few more."

When I tip the container, a pile falls out, but I keep them down there for her. "Better not waste them."

Her tail flicks, and then I meet Claire at the door. "Ready?"

She gives me a nod, and we walk outside.

"They weren't shittin' us when they said it was an arctic blast movin' through," I say, opening the door for her, and she climbs in, blowing her warm breath into her hands.

I crank the truck. "Can't turn the heat on yet. Gotta get the engine warm."

She smiles. "It's fine. Reminds me that I'm alive."

I look over my shoulder, back out of the driveway, and head down the old gravel road. We drive past the rows of Christmas trees covered in frost and the building where customers line up to pay. Another half mile down the road is my parents' place. Their house sits up on a small hill and somewhat overlooks the farm. Smoke drifts out of the chimney, and I know Mom didn't tell Dad we were stopping by. He's too proud to ask for help most of the time, even if I offer first.

I park next to the SUV in the garage. When all of the boys were still at home, we used to fight over who got the third parking space. Now, anytime I snag it, it feels like a victory.

We walk through the side door that leads through the mudroom and into the kitchen.

"Honey!" Mama says when she sees me. Then Claire comes into view, and her mouth falls open before twisting into a smile. "Oh, goodness. Who is this?"

She looks between us, then forges on before I can answer. "I'm Evelyn Jolly, Jake's mother. It's so nice to meet you." My mother doesn't care about personal space or boundaries and immediately pulls Claire into a tight hug.

I shake my head and mouth, *I'm sorry*.

"I'm Claire Chester. It's very nice to meet you, too."

Mom turns to me with raised brows. "You didn't tell me you were bringin' a beautiful girl home. No warning or nothing! I would've at least fixed my hair."

"You look great," I tell her, placing a kiss on her cheek. "Also, I didn't plan on having company, either. It just kinda happened."

"What does that mean?" Mom looks between Claire and me, then holds up her hand to stop us from explaining. "Wait, let's do introductions in the living room so your father can be on the same page and you won't have to repeat yourselves."

"Ma," I sigh. "It's not a big deal. Claire is just a guest. That's it."

She doesn't listen and shuffles through the kitchen. I glance at Claire and place my hand on the small of her back to guide her into the living room, where my father is reading in his recliner. His glasses are sitting on his nose, and when he looks up from his paper, he's shocked.

"Howdy," he says with a grin.

Claire turns and whispers, "Your dad is freaking Santa Claus?"

I nod. "Yeah."

Dad lets out his infamous *ho-ho-ho* so she gets the full effect. Claire walks over to him and politely introduces herself.

"Nice to meet you. So Jake didn't tell you I've got a list of who's naughty and nice and I check it twice?"

"Actually, no," she says with a kind smile, but there's a sparkle in her eyes. "I've seen your picture online at least a thousand times. You're a legend."

Dad folds the newspaper and sets it down on the small table next to his recliner. "I do get around, as Santa does."

Claire laughs. "I have so many questions."

"Please have a seat," Mom offers, and Claire moves to the small couch and sits on the edge. I plop down next to her.

"I can't believe you didn't tell me," she whispers.

Doesn't help that Dad is wearing red pants, a white shirt, and suspenders. In December, he's never caught without his signature gear. Even when the town is shut down and everyone is locked inside, he's prepared.

"Honestly slipped my mind," I tell her truthfully. I'm so used to everyone already knowing that it's not even a point of discussion.

Mom clears her throat. "I thought we'd bring the

conversation in here. Jake was just gettin' ready to tell me how he and this young lady met."

"Mom," I say, "it's not like that. We're not together," I explain again.

Dad looks at me with his eyebrows raised. "Yet."

"No." I give both of my parents a look of warning. "I'm sorry," I whisper to Claire, but she's grinning in delight. I honestly think she enjoys seeing me squirm because that's what this conversation is doing to me.

"So I found Claire walking into Merryville."

Both of my parents snicker.

"I'm not kiddin'." I look at Claire. "See, I told you they wouldn't buy it."

"It's fine if you two are datin'. We approve," Mom says. "Claire, you seem like a very nice young lady. Did you two meet online?"

"Mom," I groan.

"Online datin' is a way of life now," Dad offers with a knowing nod. "There is nothin' wrong with it."

I place my face in my hands, and Claire puts her hand on my shoulder and squeezes.

"He really did pick me up off the side of the road. My rental broke down, and Jake rescued me from the storm after an issue with my reservation at the inn."

Neither is convinced.

"You two really seem to hit it off quickly. I'm sensing some chemistry," Mom observes. The last time I brought a girl home was over five years ago. Too long. But this isn't that, and I wish they'd stop.

"Anyway," I interrupt before this can go on any further, "I'd like to bring Claire to Christmas dinner if she's still in town."

I glance over at her, and she's beaming.

"Oh, we would love that. Would give you an opportunity to meet the rest of the family, too," Dad says. "However,

Christmas Eve is a big night for me. Flyin' around, delivering gifts around the world."

He offers Claire a wink, and she giggles.

"How long will you be stayin'?" Mom asks Claire.

She swallows. "I was supposed to stay until the first week in January to get the full Merryville experience. I've heard the town has an incredible New Year's Eve celebration, with a ball drop and fireworks."

"It's worth staying for," Dad says. "I'd much rather be in Merryville than downtown New York. I've heard people wait all day and wear diapers if they have to relieve themselves. Can you imagine?"

Claire laughs. "It's true. Did you also know that the celebration started in 1907?"

"Really?" Mom looks at Dad. "Didn't realize it had been goin' on that long."

"It originated in 1904. However, the first year of having a ball was 1907. There were a few years when it was suspended due to wartime."

"The more ya know," Dad says. "Mrs. Claus, I'm gettin' hungry. Are you?"

I chuckle at the nicknames they use for one another, even when they are off the clock.

Mom nods. "You kids wanna stay for breakfast? Was just gettin' ready to make some French toast."

I meet Claire's gaze, and she nods.

"Sure, we'd love to eat. But let me bring in the rest of that wood for y'all first," I say, standing.

Claire does the same. "I'll help."

"You sure?"

She nods.

"Breakfast will be served when y'all finish up. Twenty minutes," Mom tells us.

"Great, guess we better get to it." I lead the way out the back door, with Claire following behind me. We track around the side of the house to the shed where my parents keep their wood.

"You weren't kidding when you said they'd think we were together." She helps me stack wood in the wheelbarrow that's sitting outside the door, where Dad left it earlier.

"I told you. They're hardheaded and believe what they want. Even after explaining the truth, I knew they wouldn't believe me." I make quick work of our task, knowing Mom likes to serve food hot.

It's below freezing, but the wind isn't blowing, so it's not as bad as it could be.

Claire snorts.

"What?" I turn to her.

"You could've knocked me over with a feather when I saw your dad." She shakes her head. "I was shocked."

"At least you didn't sit on his lap."

She giggles as we walk toward the house with a load.

"I thought about it but didn't want to make it awkward."

I turn my head and lift a brow at her. "You got a Santa kink?"

Laughter escapes her. "Oh God, no. I've got a thing for tall, muscular men my age."

"Lumberjacks on that list?"

Claire shoots me a wink, and my heart rate picks up. "And what if they are?"

"I think you shouldn't start something you won't be able to finish."

Once we make a few trips inside to unload our first round, I smell the sugary sweet aroma of breakfast, and my stomach growls with anticipation.

"Thanks, y'all," my father tells us over his newspaper. "I wish I could help."

"No prob, Dad. We've got this."

"Breakfast is almost ready," Mom yells from the kitchen.

"Better get back to it. Don't want anyone gettin' hangry." I place my hand on Claire's shoulder as she leads the way outside. A few more trips and we'll be finished.

As we get ready to step off the back porch, Claire turns around, wraps her arms around my neck, and presses her warm lips across mine. I'm shocked. Not sure what's going on, but not going to look a gift horse in the mouth. The kiss deepens when she slides her tongue between my lips and lets out a pant. It shouldn't feel this good to cross the line with a woman I barely know, but there's something more simmering between us. I run my fingers through her hair, holding her, kissing her, and she moans against me.

When we finally break apart, I study her, getting ready to ask her why she kissed me, knowing we lost control. But before I can speak, she points up. That's when I see the mistletoe hanging.

"Of course. They've always got it around the house during this time of year. The placement changes, but, well, I never have anyone around that's worth smoochin'." I shoot her a wink.

"It's said to be bad luck not to kiss under it. I've had enough of that lately." She places her hand on my chest and meets my gaze.

"Your bad luck streak is over," I whisper in her ear. "But now my parents are *never* gonna believe we aren't together. Pretty sure my ma saw that from the kitchen window."

A hint of blush hits her cheeks, and I try to calm my racing heart.

"Whoops." She shrugs as she chews on her bottom lip.

I'm tempted to kiss her again, just for the hell of it, but she changes the subject.

"Guess we should probably finish up?"

"Yeah, I think after this we should be good. Want to make sure they got enough for the week since Dad pulled his back."

Her eyes go wide. "Aww, he's hurt?"

"Yeah, he might be Santa, but he's still stubborn as a mule. Don't let the white beard and rosy red cheeks fool ya."

We make the last few trips and finish loading the wood into my parents' house. When we put the last log on the stack, my ma comes in and lets us know the table is set. Dad is no longer sitting in his chair, and when we walk into the dining room, Claire is amazed by the feast my mom has prepared.

I pull the chair out so she can sit, then slide in next to her. Mom made fat stacks of French toast, chocolate croissants, bacon, and eggs. Claire loads her plate up with everything. I do the same as Mom passes the butter.

I slap a large pat down on my French toast. "The secret ingredient."

"Whoa," Claire says. She covers her mouth as she continues to speak. "This is...the best French toast I've ever eaten in my life."

Mom gives her a grin. "I like her. She's a keeper," she tells me, pointing her fork toward me with a laugh.

Claire blushes again. "Thank you for this."

"And she has manners, too?" Dad adds.

"Y'all, stop," I say. "Claire really isn't my girlfriend. She's more like my roommate at this point."

"Are you sleeping in the same bed?" Mom asks.

"Ma! That's inappropriate," I tell her. "Shame on you."

Dad lets out a *ho-ho-ho*, and we all fall into a fit of laughter. Dad talks about his job, and Mom chats about the weather. When we're finished eating, I offer to clean the dishes, but Mom won't let us help.

"No, it's fine." She shoos us away with a dishcloth, and neither one of us dares get in the line of fire. As we prepare to leave, Mom and Dad both hug Claire.

"Can't wait to see you at Christmas," Mom says with a wink.

Claire gives them both a grin with a nod, followed by another thank-you. She's nearly skipping as we head out to the truck. When we're inside, she leans her head back against the seat and looks over at me.

"Your parents are incredible."

I laugh. "Thanks. It's been interesting growing up here."

"I can only imagine," she says. "It almost seems like a fairy tale."

"It's been incredible. I have a loving family, but it's not always been easy. The business has gone through ups and downs over the years. I've personally watched it take a toll on my family. It's getting better. There is lots of love, adoration, and respect, but it's hard work."

She nods. "I understand. However, your family has things money won't ever be able to buy, Jake. And you should be proud of that."

I nod, smiling. "I am. Very proud."

I think about the current struggles with the farm. Being shut down for a few days because of the storm isn't helping the bottom line. But I've learned over the years to worry about the right now while keeping the future in mind.

It's gotten me this far.

I just hope it's enough.

CHAPTER 11

CLAIRE

The next morning, I slide out of bed, not disturbing Jake or Tinsel. I use the bathroom, then realize I haven't spoken with Emma recently, and I start to have a mini panic attack. She *will* call the authorities.

The cool temperatures make me shiver, but I try to ignore it as I head straight for the kitchen, where my phone is plugged into the extra battery bank. I don't know what time it is, but I don't need her enacting our sister pact.

Once my phone is on, I'm bombarded with a barrage of messages. As soon as I see Dale's name, I ignore the messages and hit "reply," my fingertips stabbing the screen hard enough to wake Jake.

CLAIRE

We are over. Leave me alone.

Then I blocked him, just as I should have before. I'm sick of empty promises and lies. I won't fall for it again.

Then I scroll down to see Emma's texts and reply.

> I'm fine, please don't send out a search party.
> I love you, and I'll call you as soon as I can.

I glance at the time and it's just past five. She'll be up soon because she attends an online yoga class every morning and she's an hour ahead of me.

While I wait for her reply, I throw a few logs on the fire and sit on the couch, watching the flames as I think about yesterday.

Meeting Jake's parents was a highlight of my trip. I'm not used to the hugs, the food, or friendliness. They're adorable, the type of personalities that television parents are based on.

However, it confirms how different we are from one another. Yesterday, as we laughed at the table and ate French toast, I was envious of Jake and what he had. His family home is filled with love, laughs and support.

I can only imagine his childhood and know it was the opposite of mine. While he was playing on the farm and getting dirty, I was wearing a pressed uniform at boarding school.

I've never kissed anyone under the mistletoe in my life or met a real Santa Claus. Yesterday was a great day. But I can't stop thinking about how good his lips felt on mine. When we returned home, Jake acted as if it hadn't happened.

I shouldn't have crossed that line, but I don't regret it.

Something twisted inside of me as I tasted the hint of coffee and mint from his toothpaste. Jake Jolly is kind, generous, and sexy as hell. He's too good to be true, almost as if he's the perfect man I've been searching for my entire life.

But he's Texas and I'm New York, and while being with him is fun, I don't think it would ever work out. I only hope staying with him won't be my biggest mistake yet.

We've officially been without power for longer than I expected.

But it's not as bad as I'd thought it would be. As long as we continue to have hot water, a fridge that keeps our food safe, wood, and a gas stove, I'm okay. I wouldn't say I'm thriving, but I'm realizing the simple life isn't as awful as I'd imagined it to be. I'm trying to live in the moment because one day, I may wish for this escape from my reality.

The outside world and my worries have faded while I'm in this little cabin in the woods. It's like a detox from my responsibilities.

I've not had to do a thing while I've taken space in Jake's house. A tinge of guilt covers me when I think about everything he's done for me. He's treated me with kindness and respect. He shared his space, his books, and even his bed.

My phone buzzes in my lap, and it's so quiet—and I'm still half-asleep—that I jump, nearly dropping it on the floor.

Tinsel jumps up next to me on the couch.

I reach over and pet her, and she purrs before she plops down.

"Aww, do you like me now?" I try to pet her belly, and she playfully swats at me.

"Okay, I understand that. Boundaries. Got it."

I bring my attention back to my phone to see a message from an unknown number.

UNKNOWN

You can't avoid me.

I read the threatening tone in the message, knowing who it is —Dale.

"Good mornin'," I hear from behind me in a gruff voice.

The panic rises inside of me and I scream, my phone flying out of my hand.

Jake walks over, sets his hand on my shoulder, and squeezes. "I'm sorry. I didn't mean to scare you."

I place my hand over my heart, needing to calm down.

"You added more wood?"

I turn and look up at him over my shoulder. "Yes."

"Good girl," he says with a smirk. And he's got those damn glasses on.

He makes my internal temperature rise.

"Coffee?"

"I'd love some," I tell him, turning off my phone and closing my eyes as he goes to the kitchen.

Once the grounds have steeped and we both have cups in our hands, Jake joins me on the couch. Tinsel curls up on his lap. We sit in silence until our cups are empty, then he excuses himself. Tinsel hisses; she's pissed that he disturbed her, and I understand the sentiment.

Maybe she and I do have a lot in common.

I lean back on the cushions. I must've drifted off because Jake's words wake me.

"I need to chop some more wood. We're getting low," he tells me, beanie already on his head as he slides on his coat and boots.

"Outside?"

He nods with a half grin. "You can come with me if you'd like."

I turn and look at Tinsel, who's now stretched out on the rug in front of the fireplace. She looks warm and comfortable. I look back at Jake, knowing that each time I've told him yes, I've had an experience. That's been the case from the first time we met.

"Okay, I'm coming. Give me a few minutes to get dressed," I say, going to his room and wheeling my suitcase to the middle of the floor. I open it with a thud and grab a thick sweater, jeans, and socks. Then I look at my shoe choices and decide running shoes are the best option.

I throw my hair into a low ponytail and slide on my beanie with the fuzzy ball on the end.

When I meet back up with him, he's standing with a smirk and his arms crossed over his chest.

"You opted out of your boots today?" He snickers.

My mouth falls open. "Are you poking fun?"

"I just don't understand why anyone would wear anything with a heel like that, knowing there will be ice. Makes no sense."

I playfully purse my lips. "Do you have any idea how much they cost?"

"No, but you should probably give them away."

"They were three grand!"

His eyes go wide. "Please tell me you're jokin', and you did not pay that much."

"I didn't. They were a gift, but still very expensive."

He laughs as he reaches for the door. "Sounds like somebody got swindled. I'm in the wrong business."

He leads me outside to the shop across the driveway from his house. It's cold outside, but the sun is shining, so it's not bad. Frost covers the ground, and with every step we take, there's a crunch under our feet from the ice and gravel. Jake swings open the double wooden doors and allows me to enter.

I look around in awe at the hyperorganized man cave. Neon signs are hung on the wall, and gardening tools are neatly stacked on one side of the room. There is also a motorcycle with a cloth draped over the top.

"I'd turn on the lights, but ya know." He moves to an area of camping gear and pulls out a spare lantern. Within a few clicks, the flame slowly comes on before catching the wick. "Kerosene."

There are several windows in his shop, so it's not entirely dark inside.

He grabs his axe and looks at the blade. "You ever chop wood before?"

I give him a look like he's lost his mind.

"I'll take that as a no, then. Wanna learn?"

My expression doesn't falter.

"Heard loud and clear, but you're comin' with me once I sharpen this blade. It's a good skill to have just in case you need it in the future."

I hold back laughter. There is no way I'll ever need to know how to do this, but I'm curious. Besides, I've seen some lumberjack TikTok videos and figure the visuals alone will be worth it.

Jake sets the axe down on the large table and then grabs something that looks like a stone. Carefully, he slides it across the blade several times, and I imagine how his muscular arms flex beneath that shirt. He's mesmerizing as he pays close attention to detail, running his finger over the end to feel its sharpness. He flips the blade over and takes care of the other side until the metal edge is silver. "Cutting wood with a dull blade is how people get hurt. But I think we're good now."

He holds it up, examining his handiwork before turning on his heels. "Ready?"

"As ready as I'll ever be."

The wind howls against the building and blasts me as soon as I exit the doors. He leads me to the side, where a huge blue tarp is stretched over a large mass. He removes it, and the water from the melted ice falls to the ground. Under it are large slabs of tree trunks.

"Why can't we just burn that?" I ask, tucking my hands into my pockets, really wishing I had a pair of gloves.

He chuckles, his hot breath immediately evaporating into

smoke. "Because smaller logs catch easier and provide more heat. Just gotta chop some of this up, and we'll be good to go for the rest of the week."

"Be my guest," I say as Jake lifts what looks like the entire trunk of a tree and sets it down on a clear spot on the ground. Then he lifts the axe above his head, slamming the blade on his target. The wood splits, and he continues his assault on it until it's divided into six smaller pieces.

"Want to grab the wheelbarrow out of the shop?" he asks me over his shoulder.

"Sure," I tell him. "Where is it?"

"Inside, directly to your left, leaning against the wall. Can't miss it."

I nod, wanting to be helpful. He's still chopping, and I hear the blade's steel cracking through the wood as I enter. I spot it immediately. As I move forward, I notice a board with pushpins all around, then I see a picture of an older man and two little boys. I lean in, trying to get a better look, when I'm startled by the clearing of a throat.

"Did ya get lost?" Jake asks in a light tone, moving toward me.

I'm still staring at the photo. "Who's in this picture?"

Jake grins wide and points at the smaller boy holding a tiny axe in his hand. "That's me. That's my older brother Hudson. And my grandfather. Rest his soul."

In the background, I see rows of Christmas trees as they stand proudly together like they're having the time of their lives. Everyone is dressed in layers, so I imagine it was taken in December.

"I'm sorry."

"Nah, it's fine. I miss him every day. But he lived a very full life. Never saw him upset once."

"Sounds like he was a treasure."

"He was." He lingers on the photograph.

"How many siblings do you have?" I ask, realizing I've not

learned much about him besides what he's willingly offered in conversation. The fact I want to learn more about him nearly scares me.

I'm not one who usually cares, especially when I'm dead set on accomplishing my goals. But being with Jake is different.

"An older brother and a younger one. This was before Luke was born, though. It was just me and Hudson. Oh, I've got a shit ton of cousins, too. I should introduce you to everybody. Y'all would probably get along great."

"That'd be nice," I say, but I doubt I'd have anything in common with anyone here. My life is on the other end of the spectrum from anyone who lives in Merryville. "Growing up on a Christmas tree farm must've been magical."

He smiles and nods. "It was. Can't wait for my kids to experience it."

"You want children?"

He turns and meets my gaze, and our bodies are close. Almost too close. I can smell the mint of his toothpaste and the hint of his soap.

"Maybe one day. Isn't that the natural progression of life? Live it to the fullest with the love of your life?"

"Sounds like a romance book."

This makes him crack a smile, and he sucks a deep breath. "Easier said than done, I guess. But one day, yes, I'd like a family. My nephew is—"

"You're an uncle?" It comes out almost like a surprise.

"Oh yeah. My brother has a son. Colby. He's such a sweet kid. Kind. Helpful. Very chatty. He's three. Been having a rough time since his mama left them, but my brother is making the best of it."

My jaw nearly falls to the ground.

"I know, we were shocked, too. Anyway, wanna see a picture of him?"

I grin. "Yes, absolutely."

He pulls his phone from his pocket and scrolls briefly before turning the screen around. It's a picture of Jake and Colby sitting on his couch. Tinsel is on the little boy's lap, and his tiny hand rests on her back.

"Wow. He is the cutest kid I've ever seen. Look at his dimples and big green eyes. And Tinsel loves him?"

"She adores him, even though he wants to pick her up and carry her awkwardly around the house." He laughs. "She likes to play with him and chase him around, too."

"That's so sweet. I'm happy for you."

"Thanks. I'm a proud uncle." He glances at the picture one last time before locking his phone and sliding it in his pocket. "Now, let's get this wood loaded."

"Good idea."

Jake carefully grabs the handles of the wheelbarrow that was leaned against the wall and sets it down on the ground. "After you."

He holds out his hand, allowing me to go outside first as he wheels it behind me. When we're close to the small stack he's cut, I bend over and help him load them into the bed of the wheelbarrow.

"Okay, you have to try to chop at least once. You're not leaving Merryville without the full experience."

I tilt my head. "You can't be serious."

He lifts his brows. "Do I look like I'm kiddin'?"

"I don't know how," I explain. "I've never held an axe in my hand before."

"Luckily, you've got a pro teachin' ya." He waves me over after he sets a log upright for me.

"Okay, now what? I just swing it?"

"You're adorable. Let's get your grip right," he says, picking up the axe and standing directly beside me. "You're going to want to put your hands around the wooden handle like this. Keep your grip firm so you don't lose it when you lift it over your head."

I look down at it, and Jake grabs my hands and places them exactly where they need to go.

Not knowing the weight of it, I lift it. "You really think I can do this?"

"You don't know until you try. But if your strength is anything compared to your stubbornness…"

I elbow him in the ribs, and he chuckles.

"Hey, I'm Team CeCe. I believe in you."

I look up into his green eyes, and I think he might be the only person other than my sister who's ever told me that. I swallow hard, my heart fluttering, more determined than ever to chop that wood into two.

"Like this?" I ask, repositioning my hands.

He slides them farther up on the handle. "Right here." His voice is low. "Now, I'm going to step back. You want to focus on where you want to hit. So look where you want the blade to go."

Jake moves toward the wood and points his finger right in the center of it. "Right here. Oh yeah, one more thing."

He moves beside me and slides his strong hand between my thighs, parting my legs slightly. It might be cold outside, but my body is so hot I feel as if I'm sweating. "Shoulder-width apart. You want the stabilization when you swing."

"Okay," I say breathlessly, swallowing hard. He stands beside me and walks through the motions, explaining how my elbow should be, using my body weight to bring the blade down onto the wood.

I chuckle.

"You gotta tell me what's funny."

"This reminds me of the golf lessons I took."

He shakes his head. "First sailing. Now golf. Your hobbies are too fancy for me."

"Oh, don't worry, I hate golf, too. Now that I think about it, I pretty much dislike all the hobbies that I have. If you can even call them that."

He gives me a puzzled look. "Then why do you do them?"

It's not a question I've ever asked myself. I'm so used to doing what I'm supposed to that I've never thought about it. "I guess because of expectations."

Jake shakes his head. "Fuck expectations. Life is too short. You gotta start doin' the things that make you happy, CeCe."

"Truthfully, I don't know what does," I admit, lifting the axe and slamming it down on the wood before he can pity me. The blade crashes where it should, and the wood cracks and splits nearly to the bottom.

Jake lets out a hoot. "You're a natural!"

I'm giddy with excitement that I actually did it as he helps remove the blade and pulls the two pieces of wood apart before throwing it in the wheelbarrow.

"Want to do another one?"

"Yes."

Immediately, he sets it up for me.

I think about my life. I think about all the motions I've gone through just to make everyone else happy, to fit in, to be the perfect mold of my father, down to sailing and golf. And the only person that I have to blame is myself. I lift and swing, bearing my body weight down as the sound of the axe slices through the log. I did it! And accomplishing something as simple as this gives me so much satisfaction.

"Good girl," he encourages, and butterflies flutter inside me as he comes closer. "If you ever need a backup job, lumberjill might be in your future."

I snicker. "I can't even imagine."

Jake gives me more praise, and I'm over the moon. After that, he shrugs off his coat and takes over. I stand back, admiring him as he lifts and swings. I help pick up the chopped wood and smile at him when our eyes meet. He continues until the wheelbarrow is full of logs for the fire. He wipes the sweat from his forehead with the back of his sleeve. "I think this is enough."

I give him a nod, then we unload it.

After dinner, Jake and I sit on opposite ends of the couch. He carries the bottle of moonshine and drinks straight from the top while watching the flames lazily lick up the fireplace.

"Want a drink?" he asks, offering me the bottle.

Against my better judgment, I take it. "Thanks."

Once I down two big gulps, I exhale spice and cough. Jake takes the bottle from me with a chuckle. "Gotta be careful. Too much moonshine and you'll lose time."

The fire draws our attention back. "I can't seem to understand why you're single."

He blinks a few times, and I wonder if he even heard me. Another swig, and then he speaks. "Me either. If you want to know what happened, you're welcome to ask."

"I didn't want to pry." I reach for the bottle again, and he hands it to me.

"Long story short, she said I made her miserable."

I can't help the expression on my face. Disbelief. Pure ridiculousness. He laughs, but I know he doesn't think it's funny.

"She waited until I proposed in a very public way to tell me. It was one of the most embarrassing days of my life, I think. The whole town was there when she said no."

A gasp escapes me. "I'm sorry. I can't imagine how that felt."

"Yeah. I felt this big." He holds up his fingers, showing about an inch of space. "And what about you?"

My heart pounds in my chest. "I don't think I've had enough booze to discuss it."

"Three more gulps of that, and you're gonna be on your ass," he warns, so I drink that amount.

When I hand him the bottle back, my esophagus is burning, and so is my stomach. I feel as if I can breathe fire at this point.

"Where is she now?"

He sucks in a deep breath. "She's still around. I run into her often."

"That must be hard."

"Sometimes it is. During the holidays, it's harder. But this time, it's not quite as bad."

I scoot closer to him, and we fall into silence and take turns drinking as we listen to the wood popping and crackling.

"How long have you been single?" He asks questions I didn't expect. It catches me off guard, but I think about it.

"That's hard to answer," I admit, feeling the liquid courage soaring through my veins. My thoughts are all over the place, and my mouth almost feels numb. I take the bottle from him again and take another drink. It's at the point where it goes down like water.

"Whoa, better slow down on that stuff. Like I warned ya earlier, it will put you on your ass. Now, you were sayin'?"

I suck in a breath. "The last man I was dating...was married." Jake's kind expression doesn't change, but I can tell he's curious. "There is obviously something on your mind. Just ask what you're thinking."

"I don't wanna be rude."

I shrug. "I won't think it's rude."

He takes another swig. "Did you know he was married?"

"Are you asking if I'm a home-wrecker?"

He chuckles. "No. I'd never think that about you. Just curious how that happened."

The memories flood my mind, and I remember the first time that Dale and I spoke. "He told me they were separated and they were getting a divorce. And I believed him. His wife found out, and it was a disaster."

"Fuckin' prick." Jake shakes his head. "You deserve better than that. Someone who will commit to you, who wants to make you happy."

I don't know why I feel my emotions bubble, but I force it

down, something I'm used to doing. "That's easier said than done. I intimidate most men."

He bursts out laughing, and I take the bottle.

"What? I'm serious!"

He leans back on the couch, and I twist to face him.

"I'm not intimidated by you."

"I've noticed," I say. The world feels as if it's tilting on its axis. Is it the booze, or is it Jake?

"Should I be?" His brow is lifted.

"Yes," I tell him.

Laughter escapes him again. He finds it so funny that even I start laughing. I lean against the couch, our arms brushing together as he turns and looks at me.

"I'm happy you're here. I honestly can't remember the last time I've had this much fun."

I'm smiling, a genuine smile, something I haven't felt in a long time. "I agree. It's been nice."

As our gazes meet, I feel drawn to him. His lips look soft and kissable, and I'm tempted to slide my mouth across his and taste him again. I find my courage, and as soon as I decide to go for it, my phone buzzes on the table, pulling my attention away.

"I think that's yours," he says. I almost forgot I turned it on before dinner.

"Yeah." I walk over to it. When I see the name flash across the screen, my heart drops.

It's my father.

CHAPTER 12

JAKE

Claire answers, and her tone immediately shifts.
She's more serious, all business and no bullshit.

I look over my shoulder at her, and she points to my bedroom, then continues the conversation down the hallway. The door snaps shut.

Claire hasn't acted like that since I picked her up from the side of the road. I'd like to think I've broken through her hard shell, but her walls went up fast. I wonder who's on the phone and what they said to sour her mood. I'd never ask, though. People will share what they want when they're ready. But I know there's more to her than what meets the eye.

Twenty minutes later, she sits next to me on the couch. She's pale, like she just saw a ghost, as she stares at the fire.

"You good?" I can feel her emotionally pulling away. "You want to talk about it? I'm a fantastic listener."

She sighs, grabbing the moonshine from the table and taking several gulps like she's trying to erase a memory. "Have you ever wanted to take risks? Against your better judgment?"

I study her as she scoots closer and crawls onto my lap. Then she looks down into my eyes.

"What're you doin—"

She places her finger over my mouth. "You said you were a great listener."

I hold her tight, my thumbs digging into her hips as she rocks against me and groans.

"The moonshine," I whisper, trying to give her an excuse, an out.

She shakes her head. "It's not that."

The shared physical attraction is undeniable.

It's been simmering for the past three days, or has it been four?

Hell, a week?

I don't know.

The days have melded together, and it feels like time stopped when Claire arrived. Every day is the same, but also different. We've been inseparable, spending every waking moment together. Without her here with me, I'd have been lonely.

I groan, my cock growing hard as she continues to rock against me.

"I know you'll deny me, Jake, because I always get pushed to the side. But it's nice to pretend you won't."

My brows furrow and my heart breaks for her, but I understand.

I've been no one's priority, either.

"Your silence says it all."

"CeCe," I whisper as she stands to create space between us.

After one sad look, she walks away.

Every logical part of my brain tells me I shouldn't follow her, but she's opened Pandora's box. I'll be damned if I allow it to be slammed closed so quickly.

"Claire." I get up and repeat her name. She turns toward me, disappointment on her face.

I take her hand and pull her against my chest. She studies my lips, and I tuck loose strands of her hair behind her ears.

"I've been waitin' all day to do this," I admit, crushing my mouth to hers and diving into the kiss. It happens too fast. She whimpers as our tongues tangle together. I want this woman more than anything. She reaches down and unbuttons my jeans.

"Darlin'." I gently grab her wrist to stop her. "I haven't been with a woman in far too long."

"Do you want me?"

I release my grip on her. "How could I not? You're fuckin' gorgeous. Intelligent. Kind. Unpredictable. But also a bit drunk."

"Great, I want you. You want me. We're adults, consenting."

I study her expression. "We can have this conversation tomorrow when a hundred fifty proof ain't flooding our systems. I don't want to be your regret. Decisions like this need to be made with a clear mind."

It's not the answer she wants, but I respect her too much to take advantage of this situation. In the morning, I don't want to wake up and have it be awkward between us.

She sighs. "You're such a cinnamon roll of a man, Jake Jolly. And too damn logical."

I return my lips to hers and softly kiss her. "And you're a Stubborn Susan."

"You probably think I'll forget about this tomorrow, but I won't." She relaxes.

"I'm prayin' to any God that will listen that you don't."

I lead her to my bedroom, and we undress and crawl under the covers. My eyes are heavy, and I open my arms, allowing Claire to rest her head on my chest.

I don't know how we got here. Is it the isolation? The moonshine? Regardless, I'm not complaining.

As I gently run my fingers through her hair, her breathing slows. Within ten minutes, she's asleep, and I follow her to dreamland.

The following day, I wake up to Claire in her bra and panties, straddling me.

At first, I'm convinced I'm dreaming—until I realize her soft lips are kissing up my chest and neck and are tracing the shell of my ear.

"Good morning," she whispers. "How are you feeling?"

I grin, placing my arms behind my head, and watch her. "Good mornin', beautiful. I'm feelin' mighty fine."

"I'm ready to finish our chat from last night."

A smirk touches my lips. "Oh, so you were serious?"

"You didn't think I was?" She rocks against me as my cock begs to be buried deep inside her.

I flip Claire over on her back, my lips inches from hers. "I'd never take advantage of you."

"I don't deserve your kindness," she says as I move her hair from her face.

"You deserve more, CeCe." She meets my eyes. "I don't want to be one of your regrets."

Her face softens, and she reaches up and places her palm on my cheek. "Never. But also, I don't want to be one of yours, either."

I chuckle. "You burst into my life like a tornado. I've been enjoyin' this little adventure we're on, but once we cross this line, there's no goin' back. So you have to be sure."

"I know. And I am." She sucks in a deep breath. "There's one rule, though."

I meet her gaze. "Shoot."

"Oh, Texas slang. Almost forgot." She hesitates. "I can't fall in love with you, Jake."

"I understand. You and I both know that's risky." But I also know, based on experience, it's impossible to control who you fall for. By agreeing to this, are we setting ourselves up for heartbreak? I don't know. And I refuse to worry about that right now.

Her smile softens. "You're right."

"I haven't wanted to be with anyone until you barged into my life, lookin' gorgeous as fuck, sayin' all the right things, sleeping in my bed, and whispering my name in your sleep."

"Did I?" Her brows furrow.

"Fuck yes."

She pushes herself up on her elbows. "I want you, Jake. There's been something bubbling between us since the moment I climbed into your truck. Yes, we're strangers, but it feels like I've known you forever. I never click with people. I don't trust anyone other than my sister. But it's different with you."

"It's because I've seen the real you, darlin'. Not that persona you hide behind. And I like the real CeCe. The girl who laughs and smiles and isn't so damn serious."

She wraps her hand around the back of my neck and brings my lips to hers. Our mouths greedily crash together, and her breathing increases. I slide my hand farther down her body and her back arches. When my fingers glide over her pink panties, she gasps.

"No strings attached. No falling in love." I give her the rules, desperate to make sure we're on the same page.

She pants, nodding with her eyes closed. "As long as you're mine until I leave."

"It's a deal," I mutter against her lips as I add pressure to her clit.

"Yes," she hisses as I kiss down her mouth. She lifts, unsnapping her bra, and her beautiful breasts and pink, perky nipples are on full display. I capture one in my mouth and twirl my tongue around the peak. As she lies back on the bed, I slide my hand inside her panties.

"You're so fuckin' wet." My voice comes out rough as I peel the material from her body. I admire every inch of her as she lies on my silk sheets.

She tilts her head, her hair spreading out across the pillow.

LYRA PARISH

"You're gorgeous, CeCe." I gently palm her breast, our lips locking together once again. "I need to taste you."

Her heart rate increases, and I see the pulse throbbing in her neck. "No one..."

"What was that?" I say, kissing down her stomach, above her belly button, and memorizing the softness of her inner thigh with my lips.

She lifts herself on her elbows again and meets my gaze with hooded eyes. "No man has ever gone down on me."

My brows furrow as I whisk my fingertips across her bare pussy.

Claire continues. "And no one has ever given me an orgasm."

"What?" The question comes out a little shrill just because I'm so appalled.

She sits up in bed, pulling the sheet over her body.

"Have you ever had one before?"

This makes her laugh. "Of course I have. All self-induced, though."

I lift a brow. "Will you show me how you touch yourself?"

I can tell she's intrigued as a sly smile touches her lips. "Only if you do the same."

I smirk, standing. My cock is hard as concrete, and my joggers tent out. She raises her brows, wearing an adorable grin as I slide them down my body.

Claire gulps, and her mouth falls open as she looks at my dick. "I...uh... That thing will not fit inside me."

I burst out laughing, my cock pulsing at the thought. "We'll take it slow. There ain't no rush."

"JJ," she whispers, scooting to the edge of the mattress and placing her feet on the floor. I take a step forward, moving closer to her, as she reaches out and grips my cock, stroking it a few times. Precum glistens on the tip, and she licks it off, smiling before taking me in her hot mouth.

114

"Feels so damn good," I groan. My head falls back as her tongue twirls and teases my head.

I run my fingers through her hair and watch her watching me. The eye contact is intense, and she's so fucking sexy that if she doesn't stop, I won't be able to last.

"Fuck," I hiss as she tries to take me down her throat. She gags, her eyes watering, and I slowly pull away.

Then I drop to my knees, face to face with her, cupping her cheeks. "Can I make you feel good?"

"What if I can't come? What if I'm broken?" Anxiety fills her tone.

I shake my head. "You aren't the problem. You just weren't the priority. That changes now."

She leans forward with her ass on the edge of the mattress and kisses me. Emotions soar, and it breaks my damn heart that she's not been worshipped the way she deserves.

"I want you to be comfortable. If at any point you're not or you want me to stop, please speak up, okay?"

"Okay." Her eyes twinkle as she bites the corner of her lip.

Gently, I spread her legs wide, admiring her beautiful pussy, noticing how wet I've made her.

"Mm, fuckin' beautiful," I growl and move my face closer to her.

She gasps, and her head falls back as I take my time, adding gentle pressure to her clit. I allow her to relax and get used to the sensation of my tongue between her legs. There's no rush, only right now. This is about her and making her feel good. She groans, rocking her hips forward as I lap my tongue against her swollen bud.

Her breathing increases as she threads her fingers through my hair and tugs. I move, darting my tongue into her sweetness, lapping her up, loving the way she tastes. I lick and suck her clit and slide my tongue up and down her slick slit.

"Oh God," she growls, breathing more heavily. Claire thrusts her pussy forward and leans back with her body arched, giving me more access to her cute little cunt. I smile against her soft skin, knowing she's teetering on the edge as her hips rock against my face, but I don't let her come yet.

Her moans fill the room, and I love to fucking hear it, knowing that I'm giving her something she's never had.

I lift her legs, resting them over my shoulders as I slide my hands under her ass and squeeze.

She grinds against my mouth, her pants growing more ragged. "I'm…so close. So, so close."

"Enjoy it, darlin'," I say, giving her all the permission she needs as I slide my finger deep into her tight, wet hole.

"Yes, yes, yes." She tweaks her nipple as every muscle in her body tenses.

Time seems to stand still as I slow my pace. "Jake," she pants. "I'm…"

She doesn't finish her sentence as her body convulses and her pussy pulses around my finger. I massage her clit, letting her ride the orgasm, then I tongue fuck her, enjoying the taste of her cum, indirectly continuing to stimulate her bundle of nerves because I know it's sensitive after coming so hard.

"Fuck, you taste amazing," I murmur. If she were my last meal, I'd die a lucky man.

Claire grabs her ankles, keeping her legs wide open, allowing me to lick around her clit.

"It feels so damn good," she says, her voice a whisper. "Don't stop. Not yet."

I smile against her mound, realizing she just gave me permission for round two.

CHAPTER 13

CLAIRE

I'm having an out-of-body experience as Jake worships my pussy. The orgasm takes hold of me and doesn't let go. Every muscle in my body convulses as I spill over, throbbing so hard around his finger that nearly fills my tight hole. I groan; I've never experienced an orgasm so intense I feel like I've transcended to another reality. My nipples are hard, and my body begs for more of him, all of him.

I'm greedy; I need to experience him again. He hasn't pulled away, just slowed down, and each time the flatness of his tongue grazes the side of my clit, my pussy throbs. It's sensitive, but he gives me a chance to come down from my high, massaging my bundle of nerves. The scruff on his chin feels so fucking good between my legs, and I don't want him to stop.

Breathing rapidly, I lean up on my elbows and look at him with hooded eyes. I meet his green ones, and he smirks. "You good?"

"More than good," I pant. "But…" I lick my lips, barely able to speak. "I think I'm going to come again."

He smirks and playfully slaps my pussy, making me pulse with anticipation.

LYRA PARISH

"But," I tell him, "I want to return the favor."

"This is about you, darlin'." Jake trails kisses onto my inner thigh, and I love how his scruff feels against my skin. "Tell me what you want."

I break our eye contact, almost embarrassed. I'm not used to communicating in the bedroom, and sex has always been something I did to make my partner happy. But this, it's different—it's personal, it's about me.

He notices my reaction and stands, then hovers above me to kiss my lips. I taste my orgasm on his tongue. Another first. He strokes the backs of his fingers against my cheek. "Don't be shy. There ain't no room for that in here."

"I want you to come in my mouth." I swallow, meeting his smoldering gaze. "While I ride your face."

He smirks. "Music to my fuckin' ears."

"I've just never—"

His lips crash against mine. "Making you feel good and giving you what you need is my only priority, Claire. I have no limits."

Heat floods through me as butterflies flutter in my tummy. "I don't know if I do. But I guess I have a month to figure it out."

He pulls my bottom lip into his mouth and sucks. Then he lies beside me on the bed, brushes his hand over his mouth, and smirks. "Cleared off a place for you to sit."

I laugh.

"Now, put that sweet pussy in my face," he says, and I nervously crawl closer to him. "You're in control."

It's all the encouragement I need to put my insecurities aside and straddle his head. I've never explored different positions. I've never been with someone willing to do anything like this. Sex has always been a thing I've checked off my to-do list to make my partners happy. But Jake is right: I've never been the focus—until now.

With each compliment he gives me, my confidence soars.

118

You're sexy. You're beautiful. I love the way you taste.

"Fuck," he hisses, grabbing my ass, pushing me harder against his face. I hold myself up with one arm, sinking against his hot mouth, rocking my hips against his scruff. I groan out as he massages my clit with his tongue, giving the perfect amount of pressure.

How is it possible he already knows what my body needs and wants?

I grip his length and stroke before taking him in my mouth. The precum on his tip is sticky and salty. His hips buck upward and I hollow my cheeks, wanting to please him, wanting this experience to be as good for him as it's been for me.

With firm hands, Jake grips my ass, encouraging me to grind harder against him. I throw all my inhibitions away, letting go of my control and giving myself over. His guttural grunts encourage me to keep sucking as I gently massage his balls. Our pants and moans fill his room as we lose ourselves with one another.

The orgasm builds quickly, almost too fast, and every muscle in my body tightens. My toes flex as heat floods me, and then I can't hold on any longer. Pleasure tears through me, ripping my reality to shreds. I rock against him, fucking his face as I let go. I scream out his name, continuing to stroke him as I come.

As I take him to the back of my throat, I use my hand to stroke, working him so fucking good.

"CeCe," he grunts. "I'm gonna—" he warns me as his balls tighten. Then he pumps into my mouth, and I swallow every salty drop of him.

My muscles are like gelatin as I lie down on the mattress. We both stare at the ceiling, panting like we just ran a marathon.

Jake glances at me, and I turn to meet his hooded eyes. "Well?"

I scoot closer, and he holds me in his arms. "I guess I'm not broken."

"Satisfied?"

I nod. "I think I want to do that again."

"Right now?"

I smile against his chest. "I don't think I could handle it. Two was more than enough. Never had them back to back before."

"No?" He gently brushes his fingertips over my arm as he holds me. I can hear his heartbeat slow as our bodies relax. We just woke up, but I could go back to sleep again.

I let out a contented sigh. "I never knew it could feel like that."

He kisses my hair but says nothing, which is a relief. My sex life, my relationships, they've all been shit, and it's because I've chosen men for the wrong reasons. My eyes grow heavy, and I close them as Jake holds me. I'm relaxed, comfortable, and satisfied, but deep down, I know I don't deserve any of this. Being with him so intimately is too good to be true. If I'm dreaming, I don't want to wake up. I just want to stay here a little longer.

I open my eyes and sit up, my hair a mess. "I fell asleep."

He's smirking. "I know. You were talkin' in your sleep again."

"What did I say this time?"

His smile widens. "You were just sayin' how I'm too good to be true and how you hope this isn't all a dream."

"God, how embarrassing."

His thumb traces along my bottom lip, and those butterflies return. "I welcome it."

Leaning forward, I kiss him. "Did I say anything else?"

He pretends to think about it. "You did."

"Tell me."

"Who's Dale?"

I slam my eyes closed, not wanting to have this

conversation but knowing I need to. "My shitty ex. The married one."

"Ah. That explains a lot. Don't worry. You said nothing that probably shouldn't have been said. Just a bunch of 'Fuck you, Dale,' and you mentioned his dick being tiny."

A howl of laughter escapes me, but I still shake my head. "I have to get my sleep talking under control."

"I think it's adorable. You know, sometimes you answer questions. I thought you were awake until I realized your breathing was slower."

"Yeah, it's a problem. It's gotten me into trouble a few times, and I need to control it, but there's nothing I can do about it except hope I don't say something that will incriminate me."

"It's happened before?"

I slowly nod. "It's how my sister found out about Dale." I suck in a deep breath. "He works with my father."

Jake sits up, facing me. "He sounds like a piece of shit. Tiny cock. Can't make you come. You're definitely better off without him."

"I don't miss him," I admit. "I've tried to understand why I was obsessed. He's older, much older."

"Daddy issues?"

I chew on the corner of my lip. "My dad wouldn't have approved, which made me want to pursue the relationship more. We snuck around often, but I realize now it was because he was still married." I think about the relationship. "He asked me to stop taking my birth control."

Jake searches my face. "Why?"

"I think he wanted me pregnant."

His mouth falls open. "Did you want that?"

"No." The word comes out without hesitation.

"CeCe."

Placing my finger on his lips, I shake my head. "I've made a million mistakes with men—more than I want to admit or even think about. I fall for the wrong guys for the wrong reasons, and I've realized that. That's in the past now."

He kisses my finger before placing it in his mouth and sucking on it. It's an erotic sensation, and I can't stop watching him as he stops and smirks. "What were you sayin'?"

"I don't remember."

"How about some food?"

He's distracting and all-consuming. "You're a tease."

"I know." He slides off the mattress. "I've been told that a time or two."

I can't stop staring at the muscles that cascade down his back as he bends over to slide his joggers over his perfect ass. Jake looks over his shoulder at me and chuckles.

"Still a tease! Without even trying!" I stand, and he pulls my naked body against his and places a soft, seductive kiss on my lips. Then I sigh against his mouth. "I'm doomed."

He grabs a handful of my ass. "Don't worry, darlin'. Feelin' is mutual."

CHAPTER 14

JAKE

When I wake up the following day, the power is still out, but I've stayed warm with Claire snuggled against me. If we never leave the cabin again, I won't complain. I want to make her happy. I want to keep her sexually fulfilled, showing her how she should be a priority. Encouraging healthy conversations about sex and her desires is one of my goals, too. We haven't gone all the way, but I'm letting her call the shots. There is no rush. Whatever piece of her she's willing to give me, I'll take it.

When I walk into the living room, Claire watches me over the book. I meet her eyes, catching her, and she tries to hide her smile. The woman is fucking flirty, and just a simple look from her makes my heart pitter-patter.

There are too many side-glances and unspoken words, but I'll keep my rules in place—no falling in love and no strings attached.

I'm taking it one day at a time. And she is, too.

Claire huffs, shutting the book and sitting up. I glance over at her.

"What just happened?" I'm curious.

"She left, and I'm very frustrated."

"Ahh. Just gotta keep going."

Once she sits upright, Claire lifts her arms and stretches. She's not at the part that will break her yet, but I look forward to watching her holding back emotions. She's tried to convince me she's tough, but I know better. I saw through that act the first day we met.

Just as I get up to make some more coffee, my phone buzzes in my pocket. I pull it out and see Hank's name on the screen. I'm almost surprised to see him calling, but I answer.

"You two kiss yet?"

"Shut up," I say, but I can't hold back my grin.

He hoots. "By the sound of your tone, it's a lot more than kissing."

I ignore him, knowing if I say too much, he'll get the truth out of me, and I'd love to keep us to myself for now. "Whatcha want?"

"The power should be on any minute," he announces.

"Really? That's good news."

"Yeah! Downtown has electricity. Glenda's been cooking all day for all the electrical workers. Many of them are camped out because there ain't nothin' open anywhere else."

"Damn, I might take a drive down there if that's the case," I admit, wishing I could get one of her renowned chicken potpies or some potato soup. When the temperature drops, it's usually my go-to. "Thanks for lettin' me know. Was that it?"

"Just one more thing. I got an update on the truck you had me tow back to town. But I want an update from *you* first," he says.

"There ain't nothin' to talk about." I put a pot of water on the stove and let it boil.

"That's great news, then. Been thinking 'bout all the places I'm gonna ride that Harley to over the summer."

I shake my head, not wanting him to get too cocky, but

also not wanting to play this game. I'm hyperaware that Claire is within earshot. "Oh, I nearly forgot to mention she's stayin' until January seventh, so if you'd needed more time on the vehicle, it would've been fine."

"Really?" His voice goes up an octave like he's perplexed. "I thought she wanted to fly back to New York ASAP."

I chuckle. "You almost sound disappointed."

"No, I just didn't think you'd have a chance in hell with that one."

"Boohoo. Just bein' my usual self," I tell him.

"Isn't this fuckin' great? Playboy Jake is back in action. Hot damn." He lets out a whoop. "Let the games begin."

"I don't know what you're talkin' about. Anyway, the update?"

"Oh yeah, about that. There was nothing wrong with the truck."

My brow furrows, and I freeze. "What?"

"Yeah, just conveniently ran out of gas."

"No way."

"Mmhmm, so now I'm back to my original thought. Are you sure this woman isn't here to scam ya out of everything you own?"

I think about his question, and then my mind replays what Claire and I have shared over the last few days. It is real, but I keep my answers neutral. "Nah. I don't think so."

"She seems smart, though. She could've set the whole thing up and ran out of gas on purpose to help her find her next victim."

I shake my head, refusing to entertain the idea. "I think all the reality TV you've been watchin' has given you brain damage."

"Whatever you say, man. Just be careful."

"Always am," I admit, glancing at the back of Claire's head.

"It's ready, and the roads are clear if you wanna come get it today. Even filled it up."

"Thanks. What if I stop by in about an hour? Will that work?"

"Sure thing, man. I'll be here 'til six. Be careful. The roads are still slick."

"Will do. See ya soon."

I end the call and shake some coffee grounds in the bottom of the French press, then carefully pour the hot water into the top.

While it steeps, Tinsel waits at my feet. When I look down, she meows, so I bend over to pet her. She raises her body upward and meets me halfway. When she gets like this, it usually means she wants to be held.

Since it's not something that happens often these days, I take it when I can get it. Carefully, I hold her in my arms like a baby. She immediately purrs when I kiss her head, then nuzzles her face against mine. If cats could smile, I know she would be.

"You're such a heavy girl. Guess I should start cuttin' back on those treats."

Tinsel blinks slowly, her way of telling me she loves me and knows I would never do such an awful thing to her.

I walk into the living room carrying the fluff ball and stand at the end of the couch. Claire looks at me from over the top of the book. She must've picked it back up when I was talking to Hank.

Her eyes fly over the page, and when she notices me staring, she stops.

"Just tell me what happens," she begs.

"Nope. The suspense of it all is what keeps you turning the pages. Plus, it's romance. You already know how it ends."

She huffs. "I'm impatient."

"And you're stubborn, too. What's your point?"

She playfully groans, but she knows I'm right.

"Hank called. He fixed your truck." I gauge her reaction, seeing if there's any tell since she's a terrible liar.

"That's great news! I hope it wasn't something difficult."

I meet her gaze, noticing no change in her demeanor. "You ran out of gas."

She sits up, looking confused. "What? How is that possible?"

Carefully, I reposition my arms to keep Tinsel held against my chest. She's heavy, at least fifteen pounds of fluff. "Did you drive it from the airport without stopping to fill it up?"

Her head tilts like she's trying to remember. "It's a truck. Don't they go farther than cars? Have bigger fuel tanks?"

Tinsel gets fidgety, and that's when I know my time is up. "Okay, okay. Love you, too." I place one soft kiss on her head before setting her back on the floor. She zooms off, the bell on her collar jingling as the pads of her feet skirt across the wood floor.

I sit at the end of the couch. "I have to ask you a serious question."

My heart thumps in my chest as I meet her eyes and think about how to word this, knowing that we've shared so much already. I hope she'll tell me the truth. "Why are you here?"

"To learn more about the town. To enjoy Christmas outside of the city. And I was looking forward to eating some homemade taffy and people-watching, but the weather didn't cooperate." She doesn't miss a beat with her answer.

"That's it?" I study her soft features, relaxing.

"I'm also into real estate, too," she offers.

"Real estate?" I ask. "Like an agent?"

She smiles. "Yeah, in a roundabout way. But it's more like management."

"Is that why you travel around so much? Like you visit different towns and research them and all that?"

"Yeah, that's a good way to describe it."

"Makes sense. There are a few people who do that in town."

She nods. "I know. And they were booked for the next year, so I settled on the inn. Seems as if there is a market for it here. Lots of demand, especially during the holidays. People love Merryville."

"They do. Well, if I can help you, please let me know."

She nods again. "Thank you. I appreciate that. So I guess we'll pick up my truck today?"

"Yeah, and I thought maybe we could grab dinner from the café since Glenda is open."

Claire's grin widens. "Yes, please. That sounds amazing."

I lift a brow. "Was my cookin' not good enough?"

"It was perfect. But I have an entire menu to eat through before I leave town." She shoots me a wink.

"When it's cold, she makes the best damn potato soup I've ever tasted. It's a must-have."

Claire springs up. "Give me ten minutes, and we can go. Might even treat myself to a slice of strawberry or chocolate cake."

"Can't go wrong with either. Maybe you should get both?"

She squeals and picks up her pace down the hallway. I laugh, returning to the kitchen. I add some milk and a few sugars to the bottom of my travel mug, then fill it full of coffee. After I mix it, I take a drink and sigh from the pleasure of a perfectly prepared sip.

Once she's dressed in jeans and a sweater, I slide on my boots and coat, and we leave.

Hank is right. The roads are slick with ice, so I take my time driving. Icicles hang from the power lines and tree branches, and the field is silver white.

"I've seen nothing like this before," Claire whispers. The heat of her breath causes the window to fog. "Tons of snow, yes. But ice? It's...magical."

"But also a pain in all of our asses." I keep my hands

128

gripped tight on the steering wheel. Thankfully, no one else is on the road, just us.

There are no parking spaces in the downtown area. We stop at every intersection, and the sidewalks are packed. All the shop lights are on, a total difference from when Claire first arrived. She people-watches out the window, and I can feel her excited energy. "Oh, the theater is open. Can we visit one day?"

"Sure! But they only play old stuff there, like the things you can watch on the streaming channels."

"So what? It's for the experience," she explains.

We park and walk into Hank's shop together. As soon as he sees us, he lifts a brow.

"Howdy," he says directly to Claire, then glances at me.

"Hello," she returns. "I heard I ran out of fuel?"

Hank chuckles. "Dry as a bone."

She shakes her head. "I drive very little, and they gave me a vehicle I didn't reserve. Was flustered and not thinking properly. I'm honestly embarrassed."

"Oh, you must be one of those spoiled city folk." He hands her the key, and I think I see her blush. "It happens all the time, though. There's one gas station you have to fill up at, or you're pretty much screwed. Makes for good business, though." He chuckles.

"Thanks for this. How much do I owe you?"

Hank shakes his head. "Don't worry about it."

Her mouth falls open. "Please allow me to pay for your time and the fuel you put in it."

"It ain't the Merryville way, ma'am. I'd feel bad. Was no problem at all."

Claire looks at me, and I shrug. "He's hardheaded."

She reaches for the business cards on the counter and tucks one into her pocket. "I'll leave you a review online."

"See, now that's priceless." Hank taps his knuckles on the counter, then gives her a wink.

Claire laughs, not taking him seriously. "Thank you for this," she says.

"Thanks, Hank," I tell him. "We're gonna go eat. You want anything?"

"Nah, I'm good. Y'all need anything else, lemme know," he says just as Mrs. Reindeer enters.

I give him a wave, and we walk outside.

"Wanna come back and get it later?" Claire glances at the gigantic truck backed up in the parking lot. It's almost comical that they gave her something so large.

"Sure. Let's get some food."

She moves closer to me as we walk to the truck, and I open the door for her. Then we make the short drive to Glenda's. The parking lot is full, but as soon as we arrive, someone leaves. It's right up front. I glance inside and notice nearly every table is taken.

"It's packed," Claire says.

"If you don't want to wait, I can call it in to go. It's a local trick," I tell her.

"Let's go check it out. We might get lucky."

I open the door, and we enter. Music plays overhead, and chatter fills the room. Glenda and her staff are running around, but there isn't an unhappy person in the building.

"Two of y'all?" Chelsea asks. She came to Merryville a few years ago, and instead of going back home, she stayed. Glenda hired her, she found a small house to rent, and the rest is history. Sometimes that happens.

"Yep," I tell her.

"Once they pay, that table right there is all yours." She points across the room, and I see the guy take a sip of his coffee.

I smile at her, and then Claire and I sit in the waiting area in the front by the door. I put my arm across the back of the bench, and she leans into me.

Claire turns and looks at me, and just as I get ready to say something to her, my attention is being pulled away.

"Jake?" It's a voice I'll never forget. My ex. Lacy. The woman who destroyed my heart.

My smile fades. Claire notices and turns to look at her.

"How have you been?" Lacy asks.

"Fantastic," I say as Claire leans into me further.

"My manners," Lacy apologizes, but she sounds anything but sorry. "And you are?"

"Claire." She stands, meeting Lacy eye to eye. "My friends call me CeCe."

My ex holds out her manicured hand. "Lacy. That's *cute*. JJ and CeCe."

Claire gives her a tight smile. "Isn't it? Lacy… Oh yeah, I've heard *a lot* about you."

I don't know what she's doing, but I see the fake smile on my ex's face fade. I think this is the first time I've ever witnessed someone get under her skin—other than her mother. And it's…comical.

"All good things, I hope," Lacy adds. I almost burst into laughter. The audacity.

Claire strategically pauses, then lets out a laugh. "Oh yeah. Of course. All great things."

The sarcasm could be heard from a mile away. Her words are literally dripping with it.

"Are you two togeth—?"

"Yes," Claire says, proudly smiling, before Lacy finishes her question.

I'm almost intimidated by Claire's confidence, but I'm enjoying watching Lacy squirm. When we ended things, I was broken and thought she'd live rent-free in my head for the rest of my life. Thankfully, that passed. Even though I've got no love for her any longer, seeing her is still a constant reminder of what could have been. I've not dated anyone since the breakup, so I guess she has reason to be surprised. Her cheeks are pink, and I can see her pulse ticking in her neck. I'm sure Claire notices, too.

"Sweetheart," Claire says, reaching her hand out toward me. I stand, moving next to her, and take it. "I think our table is ready." She looks up into my eyes and grins widely.

I tuck a loose strand of hair behind her ear, my thumb trailing on her cheek. She leans into my touch, but I know this is a part of the act. Isn't it? Either way, I'm down for this. The couple sitting at our table walks past us, and Chelsea waves us over, pointing at it. "Oh, you're right. It is. Anyway, nice seein' you, Lace," I say, using her nickname as Claire leads me away. "Hope you've been well."

"Yeah, you too."

I don't even look back at her. I slide into the booth first, and Claire sits beside me. And she's close, so close I can feel the warmth of her leg against mine.

I wrap my arm around her and lean in to whisper in her ear, "You know, this is how rumors get started."

She giggles. "I hope the whole town knows by the time the sun goes down."

"That's the thing: they will. I hope you know you're playin' with fire. She's evil and very jealous."

"I'm not concerned about her," Claire states. "I'm not easily intimidated."

"I noticed," I tell her just as Chelsea slides two menus in front of us. "You have the potato soup today?"

"You know it," she says. We order two coffees, and she leaves us be.

"What would you suggest?" Claire asks me, flipping the menu over.

"Potpie. Chicken and dumplings. Potato soup. Tomato bisque and an adult grilled cheese."

She sighs. "Too many choices, but that last one sounds good. That's what I'm having."

I move the menus to the table's edge and order for us

when Chelsea returns. As I'm pouring cream into my coffee, I turn to Claire. "You don't have to stay on this side of the table with me."

She bumps her body against mine. "I don't mind it, actually. You're warm. Feels good."

I smile over the rim of my mug. "Keep it up, and I might miss you when you're gone."

She raises her eyebrows. "I can toast to that. I'm worried that when I leave, I will miss your company as well. It's been a while since I've detoxed from my life, so it's been exactly what I've needed."

Moments later, Lacy sits at a booth across from the restaurant, facing us. Claire leans in and whispers, "She's staring."

I keep my gaze focused on her lips as she picks up her coffee mug.

"I know. Out of all the people we had to run into today," I mutter.

Moments later, Glenda walks over. "There's my favorite holiday couple!" she crows.

"Oh, stop," I say as a few heads in the restaurant turn.

"Food should be right out. Y'all are cute," she tells us and then greets another table.

"Yep, my mama is going to be calling me about this. Too many of her friends from church are in here."

Claire laughs. "You're too easy."

"Easy?" I reach across my body and tickle her.

She lets out a loud yelp and squirms, and we draw even more attention. "Shit, you really are ticklish."

"I told you! I didn't say it in jest."

"So proper, CeCe. Also, I loved that you introduced yourself using your nickname."

"It seemed like the right thing to do," she says. "Plus, it's somewhat cute."

"Somewhat?" I hold my hand over my heart as if I'm offended.

Before she can respond, our food arrives.

"Mm, this looks great," Claire offers as Chelsea refills our coffee.

"Y'all need anything, just holler," she says, and we both nod, immediately digging in.

"Oh my God," Claire moans out. "This bisque is fabulous."

"Everything on the menu is. Taste my potato soup."

Claire nods, and I dip my spoon in the bowl and hold it to her mouth. She meets my eyes before I feed it to her. She covers her lips, chewing and then swallowing, her eyes widening with surprise. "I'm getting that next time."

I chuckle. "You can have as much of mine as you want, but I wanna taste yours."

I try to dip my spoon in her bowl, and she shakes her head. "You feed me. I feed you."

"I love a woman who reciprocates," I mutter.

As she moves the spoon to my mouth, I stare into her eyes. She slides it in with a brow popped, and I swallow, nodding. "Okay, yeah, that's as good as I remember it. But you gotta dip your sandwich in it."

She makes a face.

"Don't knock it until you try it. Go on," I tell her, scooping up a few more of the tender potatoes as I watch her.

She chews, then swallows. "I'll never doubt you again."

"Thank ya." I shoot her a wink.

When I glance up, I notice Lacy's eyes pinned on me. I give her a small smile, and she looks down at her plate. I'm glad she finally understands how I've felt seeing her blaze through men like she's running out of time. Luckily, I've had years to get over it. She seems destroyed seeing me with someone else. The last thing I want to do is hurt her, but did she expect me never to move on after her?

I have to remind myself that Claire and I are not together and that she will only be here temporarily. All the stares will eventually fade, and new rumors will spread.

"Everything okay?" Claire asks.

I force a smile and nod. "Yeah. It will be. It always is. What do you want to do after this?"

"Can we go to the antique store on Main?"

"You got it, babe."

CHAPTER 15

CLAIRE

After we finish eating, Jake pays again. When we leave, he places his firm hand on the small of my back and leads me out to the truck, where he politely opens the door. It doesn't matter that his ex is watching our every move. Jake would act like a gentleman without an audience; I know that to be a fact. However, making her squirm after what he shared about her satisfies me.

By how his expression changed when he mentioned her, I could tell how badly she hurt him. Seeing her in the flesh, hearing her high-pitched voice, and seeing the way she looked at him like she owned him infuriated me. She's a pretty girl, but honestly, he can do better.

Jake isn't a toy for her to snatch back when it's convenient. And if I teach him anything while I'm here, it will be that.

I don't think he realizes how much of a unicorn he is. If he ran within my circle, he'd be snatched up so fast and married before he could blink twice. Good guys are elusive.

He drives us to the antique shop, and when we walk in, I'm amazed by how deep it goes. The building is the entire length of the block from Main Street to Gingerbread Lane. It smells like an old library, and I make an immediate left.

Shelves full of knickknacks, picture frames, and random dishes go from floor to ceiling.

"Do you antique a lot?" Jake asks, watching me with amazement as my eyes trail over every item.

"I like to look, but I hardly ever buy anything. Although I've been known to purchase the occasional snow globe."

He gives me a wide grin. "You collect snow globes?"

A blush hits my cheek. "Yeah, it's dumb. I know."

"It's not. But this means you have to meet my mawmaw. You'd love her collection. She has several passed down from her mother and ones she's collected as a young girl."

"Ooh, I'd love that. I have a shelf in my bedroom with all the ones I've found over the years. Funny story, though: I always get stopped by security for carrying it in my bag."

"Really?"

"Swear."

"Did you know there is controversy on when the first snow globe was invented?"

He chuckles. "Oh damn, snow globe drama."

I nod, continuing to make my way toward the back. "Oh yeah. The first one was seen at the 1878 Exposition Universelle. Then, in 1900, a man named Erwy Perzy patented it. The collection of the originals went up for sale a few years ago. I almost bought them. Probably should have."

"Wow, that's interesting. I didn't realize they aren't that old of an invention. I guess my grandma has some early ones, then."

We pass a rack of goofy hats. Many look like they came from detective shows from the 1940s. Against the back wall, there is a glass cabinet, and inside are different jewelry boxes. I'm a little disappointed; I thought I'd found the snow globe haven. Most antique shops I've ever visited have had one. I never ask the clerks where it's located, either. It's like my personal treasure hunt. Sometimes, they're even randomly sprinkled around among the junk. That's when it's entertaining.

"What other facts do you know?"

I burst out laughing. "Oh God, way too many. They are mainly useless things, though. When I had panic attacks as a kid, my mother would start listing off random facts she knew to calm me down. After she passed away, it became an obsession. For example, did you know the Texas state sport is rodeoing?"

His face contorts. "It's not football?"

I shake my head. "Did you know there is a ranch in Texas larger than Rhode Island?"

"Okay, that's believable. Texas is a huge bitch."

"All peacocks are male. Females are called peahens."

He snorts. "Ha. Cocks. That's easy to remember."

"William Shatner sold a kidney stone he passed to an online casino for twenty-five thousand dollars, then donated the money to charity."

His mouth falls open. "Okay, wow. I could have you tell me this random shit all day long. A kidney stone? That's... weird as hell."

I shoot him a smile. "Green eyes are very rare. Only two percent of the population has that eye color, and it's even rarer for men."

Jake bats his eyes at me. "Oh, so I *am* special?"

"In more ways than one." I wink. "When I first met you, it took every bit of control I had not to share that tidbit."

"Interesting. Didn't know any of that."

I appreciate Jake not rushing me. Instead, he grabs random things and looks at them.

"Have you ever been in here before?" I ask, picking up a hand mirror with gold embellishments.

"When I was a kid, my mama kept her hand on my shoulder so I wouldn't break anything. I don't think a thing has changed since then. Even has some of the same items." He chuckles, looking at a candlestick.

Several rooms are filled with random items, and when we cross to the other side, I find what I'm searching for.

"Ooh," I whisper, picking up a snow globe with downtown Merryville inside. "I have to get this one."

He steps closer as I shake and lift it to the light. Flecks of glitter fall around the globe, and I smile.

"Can I see?" He holds out his hand, and I give it to him. He flips it over and reads a date from the bottom. "Whoa, this thing is thirty-five years old."

"Really?" I ask, and he passes it back to me. I hold it in my hands and can't help but grin wide. "Wow. It's a real antique."

He chuckles. "Aren't most of the things in here?"

I glance at the smaller globes on the shelf and point to another. "This one is cute."

Inside, a couple is walking down a sidewalk, holding hands. It's basic, but there's something special about it, something I adore. "Dang it. Now I have to decide which one I want."

"Just get them both," Jake says.

"I've got a personal rule that I've always followed: I can only buy one." I hold them both out in my palms. "If you had to choose, which would you go with?"

He looks between them and points to the Merryville one. "It makes more sense. You're here in town experiencing it, ya know?"

"Yeah, you're right." I set the other globe back where I found it, and then we move to the other side of the store.

There are tons of pottery, dishes, chandeliers, and children's toys on this side. One thing I can say about this place is there isn't a method to how most items are placed. It's a treasure chest of junk, and I love it. When I was growing up, everything had a place, even me and my sister, so this reminds me that not everything is like that.

"How's this look?" Jake asks with a top hat on his head.

"It's kinda hot," I admit. "All you need is a tux and bow tie and you'll look like Prince Charming. Oh…one sec."

I pull out my phone and take a picture. I show him and then text the image to my sister. At any moment, my phone will buzz like crazy.

"I kinda look like Jim Carrey in *Dumb and Dumber*. Goofy as hell."

I let out a snort. "Well, now you've ruined it."

He shoots me a wink and returns it to the coat rack that's leaning slightly less than the Tower of Pisa.

We take our time, walking down every aisle as we make our way up front. The woman behind the register smiles at us as I set the globe down on the counter.

"Oh, this is perfect." She shakes it, and the glitter falls around the small town. It sparkles in the light, and it brings me so much joy. "Six dollars. That sound fair?"

Jake pulls a ten-dollar bill from his wallet and tells her to keep the change. She grins widely and wraps the globe in brown paper before stuffing it in a recycled plastic bag from the grocery store.

"Y'all come back, ya hear," she tells us as Jake opens the door and I step outside.

I hold the bag up. "Thank you for this. It was a steal!"

"Consider it a gift from me to you. Now, when you return to New York and place it next to the others, I hope you'll always be reminded of this moment."

"Me too," I admit, a smile touching my lips. "It will be the perfect addition to my collection. So now what?"

"Want to head home?" As soon as the words leave his mouth, my phone buzzes like crazy in my pocket. I try to ignore it.

"Yeah, that would be great," I tell him as we walk down the busy sidewalk.

"You need to answer your phone?" he finally asks.

As I expected. It's my sister calling. "I should probably take this."

He nods, and I step away.

When I answer, she's chatting with someone in the background.

"Hey! What's up?" I'm smiling, watching Jake type on his phone. I can't seem to keep my eyes off him, and when he meets my gaze, my heart flutters.

I'm doomed. I'm fucking doomed.

"Did you hear me?" she asks.

"Sorry." I shake my head and turn my back so my attention isn't pulled away again. "Can you repeat that?"

"Did Dad call you?"

I think about the conversation we had the other night. "Yes."

"You told him you were in Merryville?" I can hear the disdain in her tone, and I can tell she's not happy.

"No, I didn't. I told him I was taking a holiday vacation but kept it vague."

She sighs. "Claire. He knows what you're doing and that you're there to scout the property for the business."

My mouth falls open. "How could he possibly know that?"

"Dale," she states.

I suck in a deep breath, almost forgetting that we were still together when the reservations were made. He probably realized it after I refused to tell him where I was.

"Shit." I shake my head. "I'm so stupid. This is a disaster."

"Yeah, it is, especially if I'm hearing about it. What will you do now?"

I squeeze my eyes closed. The panic rises, and my chest feels tight. I search my mind for useless facts, but nothing comes. Random people are walking down the sidewalks, and I close my eyes, trying to avoid their looks. I'm frozen in place and can't move. I'm a prisoner to my thoughts as I spiral.

The only thing that brings me back to reality is the gentle touch of a hand on the small of my back.

Jake.

"You good?" He searches my face.

"Oh my God, is that him? His sexy voice is giving me life! And I saw his picture! Please tell me he has brothers who are hot and single, too." She says something else, but I don't comprehend her words as my heart races. I can't suck in air quick enough.

"I gotta go," I force out. Then I end the call and shove my phone into my pocket. My breaths are ragged, and he pulls me into his arms. His warmth blankets me as he kisses my hair.

"Hey, everything is fine. Nothin' to worry about. You're safe, CeCe." He holds me against his chest so tight that I know he won't let me go, not until I'm ready.

I close my eyes tight, sinking into him, focusing on how he smells. It's a mixture of evergreen and man.

He noticed me and saw something wasn't right and took action. No one has ever done that before.

After five minutes, Jake pulls away. He lifts my chin with his fingers, gently encouraging me to meet his eyes. When I do, he smiles, and that's all it takes for me to realize that this man is what dreams are made of. And the last thing I want to do is hurt him.

Though that might be inevitable.

CHAPTER 16

JAKE

I t's a new day, but the first one we've had with electricity in
a week.

"It's so much different being in here with lights," Claire
says after we finish breakfast. "It's a Southern vibe with the
curtains open. I like it. However, just a tad sad that you're not
wearing your glasses."

"I never do when I'm on the clock. If you knew how many
pairs I've broken over the years, you'd understand. They get
knocked off my face, and a crunch always follows."

"Oh no. I mean, I'm not complaining at all. The view is
still great. You go from boy next door to alphahole in a snap."
She smirks, then breaks our eye contact to glance outside. All
the ice has melted, revealing the dormant grass.

She looks down at her mug. "Want another cup of
coffee?"

"Sure. Do you know how to work the machine?"

I think I hear her giggle. "It can't be too hard, right?"

As Claire comes up beside me and grabs my mug, she
leans in and steals a kiss.

I wrap my arm around her waist, not letting her go.
"You're not making leavin' you here today easy."

She pouts. "I know. I'm sorry." When she tries to walk away, I pull her back to me and slide my mouth across hers. Her tongue dips in and massages against mine.

"Fuck. If I didn't have to be at work in fifteen minutes, I'd swing you over my shoulder and carry you to bed."

With her hand on my chest, she laughs. "Caveman style? Don't threaten me with a good time."

"You're a tease," I whisper against her lips before she slithers out of my grasp and makes us each a cup of coffee. I admire her ass and her long legs and love how she bats her lashes at me. This woman might be my undoing.

"Me?" She places her hand on her heart. "No, you're the tease with a capital *T*. Messy hair. Perfect smile. Green eyes. Lumberjack."

"All it took was one look, huh?"

She rolls her eyes. "Don't get cocky."

I chuckle as she grabs the cream from the fridge and adds sugar to my coffee. When she hands it to me, I can't hold back the smile.

"What?" She returns to the stool opposite me and blows on the top.

"You made it the way I like."

She shrugs. "Why not?"

"Not sure I've ever had a woman do that. That's all." I take a sip. "And it's perfect. Good job."

Claire lifts her mug, and I tap mine against hers with a clink.

"To being considerate," she says. "Even if I learned it from you."

In a split second, Claire screams, spills her coffee, and then bursts into laughter. "Tinsel!"

It happens so fast I don't have enough time to ask what happened, but I hear Tinsel bolt across the floor and run into the living room.

"She attacked my leg! I wasn't sure what was going on,"

Claire explains through giggles, grabbing a dish towel to clean up the mess.

"That's usually a good sign." I look over the rim of my mug at her.

"Yeah? You think that little fuzzball might actually like me?" She glances over at Tinsel, who is glaring at her.

"That's still to be determined," I say, checking the time. "Shit. I really gotta go. If you need anything, anything at all, call me."

"Call you? I don't have your number." Claire picks up her phone. She unlocks it and raises her brows. "I'll text you."

I read off my number to her, and a few seconds later, my phone buzzes. I unlock it to add her contact, and when I see she sent me a picture of herself, my mouth falls open. "Fuck, you're gorgeous."

She's standing in what I assume is her bedroom, wearing a tiny white T-shirt and a pair of panties. Her hair is messy, and she's smiling in the long, full-length mirror.

Her lips turn up into a grin. "When you miss me today, open your phone, and I'll be there."

"Hell yeah." I finish my coffee, then, as I pass her, I stop to steal a kiss.

"What was that for?" She bites her bottom lip.

"You looked like you could use one. But now I gotta go." I boop her on her nose. "Try not to give Tinsel too many treats today."

"We'll see," she says as I move to the door to slip on my boots. Then I tell her goodbye and leave.

There's a permanent smile on my face as I drive the short distance to the Christmas tree farm. The road to the farm is full of cars parked on the side. I should've known we'd be overwhelmed with customers today, considering we were shut down for a week. Now, people are scrambling.

I pull up to the large barn and park the old truck on the side, then walk a short distance to the staging area. Holiday music plays overhead as I make my way through the crowd to find my older brother Hudson, who's passing out assignments to all of the employees.

"You're late," he says.

"No, I'm not," I tell him, pulling my phone out of my pocket and showing him the time. "Loosen up."

Ever since his wife left him and his son, he's been a Scrooge. The holidays bring out the worst in him. And while I know it's because he's lonely, I also don't let him act like a dick just because. He hands me my duties for the day; it looks like I'll be restocking the precuts, which I'm happy about. Time always passes by quickly when I'm out in the field.

When I walk away, he says my name, drawing my attention back.

"What's up?" I ask, shoving my gloved hands into my pockets. The temperatures aren't below freezing, but the upper thirties aren't exactly warm, either.

"Mom and Dad told me you had a girlfriend. Is that true?"

I snort. "No. Long story short, a woman is currently stayin' at my house."

"What?" He lifts a brow.

"It's a story for another day," I explain, noticing many people walking up to the pay station. Hudson sees everyone, too, but ignores them.

"I've got time."

"She was walkin' into Merryville, and I picked her up." Then I explain what happened at the inn and then the storm.

He's giving me the same expression that Hank did.

"It's going to be fine. I'm still alive, aren't I?"

He's not convinced. "I dunno, Jake, are ya?"

"She's incredible. Honestly, you'd love Claire. You're both kinda grumpy and serious."

His eyes are wide as saucers. "You like her."

"What? What makes you say that?"

"The way your demeanor changed when you mentioned her. It's obvious."

I shake my head. "It's not like that."

"Who are you tryin' to convince?" He stares me down.

"So what if I do like her? What's the worst that could happen?" It's a question I immediately regret asking. "I'm sorry," I tell him, knowing he's thinking about his ex. I'm hyperaware of his insecurities regarding failed relationships, even more than my own.

"I just want you to protect yourself. And your heart. That's all. So who is she?" I start to walk toward the barn, and he follows.

"Her name is Claire Chester and…" I think on this for a couple of seconds too long. He lifts his eyebrows, waiting. "She said she's in real estate."

"That's it? That's all you know about her?" He presses his hand to my forehead. "No fever."

"I know she talks in her sleep and likes baths the same temperature as mine. I know she has stupid expensive boots that ain't good for nothin', and she's hard on herself when she shouldn't be. I also know she loves Christmas and snow globes and pretends to be tough as nails, but it's all an act. She has a soft side and can't cook for shit. She also drinks her coffee like a serial killer. And sometimes, she gets so overwhelmed that panic attacks take over. She's dated asshole men and has a chip on her shoulder because of it. But she's kind, a little shy, and has no street smarts. Stubborn as hell, though. So, if you're wondering, I know a lot about her. The real her. Not the bullshit you brag to your family about. None of that matters to me, anyway."

He huffs. "Well, I stand corrected. When do I get to meet her?"

I shrug. "Christmas dinner?"

"Sooner than that. I ran into Hank, and he said he was planning a get-together at the bar. If he does, you should bring her, let her meet everyone at once." He places his hand on my shoulder. "Take care of yourself, okay?"

I give him a nod, then we go our separate ways. He means well. I know he does. But no one has experienced Claire in the ways I have. I might not know everything about her everyday life, but do I need to? She's leaving. That much is certain. So, in a way, the less I know about her, the less to fall in love with. And at the end of the day, that's better for us both.

Just as I predicted, time is soaring. Randomly throughout the day, I text Claire silly selfies. She's a good sport and texts funny faces back.

JAKE

You're adorable.

CLAIRE

Keep telling me that, and I might begin believing it.

I send her a picture of me leaning against the truck.

JAKE

Could use a lumberjackqueline right about now.

My joke makes me chuckle, but I gulp when she sends me a picture of her in my bathroom, standing in her bra and panties. Her nipples are rock hard, and she's chewing on the corner of her lip. She's not looking at the camera but rather down at her phone, with her brown hair flipped over on one side.

. . .

CLAIRE

Could use a lumberjack right about now.

"Fuck," I hiss, ready to throw this chainsaw on the lowboy full of cut trees and go home. Not like I would get fired, but I also take pride in being a team player. My cock grows hard thinking about her naked in my shower.

I force the thoughts away and think about abandoned kittens. I try to move my thoughts to anything other than her. But when I close my eyes, I envision being buried between her legs as she moans out my name.

"Jake!" I hear a deep voice say.

It's not the tone I wish was yelling my name right now. I turn around and see my brother Lucas walking toward me with a smirk. He's in his early thirties, but people always think he's my twin.

I pinch the bridge of my nose, wanting little Jakey to calm the fuck down as I keep my body facing the metal of the truck.

"What's up?" I say, readjusting myself.

"Are you okay?" His face contorts. "You look ill. Hudson warned me that you were lovesick, but damn, I didn't realize it was literal."

I roll my eyes. "I'm fine. And don't listen to him. He's just mad a stork didn't drop a pretty woman on his doorstep."

Lucas nearly doubles over laughing. "You're wrong for that."

I wait for him to catch his breath. "Yeah?"

"I was told to tell you to hurry the fuck up because they need these trees at the loading area immediately. There are about sixty cars waitin' for them."

The number catches me off guard, and I know I must've misheard. "Sixteen?"

"Six-zero. We don't have time for you to be lollygagging. Hudson is ready to blow a gasket."

I shake my head. "He needs a vacation."

"He needs a wife," Lucas says. "Need any help?"

"Nah, I'll meet you up front." I give him a wave and make my way around the front of the truck, then climb in.

I carefully haul the trees to the unloading area. Then, I help wrap them in wire and secure them to customer's vehicles. I do this for the rest of the day and am relieved by the afternoon shift. I take my work gloves off and hold my arms over my head, sore from the lifting I did.

"I'm starving." Lucas pats me on the back. "Want to go to Glenda's?"

"Nah, can't." I smile at him.

"Ah, almost forgot. Well then, good work today." He gives my hand a firm shake. "Have fun with your lady friend."

"Yeah, thanks."

We go our separate ways, and the only thing on my mind is Claire. Being away from her was more complicated than I thought it would be. I'm looking forward to cooking a hot meal and having her for dessert.

I turn off onto the gravel road that leads to my cabin on the property. As I'm happily driving along, I see red flashing lights. When I round the final bend, I see the volunteer fire department outside my house.

My heart immediately sinks as I park.

What the fuck is going on?

CHAPTER 17

CLAIRE

I'm a blubbering mess as the fire trucks surround the house. My nerves are shot, and I've *almost* shed a few tears from the stress. It's not something I do, so it was shocking for me, too.

When I look up, Jake rushes toward me, grabbing my shoulders and asking if everything is okay.

"CeCe?" he asks, looking around, and I point up to the tree where Tinsel is meowing.

Jake's eyes widen, and I'm worried about what he'll say or how mad he'll be. I nearly lost his pride and joy; she's been in that tree howling for the last hour. Poor thing is probably scared to death, and it's all my fault because I didn't pay attention.

"I'm so sorry," I say, my bottom lip quivering.

He places his palm on my cheek, then he bursts into laughter. "I should've warned you that she's great at opening doors if they're not clicked closed."

I look into his eyes, and he smiles, a reaction I didn't expect. "It's not a big deal, babe. But I better get her down before she works herself up." Jake goes to the base of the tree.

"Tinsel! You turd!" he hollers, passing one of the guys dressed in full firefighter garb.

Jake talks to the man with the ladder, and I overhear their conversation.

"If she climbs any farther up, we're gonna have to call Henry's Tree Service to get someone with harnesses to get her down."

I want to disappear.

"Nah, that won't be necessary. Do you mind?" Jake puts his foot on the bottom rung of the ladder and climbs up. With his height, it's no issue for him to reach out and grab her. She fusses bitterly all the way down as he holds her against his chest.

"You're okay," he whispers, kissing her. "You're fine."

"Another successful day," one of the volunteers says, patting Jake on his back.

"Thanks for coming out. Appreciate it," he tells them. "Gonna get this old woman in the house." He glances down at Tinsel. "You're grounded."

They load the ladder, give us a wave, and then they're gone.

It's like it never happened.

We go inside, and he still has Tinsel wrapped in his arms. Her claws dig into his sweater, and he peels her away. As soon as her paws are on the floor, she hisses, then trots away. "Someone's got a cattitude. Too much attention?"

I can't stop watching him. I feel like total shit. Jake moves closer and wraps his arm around my waist, pulling me against him. "Have you had enough commotion for the day?"

"I think I've had enough for the rest of the month. I was so scared that something bad was going to happen. And it would have been my fault. Are you sure you're not upset?"

"Not even an ounce, but I gotta say it's cute that you cared so much about her furry butt that you were on the brink of tears."

I playfully smack his arm. "It's not funny. My thoughts were everywhere, and I knew if something happened to that cat on my watch, you'd hate me. She's basically your child."

He shakes his head. "I'd *never* hate you, CeCe. Accidents happen. Now, if you purposely put Tinsel outside, that would be different. Plus, she wouldn't have gone too far. She acts brave but always comes back."

"It wasn't on purpose, I swear. I planned a trip to town to buy some ingredients to surprise you for dinner. Work on my domestic skills, considering I have zero."

His expression softens as he studies my lips. "That's sweet. What were you going to make?"

"Lasagna. I found a video on YouTube. I even made a list of everything to buy. But as I walked outside, Tinsel ran past me and trotted down the steps in front of your house. I tried to coax her to come to me. I even said all the magic words like food, treat, nap."

He laughs. "And that didn't work."

"No, it didn't. I chased her for nearly thirty minutes. Fell a few times. She'd bait me. Wait until I was close, then would bolt away. The final time, she darted up the tree but kept climbing. She was meowing like she was in pain and was begging me to help her. So I did what people on TV do and called the fire department. I'm actually shocked they came."

"You could've called me," he says, placing a soft kiss on my forehead.

"I wanted to solve this problem alone so that you wouldn't worry."

He pulls away and rubs his thumb across my bottom lip, causing my breath to hitch. "That pride of yours is going to be your downfall, CeCe. If you *ever* need me, I'm there for you. If there's a problem, we can solve it together."

I swallow hard.

"I thought something bad had happened to *you*. I was worried."

"I'm fine. Just have a bruised ego, but I'll be okay if Tinsel is okay."

He tucks a loose strand of hair behind my ear and glances at Tinsel. She's cleaning her paw in front of the fire. "That cat gives no fucks about what happened."

I chuckle and shake my head. "I can't believe I cried."

"Maybe you'll end up turning into a softy on me."

I wrap my arms around his neck. "I'm sorry I messed up your surprise."

He shakes his head. "It's the thought that counts. Are you hungry?"

I slide my hands down his chest and fist his shirt, smelling his cologne mixed with sweat. "For you."

With a brow popped, he smirks. "Mm. I need a shower first. Want to join me?"

"Yes, yes, I do." I don't care that I've already taken one today.

He chuckles, hooking his arm around my shoulder. "Good girl."

Each time he says it, I nearly melt in his hand. "I like it when you say that."

"Oh yeah?" He leads me into the bathroom, his fingertips brushing across my stomach as he lifts my sweater over my head. His lips trail across my collarbone, peppering kisses up to my neck. Jake's hot breath is in my ear as he nibbles on my lobe. "You're a very good girl."

My knees nearly buckle as he hums against my neck, unbuttoning my pants and sliding them down my body with my panties. My head falls back as I revel in his touch. I step out of my jeans and reach behind to unsnap my bra, allowing it to fall to the floor.

"Mm." Jake takes a step back, his heated gaze sliding down my body and up again. I'm not self-conscious, and I enjoy being the center of his attention. A small smile touches my lips, and he notices. "You're so goddamn beautiful."

I remove the space between us and peel the hoodie off his body. My fingertips graze over his abs, and before I can unbutton them, he drops to his knees, kissing my stomach down to my pussy. As I run my fingers through his messy hair, he meets my gaze and lifts my leg over his shoulder. I steady myself, giving him full access to me. At first, I tense, but as soon as his tongue grazes against my clit, I'm putty in his hands.

A sigh escapes me as I sink into his mouth and rock my hips. "Yes, darlin', take what you need."

"I have a confession to make." A whimper escapes me. "I came earlier...thinking about your mouth being between my legs."

He smiles against me, but his tongue doesn't stop its assault.

"How was it?" he whispers before darting his tongue inside my cunt.

I groan. "Mind-blowing."

He chuckles. "I still want to watch you touch this cute little clit of yours."

My breathing increases. "Yes. Just thinking about you watching..."

The fantasy nearly overpowers me as he draws a circle on my clit with his tongue. It's slow and methodical, and the orgasm takes hold so fast, without warning. I grind against his mouth, riding out my release as he grabs a handful of my ass, creating more friction but also steadying me.

His name releases on my lips as he continues lapping me up like ice cream on a sugar cone. He carefully places my leg on the floor, grabs my hips, and then stands, wearing a smirk.

"You came fast." He kisses me, sliding his tongue into my mouth. "See how fuckin' good you taste? You've quickly become my favorite flavor."

"I used to think there was something wrong with me and that was why no man ever wanted to please me like that."

Jake lifts my chin and shakes his head. He's wearing that serious expression, the no-bullshit one I sometimes see. "No, darlin'. The problem is you weren't with men."

I tuck my bottom lip into my mouth. "I'm glad it was you."

He grabs my ass. "Fuck, me too. Now, it's time to get my dirty girl all clean."

Jake finishes undressing, and his cock is at full attention. I grip it, stroking him a few times as he leads me to the shower. Then I admire the thick veins and how perfect he is.

"Likin' what you're seein'?"

I smirk. "Pretty sure you're a Greek god. Muscles like stone and an anaconda cock."

He howls with laughter as the water splashes down his body. "First time anyone has ever said that to me."

"Really?" I'm shocked. "I'm pretty sure your ex didn't know what she had."

He shakes his head. "I don't want to talk about her, CeCe. Not while your beautiful tits are pressed against me."

"I understand." I rub the bar of soap between my hands until suds form, then I grip Jake's thick cock again. He leans his back against the shower wall as I stroke him. When it throbs, my eyes go wide. "You made it do that?"

I love the sound of his laughter. "Yeah, of course."

"Can you make it do that...*inside* of me?"

He growls and nods as I continue to fondle him. We've only been fooling around for the last few days and haven't gone all the way yet. It's the next step in this...whatever we're doing. I cup and massage his balls as I stroke up and down, rubbing my thumb across the head. Jake groans, and I get so much satisfaction from making him feel good, knowing I'm in control and I'm the one who will make him come.

"Will you fuck my mouth?"

Desire dances in his expression as I drop to my knees and hollow my cheeks. I guide him inside of me and adjust my mouth to his length and girth. He blocks the stream of water with his broad shoulders, allowing me to look up and watch him watching me.

"You're so sexy," he growls as my hair falls in wet strands around my face. I place my palms on his thighs, giving myself more stability as I pick up my pace. He doesn't thrust and gives me complete control to take in as much of him as I can. This time, when he hits the back of my throat, I don't gag. He doesn't fit all the way, but I try.

"Fuck," he groans, his voice deep and low. The sound of it has my pussy clenching with desire.

Jake threads his fingers through my wet hair, placing his hand on the back of my head. It only encourages me further. I want this man to remember me, to remember this, for the rest of his life. I don't want to leave and have him forget everything we experienced together because I won't. I'll never forget Jake Jolly. I'll never forget his perfect cock or the way he pleasures me, or how he sees me. The real me. The me I've hidden from everyone my entire life. I don't know how he unlocked this part of me so quickly.

"Claire," he moans out my name, fisting my hair. "If you keep goin'..."

I nod, knowing and wanting him to pump into the back of my throat. The thought of swallowing always made me sick, but with him, I want to. I enjoy the taste of him—salty and sweet—knowing I'm responsible for his pleasure.

His balls and quads tighten as he finally gives me what I want and fucks my mouth, thrusting his release into my throat. I swallow him down, licking every drop of cum off the tip of him.

"Mm." I stand, crashing my mouth to his, allowing the two of us to mix together. "How was it?"

"Perfect. Such a good fucking girl." He holds me against his chest.

"Shit. I do have a praise kink."

He dips down and nibbles on my lip. "We're going to have a lot of fun with that. Now let me clean you up, darlin'."

Jake spins me around, massaging my shoulders. "You're tight," he whispers, his strong hands kneading at the knots in my shoulders.

"Just wait until you're inside me," I say, feeling his cock against my back.

I glance over my shoulder at him, and he captures my lips. As the kiss deepens, there's a loud pounding on the door. Our eyes fly open.

"Did you hear that?" he asks, and the sound returns.

"Yeah," I whisper.

"Shit," he says. The knocking is persistent. "Whoever it is ain't goin' away."

Jake steps out of the shower and dries off, then quickly wraps a towel around his waist. I finish rinsing the shampoo from my scalp and quickly condition it, then turn off the stream so I can see what's going on. One of his robes is hanging on the back of the door, so after I twist my hair into a towel, I slide it over my shoulders and then tie it in the front. It takes me less than a minute.

As I rush out of the bathroom and down the hallway, I see Jake, his arms crossed over his chest, water dripping from his hair.

He stares at the woman who broke his heart all those years ago.

CHAPTER 18

JAKE

My nostrils flare as I stare at my ex.

She smiles sweetly, her gaze wandering around the cabin until finally landing on me.

Then I notice how her eyes trail to my lips, down my stomach, to my cock. I step to the side, letting her in so the warmth doesn't escape. "It looks great in here." Considering I built this place for us and wanted her to move in with me once we were engaged, her commentary on the appearance of it feels bitter.

Conveniently, my question is ignored. "What are you doin' here?" I ask again.

"Oh, I was just visitin' your parents and told your mama I was stopping by, so she gave me some leftovers to bring you."

I look down at her hand, seeing food in a plastic bag.

Claire strolls down the hallway, dressed in one of my robes, her hair wrapped in a towel. I expect her to stop walking when she sees Lacy, but she doesn't. No, that air of confidence quickly swallows her whole, and she struts through the living room, petting Tinsel on the head before standing next to me.

The smile on her face is saccharine sweet. "Oh, hi. What's the occasion?"

I see the color fade from Lacy's face. "I didn't realize you were still here."

Claire lets out an adorable laugh and interlocks her fingers with mine as she looks at me. "I'm not going anywhere."

She stands on her tiptoes and kisses me, and for a brief moment, everything in the room completely fades away.

Lacy clears her throat, and Claire apologizes, but she doesn't mean it.

"Why are you still stopping by my parents' house?" There is no reason for her to do so, not when we live on the outskirts of town.

"I found a few pictures of us together and know how much your mama loves keepsakes, so I wanted to gift them to her."

I shake my head, my brows furrowing, wondering if she thinks I'm fucking stupid. "Stop whatever it is you're doing."

"I don't know what you're talkin' about."

Claire steps forward and grabs the food from Lacy's hand, then struts to the kitchen. She sets it on the island and pulls the containers from the bag. "Ooh, this smells delicious. Your mom packed enough for us both. I just love her."

I glance at her and then back over to Lacy, who looks like she's chewing rocks. When we were together, I saw that look many times.

"Anything else?" I ask, standing my ground. Tinsel jumps off the back of the couch and saunters toward Lacy. As soon as she's close, she hisses.

"It's okay, baby."

"You still have that stupid cat?"

I suck in a deep breath, remembering how much Lacy hated her. The feeling was mutual, though.

"I think it's time for you to go," Claire says from the

kitchen. She wipes her hands on a dishrag, walks past me, and places her hand on Lacy's shoulder. "Thanks for stopping by."

Lacy looks at me over her shoulder as Claire gently guides her to the door.

"Do I owe you a tip?" Claire asks with great sincerity.

"Excuse me?"

I've never seen Lacy look so offended in my life.

"For the food delivery."

When Lacy lets out a huff, Claire shrugs and then slams the door in her face. Before walking away, she locks the dead bolt.

My mouth falls open. I think I'm in shock.

"Some people can't take hints, can they?" Claire moves toward me, wrapping her arms around the back of my neck.

I place my hands on her hips, pulling her against me, then I fall into a fit of laughter. "I can't believe you did that."

"Your boundaries deserve to be respected, Jake."

"No one has ever stood up to her before. Not her parents. Not mine. Not me."

She lifts onto her tiptoes and places a kiss on my nose. "And that ends now."

Tinsel rubs her body on the back of my leg and then does the same to Claire. "I think she approves," I say.

"Finally. Especially after the day we've had together." Claire bends down and pets her head with the back of her hand, then scratches under her chin. "You might turn me into a cat lady," she tells her sweetly.

Tinsel nips at her and then runs off.

"That's her way of saying she likes you." I kiss the soft skin on her neck, then add a little pressure with my teeth.

"Ow." She playfully pats at me. "Bites from both of you. That food smells delicious. Do you think it's safe to eat?"

"She's a bitch, but she's not stupid. I don't think she'd tamper with my mama's cookin' like that. Too many repercussions."

"I trust your judgment. Kinda." She winks and leads me into the kitchen, and I peel the plastic lids off the containers.

She peers down and looks comically disappointed. "What is it?"

"Shepherd's pie and corn bread."

"Uh…" She hesitates.

"Ignore how it looks. It tastes amazin'." I grab a fork from the drawer and scoop some up. She opens her mouth, and I feed it to her. After she chews and swallows, she smiles at me.

"Please, sir, I'd like some more."

"I'll teach you how to cook this one day if you'd like." I chuckle.

"I'd love that," she says.

I pull two plates from the cabinet and another fork. My towel falls from my waist as I divide the food onto our plates. Claire's eyebrows pop up, and she studies my cock. "Is that for dinner?"

"I thought you'd had your fill already."

Laughter escapes her.

"Gonna go put some joggers on. I'll be right back." I walk away, and when I glance over my shoulder, Claire's staring. I shoot her a wink, then go to my bedroom and slide on a pair of dark-gray jogging pants. Before I return to her, I remove my contacts and grab my glasses.

When I walk into the kitchen, I find her gulping down her food. She eyes my pants and says, "Damn. You're really trying me, aren't you?"

"Not sure what you're referring to."

She holds out her hand. "You're not real. There's no way."

I sit on the stool beside her, resting my hand on her inner thigh and gently squeezing. She sucks in a deep breath. "See? Just one touch and I can't concentrate. You sure she didn't poison our food?"

Even though I'm shaking my head, I'm smiling. "You flatter me."

Claire bumps her shoulder against mine. "Learn to take a compliment every once in a while. Just don't get too cocky. A humble man is hot."

As we eat, our legs rest against one another, and I place my hand on the small of her back, a simple gesture, one that tells her I'm here. We don't need to fill the space with pointless chatter as we eat. The stolen glances are more than enough.

"So what's for dessert?" she asks when we're finished eating.

"You," I suggest, and that's when I realize I'm too comfortable with this woman.

"That sounds like a good night."

"But there's one thing we have to do first," I tell her as she clears her plate. I try to grab them, but she takes them first and carries them to the sink.

"I'll take care of that."

"Washing a dish is one thing I can do without messing it up," she says, turning on the sprayer. I move behind her, wrapping my arms around her waist. Softly, I place kisses behind her ear, and she tilts her neck, giving me more access. She drops the fork in the sink, and the clank makes her jump.

After she cuts off the water, Claire turns to face me, her back against the countertop. She studies me, words on the tip of her tongue, but she doesn't speak.

"What?" I ask, my brows lifted, waiting.

"I'm scared I'm growing attached to you."

I swallow hard, a lump forming in my throat. "We have rules, CeCe."

"I know," she says, studying my lips.

We don't say anything else because it's understood. She's leaving. She has a life outside of Merryville, and while it's fun to pretend that it's just us against the world, that's not reality *for either of us.*

"Don't," I whisper, brushing my lips across hers. "I don't want to think about you leavin' me. Not tonight. Not tomorrow. We'll cross that bridge when we get to it."

She nods, slamming her mouth to mine as too many emotions swirl between us. "What did you want to do? You'd mentioned something but never told me."

I'm glad for the change of subject. I clear my throat. "Well, I thought we could build a gingerbread house together."

A wide smile fills her face. "Really? I've never done it before."

"Even better," I say. I grab the homemade dough from the fridge and some eggs so they can get to room temperature.

Claire points at the brown ball, puzzled. "You just have it waiting in your fridge at all times?"

I kiss her forehead, then wash my hands. "I defrosted it in the fridge a few days ago for this occasion. It's a staple around here during this time of year. You can freeze it for up to three months, then pull it out when you want some cookies or a gingerbread house."

She snorts. "You're so nonchalant about it."

"This stuff is my grandma's recipe. Now, let's get to baking. Remember, your eggs need to be at room temperature for our royal icing. It's a key step."

She repeats it. "Wait, royal icing? That sounds very fancy."

I laugh. "It's the sugary glue that holds it all together. Without it, the whole thing will collapse. We don't want that."

Claire is overly excited about this as she removes her damp hair from the towel. After she throws it in the laundry room and returns, she washes her hands. "All right. Teach me your Jolly ways."

I grab some flour, parchment paper, and a rolling pin and set it on the counter. Then, I go through the steps with her as I preheat the oven.

"You'll flatten all this out so we can make the walls and roof," I explain as she tries to smoosh it down with her palms. "Gonna take more elbow grease than that, but you've got this. Start at the edges with the pin and roll your way up," I encourage.

"This smells so good," she says, inhaling the cinnamon and ginger.

As Claire continues to flatten it, I measure the sugar and pour it into the mixing bowl.

"How's this?" she asks.

"Almost there." I give her an encouraging smile, and she continues.

"I think I already have more of an appreciation for the art of this."

This makes me chuckle. "And we've only just gotten started."

"So you have the steps and ingredients memorized?"

"Learned them by heart. It was something we'd do every year growing up. The tradition started a long time ago by family when Merryville was first established. I've probably made a whole neighborhood of houses in all different shapes and sizes over the years. What about you? Any holiday traditions?"

She shakes her head. "Not unless you'd count drinking wine alone as one."

"It doesn't because you can do that every day of the year, and no one would think twice about it. If you made a fuckton of gingerbread houses in March, and you didn't live in Merryville, people might give you the side-eye."

She snorts. "You're right. But maybe, after tonight, this will be my new one. Probably need to learn how to make the dough, though."

"No can do. It's a secret recipe."

She gasps. "You wouldn't tell me?"

I shake my head, smirking. "Not unless you let me put a ring on that finger. Only family knows."

"Tempting," she purrs. "But I totally understand. Wouldn't want me stealing the recipe, then distributing it across the country."

"Pfft. Not worried about that. However, you can probably search some recipes online and find something comparable."

"As long as it has butter, right?"

I nod. "You've got it."

Once the dough is the correct thickness, I move closer to her, sliding the robe up her body and palming her bare ass. "I think this is the most fun I've ever had making one of these."

"Same," she quips.

I look over her work. "Great job."

She pouts.

"I mean…" I turn her around and lean in, nudging my knee between her thighs. She sighs, and I give her the words she fucking craves. "That's my very good girl."

She shudders. "Stop distracting me."

"Me, distracting you? You're the queen of it."

The oven beeps, and Claire nearly jumps out of her skin. "Scared the shit out of me."

I open the drawer where I keep the patterns for the shapes of my walls and roof, then lay them on top of the dough. "Do the honor."

"Really?"

"Yes, ma'am." I hand her a baking knife, and she carefully cuts the squares and then freehands a window.

When she realizes it's crooked, she frowns. "Ugh. I messed it up."

I grab her chin and shake my head. "It's not a mistake. It just adds character. May I?"

She hands me the utensil, and I cut an oddly misshapen window on the other wall. Her smile returns. "I like that."

I don't like how she's so hard on herself. When she has the

slightest mishap, she becomes her own worst enemy. If she learns anything while she's here, I want her to know it's okay to be human, to fuck up every once in a while. I think her and her happy mistakes are perfect. They prove she's not an emotionless robot who does everything as it should be.

Once our shapes are cut, we place them on a cookie sheet, then put them in the oven. I set a timer, then we go back to the icing.

"What's next?" The excitement returns to her tone.

"Royal icing, for my queen." I shoot her a wink. "What did I tell you to remember earlier?"

"Eggs at room temperature."

"Exactly." I pick one up, feel it, and hand it to her. "As if it came out of a chicken's butt."

She snorts, unable to hold back her laughter. "Didn't expect that to come out of your mouth."

"I got all sorts of Southern shit like that to share at the most random times." I show her how to quickly get rid of the yolks since we're only using the whites, then we turn on the mixer.

Claire watches it carefully, making sure it doesn't overmix, and when there are peaks, she turns it off. "I think it's ready."

I glance into the bowl, dipping my finger inside, then placing it in her mouth. She sucks and moans, devouring all the sugar. My cock instantly hardens.

Claire turns around, scooping some up with her finger. I expect her to put it in my mouth, but she opens the robe and places it on one of her hard nipples. I don't wait before I suck and lick up every bit of it. She braces herself against the counter when my hand slides down to her clit, then inside of her. Her eyes roll into the back of her head as I slide another finger into her dripping wet pussy. She holds on to me for dear life, and when I think she's close, I pull away, putting my two fingers in my mouth and tasting her.

"You're going to leave me hanging like that?" she asks like

she's offended, trying to catch her breath. Her pulse is ticking hard in her neck.

"One thing at a time, darlin', because once we get started, I'm not stopping for anything. Gingerbread house first, then your sweet cunt is mine."

She glances down at my dick, and I tuck it up in my joggers, the head on full display. With just one look, she makes me hard, and having the power to make her come within minutes has me nearly exploding. I know her body already. I know what she likes, what brings her to the edge, and what roughness she craves. By the end of the trip, I have a feeling she'll be just as addicted to me as I am to her.

The timer on the oven screams out, letting us know the gingerbread is finished baking. I force myself away and grab a mitt, then set the pan of gingerbread on top of the stove. Claire reties her robe and inspects our work. "Wow, it looks legit."

"Because it is. Now we just have to wait for it to cool." I take our structure and place it on a mat on the island. "Let's finish the icing while we wait."

Claire steps back and watches me put the icing into a plastic bag with a tip.

"I'm impressed," she says.

"Just wait until I teach you how to decorate."

She shakes her head. "No. I can't. I'm not an artist. Trust me, I've had plenty of lessons. Bad at sports. Bad at drawing. Bad at painting. Bad at dancing."

"And you're going to be great at decorating a house made of bread. Come on, we'll do some practice runs. You're gonna be amazin'. I can see the determination in your eyes." I wave her over and slide one of the extra squares I baked just for this purpose in front of her.

I stand behind her, wrapping my hands around hers, adding the perfect amount of pressure to the bag so she can get used to how the icing spreads.

"See? Pro level," I say in her ear, and she smiles. "Feelin' confident?"

"I think so."

"Great, because we're gonna assemble it tonight and decorate later."

"What!" She turns and glares at me. "Decorating is the fun part!"

"It's the rules! If we decorate it too early without letting everything settle, it will crash and burn. Okay, well, not burn, but it'll fall apart."

"Patience is not one of my strengths."

"Luckily, it's one of mine. Now, let's build this house so I can focus on you the rest of the night."

"Actually, now that you mention it, I'm totally on board with this plan."

I chuckle. "Hardly needed any convincing. Let's do this."

I grab a glitter board from the pantry and set it in front of her. Then I walk her through how we'll glue it all together.

"Like this?" she asks, setting the bottom of one wall upright. I reach forward, holding it so it doesn't fall as she does another.

With care, she lines the edges where the roof will go, then places it on top. The smile on her face might be permanent as she takes a step back and admires her handiwork. I lift my hand, and she gives me a high five.

"Good girl. Now, you'll want to reinforce the seams with some icing, and then we'll let it rest for a few days."

"Days?" Her brows furrow.

"Constructing is the hardest part."

"Seriously?"

I laugh. "Google it. People rush, want to bake and decorate and do everything at once, but it doesn't last. Building a gingerbread house is like dating. Gotta give it time to settle, make it sweet, then sit back and admire it."

"And gobble it up?"

I shake my head. "Not exactly."

"Then you're making me some cookies to experience that dough! But not right now."

I grab her hand, leading her out of the kitchen and into the living room. I throw a few logs on the fire and flick off the overhead lights so we can enjoy the ambience of the Christmas tree. "Are you happy?" I ask, loving her demeanor.

"Yes," she whispers. I pull her into my arms, and our bodies sway together. As I grab her hand, I twist her around, and she giggles.

I hum "'Please Come Home for Christmas'" as we slow dance in front of the fire.

When we're done, she pulls away. "Why that song?"

"My grandpa used to sing it a lot."

"It's depressing."

I laugh. "Getting soft on me?"

She pops out her bottom lip, and I remove the space between us. "I'll be here for Christmas. I promise."

"You better be," I tell her as our lips press together. Claire pulls me to the floor in front of the fireplace with her.

She lies flat on her back, and I tucked into her side, propped up on my elbow. The flames dance in the fire, and when she smiles, my heart races.

"I'm glad you picked me up," she whispers.

"I'm glad you didn't put gas in your truck."

Laughter escapes her. "So dumb."

I brush hair out of her face. "Sometimes mistakes end up being miracles in disguise."

Her palm presses against my cheek, and I dip down to kiss her again.

Before I pull away, she whispers against my lips, "Make love to me, JJ."

CHAPTER 19

CLAIRE

W hen the words come out, it feels right.
"Darlin', ya sure?"

"Yes, please."

"Mmm, kinda sexy to hear you ask so nicely." He smirks.

Being here in this moment with Jake is everything.

I untie the robe, revealing myself to him. I'm on full display, loving the way his eyes drift over my naked body. He captures one of my hard nipples in his mouth and slides down his joggers, his hard cock at full attention.

Our lips dance together as Jake positions himself above me. I open my legs wider, anticipating every thick inch of him, but he stops, waiting outside of my entrance.

"We'll go slow, okay? If I hurt you, ple—"

Placing my hand on his cheek, I whisper, "I trust you."

As he rests his forehead against mine, he slowly thrusts forward. I gasp, and he freezes, meeting my eyes.

"I'm okay," I say, further adjusting to him.

"Fuck," he hisses, giving me a little more. "You're so tight."

I swallow hard. I'm already filled so full, but I want to keep going.

"You good?" he asks, as he always does, with care and sincerity in his tone.

"I want all of you," I whisper, my breathing ragged, the sensation overpowering every thought.

He carefully continues, and a moan escapes me, my muscles contracting. My pussy clenches around him once our ends meet. He doesn't move, and we just kiss, knowing we're the closest that we will ever be. The lines are blurred and have been crossed. There is no going back. And when I meet this man's heated gaze, looking at me with so much compassion, I feel nothing but satisfaction.

We're complete opposites, and somehow, we've found exactly what we need in each other. It's like finding two needles in a haystack—the odds of that happening are astronomical.

Jake rocks his hips, adding just enough pressure that I think I might rip in two. But he keeps me safe. He moves at a steady pace, allowing my body to conform to him as the pleasure builds.

His lips, mouth, and teeth graze across my skin as I have a near out-of-body experience. Each time he goes deeper, he hits my G-spot, and I think I might explode. It's a sensation I can't quite explain.

My back arches off the rug as I rock my hips.

As the warmth builds inside me—an unstoppable fire that will leave me burned to a crisp—I whisper his name.

"Such a good fucking girl," he mutters, the low timbre of his voice coming out like a growl. Goose bumps trail over my skin.

I have all of him, but somehow I need more. I'm greedy when it comes to this man, too greedy, and I know tomorrow I will feel where he's been.

"Harder, please," I groan, scratching my nails down his back. The warmth swirling inside of me transforms into something completely different.

He holds me, kisses me, and fucks me precisely the way I want and need.

"Oh. Oh. Oh." I'm breathless. "Jake. Shit!" I say, not knowing what's happening as an orgasm, different from anything I've ever experienced, takes over.

"Yes, darlin'," he says, continuing to impale me with his monster cock as my body seizes up and clenches around him.

He's so deep. He rocks my fucking world as I come. Everything seems to fade away, and I'm captured by the intense pleasure that takes hold. Nothing in the world matters right now, but I know he's close, too. His breathing grows ragged, and his muscles tighten. But he slows down, moving hair from my forehead as he studies me. This is different. This feels deeper than just fucking as I study his green eyes.

"Cum inside of me," I whisper. "I want all of you, Jake."

"You're sure?"

"Yes, *please*. I'm on birth control."

And seconds later, he does. His cum fills me, and the warmth spreads. We stay connected as we struggle to breathe, my heart rate ticking in double time.

He brushes his nose against mine and smiles against my lips as his eyes flutter open. "It's never felt that way before."

I swallow hard. "For me, either."

He rests his head in the crook of my neck, staying inside me for another moment. When he finally pulls away, one of his brows pops up. "Didn't know you were a squirter."

I push myself up on my elbows, shocked to see the robe is soaked. "I didn't know I was, either. News to me."

"Fuck, CeCe, I'm addicted to you," he admits with hooded eyes, running his fingers through his hair.

"I am addicted to you, too."

"What are we gonna do?" he asks.

"For once, I don't know," I admit, and it's the truest answer I've ever given. Each day we spend together is one day closer to me leaving, not to mention the reason why I'm here.

Rock, meet hard place. I'm officially fucked, and I don't know how I'll survive any of this. But if making my father proud means hurting this incredible man, I'm not sure I can do it anymore.

Maybe my father was right, and I don't have what it takes to be like him.

My body is like gelatin as I lie in Jake's arms on the fuzzy rug. The warmth of the fire feels incredible against my skin.

"I don't want to get up," I tell him, knowing we must.

He hums against my ear. "Let's take a bath."

I smile. "Can you carry me?"

Jake stands, slides his hands under my naked body, and does exactly that. I don't know why I'm shocked that he can lift me with such little effort, but I am.

I giggle, wrapping my arms around his neck as he carries me down the hall. "So you *really* could have thrown me over your shoulder like a caveman and put me in your truck?"

"Did you doubt me?" He lifts a brow, then sets me down in the bathroom.

He turns on the water, adjusts the temperature, then holds his hand out for me. I saunter over, and he helps me slide down into the tub since I'm wobbly on my legs. I watch him as he walks away and then returns with several candles. After they're lit, he flicks off the lights and approaches me.

His shadow dances on the wall as he slides in behind me.

The water is warm and relaxing, and Jake was right—I already feel where he was. I lean my back against his muscular chest as his legs and arms encapsulate me.

We don't speak. I'm not sure what words I would say to him, anyway. Leaning forward ever so slightly, he grabs my loofah and soap, then carefully washes between my legs. I close my eyes, reveling in his gentle touch, not knowing what I did to deserve this experience but grateful for it nonetheless. No man has ever treated me as reverently as he does.

"How does that feel?" He's so kind and attentive I may never leave this tub.

"Incredible. But I can't help thinking I don't deserve this."

He kisses the back of my head. "If not you, then who?"

The question catches me off guard.

"You're worthy of love, CeCe. And the sooner you accept that the quicker you'll stop dating assholes who don't worship the ground you walk on."

I suck in a deep breath. His words slice through me like a knife.

"It's not about me, though. It's about *you* deserving someone who can give you what you need."

He exhales. "That's the thing: you don't understand what you bring to the table. I wish you could see yourself through my eyes. Fuck, I wish you could."

"Jake," I whisper. My emotions are a tangled mess. This wasn't supposed to happen.

He continues. "I've come to terms with my loneliness and accepted that it's a byproduct of living in a small town. It's the relationship card I've been dealt. But that doesn't mean I won't cherish the fuck out of every moment you're here. Time is precious, and right now, there is no other person I'd rather be with than you, Claire. I'll worry about what I'm missing when you're gone."

I sit up, the water sloshing, and meet his gaze.

He tilts his head. "Please don't be upset."

"There's so much I wish I could tell you. But I don't know where to start. I'm scared of falling for you. I'm scared that in January, I'll leave and ruin your life. It's just…" I swallow hard, not wanting to seem weak. "There are things in New York that I can't walk away from."

He nods slightly. "Is there someone else? If there is——"

"No." I shake my head. "No. It's my father."

He tucks hair behind my ear, and I lean into his touch, wishing he knew the internal war I'm fighting. And it's one I'll ultimately lose because I have no other choice. Staying in Merryville isn't an option. We knew that when we started this and created those stupid rules. "We'll figure it out, okay?"

"Okay." I nod, and I want to believe his words.

Jake uses his strong fingers to massage my shoulders. I'm so relaxed that I nearly fall asleep.

When we exit the tub, he grabs a towel, drying every inch of me. "This must be what a queen feels like," I remark.

"Anything for you, milady." He does a bow, then grabs my hand and kisses my knuckles. Afterward, we go to his bed and slide under the blankets. Jake opens his arms, and I crawl into his embrace. I'm so tired that I immediately drift off. The last thing I remember is Tinsel opening the door and climbing onto the bed.

The morning comes early, but I wake up rested. I roll over to find Jake, but the bed is empty. I feel a tinge of disappointment.

Usually, I'm a light sleeper, but I didn't notice he left. I reach over and feel where he had been, and it's cold to the touch.

I put my feet on the floor, somewhat disappointed, because I was hoping for round two. Though, when I stand and feel sore from the inside out, it's probably for the best. I laugh to myself, almost feeling like a virgin again.

After my quick routine, I get dressed and go to the living room.

Jake is nowhere to be found.

I walk into the kitchen, where there's a note next to a coffee mug.

CeCe,
Had to work this morning. I miss you already. I'll be home around five.

JJ

"Aww," I say, looking at the crooked heart he drew, just as Tinsel jumps on the counter and pulls my thoughts away. She hasn't done this once since I've been here, and I feel like she's testing her limits.

"Tinsel! Get down!" I walk over to her and pick her up. She's heavier than I thought, but she immediately starts purring. Her claws dig into my shirt, and I don't know what to do. So I awkwardly hold her until she wiggles out of my arms and jumps onto the floor.

"Meow?" She blinks up at me.

"Did you not get fed?" I ask, wondering if Jake forgot. I narrow my eyes at her. "Or are you a lying liar?"

I move to her bowl, and it's empty. So I pour a can of her food inside her silver dish. She takes a few licks and then snubs it. This reaction doesn't surprise me.

After I make a cup of coffee, I move to the couch and text my sister.

CLAIRE
Are you around?

EMMA
Will be in about five minutes.

CLAIRE
Call me when you can.

She sends me a thumbs-up emoji, and I set my phone beside

me. Since the electricity has returned, it doesn't seem like much has changed other than the lights are on.

While I wait, I pick up the romance book I'd promised Jake I'd read without crying. The further I get into the story, the more of an emotional tug I feel toward the characters. I'm afraid this might break me just as much as leaving Jake. Knowing everything to come in January, I should probably plan to escape somewhere. Maui, maybe. I've never had a bad time when I visited.

As I reach for my phone to contact my travel agent, it rings. But it's not Emma; it's my father.

I suck in a deep breath. "Hi."

"Claire. Progress update, please?"

I try to act dumb, as if I'm not sure what he's referring to, but if Dale has opened his big mouth, lying will only frustrate my father. The mental gymnastics immediately begin.

"Progress?" I act oblivious.

"On your activity in Merryville."

"Father. I'm on vacation. And that's it."

He clicks his tongue. "I've spoken with Dale and the legal counsel. I know you're there to purchase property, and I'd appreciate it if you didn't insult my intelligence."

I feel like a little girl being scolded. I swallow down my insecurities regarding him and find my strength. "I don't care what Dale told you. Plans change. Also, you realize this is his way of retaliating to get what he ultimately wanted: to be in your good graces."

The line is silent, and I watch the seconds on the call timer pass by. We've only been chatting for one minute, and we're already at a stalemate.

"I knew you wouldn't be able to follow through."

Then the line goes dead. I stare at the screen, my thoughts all over the place. The panic swells inside of me, and I realize one of my triggers is my father and his expectations.

I've known it for some time, but right now, as my heart rate increases and I feel the hard pounding in my chest, it's confirmed. As I'm spiraling, Tinsel jumps on the couch. I close my eyes and feel her soft fur and wet, cold nose nudge against me.

"I'm safe," I whisper, wondering if this will be the time that my heart explodes out of my chest. If Jake will be the one who finds me. More adrenaline pumps through my body, and I try to focus on the gentle purrs that Tinsel releases as my hand rests on her back. Then she bites me, and my eyes bolt open.

"Ouch!" I yell, looking down at the indentations of her teeth on my skin as she sits upright, staring at me.

"Meow." She nudges me hard, and I rub her pointy ears between my fingers as she settles down. Lazily, she lifts a claw, places it on my lap, then digs into my leg as her tail flicks. But she doesn't take her focus off me.

"What? You like me now?"

She stretches, lets out a groan, and flips over. I see the little patch of white on her belly and run my fingers through her long hair.

Then I realize I'm on the other side of my episode. And it's because of this ball of fur and her persistent need to give me conflicting signals. Cats are strange creatures, but I appreciate how they decide if you're worthy. Right now, I want to kiss her cute little face, because she saved me from myself.

Ten minutes later, my sister finally calls me. I decide to keep last night between Jake and me, wanting it to be something I keep tucked deep inside for now. It's not a secret, but I don't want to talk about the emotions he's stirred inside me.

Falling so fast and so hard has my head spinning, and I'm not sure what to do.

January is coming, and I have decisions to make that can potentially ruin not just my life but many others. I usually have all the answers, but right now, I have none.

CHAPTER 20

JAKE

After my shift, I stop by my parents' house to discuss what happened yesterday with Lacy. It's essential that they know that it's not acceptable. Claire was right when she mentioned my boundaries being stomped on, and I need to make it clear to everyone so it doesn't happen again. I'm standing up for myself and my personal space and will let my family know that Lacy isn't allowed to be in my life in any capacity. That ship has sunk.

When I walk in, my mama is in the living room, knitting something that looks like a scarf. It's thick, with alternating red-and-white stripes.

"Hey, honey," she says, looking up, seeming almost surprised to see me. I didn't tell her I was coming because I knew she was home since I chatted with her earlier. Right now, my dad is in town taking photos with children and tourists. A few hours ago, I'd heard the line was four blocks long and growing.

"Hey, Mom." I sit on the small couch across from her, interlocking my fingers.

She sets down her needles and grins, but my mood is serious. "What's goin' on?" she asks.

"First of all, I wanted to say thanks for the shepherd's pie yesterday. It was great." I hate having conversations like this, but discomfort makes change possible.

Her brows lift. "Oh, you're welcome. You know I always make extra. Did Claire enjoy it?"

"She did. Told me to send her thanks as well. She'd never had it before, and I told her I'd teach her how to make it."

"Please tell her I said she's welcome, and there's a lot more where that came from. But I have a feeling there's more on your mind."

I nod. Not much gets past my mother. When something bothered me as a kid, I couldn't fool her, and it's not any easier as an adult. She knows my mannerisms and can probably predict what I'll say, but I speak up anyway. "I wanted to discuss Lacy delivering it."

"Sure, dear."

I take a moment to put my thoughts together so I don't misspeak. "I'm not sure how to say this, but I never want her to step on my property again. It was awkward, and I didn't like how it made me feel."

Mama's smile quickly fades. "She brought me pictures of you two and announced you were getting back together, that the past was water under the bridge. Then she mentioned she was headin' over to your house to chat with you. Since you were very clear about you and Claire not being together, I believed her. I realize now that's not the case."

"No, it's not. Mama, she's delusional—and extremely jealous now that she's seen me in public with Claire. She's not used to that. But there isn't a future where she and I are together again. And there won't ever be. I can never give her a chance again after what she did, and I thought I'd made that clear in the past."

"Sweetie, I'm so sorry. She said a lot of things about time passing and missing you, how she saw you in town and stopped by to see how we were doing. I apologize for that and know that must've been hard."

I shake my head. "It's not your fault. I just want it to be known that there isn't anything left between us. I don't have feelings for her, and I won't spend the time to repair what was lost when we broke up. There was a time when I wished to have her back, but I'd rather be alone than with someone like her."

She nods, listening. "I should've known better and understood she was using us to get to you. At the very least, I should've called or texted you and asked."

"It's fine. Claire got rid of her." I smirk, thinking back to what happened yesterday and how she offered her a tip for delivering the food while forcing her out. It was boss moves.

Mom smiles wide. "I like her a lot."

"I do, too," I breathe out.

"Why did you say it that way?"

I move my gaze to the floor, reliving last night and the words we exchanged. "Because she's leaving."

"And?"

I make a face. "It means she won't be in Merryville anymore."

"And?" she repeats.

"Long distance won't work. She travels too much. We won't be able to pursue one another and find out if there is room for a relationship."

Mama immediately shakes her head. "Honey, that's just not how love works. When you fall for someone, no amount of space between you matters. Sure, you both could say you don't want to date because of distance or whatever is the case, but love always finds a way. It will work itself out if you two are meant to be together. Have faith."

"But what——"

"Faith, Jake, means you stop trying to control every aspect and just let what will happen happen."

183

I open my mouth again, and she holds up her finger. "Eh. That's the end of the conversation."

Mama picks up her knitting needles. "Now, if little Miss Lacy comes over here again and lies to my face in my home, I'm gonna chat with her mama after church. I don't appreciate her tryin' to manipulate my or your father's kindness in such a manner. I might talk with her mother anyway, depending on my mood when I see her."

"I wasn't tryin' to start any trouble. I just don't want it to happen again," I explain.

"I understand. And I don't, either. She disrespected me, and you. I don't appreciate that. I can forgive, but I won't forget."

Knowing this conversation is almost over, I stand and stretch.

Mama stands, too. "There is something I wanted to show you that I received today in the mail."

I follow her to the kitchen, where a certified letter is on the table. "Open it," she tells me.

I slide the paper out of the thick envelope and read the first few lines.

NOTICE OF TAX SALE

"Mama," I whisper, quickly reading the rest. "They're auctioning the property?"

She sucks in air. "I felt like this was coming after the last notification I received. I'd hoped a miracle would happen and this season would be financially successful so we could catch up."

"I knew Mawmaw owed a lot, but this is more than I

thought. Where are we going to get that much money?" I look down at the number again. "Even with the agriculture credits, it's still outrageous."

Mom covers her mouth with her hand, and I move to her, wrapping my arms around her neck. "It's going to be fine. I'll see if I can get a loan. Empty my savings. Do whatever I can to stop this from happening. We have until January fifth, right?"

"Yes. I've contacted the family lawyer. He told me that even if it goes to auction, we may still have two years to purchase it back."

I suck in a ragged breath and nod. "We'll figure it out."

After giving her another tight hug, I leave feeling like a black cloud is over me. Needing some time to process, I drive to town and order some food for me and Claire.

On the way home, I get a call from Hank.

"Ew, you don't sound like yourself. Is there already trouble in paradise?"

"Actually, no. Just got some bad news from my mama a little earlier. Everyone is fine, though. It's nothing like that," I explain, not wanting him to worry but also not wanting to discuss it, either.

"Ah, well. I was callin' to invite you out tomorrow night. You can bring Claire, too. There's a band playin' at Moonshiners."

"What time?"

"Seven. The whole gang will be there. Gonna be a helluva time. Might cheer ya up."

"Maybe. Depends on how I feel after work tomorrow. Been busy. That week off did me in," I admit with a smile, not regretting a moment.

"Shit," he whispers. "Gotta go. Hope you show up."

Just as he ends the call, I turn down the gravel road that leads to my cabin. If the property goes to auction and is sold, everyone who lives on the five hundred acres will have to move. My parents. My brothers. My grandmother. And me. Losing the property that's been in my family for several decades can't happen.

I pull up to the house, see the chimney smoking, and smile because that means Claire started the fire alone. It brings me joy to see her take charge of tasks she's never tried before. At least when she returns to New York, she'll have quite a few experiences to cross off her list. Maybe she didn't get to people-watch and eat at the café daily, but hopefully, I've made it worth her while.

When I enter, Tinsel is stretched out on the back of the couch with her leg hanging off. As I walk closer, I notice Claire is asleep on the couch, covered with a blanket, the book she was reading on her chest. I take a moment to admire her features and notice I'm smiling. Looking at her puts me in a different mood, and the overwhelming need to protect her consumes me.

Her eyes flutter open. "Hi."

"Hi."

She sits up, smooths her hair down on her head, and stretches. "I must've dozed off waiting for you. This couch is a bit too comfortable. It sucked me right in."

"It will do that. Catch up on some rest?"

She smiles. "Yeah. It was nice. Dreamed about you."

"Me?" I smirk.

"Yeah." She stands and walks over to me, noticing Glenda's logo on the outside of the paper bag in my hand. "Ooh."

We make our way to the kitchen. "Potpies."

"I don't think I've ever tried one before." She studies it.

"Darlin', I'm startin' to believe you're from another planet."

She snort-laughs. "After being here with you, I think the

same. The South is different from what I'm accustomed. The politeness. The accent. The food. Hugs. I could list an overwhelming amount of culture-shock moments I've already had."

I smile as I grab some utensils for us. Being around her for this short time has changed my demeanor already.

"So, Jake Jolly, inquiring minds want to know: have you always been a nice guy?"

"Of course. I learned a long time ago it's too hard to keep up the bad boy asshole persona. It's easier just to be myself. Then there's no pretending. Just waiting around to find the right person to appreciate me, though. What about you? Always been the serious type?"

She nearly chokes, then scrunches her nose. "Serious?"

"Sailing—check. Golf—check. The overwhelming need to be perfect—check."

"I see what you mean. Yeah, guess I have. But being here is inspiring me to change my ways."

"I hope you do. Oh, tomorrow my friends are getting together at a local bar. Moonshiners. You wanna go?"

"Do *you* want to go?"

"You can't answer my question with a question."

She takes a bite of the flaky crust. "But I did. So?"

"I think it would be fun. I'd love for you to meet my brothers and cousins, too. They'll all be there."

"Then I'd love to. What's the dress code?"

"I'd say casual. A lot of locals go there after work."

"Hmm. I think I've got the perfect outfit." Her eyes flash, and I see something behind them.

"If it's too sexy, we ain't leavin'. I'm gonna keep ya all to myself."

"Speaking of…" She sets her fork down and wipes her mouth.

I give her every ounce of focus I have.

"I'd love a repeat of last night." Fire dances in her eyes as a cute little grin plays on her lips.

"I think I can help make that happen."

When I'm with her, the world around me disappears. She's the escape I need to pull me away, and I'm so damn grateful I was persistent about her getting in my truck.

CHAPTER 21

CLAIRE

W hen I was a teenager, I'd dreamed about being successful.

Finding love was never on my life list. Sure, I wanted someone to share special moments with, but over the years, I've realized my relationships were transactional and without depth.

My father has fucked around with random women since my mother died and hasn't found anyone to fill that void. Money and power aren't enough; he's proof. Sex isn't, either. He's constantly searching for the wrong things in the wrong people, and that's why he'll never be in another healthy marriage.

Some people aren't replaceable. My mother wasn't.

I put on my pearl earrings as Jake slides a belt into his slacks, and I realize he's not, either. This man is one of a kind.

I smile at him, and he smiles back. Happiness spreads over me like a warm blanket.

"Almost ready?" He walks up behind me, wrapping his arms around my waist, and kisses my neck. "You smell so damn good."

I turn and brush my lips across his, humming against his mouth. "You do, too."

He takes a step back, his eyes sliding down to my red lips, my breasts, and back up again. The sweaterdress I'm wearing hugs me like a second skin. "Those boots again."

"I was anticipating you mentioning them."

He pulls me into his embrace. The scruff on his face tickles, and goose bumps trail up and down my body. "You're gonna be the center of attention tonight."

"Everyone will know I'm yours," I confirm as his heated gaze meets mine.

"Then I guess we should give them something to talk about."

I don't know why I grow nervous on the way to Moonshiners, but I do. I've already met Hank, but knowing I'll be introduced to his brothers makes me anxious. What if they hate me? The thought makes me laugh because I can't recall a time when I've ever cared.

"What's funny?" Jake asks as we park behind the bar. The street is packed, and it feels like a miracle we found a close parking spot.

I shake my head. "Just a realization that I want to be liked."

"Doesn't everyone?" He leans over and unbuckles my seat belt, placing a chaste kiss on my lips.

"No. Before visiting Merryville, I didn't care who liked or didn't like me. It's why one of my only friends is my sister."

"I'm not sure I would like the other *you* that you keep telling me about," he says.

"You wouldn't. She's a bitch to everyone."

He chuckles. "Ah yes, I met her on the side of the road, wheeling a suitcase during an ice storm. Ol' Stubborn Susan, I remember her well."

I snicker as we get out of the truck and walk inside. The lights are low, other than the ones above the stage where a band is setting up. Jake places his hand on the small of my back as the heels of my boots click against the wooden floor. A long bar stretches the length of the room, and they're serving drinks of all different colors.

"Moonshine," he whispers. "It will knock you on your ass."

A few heads turn and look at us, and I'm aware of how good we are together. At six foot three with muscles stacked in all the right places, he's the perfect height for me in heels. I feel small as he towers over me, and I like that…*a lot.*

Eventually, we cross the room to a table of guys. All of their eyes widen when they see me, except for Hank. "There's my favorite city slicker," he says, giving me a side hug. "You clean up nicely."

I roll my eyes but can't stop the pleased smile that creeps across my face.

Jake clears his throat. "CeCe…this is my older brother Hudson."

He and Jake have the same features. It's undeniable that they're related.

Hudson stands and grabs my hand, then kisses my knuckles. "Nice to meet you."

I blush and giggle, then Luke introduces himself. They're cut from the same mold and are polite, with Jake's demeanor.

"Ahh, my two cousins, Wendy and Bella." The girls meet up with us and immediately compliment me, but they're sincere. I thank them. Kindness genuinely runs in their family, and it's easy to be comfortable.

"So you're JJ's new girlfriend?" Bella asks. She brushes her black hair over her shoulders, revealing her green eyes.

A wide smile touches my lips as I look up at Jake. He wraps his arm around me and pulls me into him. Immediately, I'm comforted by his warmth and his closeness.

"Y'all don't give her a hard time," he playfully warns everyone but doesn't deny it.

"Yep, she is," Hank says, but I notice how his eyes meet Wendy's. It's obvious he has a thing for her. I'll have to ask Jake about that later.

The band quickly warms up, and when they open their set, the dance floor fills with people. Wendy stands on the other side of me.

"Would you like a drink?" she offers.

"My manners," Jake says with a cluck of his tongue. He leans in and whispers in my ear, "Be right back."

Once I'm alone with his family, I feel the pressure. Luke speaks up. "So I heard you met our parents."

"I did. They're lovely."

He grins. "My ma adores you already."

"She's kind and cooks amazing food. I wish I had her skills."

Moments later, Jake returns with two drinks the color of honey. He hands me one. "Careful with this. Might make ya take off your clothes." He gives Bella the stink-eye. "She nearly got us kicked out last time because of it."

"It was hot as hell in here," she protests. "I was literally sweating. It wasn't the drink." She snickers and then shrugs. "Or maybe it was. I had three of them."

Jake nods. "See? Gotta be careful who you bring out these days."

I take a sip, and it tastes like liquid honey on ice. It's sweet and causes my taste buds to come alive. "It's... delicious."

"And that's why it's dangerous," Wendy warns with a little elbow nudge.

While Jake warned me to take it slow, I finish it within five minutes. My head is slightly swimming, but I like that my nerves are calm. Jake notices that I've finished, and he lifts his brows.

"May I have another, please?" I bat my eyelashes at him, and he slurps up the rest of his.

"Sure," he tells me. When he returns, he's carrying my drink and two glasses of water.

"Always so responsible." I give him a thank-you, but dive into the moonshine first. When the glass is empty, my cheeks are hot, and I smile.

"Want to dance?" Jake asks me when the music slows and the lights in the room lower.

"I suck at it," I admit. "Even after all of the ballroom dancing lessons."

He laughs. "Adding another shitty hobby to that ridiculous list of yours."

Taking my hand, he interlocks his fingers with mine and leads me to the middle of the room. "I'm a very good teacher."

"I'll try." I look up into his sparkling green eyes as he places his hand on my hip, resting his palms slightly above my ass. I'm his, and everyone in this place knows it.

I put my arms around his neck, and we rest our foreheads together. "I don't want this night to end," I admit.

"I'm glad you're havin' a good time."

"Are you?" I ask, hoping this isn't boring.

"The best, but that's always the case when you're around. You're happiness, Claire."

I laugh. "There are many people who'd disagree with you. I think you're sunshine and just bring out the best in me."

"I can live with that."

Right now, I want to feel his lips against mine. It's a want so deep that it nearly overpowers me.

I want him to claim me on this dance floor so no one has any doubt in their mind who I belong to. Public displays of affection aren't something I've ever wanted, but with him, it's different. I'm not embarrassed, and it never feels forced. "Please kiss me," I whisper, swallowing hard, craving his taste so damn bad it nearly hurts.

Jake continues swaying to the music, licks his plump lips,

then crashes them against mine. Our tongues twist and twirl together, and I run my fingers through his hair with a moan. I need this man like I need air. It's almost as if nothing in my life made sense until he entered it, and I want to revel in that.

His firm hand grabs my ass, and he pushes me against him. He's rock fucking hard, and I know he wants me as much as I want him. When we pull apart, we're breathless and stare into each other's eyes.

He leans in and whispers in my ear, "You wanna get out of here?"

"Yes," I say, allowing my desires to overtake me. "Should you tell everyone bye?"

He shakes his head, grabs my hand, and leads me outside.

The chilly night air has me shivering, and Jake takes off his jacket and gives it to me. We pick up the pace to the truck, and once inside, he cranks it and turns the heat on high.

"I can't wait until we're home. I need you. Right now." I scoot to the middle of the seat, and as soon as I'm close enough to him, our lips smash together. He's still hard as I undo his pants, pushing them down.

He growls, giving me permission.

I place my mouth on his cock and go down on him. He grunts, tugging on my hair as his hips buck upward. I'm so wet that I need him inside of me. As if he reads my mind, Jake scoots over, giving me room to straddle him. I hike my sweaterdress up my legs, and he smirks.

"No panties? It's almost as if you planned this."

I carefully straddle him, placing my leg over his waist, the tip of him waiting outside of my wet entrance, then I slowly slide down on him until his thick cock fills me full.

"You're so wet, darlin'."

"Yes," I sigh, not able to find the words. "I've wanted you since we left."

I rock my hips forward. The windows fog as we greedily fuck like tomorrow will never come. My body adjusts to him, and I pick up my pace, grinding hard against him. His groans satisfy me in ways I can't explain.

Jake pulls the front of my dress down, capturing my nipple in his mouth. He adds just enough pressure with his teeth as I bounce up and down on his dick that I feel a world of pleasure course through me.

"Fuck, baby. You feel so good," he groans out. "You're mine, Claire."

"Yes, yes, yes." I slow my pace, placing my forehead against his. "I want to be yours."

I need him, all of him, like I need air in my lungs and blood in my body.

I take him from the tip to the bottom of his shaft, and he bucks his hips upward, giving me more friction. The sounds releasing from my throat aren't like any noises I've ever made. It's unrecognizable, but so is the orgasm that's begging to be released.

"I need more of you," I growl. Not sure how that's possible, considering he's balls deep inside of me, but it's not enough. It's never enough when it comes to him.

He smirks, places his finger in his mouth, then reaches around and slowly slides it into my ass.

"Fuck," I hiss, throwing my head back, loving the pressure it added. It's overwhelming but in a good way. As I bounce up and down on him, I keep up my assault, allowing him to press deep inside of me. Each time he hits my G-spot, my body convulses and my pussy clenches.

"Darlin'," he whispers, and I know he's just as close as I am. But I can't say a single word as the orgasm takes hold, nearly pulling me under and drowning me. My entire body tenses and then releases as he pumps inside of me, his warmth filling me full.

I'm breathless and still so greedy for more. I'm addicted, and Jake is my drug of choice.

He wraps his arms around me, and I rest my head on his

shoulder, trying to come down from the alternate reality we visited. Our hearts thump rapidly, and I think, *This is the way it's supposed to be.* I crave him more than I crave success because I know Jake Jolly leads to ultimate happiness.

"That was incredible," he mutters, still breathless, as I close my eyes.

"I needed you so bad it almost hurt."

"The feeling was mutual," he assures me. "But we gotta get you cleaned up."

I have the overwhelming urge to tell him how I feel, but I hold back my words, not wanting him to think the moonshine is making me emotional. I've already been through that with him once.

It's not the booze… It's him and how he's captured my heart.

I move off from him, and he opens the glove box, where there's a stack of napkins, and we do the best we can with them. Just as I smooth my dress back down my body and Jake puts his penis of mass destruction away, there's a knock on the fogged window.

I make a face, and so does he, but he rolls it down anyway.

"Jake. We need to talk."

And that's when I recognize the high-pitched voice.

CHAPTER 22

JAKE

I glance over at Claire, who is just as confused as me.

"Actually, no. I'm good." I roll up the window, and Lacy knocks again.

Claire's eyes are wide, and she stares at me. "I don't think she's going away," she whispers.

I grasp the bridge of my nose and add pressure. I've only had one drink tonight, and that was hours ago. I'm not intoxicated enough to want to hold a conversation with my ex, but there isn't enough liquor in the world that would make me want that. I know how this conversation will go without even starting it. She'll talk over me, control the narrative, and expect me to agree. I won't allow her antics to ruin my good time.

"No. I don't care. I'm not doin' this." I put the truck in reverse, and Lacy stumbles back as I put the truck in gear and drive away.

I glance at Claire; she's beaming. "I'm so proud of you."

"I'm proud of me, too." I tap my palm against the steering wheel, singing with the Christmas music on the radio as Claire sits beside me with her hand on my thigh. I'm turning over a new leaf and protecting my boundaries, the same ones I'd allowed Lacy to decimate before.

For years, I did whatever I could to make her happy, to make her want me more, to be the perfect man. It wasn't enough because she was never in love with me, just the *idea* of me. It's why our relationship never progressed to the next level and why she refused to commit. I'd have married that woman, but I'm grateful I didn't.

When I turn onto the road that leads to the cabin and we drive under the worn sign for the farm, I make a promise to myself to repaint it.

We park in front of my place, and I open Claire's door. Once we're inside, I turn to her. "You know what you've helped me realize?"

"Hmm?"

"I don't have to give away my joy and be miserable to make someone happy. It's not a barter system or an exchange."

"You're right," she says. "Your boundaries matter. You matter."

I lift her chin with my finger, and her baby blues meet mine. "I have you to thank for that."

"No, JJ. You learned that through heartache. I can't take credit."

I kiss her softly, and we walk inside. I glance over where our gingerbread house is waiting. "Want to finish decorating?"

She returns my smile with one of her own. "I thought you'd never ask. But I want more moonshine."

"Your wish is my command." I pull the bottle from the fridge and remove the top. "Want a glass?"

She shakes her head and drinks it straight. "Mm. So good. Now, let's get to decorating this house."

I wash my hands and make more icing, then hand the bag with the tip to Claire and grab jars of candy from my pantry.

"This icing is a little bit different from the other stuff."

She dips her finger in the bowl, and her eyes widen as she tastes it. "Mm."

I chuckle, kissing her. "Now, what I like to do is outline the doors and windows, then add candy to it. But there are zero rules, so go to town."

She gives me a look.

"It means to do whatever you want," I clarify, chuckling. "Like have fun."

"More slang to add to my Texas lexicon." She winks, then takes a small sip of the booze before doing precisely that. "You owe me gingerbread cookies."

"You're right." I take the extra dough from the fridge and roll it into small balls before smashing them on a cookie sheet. As the oven preheats, I grab the moonshine and take a sip. It burns going down, but I know if I keep drinking, it won't. I place my back against the counter and face Claire as she outlines the roof and side walls with icing. Every few minutes, she dips her finger in the bowl and steals a taste.

"When the cookies are ready, we'll decorate them, too."

"I can't wait," she says.

I love seeing her happy and carefree. The woman standing in front of me isn't the same one who was trekking her ass to Merryville, refusing to get in my truck. This is the version of Claire I adore.

"What?" She grabs a few candies from the jar and presses them against the icing line she made around the door.

I shake my head. "Nothin'. Just admiring you."

"Keep it up, and I might get used to it," she warns.

A side smile meets my lips. "I hope you do."

As she continues decorating, the oven sounds off. The house smells delicious, like cinnamon and ginger and sugar. I put the tray on the stovetop, allowing the cookies to sit for a minute before sliding them onto a mat on the counter.

"They're still very hot," I tell Claire as she reaches for one. Not caring, she picks it up, tossing it between her hands. "Stubborn Susan came out to play tonight, didn't she?"

She sets the hot cookie down, waving her hands for a few seconds to cool them. It won't do much good, considering they were baking at three hundred and fifty degrees. "Should've listened."

"Give them ten minutes and they should be okay to eat. Let me show you how to do the roof."

Claire hands me the icing bag, and I draw wide *U*'s across the top in a row, just like my mama taught me all those years ago. "Then you just keep going."

I give it back to her, and she continues it down and on the other side. Then she fills in every space with icing, adding green and red candy all around. "Oh, do you have a peppermint?"

"Actually, I do." I grab the bag of them out of the pantry. She untwists one and places it right above the door, then steps back and admires her masterpiece.

"This is the best little gingerbread house I've seen in a long time." I grin, loving how she's strategically placed everything, and then I see CC and JJ written on the front. "Nice touch."

She wraps her arms around me and looks up into my eyes. "Now, can we eat those cookies?"

"Ever had a gingerbread sandwich?" I ask. "Don't make that face. You're gonna like it."

I squirt a bunch of icing on one cookie, then stack another on top, squishing it down. I pick it up and hand it to her. "Bet you can't just have one."

Claire grabs it and takes a small bite. Her eyes go wide, and she covers her mouth as she talks. "This is...*incredible*."

"And that's why it's a secret recipe."

We eat cookies and drink moonshine. It's not the best combination, but I don't care. We've got crumbs on our clothes and sticky fingers, and we're happy. Genuinely happy. Not that bullshit, pretend, trying to impress someone after a night at the bar happy. I'm comfortable with her in ways that are hard to comprehend. I don't know much about her past or her life in New York, but as we stand in my kitchen enjoying each other's company, I don't give a fuck.

After we eat almost all of the dozen cookies I baked, Claire moves to stand before me, parting my legs as she wraps her arms around my waist. I kiss her, tasting the sweetness of the alcohol and cookies combined. She moans against me, fisting my shirt with so much need and desire that I don't know if I'll ever be able to get enough of this woman. At this rate, I won't.

Her gaze heated, Claire takes my hand and leads me to the bedroom. I start the fire as she undresses. When I turn around, she's naked, and in her hand is a bright-pink vibrator. "I promised to show you."

She places it in her mouth until it's wet, and my cock nearly bursts from my pants at the sight of her.

"Shit," I hiss.

"I have rules, though. No touching me. Having your eyes on me is enough. And you promised to show me, too." She glances down at the tent between my legs.

"I have a request: no toys. I want to see you come without that."

"Okay," she whispers as she props a few pillows up, then climbs onto the bed. "I have another to add to our list. You can't come until I do."

I smirk. "Deal. I love a challenge."

I remove my collared shirt and pants until I'm naked and stand at the end of the bed, loving that she's on full display. It's a show I'm eager to watch.

"You're so fucking gorgeous, Claire." I grab my cock; it's thick and hard and begs to be inside her perfect pussy, but I'll play this game.

Her eyes pierce through me as she widens her legs and slides her hand down to her clit. Slowly, she rubs circles, and a huff of breath escapes her while her pink nipples harden to rocks. Her breasts rise and fall as she teases herself.

I stroke myself, matching her pace. She sucks her bottom lip into her mouth, then slides her two tiny fingers inside her slick cunt. She's gentle, moving in and out as she gasps. My focus is on her as she rubs sticky cum between her fingers before placing them between her lips.

"I have a confession," she says, moving her opposite hand back to her clit as she enjoys the flavor. "I've never tasted myself before you."

I grunt, loving these confessions she's giving me. "You like it, don't you?"

"Yes." Her breaths grow desperate, and when I think she might explode, she pulls her hand away. I lift a brow, watching her be the prettiest damn cocktease I've ever had the pleasure to see.

"God." She smacks her pussy, and I watch her tight hole clench. "I want to come so bad right now," she pants.

It takes every bit of willpower I have not to keep stroking myself. As she watches me, I guide my finger over the tip, and the precum glistens.

She rubs her fingers from her clit down into her pussy and back up again, allowing her hips to guide her. The moans that escape her nearly make me fucking crumble.

"Jake, fuck," she growls, closing her eyes tight. "It feels good. And I'm so wet because I'm imagining it's you." Her red lips fall open as her fingers go deep inside, all the way to the knuckle. I love watching her work her pussy. I love seeing what she's done to get herself off all of these years since no man has ever been able to do it for her—until she met me.

She keeps up her slow assault until she's close again and stops. Her cunt clenches, her precum wet and glistening, as she grabs both nipples and tugs them hard. She growls, frustrated with herself, and I know she wants a release. The wet spot on my sheets, paired with her desperate pants, tells me as much. But I'm right there with her, teetering on the edge. It's almost too much to watch, and I don't know how much longer I'll be able to hold back.

"Okay," she sighs, as if she's finally giving herself permission. And then, like someone opens the floodgates, she comes. I can't stand there and watch and not touch her.

"Fuck the rules." I climb on the bed, and she nods, giving me all the permission to give her what she wants. I place her legs on my shoulders, opening her wide, then fuck her perfect little pussy until she comes again.

We get lost in one another, and I look into her eyes, hearing her soft pants as we come down from our highs. She kisses me, and I can't help but feel like this is a goodbye. Time is running out. But as I stare into her ocean-blue eyes, I push the thought away. I'm falling in love with her, and there's nothing I can do to stop this.

An avalanche of emotions crashes down on me, and I try to push it away.

"Thank you," she whispers.

"For what?" I ask, kissing the softness of her neck.

"For showing me what it could be like."

"What it *should* be like," I correct. "If you were mine…"

She places her finger over my lips. "I wish it was possible."

Neither of us wants this to end.

CHAPTER 23

CLAIRE

"Almost ready?" Jake asks from the bathroom doorway as I finish blow-drying my hair, and I nod. It's gotten to the point where I can't look at him without feeling that electrical jolt throughout my body. Just a simple smirk has my heart fluttering.

I'm fucked, but I'm trying to make the best of it.

After I've put on some lip gloss and mascara, I meet him in the living room, where he's holding Tinsel. He's smiling, kissing her on the top of her head as she kneads in the air. It's the cutest sight.

"Sorry, baby girl. I gotta go see Mawmaw," he tells her. She groans and gives me a growl of a meow as she runs away. "Cranky ass."

I chuckle, showing Jake my outfit. "How's this?"

"Gorgeous, as usual."

My cheeks heat. I don't think I'll ever get tired of his compliments because they come from a place of sincerity.

"What if she doesn't like me?" I ask.

"There isn't one person in this town who doesn't like you," he reassures me as he puts on his boots.

"Uh, that's not entirely true," I tell him. "I'm certain I'm at the top of your ex's shit list."

"Who cares? I'm right there next to you." He shrugs.

"About last night. Do you think…she watched us?"

He searches my face. Since I woke up, I've replayed the whole scene—me riding him, my nipples in his mouth, and coming several times.

"I don't know," he admits, running his fingers through his messy hair before putting a beanie on. "I didn't think about that."

"She conveniently showed up right afterward."

He nods, swallowing hard. "I wouldn't worry about it. Not like she saw anything anyway with how fogged the windows were." He shoots me a wink. "And if she did, oh well. But we better not leave Mawmaw waitin'. She tends to get impatient when visitors are supposed to come over."

"Right, let's go," I say, leading him outside. Jake locks the door and double-checks it. Since Lacy showed up unannounced, he's been diligent, which I appreciate.

I'm not sure what that woman is capable of, but something is wrong with her. When I looked into her eyes, they seemed hollow, like she didn't have a soul. Then again, I'm sure people have said the same about me, too.

Jake's grandma lives on the opposite side of the property, farther than his parents do. I love seeing how large the farm is, how many structures there are, and what the landscape is like. Each section is a private oasis, and each family member lives in a different area.

When we pull up to the two-story home, I'm in awe of the large porch. Behind her house, there's a pond. When we exit the truck, I see several geese and ducks waddling around.

"We can check it out afterward," he says as if he can read my mind.

It makes me smile as he leads me up the steps. Jake doesn't

knock but walks right in and starts yelling. "Mawmaw! Mawmaw! Where ya at?"

He grabs my hand, leading me through the house, which smells like vanilla. The walls are lined with different-sized frames containing photos of her kids and grandkids.

"In here!" she says.

He glances over his shoulder at me and winks. When we enter the large living room, we find his grandmother sitting on the couch with a quilt on her lap, talking on the phone.

"Oh, Bethany. I gotta let you go," she says into the phone. "Jake just walked in with his new girlfriend. Yeah, she's pretty. I'll call you when they leave. Yes, I will. Make sure your hearin' aid is turned up so you can hear the phone ring. I said, make sure your hearin' aid is turned up! Okay. Bye now."

As she hangs up, I tuck my lips in my mouth, not wanting to laugh but finding her cute.

"Mawmaw, this ain't my girlfriend," he says.

She waves him off. "Come here, sweetie. Let me get a good look at ya."

I'm more nervous now than I was when I met his parents. She's a cute older woman with curly gray hair that's cut short. Her glasses are on the edge of her button nose, and I see the resemblance between her and Jake's dad. Her green eyes shine.

I take a step forward, smiling, almost as if I should bow to this queen. She holds out her hand, and I take it.

"So nice to meet you, dear. I'm Mawmaw. That's what everyone calls me."

"I'm Claire. It's lovely meeting you. Jake has told me so much about you."

She looks at him. "He better have said I'm his favorite grandma."

"Oh, he did." I shoot her a wink.

"Have a seat. You want some sweet tea?" She tries to stand, and Jake gently touches her shoulder.

"I've got it. Claire, would you like some tea? Mawmaw?"

"Sure," I say.

"Yes, dear."

He quickly disappears into the kitchen.

"So, baby, tell me about yourself. I heard you were from outta town." Her Southern accent is thick.

"Yes, ma'am," I say, wanting her to know that I indeed have manners, even if I'm an outsider. "I grew up in California but moved to New York after my mother passed away."

"I'm sorry to hear that."

I don't know why I feel my emotions bubble, but they do. I push them away and continue compartmentalizing it, something I'm well practiced at. "I went to boarding school in Paris."

"Boarding school?" she questions but looks impressed. "That's fancy, sweetie. Never knew a person who went to boarding school. What was that like?"

"Strict," I admit.

"Just means you can follow the rules." She gives me a grin and a wink.

I chuckle. "Yes, it does."

"So where do you live now?"

I don't know what it is about this sweet older woman, but I want to tell her my life story and have her swaddle me in a warm blanket. There's an air of kindness that surrounds her, something I can't quite put my finger on. It doesn't feel like she's trying to gain information to use it against me like some people do.

"New York," I say.

She shakes her head. "You couldn't catch me in that big city. Too dangerous for a little old woman like me. And for you, too."

"I don't get out much," I explain. "I work and travel a lot. I'm hardly ever home or in the city."

Before she asks anything else, Jake enters with a tray carrying three glasses of sweetened tea. He passes them out and sits beside me on the couch opposite her.

"What were you two goin' on about?" He takes a gulp.

"Just askin' your girlfriend 'bout her life. California, New York, Paris, boarding school, all those things."

But the thing is, Jake doesn't know. I've not shared that much with him about my past. It's not something that's ever come up.

He raises his brows and nods. "Riveting."

"Hush up. Now, tell me how you two got together." She points between us.

"Mawmaw, for the last time, Claire is just my friend."

She glances down at our knees, which are touching, and how close we're sitting to one another. "You know, titles don't mean anything to an older lady like me. I can see something is brewin' between you. Have ya been kissin'?"

He looks at me. "Don't answer that." Then he turns to her. "You said you'd be on your best behavior."

She gives him a sly grin. "I know y'all have. You look good together. What's the big deal about callin' it what it is?"

"For one, titles complicate things."

She waves him off. "Hogwash."

"It's because I'm leaving in January," I admit.

"See, now that's a better reason. But why can't long distance work?"

Now I feel like I'm in the hot seat. Jake looks at me like he's waiting to hear the answer, too. I open my mouth and then close it. "I don't do long-distance relationships. I tried it once in my twenties and was hurt by someone I thought I loved. So now I avoid that. The heartache isn't worth it."

"I understand," she says.

When she opens her mouth to ask another question, Jake stops her. "Enough drilling her. Got a hundred bucks I can borrow?"

She gasps. "You didn't come over here to borrow money, did you?"

He snorts. "Nah, I heard you won at bingo the other night, though. Holdin' out on me?"

"Who told you that?" she questions.

Jake shrugs, pretends to padlock his lips, and tosses the imaginary key over his shoulder.

"You booger. It was a nice surprise, though. Betsy Jo is always winnin', and for once, I did. I screamed so loud, and everyone 'round me just groaned. Savin' it for a rainy day."

Hearing her speak makes me happy.

"You two really do look good together, ya know that?" she adds.

A blush hits my cheeks as I sneak a peek at Jake. We meet each other's eyes and then turn back to her.

"Anyway," Jake says, changing the subject. "Claire loves snow globes, and I was tellin' her about your collection. Mind if I show her?"

"Go ahead, they're in the guest room. Don't mind all that junk on the bed in there. I was cleanin' out my closet last week."

Jake stands and holds out his hand, and I take it. His grandma watches as we leave the living room and walk down the hallway. As soon as we're out of sight, he presses my back up against the wall and kisses me. I feel like I'm drowning in his touch, his mouth, his tongue, him entirely, and I want him to pull me under and take me away. His teeth graze against my cheek until he's whispering in my ear. "I can never get enough of you."

"Same," I hiss, knowing we better stop before we get caught. Jake creates space between us and adjusts himself. I glance down, seeing how hard I've made him.

I'm not sure I'll ever be able to get enough of him. I'm not sure I want to.

When we walk into the spare bedroom, I'm stunned

speechless by all the snow globes in the room. Shelves line the upper perimeter of the walls, and each globe is on display. There are small and large ones in various shapes, and they're easy to admire from where I stand.

"My grandpa built these shelves so the grandkids couldn't play with them," Jake explains. "He'd always say, 'You look with your eyes, not your hands.'"

I laugh. "He was right, though. Did one get broken?"

He nods. "Only took once. It wasn't me, though. It was Wendy. When she was younger, she was clumsy. She was skipping with it in her hand to tell Mawmaw something, tripped, and it fell on the ground and shattered. The glass was thin. Water and fake snow were all over the floor—Mawmaw about shit a brick. I'll never forget it. We all thought Wendy was gonna get a whoopin'.."

"What happened?"

"Grandma told her to stop cryin' about it and warned us kids if we ever touched her snow globes again, she'd Hansel and Gretel us."

My mouth falls open.

"I'm just kidding about that last part. You're gullible, though." He grabs my hand, pulling me toward him. "My mawmaw was right; we look good together."

I blink up at him, tugging his bottom lip into my mouth and sucking it. "We do. I've never been with a man who still has inches on me when I wear high heels. Or who can carry me to bed."

He leans in and whispers, "Or who enjoys your cute clit as much as I do."

His hot breath on my neck and ears has my eyes fluttering closed. My breasts rise and fall, and I don't know if it's me or if it's hot in the house. Every inch of me feels like it's on fire, and if I'm not careful, he'll turn me to ash.

"What are you doing to me?" I ask, hypnotized by his touch and words.

"Just returning the favor." He hums and runs his fingers through my hair. "You drive me crazy, CeCe. Even when I'm with you, I need more."

"I know," I whisper. "What will we do?"

"I wish I had the right answer." He presses his lips against mine, and the only thing that pulls us apart is the clearing of a throat.

We turn our heads to see his grandmother standing in the doorway. Thankfully, she doesn't say a word, but she doesn't have to. Busted.

"Did Jake tell you they're displayed in order of age?" She enters the room, moving past us and pointing at one corner. "Startin' there are the oldest ones. My ma collected that one when she was a young woman. 1916, I believe."

My eyebrows shoot upward. "Wow. That's early."

"You know they weren't invented until the late 1800s. Paris Exposition, I believe, if I recall the story correctly," she offers.

Goose bumps trail up and down my body. "Most people don't know that," I explain.

"Oh, honey, most people don't know their ass from their elbow."

Jake's eyes widen, and I burst out laughing.

"Pardon my language, but the truth is the truth. Anyway, I was just checkin' on you two. I learned a long time ago that when the kids are quiet, they're gettin' into trouble. But I'll let y'all get back to it." A wide smile fills her face. Then she makes her way down the hallway.

When she's out of sight, Jake chuckles. "Glad I didn't do what I wanted to do to you. Grandma might've had a heart attack if she'd walked in on that."

I step forward, grabbing his shirt and pulling him against me. "And what would that be?"

"Just let your imagination wander." His hand trails down my body and presses between my legs. I buck my hips forward, loving his touch.

"My imagination is a dangerous place," I warn, and he chuckles.

"By the way, I think you might've already won my mawmaw over. That doesn't happen often. She's usually real hard on anyone I've ever brought to meet her."

"Really?" He takes my hand and leads me into the living room.

"Yeah, she hated Lacy with a passion. And Lacy knew it, too. One time, I left them alone together, and when we left, Lacy said she'd never come over again, and she stayed true to that. Was very awkward at family get-togethers."

I tilt my head at him. "That's ridiculous."

His grandma returns carrying an orange soda. "What're your plans for the rest of the day?"

Jake shrugs. "Not sure. Claire wanted to see the ducks and geese, so we might go skip some rocks in the back."

"You should. Be careful, though." She raises a brow. "Goober is a jerk."

"Who's Goober?" I ask, looking between them.

"Just a silly goose," Jake says. "But he has been known to chase people around. I'll keep you protected, though."

"Jakey, you better not let him get her, or you'll be dealin' with me."

He gets up and gives her a kiss on the cheek. "Yes, Mawmaw. I won't let anything happen to Claire."

I lean over and hug her.

"Don't be a stranger," she tells me.

"I won't."

Jake gives her a wave and leads me into the backyard. While it's chilly outside, it's calm. I follow him to the small dock. He holds his hand out for me, and I take it. We walk with our fingers interlocked to the edge of the shore. There's an upside-down canoe a few feet away, and I wonder what summers are like here when the grass is green and the trees are full of leaves. I can almost imagine children playing and splashing with evening bonfires in the firepit that's a few feet away.

I wish I knew. Am I making the right decision?

I just need a sign. Do I choose my career or Jake? If I don't finalize what needs to be done in Merryville, I'll lose my father's respect, but I'll gain Jake's. If I could look up spoilers on my life, I would do it in a heartbeat.

It's one of the most complex decisions I've ever made. Is the risk of potentially being loved and loving in return worth losing it all? Some people search their entire lives for this and never find it. They don't know what it's like to kiss someone and feel butterflies or have sex that feels good. Or have cookie crumbs all over their shirt while they eat and laugh because they're that comfortable together. These are all things money can't buy. It's what my father has been searching for since my mom passed away.

The wind gently blows, and I close my eyes as the coolness brushes against my cheeks. I swallow hard, wanting to stay strong.

"You good?" Jake asks, noticing my reaction. Something as simple as him seeing me in that moment makes my heart pound.

"Yeah. I'm okay. It's just…" I try not to choke on the lump that forms in my throat. "My mother used to tell me that when she was gone, I'd know she was close because I'd feel her in the wind."

I've never shared that with a single soul, and my tears threaten to spill over. My entire body tenses, and I try to hold it back.

"Hey." He pulls me to his chest. My tears slowly fall as he holds me against him. I can't remember the last time I felt emotions so strongly, but here I am. Jake pets my hair, resting his chin on top of my head. "You're okay. You're safe." He kisses my hair and squeezes me tight. "It's gonna be okay."

All of this is too much, and I feel like I'm losing my grasp on the character I've tried to play to make everyone in my life happy. Jake sees the real me, and that means more than words can describe. I've quickly grown attached to him, his family, and even his cranky cat.

None of this was supposed to happen.

I planned to visit Merryville, take what I wanted, and destroy lives without a second thought. But I can't do that now. Not anymore. Because I stupidly, but without apology, fell hard and fast for Jake Jolly.

CHAPTER 24

JAKE

I adore Claire—her voice, her laugh, the cute way she scrunches her nose when she hears something she doesn't like. Not to mention her moans or how she begs me to give it to her harder when she's close and the way she screams my name as she comes. There's a lot about Claire that I'll miss when she leaves, but I'm hoping a solution will reveal itself. Like my ma told me, I need to have faith.

If we lose the farm, I'm not sure what I'll do anyway. I push those thoughts away because they're too intrusive and only cause me to worry, which isn't helpful.

If only things were different.

I think about Claire and her career and how I'll never make her choose me over her dreams. With everything she's shared, she's dedicated. Sailing, golf, ballroom dancing? All sports you couldn't pay me to do, even with desperately needing money fast.

When we arrive at my house, there's a silver Jaguar parked outside. It's slick, with smooth curves, and I don't see a speck of dirt on it, which is completely unnatural.

I look at Claire and notice there's alarm written on her face, but then her brow furrows and I'm met with anger. She's livid. Before I can ask any questions, she exits the truck and marches across the driveway. Gravel crunches under her shoes, and her hands are balled into tight fists.

A man who is sitting on one of the rocking chairs on my porch stands. I didn't even notice him there. He's on the shorter side, and he almost meets her eye to eye. Based on her hands and how her feet are spaced shoulder-width apart, I think she might deck him.

"What are you doin' here?" she screams, and I get out of the truck and follow her.

"Claire," I say, not wanting to have to beat this guy's ass for trespassing.

"Oh, is this your new boy toy?" he asks. He's older, if I have to guess, in his late forties. Too young to be her father.

"Dale, fuck off. I've told you to leave me alone."

A sneer spreads across his face. "See, that's where you've got it wrong, princess. Let's go. We have some things to discuss."

He grabs her arm, and I step up. "Sir, you're gonna take your hands off her right now."

"Or what?" He looks me up and down, tightening his grip. I don't respond with words.

I lift my fist and punch him right in the face. He falls back, crashes into the rocking chair, and groans. "You hit me!" he exclaims, clutching at his face.

"Yes, sir, I did. Now, you're gonna get your goddamn ass off my property. And be sure when you go to the sheriff you tell him you were trespassin', 'cause he ain't gonna take kindly to that. Might wonder why I didn't shoot you between the eyes. You come back, and I will."

"Are you threatening me?" He's still holding his face, rolling on the ground, dirtying a formerly pristine suit.

"It's not a threat but a promise. Now I'm gonna give you ten minutes to get the hell outta here."

I hold my hand out for Claire and unlock the door,

allowing her inside. I don't follow, though. Instead, I turn around to finish the conversation he started.

He's still sitting on the ground, trying to get up. I place my firm hand on his shoulder and squeeze. "And if you ever touch her or lay another fucking hand on her again, I will find you." I pat his back. "Now, try to have a nice day. Oh, and if no one has told ya yet, Merry Christmas. The timer starts now."

I walk inside and slam the door, then crack my knuckles before setting an alarm on my phone for ten minutes.

Claire stares at me, and I can't quite place her expression. "I can't believe you did that."

"I'm sor—"

She shakes her head, rubbing her arm where he grabbed her. "No, don't apologize. No one has ever stood up to him for me."

I hold her against me. "Has he always grabbed you that way?"

Claire doesn't meet my eyes when she nods.

I pull away, go to my bedroom, and unlock my gun safe. I remove my shotgun from inside and stalk down the hallway, anger coursing through me.

"Jake," Claire whispers as I swing open the front door. I take a few steps toward Dale and rack the shotgun. The sound echoes on my porch; it's enough to make anyone's hair stand on end.

"I've changed my mind. You're gonna get the fuck off my property right now," I growl, lowering the shotgun to point the barrel directly at him.

Claire stands in the doorway, watching the debacle, and I hear her shoo Tinsel away.

Dale gets up and stumbles off the porch, muttering something under his breath.

I let out a warning shot, and Claire gasps behind me. The loud crack echoes through the woods. "Remember what I said!" I yell.

Dale rushes to his car, and that's when I notice he's pissed himself. When he backs out of the driveway, he kicks up gravel.

I turn around. "He won't be back, and he won't be messin' with you again."

"Jake, you cannot point loaded weapons at people on my behalf," she protests.

I wrap my free arm around her waist and slide my lips across hers. "I wouldn't have hurt him."

She snorts. "No? Just blacked his eye?"

"Him roughhousin' you just ain't okay."

She looks perplexed.

"It means bein' violent. I won't allow him or anyone to touch you like that. Had to scare him a little so he understood I'm not playin'."

"Added that one to my lexicon. Thank you. I think it worked. But—" Her phone rings, and she pulls it from her pocket. She sighs. "I've got to take this."

"Sure thing."

As Claire steps outside and answers her phone, she starts to pace. Her arm moves up and down as she gesticulates angrily, and I can tell she's frustrated by how tight her lips are.

I put the shotgun away, then wash my hands. I don't have regrets about doing what I did, and he won't be back, not after pissing himself from being so scared. Men should never treat women that way, but then again, he's not a man.

When I move to the living room, Tinsel runs toward me, and I pick her up. She nuzzles against my chin and purrs. Then she yawns.

"Stop that. Those are contagious." I hold her until she's fidgety, then I set her on my lap, and surprisingly, she stays. Not long after, Claire returns, sliding the patio door closed. She sits next to me with a deep sigh.

"My father is pissed. Not at me, for once," she adds. "At Dale for coming here."

218

"Didn't work out for him."

"No." She lets out a breath. "It didn't."

"The choices we make have consequences," I tell her. "He found his."

"He did. But thank you. I don't know what I would have done had he found me on the street. Gone with him?" She looks visibly shaken up. "Hopefully, he's not staying in Merryville."

"He has nowhere to go unless he's sleepin' in a vehicle, and the town has a 'no overnighters' ordinance, so if he even tries it, they'll run him off. We know the inn is booked until next year. No one will welcome him in with that attitude, regardless of the season or temperatures. You get what you give around here. Don't think kindness is in his repertoire."

"It's not."

I think I hear her stomach growl. "How 'bout I run to town real quick and get something to cook? I'd love a nice steak with brussels sprouts and a potato."

"That sounds great."

"Wanna come with me?" I ask, knowing a lot went down. "I understand if you don't."

"If I can stay here, I'd prefer it. I need to decompress and call my sister to let her know what happened."

"Okay, just lock the doors when I leave, and if you see anything suspicious, call the sheriff. I don't think he'll be back, though. Not after that."

"You're right. He's got a huge ego, but he's a coward. What I ever saw in that man is beyond me. I was sad for myself when he broke it off. Now I'm just sad for him."

"That's progress, darlin'," I say, standing and smacking a quick kiss on her lips before I leave. I turn back to glance at her. "Maybe I'll pick up a bottle of wine, too?"

"That'd be nice. Can't wait. Miss you already," she says, grabbing her book from the coffee table and getting comfortable. She's almost to the twist, and I can't wait to see how she reacts.

On the way to the grocery store, I stop by the local florist and grab a dozen roses. Trish, one of the florists, lifts a brow. "For your new girlfriend?"

I don't deny it at this point. "Yes, ma'am."

"She's a lucky lady." She gives me the total.

"The only problem is she doesn't know that yet," I say, tapping my card against the machine to pay.

"Sure she does. Sometimes, it just takes someone a little bit longer to realize it," she says. "Need anything else?"

I shake my head, grab the flowers, and walk to my truck. Just as I reach for my door, Lacy rushes out of the coffee shop.

"Jake!"

I roll my eyes. "Today just keeps gettin' better," I mutter.

"Listen, I need to talk to you," she says, looking around. "In private."

"Absolutely not."

"I don't want to do this out here where everyone can see," she whispers, but I hear the snippiness in her tone.

"You had zero problems doing it in front of everyone when I proposed," I remind her.

"Fine." Her mouth straightens into a firm line as she steadily types away on her phone. A few seconds later, she twists it around, and I see a picture of Claire in New York, wearing a white blouse and a black skirt. She looks gorgeous. She looks important.

"I figured out who your girlfriend is and where I recognized her from," she says, her chest puffed out like she wants a pat on the fucking back. "I'm honestly disappointed in you, Jake. Claire Manchester? The heiress of Manchester Hotels? Have you not read the rumors that have been posted online?"

My mind is moving at a million miles per hour. "Excuse me?"

"The rumor about her coming here to buy your family's property at auction? I knew things were bad, but…" She shakes her head. "Get a hold of yourself. This is low, even for you."

The flowers I'm holding fall to the ground with a bounce, pink petals breaking loose from a few. Everything around me moves in slow motion. I can hear my heart throbbing in my chest, and Lacy's voice sounds like it's coming from a different dimension.

"I've gotta go," I say, not able to control my shaking hand.

"Disappointing that you'd choose her over your family. I thought you were better than that." Lacy glares at me, throws her hands up, and then walks back to the coffee shop. I get in the truck, leave the flowers on the sidewalk, and stare at the gray sky. Leaning forward to rest my head against the steering wheel, I replay everything Claire ever said about her father, being in real estate, and her overwhelming need to do everything perfectly. The sailing, golf, and ballroom dancing make sense. So does boarding school and Paris and her dickhead ex with his designer suit.

I hold my chest, feeling like my heart might explode as the betrayal takes over.

"Claire *Manchester*," I whisper, shaking my head and burying my face in my hands.

She took advantage of me. Of my kindness. Of my family. Allowed me to take her around to meet everyone so she could look them all in the eye, knowing she would single-handedly ruin our lives.

This can't be happening.

This is a nightmare. I want to wake up.

Let me wake up. *Please.*

CHAPTER 25

CLAIRE

After Jake leaves, I make sure all the house's exterior doors are locked. Then I sit on the couch and glance at the book that might break me. A few times, my nose has burned and my eyes have watered, but I haven't cried.

It's a story about two people who are meant to be together, but too many outside forces pull them apart. The hero and heroine have been through hell and back, and it's not over yet. Right now, I'm still in it to win it and haven't squirted a single tear.

As I lie back and begin reading, Tinsel jumps on my stomach and makes herself comfortable.

"You're a chunky monkey," I say, laughing, causing her head to bob. It only makes me laugh harder until my entire body and hers are shaking. Though a cat's expression doesn't change, I swear she's scowling. I pet the softness of her head and scratch under her chin until she purrs. "I'm starting to like you."

She claws through my clothes.

"Ouch. Put those murder paws away."

She stretches and nearly knocks the book out of my hand. Finishing this chapter with a cat parked on me is an unattainable goal, so I close it. I reach out as far as my arms will go and set it on the edge of the coffee table. Then I give her the attention she's begging for and run my fingers through her coat. She lays her head down, content with me being her bed.

A few moments later, my phone rings, and I have to lift my hips without disturbing the princess to pull it out of my pocket. She's immediately annoyed and jumps off me, the moment ruined. I answer the phone.

"Just my daily check-in," my sister says.

I explain what happened with Dale and how Jake reacted.

"It was dreamy. It was hot to see a man be all, like, 'you touch her and die' over me."

"Jake sounds like he fell right out of a Southern drama. Ever watched *Yellowstone*?" Emma sneezes.

"Bless you. No, I haven't, but I might start. Also, Dale was so scared that he pissed himself. It was hilarious. I've never seen him so frightened in my life."

"Have a big man pull a shotgun on you and see how unfazed you are by the ordeal."

"True." I hear the engine of his truck outside. "Jake's back. I gotta go. Talk soon, okay?"

"Please keep me updated."

"I will," I tell her, ending the call. He wasn't gone very long, maybe twenty minutes? That's a record.

When Jake walks in, I pop up from the couch and shoot him a smile, but his hard expression doesn't change.

"You good?" I ask, repeating the exact words he's said to me several times since I arrived. I notice he has no grocery bags, nothing. "Jake?"

He crosses his arms over his chest, his face hard as stone. "Claire Manchester? That's your real name, right?"

Adrenaline courses through me, followed by a bone-deep chill. "I can explain."

"You looked me in my eyes and fed me some bullshit lie

about who you were and why you knew so much about the town. Why are you here, Claire?"

This is a question I was hoping I would never have to answer, one that's haunted me since I slid my mouth against his perfect lips.

He's hurt, that much is clear, and it's because of me. I'm responsible for this.

"So it's true? You came here to buy the farm out from under my family?" He laughs sarcastically. "Now, the dates you were staying make perfect sense. You knew the farm would be auctioned off at the beginning of the year. You knew who I was the moment I told you my name."

"Jake, please."

"Did you come to Merryville to scout this property so your father could bulldoze everything and build a resort? Don't lie, Claire. You're bad at it, anyway."

"Yes," I whisper, slamming my eyes closed. "That was the reason. But things have changed."

He shakes his head. "They haven't. Your father has already started his marketing campaign, Claire. Get on your fancy device and look. It's everywhere. There are even construction plans posted." His nostrils flare, and I can see how ragged his breathing is. "I think you should go."

I open my mouth to say something, but nothing comes out. I didn't know my father had announced it to the world. I'd hoped that he would've waited to see where things stood.

The rug was ripped from under Jake, but I was standing beside him when it happened. I didn't know. I want to scream out and tell him. But the truth is I should have.

"Leave!" Jake barks. "If you can look me in the face, kiss me, make love to me, knowing that you would single-handedly destroy my family's lives..." I see the hurt on his face. "You're not welcome here. I don't want to see you ever again."

"Jake," I whisper.

He turns and walks outside, slamming the door behind him. Tinsel takes off running, and I stand there in shock.

My entire body shakes as my emotions overtake me. This is my fault—all of it. I should've told him the truth weeks ago. I should've been honest with why I'm here. I was hoping I'd never have to explain the truth once this was over, once I decided I wouldn't purchase the farm.

I immediately text my sister, and she calls me. My hand is shaking as I answer, and I can barely speak. I feel like I'm crumbling to ash, and Jake is slipping between my fingers like dust.

"Oh my God, are you okay?"

"No," I say, frantically shoving my clothes into my suitcase, trying not to cry. My dreamworld crashes around me, and I can't say I expected this today. Not after the time we've had. "I was at the highest of highs twenty minutes ago, and now I'm at the lowest low."

The panic creeps up, and I stand, lifting my hands above my head, trying to recite any facts that come to mind as my sister talks to me on speakerphone.

"Sis?"

"I need a minute," I barely get out, closing my eyes, tears finally falling down my cheeks.

Jake Jolly's dad is Santa Claus, and his grandma has snow globes predating World War II.

When Jake laughs hard, the cute little dimple he has on his right cheek pops.

He drinks his coffee with two sugars and a splash of milk, where the color is almost caramel.

. . .

He wears glasses when he's not working because, without them, he's blind.

All that comes to mind are facts about him, and when I close my eyes, all I see is him.

"I fucked up," I whisper.

"Claire, it's going to be fine. I'm sure you can explain everything. He seems like an understanding guy."

"I can't," I admit. "He knows the truth. He knows I knew about him when he offered me a ride. He knows I lied about my name and what I do for a living. And there is nothing that can change that." I suck in a deep breath. "Can you do me a favor?" I push my emotions down and bury them until I can return to New York. "Please reschedule my January flight for tonight. The latest one you can get at the airport."

"Anything else?"

"No," I state firmly.

"You don't have to act strong, like this doesn't hurt you."

"If I don't, I'm not sure I can survive the rest of the day. I'll text you when I'm at the airport."

"Claire—"

I end the call. I don't want her pity. I don't want anyone to feel sorry for me. I've got enough of that going for myself.

What did Jake tell me earlier today? Every action has a consequence, and this is mine.

Loving him would've been too easy. Losing him is what I deserve.

I understand how it looks, and if the tables were turned, I wouldn't forgive me, either. His family is everything to him, and I could've taken their livelihood away.

Had I not fallen for him, I would have. Without apology. Without thinking about how it would have affected the Jollys or the locals. It would have been business as usual.

226

The reason Merryville is so magical is that corporations like Manchester Holdings aren't in the equation. It would kill the very thing that makes it feel like home to many. Commercialization won't survive here because the locals won't support it.

Coming here wasn't a mistake. I met Jake. I learned what it's like to be with someone who cares, and I took advantage of that.

As I shove my purse, heels, and toiletries into the bottom of my suitcase, the bedroom door cracks open. I hope it's Jake, but it's not. It's Tinsel.

She trots toward me, meowing, her tail straight in the air. "Hi," I say as she rubs against my leg. "And goodbye."

I run my hand over her soft head and down her back a few times. When the purrs start, I think I might break down. She jumps on the bed, rolls over on her back, and looks at me upside down.

I grab her paw. "It was a pleasure getting to know you, Tinsel. I hope that in my next life, I'll be a cat. Please take care of him," I say, choking up.

As I drag in a deep breath, I grab my suitcase and wheel it down the hallway. I take one last moment to look around the house. My eyes scan over the big windows overlooking the backyard, the fireplace and couch, his beautiful collection of books, and the kitchen where our gingerbread house still stands.

I take a mental picture of it all, knowing I'm leaving a sliver of my heart behind. Then I go outside, struggle to lift my suitcase over the back of the truck, then get in and crank it.

The monster feels foreign, but it got me almost here and surely it will get me back. As I put the truck in drive, I get a text.

With every part of my being, I hope and wish it's Jake.

Instead, it's a confirmation from the airline that my flight has been changed. I have six hours to get there.

I'd stay in Merryville, but there is no place available. I'd do whatever I could to desperately win him back, but with how hurt he is, he needs time. The last thing I want to do is shove myself upon him, so I'll leave as he wishes.

When I woke up this morning, I had no idea today would be the last time I'd be with Jake. The last time I'd smell his cologne and sweat mixed together. The last time I'd kiss his soft lips or have him touch me. In a way, we never know when the end is coming. Cherishing every moment like it's the final one seems cliché, but now I wish I'd done it more.

As I drive off, I see the old truck in the rearview. Jake's house eventually fades away.

The guilt takes over, and I think I might be sick. As I cross under the Jolly Christmas Tree Farm sign, I pull over and dry heave. My eyes water as my body tries to release whatever it can. But nothing comes out. I'm physically and emotionally empty.

Pulling back onto the country road that leads straight through town, I realize I'm truly alone, something I haven't felt since I arrived. But it doesn't matter.

I can't fix this.

CHAPTER 26

JAKE

She's gone.

S *he's gone.*
She's really gone, as if she slipped through my fingers.

The way every woman I've ever cared for has.

I can't stand to look at her, knowing the betrayal she's capable of. I walk outside, the door slamming harder than I intend, and take a trail I've hiked a thousand times. It leads to a clearing in the woods where deer graze in the morning and evenings. The trees are tall, the leaves are long gone, and when I look up, a tiny sliver of sunshine pokes through, almost like it's telling me hope remains. But deep down, I know there's not any left.

It's over, and it fucking hurts.

I don't have the power within me to watch her leave, so I give her time to gather her things. My mind is reeling, and my heart is beating rapidly. I feel as if I'm losing my grasp on reality, and I didn't realize pain like this existed. I almost gave her everything...the farm included.

As I text Hank and tell him what happened, my fingers fly across the keys.

HANK

Shit. I just googled her. The heir of
Manchester Holdings. I don't know what
to say.

JAKE

You were right all along. She was here to
scam me out of everything. Go ahead and tell
me I'm a fucking idiot.

HANK

I'm sorry, man. Want some company?

JAKE

No. This is a lot to process, and I need to be
alone.

Alone.

The word hits me like a ton of bricks.

It was my destiny all along, wasn't it?

A part of my heart believed the two of us could make it work. That possibly, by some fucking miracle, the two of us could be together, and the loneliness we felt would vanish. It was going to take a lot of work.

How fucking naive to believe it was a possibility.

With her father's company taking the farm from under me, us being together should've been the least of my worries. I was focused on the wrong thing. Distraction was probably a part of her scheme.

Love is precious? Love is kind?

No, love is vile, and I no longer believe in it.

My future never included Claire.

It was a fantasy that I wished and hoped would come true. Because she seemed like a dream, a woman who was created just for me, my true opposite, but someone I'd be honored to protect with every inch of my being.

Why did I think she was different?

She wasn't, even after everything we so intimately shared. I thought it meant something more to her. Now I realize I was just a pawn, a chess piece she could play when needed, a faithful servant to the Manchester princess. What a fool I am.

The nice guy never gets the girl. No, we get shit on and taken advantage of.

I hear the truck crank and the engine roar as she drives away. After ten minutes, I make my way back. When I walk inside my place, every inch of the space reminds me of her, down to the gingerbread house on the counter and the book she was reading on the table.

My stomach growls; I'm starving. I haven't eaten since breakfast, but the thought of food makes me sick. So I settle on whiskey.

The first shot burns.

The second one does, too.

By the time I shoot down the third, it's not as bad.

The fourth makes my throat numb.

I'm a fucking wreck as I replay all the things she's told me about herself and her need to break all the rules to prove a point to her father. I guess sleeping with me was on that list. Hank's stupid bet comes to mind, and really, I was the one who fell for her. He'd gotten it twisted.

When I close my eyes, I see her naked body underneath mine. And last night, in her sleep, she'd clearly said she was in love with me.

Awake, Claire would never admit that, but her sleep-talking self always spilled her secrets. Even her subconscious wouldn't talk about her true identity, though. She only mentioned things about relationships, and over the last week, it's been all about me. I got used to her random mumbles about being in love and never wanting to leave Merryville. I was patiently waiting for her to come to the conclusion in her waking hours. After visiting my grandma, I felt like Claire was almost there.

Never could I have predicted Lacy would use Claire as a weapon, a knife that she drove straight through my heart. Not that I care what anyone in town thinks, but I'm sure Lacy is having a field day telling anyone who will listen. She's probably already restarted her smear campaign, making me out to be some monster who was helping Manchester Holdings destroy Merryville. My imagination goes wild, so I take another shot, hoping it will weaken the relentless thoughts that are threatening to take over.

The scenario of Claire leaving in January played out much differently in my head. It was nothing dramatic like this.

I need food. As I stand, I stumble to the pantry and look inside. Cooking isn't an option, so I grab the container of cheese balls, knowing I need to eat something. Right now, anything will do.

I plop on the couch and see the book on the table. Bending over, I reach for it and read the page where Claire stopped. I close my eyes and shake my head. It's the part where the leading lady leaves the hero. And it's fucking depressing. I grab the book and toss it against the wall, where it lands with the pages bent.

I'm numb from the alcohol but also from the shock of it all.

Every part of me wants Lacy to be the liar, but deep down, I know she is telling the truth.

I spend the next hour searching for Claire online and reading articles about her life.

Claire Manchester, the future heir of Manchester Holdings. Graduated from Harvard as a valedictorian with a degree in marketing and executive management.

She attended boarding school in Paris, just as she'd told my grandmother earlier today. I'm unsure what she's lied about besides her name and why she was here. However, those two facts are foundational.

It hurts because I felt like she was comfortable enough to tell me anything. I had no secrets, and while I didn't know things about her past, it didn't seem necessary. To learn she's Claire Manchester leaves me speechless.

Everything I learned about her finally makes sense, down to her anxiety attacks. The amount of pressure she's survived her entire life... I'm surprised she has a kind bone in her body.

I turn on the TV, the first time I've needed entertainment since Claire arrived, and flick through the channels. There's some stupid movie about love, and I keep clicking until I land on a documentary about the praying mantis. When they mention the female decapitating the male during sex, I'm ready to yell obscenities, but a knock on my door pulls me away.

"Go away!" I yell, not caring who it is or what they want, not in the mood. And Hank better not have driven over here when I told him I'd rather be alone.

The pounding stops, then seconds later, the door swings open, and I see Hudson.

"I said to go away!" I tell him, leaning my head back on the couch.

The world tilts on its axis, and I might throw up.

He walks in front of the sofa and crosses his arms over his broad chest. It's almost like looking at myself in the mirror.

"What the actual fuck?" he barks out.

I throw a cheese ball at him. It hits his shirt, leaving a splotch of orange dust in its wake, then falls to the floor. "Leave me alone."

"No." He stands firm.

Sitting up, I grab a pillow and toss it at him, but I miss.

"What happened? I just passed Claire on the road. She looked upset." He meets my eyes, and I suddenly understand why Hudson is the way he is after the love of his life left him and their kid for another man.

Next time, I won't be the nice guy, and I'll be hard-pressed to let anyone scale my walls. In the future, I'll better protect myself, and when things move too fast, I'll consider it a red flag.

"Well?" he asks.

"I told her to leave."

"Because she's Claire Manchester?"

I sit up a little straighter. "How did you know that?"

"People talk. And you've been so far up each other's asses I haven't had a chance to chat since we were at the bar. Also, I recognized her."

"No, you didn't."

He rolls his eyes. "Don't be stupid."

"You're the stupid one."

"Great comeback. So, let me get this straight. You've been fucking a billionaire's daughter and letting her live rent-free in your house and head for fifteen days, and you're mad because she didn't tell you?"

"Ding, ding, ding. You win a prize." I flip him off.

"I heard you pulled a gun on her ex."

"I'd do it again in a fucking heartbeat, too. Piece-of-shit scumbag."

He shakes his head. "Did you at least let her explain herself?"

"I asked her to tell me why she came here. She did. I welcomed the vampire in. I escorted her inside and into my bed and my heart. At the beginning of the year, she would have bought the property after I'd shown her around and introduced her to everyone."

He narrows his eyes. "She still could."

"Yeah, you're right. She probably will. We're fucked. All of us!" I pick up the whiskey bottle and take another drink.

Hudson rips it out of my hand, and I want to snatch it back, but I know if I stand up, I'll probably fall.

"How do you know she would've gone through with it? I'm not convinced."

"Everyone knows the Manchesters don't give two shits about people. They've wanted this land for thirty years, and I guess they'll finally get it. I won't be surprised if we're all escorted off the premises and she moves in here. She kept sayin' how much she loved my place. Guess it will be hers in the end."

Hudson gives me a look. "You're being dramatic now. And hey, I get it. Your heart and your dick are going through some things. But we've got bigger issues to deal with, bro. We need to figure out how to save the farm. My credit is trashed thanks to my shitty ex and her spending problems, and you won't be able to get that amount of money without signing your life away to a bank. Let's be real. Getting behind on taxes will happen again if we don't make a change. We can't keep operating at a loss and hemorrhaging money every month."

My eyes blink at two different times. "I can't have this conversation right now. I think I need a rain check."

He groans. "Tomorrow, then."

Before I can say anything, he sets the whiskey on the counter in the kitchen and then leaves. The door locks behind him. Instead of walking to my bedroom and sleeping on the sheets that smell like Claire, I grab the blanket off the back of the couch. I'm staying right here.

I'll worry about all the other bullshit tomorrow because tomorrow absolutely will come. And I'll still be living out this nightmare I call life.

CHAPTER 27

CLAIRE

ONE WEEK LATER

My life will never be the same, not after a glimpse of what it could have been. For the first two weeks of December, I was the happiest I've been in a long time. I'd almost be willing to say…ever.

I miss Texas.

I miss Tinsel.

And I miss Jake.

It wasn't the sex, but it was how he saw me and recognized me, the real me. When most people don't.

I've not left my penthouse since I returned to the city on a late-night flight. The last time I felt pain like this over a man? Never.

Every meal has been delivered to me.

Every call has been rejected, other than Emma's.

I don't want to talk to my father, and the media can fuck off. I'm confident my phone number was leaked because I've received too many random calls.

Dale made a mess of this, and I eventually learned that he was the one who encouraged my father to do the interviews about Merryville.

When I searched it online, there were dozens of articles posted. Jake and his family probably read every one of them, too. My father praised me for researching the town and ensuring no one would outbid him. With unlimited amounts of money, he's already scared any competitors away. It's pretty much a done deal.

Article after article, I am mentioned. My picture cosigned this purchase. And for the first time, I don't want my father's recognition. Years ago, I'd have felt like I'd accomplished something, having his pride and finally receiving praise, but I cringed when I read the quotes in *Business Today*. Destroying the Jollys' homestead isn't something I can or will ever be proud of.

If I could pay to have every post removed, I would. But it will stay on the internet forever. It's a lost cause.

Since Dale opened his big mouth about Merryville, I decided to release a kiss of death on his career. He was immediately terminated for harassment. My father has made it clear that I'm off-limits to anyone who works for Manchester Holdings and has fired people for less.

Some believe the rules don't apply to them, but time has proven no one is above my father's iron fist or his airtight contracts. The NDA he was made to sign keeps Dale from speaking to the media because my father will ruin him financially for breach. No one in their right mind will throw themselves into a legal battle with the company unless they want to lose everything they own and never want to work in the industry again. Most can't afford it, anyway.

But Dale will never be a worry of mine ever again. That's a promise. Between Jake's threats and my father's, I'm sure he's fled the country with his wifey. Good riddance.

As I lounge on my couch and flip through channels

without stopping on one, my sister calls. I'm tempted to ignore it, but considering she's in the city right now and only four blocks away, I don't. The last thing I need is for her to enter and see all the candy wrappers and empty ice cream containers on the floor and table. I did learn drowning myself in sugar doesn't ease the pain. Nothing does. It only reminds me of being with Jake.

As soon as I answer the phone, I realize how chipper she is by the sound of her voice. "Want to meet me for lunch? I've got some things I need to tell you."

"No thanks," I say, holding my finger down on the channel button on the remote.

"Oh God, are you zombie scrolling?"

"Nah." It would've been believable if the volume was not up so loud.

"I'll be over in ten minutes. This can't wait."

Click.

She doesn't allow me to refuse her company, though it wouldn't have mattered. She can and will get past security, and she knows the code to my door. There is a one-hundred-percent chance Emma will barge in within ten minutes. Because I'm curious, I set a timer on my phone.

I look around at the mess, and while I should speed clean, I can't be bothered. It won't stay like this forever, and right now, I don't have the energy to do anything but stay in my feels.

I'm physically and mentally broken, thanks to heartache and the elephant that's been sitting on my chest since I left Texas. My anxiety has been through the roof, and when I get like this, it's better if I'm left alone. Nothing seems to make it subside other than my meds, but even those stopped working. I've got an appointment with my doctor tomorrow because it's not okay to feel this way, even if it's of my own volition.

At eight minutes and fifty-five seconds, my door opens and

closes. I hear footsteps, then Emma leans over the couch and meets my eyes.

"Claire Caitlin Manchester. You're a goddamn mess. Look at this place. Look at you," she admonishes.

I point the remote at her and press mute. "Too bad it doesn't work on you."

"Don't you have someone who comes in and cleans your place several times a week?" she asks, glancing around.

"I told them I'd call when I was ready and explained I was going through it."

She shakes her head. "When is the last time you showered?"

I shrug. "Don't remember. Don't care. I have no one to impress. So it doesn't matter."

"I'd suggest you get your ass up. Father told me he's flying to Merryville to purchase that land in January."

I sit up and look at her. "When did this happen?"

"An hour ago."

"Shit," I seethe, my heart pounding hard.

"You need to snap out of this stupor."

I smooth my messy hair back on my head. "This can't be happening."

"Claire, you know how he gets when his mind is made up," she says.

My father is upset with me for sleeping with Dale, and I was told I've ruined my reputation—his words, not mine. It's two steps forward and three steps back for me and him. Our relationship is complicated at best and damaged beyond belief at worst. The truth lies somewhere in the middle. And I think he's going to Texas because he knows I don't have the courage to go through with the deal. I'm a weakling, just as he always implied.

No, I still have compassion and can remove the needs of the business from my thoughts when necessary. My father believes everything is black and white. You're a winner or a loser. You're rich or poor. You have what it takes to run Manchester Holdings, or you don't.

The thoughts have run a marathon in my mind since I returned. I place my face in my hands, wishing I could fix this.

"Sis, you're the smartest person I know. If anyone can stop this from happening and destroying Jake's family, you can. You've got a little over two weeks until the auction."

I think about her words. "Two weeks until the auction."

Emma watches me.

"Two weeks."

She snaps, "Are you stuck in a loop?"

I recall the contracts I've signed in the past. "But what if the auction never happens?" I turn to her, and her eyebrows furrow.

"I don't understand."

"I know exactly what I've got to do." I stand up and go to my bedroom; she follows me.

"Tell me what you're thinking," she says.

"I think I need to go to my lawyer, ask about my money, and see what I can access." I catch a glimpse of myself in the mirror. Emma is right. I do look like a fucking wreck. That's what happens when you feel sorry for yourself and stay glued to the couch for a week. I pull several outfits from my closet as Emma watches me from the doorway.

"Which one?" I ask, laying them on my bed.

"Pencil skirt with that blouse. Says you're a badass bitch who's not taking anyone's shit."

"Perfect. Can you call Nelson and tell him I'll arrive within an hour?"

"I can." She immediately pulls her phone from the cross-body bag she's wearing and dials the number as I pick out a pair of heels.

After a minute, the phone call ends. "He said he'll cancel an appointment to see you." She studies me. "Claire," she whispers, "Dad will be pissed if you rip this from under him after the media tour he's done. You'll publicly humiliate him."

"I don't care. He's never given me the credit I deserve on the deals I've landed over the years. I've tried proving to him that I'm smart enough to take control of the company when he retires. I've bent over backward to make him happy, to put the business first while not living my own life. I fucking learned to play golf and sail, and I hate them both! Not once has our father ever given me the impression that I'm his first choice because I'm not. So this is checkmate. I'm happy to beat him at his own game."

"You could lose everything."

The part of me that discredits and pushes away my feelings ninety-nine percent of the time rears its ugly head. I recognize I'm doing it and stop myself. "I have more than enough money to support myself for the rest of my life. If he removes me from his will," I shrug, "I guess you'll get it all."

"You know I don't want that," she says, searching my face.

I walk over to my little sister and hug her. She wraps her arms around me and squeezes me tight. "I love you," I tell her. "Everything will work out. This feels right."

"Love you, too, but you smell like potato chips and body odor." She laughs.

"I know. It is what it is. After I shower, I'll go to Nelson's office. I'll get his insight on how I can stop this auction from happening and will keep you updated with what he says."

We let go of one another, and I meet her eyes.

"What if this doesn't work out how you hope?" she asks.

I shrug. "What if it does? Sometimes, the risk is worth the reward. Jake is worth it, Emma. I'm tired of good guys not winning. That's changing if I have any say in the matter."

"You like this man, don't you?"

I meet her eyes. "I more than like him. And I'll do whatever I can to right my wrongs."

"That's the difference between you and Dad. If things

were as special between you two as you say, Jake will forgive you." She smiles.

"I'm not counting on it. I betrayed him. He's been hurt by women before, and I added to that."

She sucks in a deep breath, and her expression grows sad. "It's not over yet."

"No, it's not."

CHAPTER 28

JAKE

I 've been in a bad mood all day.
     Last night, I drank with Hank, and we played darts in my workshop. I should've gone to sleep earlier but didn't. Now I'm paying for it.

Hudson hands me one of the chainsaws he just sharpened. The blade is shiny silver. "Why are you being such an asshole?" he asks.

"Just taking after you." I grip the chainsaw's handle, not letting it slip, then turn to walk away. Being alone is all I want, so I've avoided people. The happy Jake that everyone expects is long gone. There isn't anything to be happy about anymore.

Just as I set the chainsaw in the back of the truck, Hudson places a firm hand on my shoulder, turning me around so I'm face to face with him.

He lowers his voice, and I know he's trying to not cause a scene, but I don't appreciate him reprimanding me, either. "You've acted this way for a week," he says. "It's time to cut the shit."

"Don't be a hypocrite," I throw back. "You act like this twenty-four seven, and we're all supposed to accept your shitty

LYRA PARISH

behavior and move on and not mention it. God forbid anyone
else be upset."

He narrows his eyes. "Lemme know when you're finished
actin' like a little bitch."

My anger takes hold, and I push him hard, putting my
weight and strength into it. As if he expected this reaction,
Hudson braces himself, keeping his feet planted, and barely
stumbles. Then his strong hands are on me. He grabs my shirt
with his fists, slamming me back against the truck. He pins me
in place with his weight as he glares into my eyes, his nostrils
flaring, and I know I've struck a nerve. Good, now we're even.
Hudson has always been bigger and stronger than me. Right
now is no different.

"Listen. I understand you're fucking hurt. I know you're
upset. No one is invalidating the way you feel. But we have a
job to do, and I'd rather you do it without walking around
with a goddamn chip on your shoulder the entire day.
Customers have noticed, Jake. And considering our financial
problems, bad reviews are the last thing we need to haunt us,
okay? So get your shit together—that's a fucking order—or
I'm putting you on leave for the rest of the season." He lets go
of me.

I'm seething and want to slam my fist into his face, but he's
not my enemy. There is just too much truth to his words.

"Go to hell," I mutter.

"I'm already there." He glares at me. "I know you were
falling in love with her. Okay? But don't forget that I also
know what it feels like to be left behind. At least Claire is still
out there somewhere, and you could potentially reconcile. It's
not over yet. Not until she signs on the dotted line."

I shake my head. "There is no reconciling. After spending
the last week thinking about it, I'm convinced what we had
and shared wasn't real. I've come to terms with it being over.
A relationship built on lies isn't one I want anyway. It's just all
fucked up."

He tilts his head. "When you're done having your pity party and have had some time, we'll talk about this. Okay?"

"Pity party? No. This is my reality."

When I meet his eyes, I can tell he's not convinced.

"Listen, I saw you two together, Jake. People can tell a lie, but they can't fake the way their body responds. It was more than obvious at the bar that the feelings you two shared were mutual. And yeah, you're right. What she did is fucked up, but nothing happened. You're pissed at the might-have-beens. You're upset that everyone in town is whisperin' about how your girlfriend betrayed you. Who gives two fucks about any of that?" He pats his chest over his heart. "Both of your truths are here, but you're too hurt even to recognize that, and honestly, I don't have time for it during the busiest days of the season. So act like a grown-ass man and do your job without a scowl. And maybe be nice to people? Shit. Never thought I'd be having this conversation with you. Lucas, yeah, with him, it's a flip of a coin. But you? Never." He turns and walks away, not looking back.

I shake my head. I'm thankful to be handling precuts because I can't put on a fake smile and pretend I'm a happy guy when I'm not. Unlike Claire, I can't fake my way through life.

For the next few hours, I cut down trees and load them on the lowboy. Typically, work like this would take my mind off anything, but right now, it's pointless. My thoughts are filled with Claire, her laugh, the smell of her shampoo, the way she sighed contentedly against my mouth when I randomly kissed her.

Was it all fake? The problem is I don't know. I'd like to believe it wasn't. But after what I've read online about her being a snake in the grass, I'm not sure.

Once I deliver my last load of trees for the day, I drive to my grandma's. She called me yesterday and made me promise I'd see her today. After I had it out with Hudson, I thought about asking for a rain check, but I've hurt enough people today. Grandma has been lonely since Grandpa passed away, and I've never ditched an invite. So I force myself to see her, knowing I might not be the best company, but I'll at least try.

When I walk in, she's sitting in the living room with a cup of hot tea in a gold-rimmed teacup. Even that makes me think of Claire.

"I made your favorite cake, honey," Grandma says. "Strawberry crème. It's in the kitchen."

I smile at her. "Want me to grab you a slice, too?"

"Sure."

I walk past the dining room and turn into the kitchen, where a tall cake sits on the counter. It warms my heart knowing she spent the day baking this for me. I'd have felt guilty if I hadn't visited after she did this. I cut two pieces, put them on plates, and then grab two forks.

When I return to the living room, I hand her one and sit in the recliner beside hers.

"What's on your mind?" Mawmaw asks.

Lying to her is the equivalent of lying to Jesus, so I lay it on her. I only leave out the sexual stuff, but honestly, that's just a tiny piece of my and Claire's relationship.

She listens, nodding and shaking her head when it's appropriate. It feels good to put it on the table. "So what's the problem?" she asks when I'm done.

I give her the abridged version and explain every detail I can, but she still acts like she doesn't understand.

"Mawmaw, I just told you what happened."

"I heard you. Do you feel like things were built on a lie when you were alone? That she was playin' a character?"

"Maybe she's a good liar," I say. "I wouldn't put anything past her at this point, not considering."

Mawmaw shakes her head and sets her half-eaten slice of cake on the small table beside the couch. "Honey, when I was younger, I could have had any man I wanted in Texas."

"Come on," I groan, not knowing where this story is going.

"No, you'll listen because I think it's relevant, even with your hee-haws about it. Anyway." She glares at me for interrupting, and I sit quietly while she finishes. "Before I met your grandfather, I could've married a very wealthy man. To everyone, he was perfect for me. He had unlimited amounts of money from a well-off family. He was charming in public because no one ever spent much time with him alone. However, I had. With people like Claire, there isn't much pretending behind closed doors. That's where you get to learn the real them. The man I almost considered marrying was a monster. He was cruel. His public persona was just a mere mask. Now, was Claire a monster?"

"No. Not at all. She was kind. Shy at times. She laughed. And smiled. We even made a gingerbread house."

"So you're mad at Claire's public persona and because she couldn't tell you who she was. Put yourself in her shoes for a brief moment. Would you want to tell her who you were, knowing the reaction she'd give? I bet my bingo money you wouldn't." She shakes her head. "The woman I met—before you shooed her away—wouldn't have looked me in the eyes had she planned to take the farm away. I'm usually a good judge of character."

We sit in silence for a few minutes.

"I think she's misunderstood, and you played right into that and treated her just like everyone in her life does: like an outcast who doesn't belong."

I suck in a ragged breath. I never thought of it that way. "So now what?"

She shrugs. "I don't have all the answers. But you need time."

"Something we don't have."

"I'll be right back." Grandma stands up and walks away while I unlock my phone and scroll through the pictures

Claire sent me of herself. I look at them, and an overwhelming amount of sadness overtakes me. Am I the one who's overreacting? Did I not give her a chance to explain herself? But she lied. If she'd lie about that, what else is she capable of?

Mawmaw eventually returns, and I lock my phone and put it away. She's carrying a jewelry box in her hand. Carefully, she opens it and pulls out a key.

"I want you to take this."

I stand, and she puts it in my palm. "What does it go to?"

"A safe-deposit box located at a bank in Dallas."

I give her a look. "What's inside it?"

"I don't know. My father gave it to me when I was about to be engaged to that awful man. He'd told me if I ever needed a way out, I'd have what I needed in that box. Thankfully, I met your grandpa, and the rest is history. Should never underestimate how easily a good man can win over the heart of a lady."

I swallow as I look down at it, and she hands me some paperwork. The date in the corner makes my jaw drop. "Grandma, this was fifty-five years ago."

"Maybe whatever is in that box will help us not lose the farm. I don't know and never needed to check it. I think right now is the perfect time. We all need a lifeline."

"Okay," I say. "I have to work tomorrow, though."

"I'll take care of it, sweetie. I'll let your mama know you're doing official business for Mawmaw."

"It's a ten-hour drive." I check the time. It's nearly six o'clock.

"And they open at eight."

I bend down and hug her. "Thank you."

"Just make sure you're back in town before the tree-lighting ceremony, okay?"

"Will do."

"Love you, Jakey."

"Love you, too, Mawmaw." I shove the key and piece of paper in my pocket and wonder what the hell I'll find.

CHAPTER 29

CLAIRE

TWO DAYS LATER

As soon as I'm off the plane, I walk as fast as I can through the airport. Many flights are delayed, and others are canceled. This all feels very much like déjà vu, but this time, I'll do things a lot differently.

I take the escalator to the rental car area and wait in line. Considering it's Texas, I don't even try for a luxury vehicle. The odds of me getting one are little to none, so I reserved what I knew they'd have— a truck.

"There's a storm rolling in," the guy at the rental center tells me as soon as I step up to the counter. I've learned that people in the South tend to use the weather as a conversation starter. I don't mind it, though. It sometimes makes speaking less awkward.

"Thanks for letting me know," I offer. He goes over every page, then I sign my name at the bottom of the contract. I'm escorted outside, where the gigantic Ram truck is parked and waiting for me. It looks as large as a bus, but this time, I made sure there was GPS and satellite radio. The guy helps load my suitcase in the back seat, but since it's a carry-on, it's not as heavy.

"Safe travels," he tells me as he shuts the door and waves. I take a deep breath and move the seat forward because whoever drove it before me was tall. Then I start it and place my hand on the steering wheel. The engine roars to life as I plug my phone into the charger. I'll be damned if I get stranded this time.

The drive to Merryville isn't much different from the last, but it's dark already. Of course, my flight was delayed by three hours, so I'm on the road later than I originally wanted and planned to be. However, nothing will stop me.

The first hundred miles pass by fast. I listen to a podcast and eventually call my sister to check in.

I'm excited, but I'm also nervous.

No expectations. It's what I've been whispering to myself since I met with my lawyer two days ago. I think it might become my life motto because, without expectations, disappointment doesn't exist.

The truck hums under my fingertips as I finally turn down the old country road that leads straight to Merryville. I press down on the gas pedal, seeing the speedometer climb to eighty-five, and I hope I can cut some time off my arrival.

A few vehicles pass me in the opposite direction, and they turn on their high beams, nearly blinding me. My wipers cross over a dry windshield every fifteen seconds, but I can't figure out how to turn them off. I'm not sure how they were turned on. Distracted driving is dangerous, so I leave everything how it is and continue on my path forward.

I'm on a mission.

When I'm forty minutes outside of Merryville, and the fuel light in the truck dings and turns on, I recognize it for what it is. And just like Hank had mentioned, I see one lonely gas station in the middle of nowhere.

Not wanting to repeat my last mistake, I slow down and pull over.

When I climb out of the truck, I go to the side and don't see a fuel door. Annoyed, I drive to the other side. I flip open the metal flap, then I look between the two handles on the pump—unleaded or diesel. I'm not sure which one to choose, so I quickly search on my phone and can't find a specific answer. My stress level begins to rise because I can't fuck this up. Time is of the essence, so I swallow my pride and go inside.

The door above the bell dings, and a teenager looks up from her phone.

"Howdy!" she says but continues to scroll. The gas station is small. In the back are cold drinks and a few aisles with candy, cookies, and chips. Because my throat is dry, I grab water and some chocolate peanut butter cups, then go up to the front. After I'm given a total, I slide my card and then clear my throat.

"This may sound stupid, but if I paid you a hundred bucks, would you pump my gas?"

She laughs and shakes her head. "Wait, you're serious?"

"As a heart attack." I hold up the hundred-dollar bill.

"Right this way." She snatches it out of my hand, and I grab my stuff, then follow her outside.

"Nice-ass truck."

"It's a rental," I tell her. "Drives great, though."

She runs her hand over the smooth, dark-gray hood and down the side. "Slide your card, and I'll get ya goin'."

So I do. Then, she removes the green cap from the fuel tank and picks up the green handle.

"It's diesel, ma'am. Had you put the other one in there, you'd have messed up the fuel system and been stranded. Ain't many people on the roads at this time. Most are at the Winter Solstice Festival right now."

"Shit, I'm glad I asked. That would've been bad."

She replaces the nozzle. "Yeah, it could have. You feel free to stop by anytime. I'm always here. My name is Ginger. My family owns this place."

I hand her another hundred. "Thanks, Ginger. I'm Claire. Hope you have a Merry Christmas. You just saved my ass."

"Aww, thank you. I could say the same about you," she tells me, shoving the money in her pocket. "And Merry Christmas to you, too. You headin' to Merryville?"

I nod. "I'd like to make it to the tree-lighting ceremony, but I'm not sure if I will."

She checks her smartwatch. "Better haul it. Starts in thirty minutes. But hey, if you miss it, it's not the end of the world. There's going to be a lot to do. Oh, and you have to try the apple cider. It's incredible."

"I will. Thanks again." I give her a wave, then veer onto the country road. When I finally pass a sign that tells me it's fifteen miles to Merryville, my heart throbs. I will make it there, or at least that's what I think until I see flashing lights behind me.

"Fuck!" I yell, hitting my palm against the steering wheel, slowing down, and pulling over on the side of the road. That's when I look at the GPS and see I'm eight miles outside of town. This is almost exactly where I ran out of gas the first time I visited.

"You've got to be shitting me. How is this even possible?" I mutter.

Moments later, the officer comes to the driver's side window, and I push the wrong button so the passenger one goes down. Eventually, I find the right option, and it slides down.

He looks at me with a lifted brow, and I can't help but

notice the cowboy hat. "Ma'am, do you know why I pulled you over?"

My anxiety grabs hold of me, and I feel a jolt of adrenaline course through my body. "No."

"For one, you're bakin' everyone with your high beams. Your windshield wipers are on, and it's not raining yet. You were going twenty miles over the speed limit and ran off the road several times."

"I'm sorry," I say, not disagreeing. I'm sure all those things are true.

"How much have you had to drink tonight?"

I look at him like he's crazy. "I'm not drunk. I just don't drive a lot, and I'm not used to this truck."

The windshield wipers groan as they nudge across the dry glass.

"Can I get your license and registration?" he asks.

"It's a rental, but I have the paperwork. One sec." I grab the contract, then my wallet, and pull out my driver's license, the real one with my legal name. I only use the fake one to hide my identity when I travel because most of my reservations are made under Claire Chester.

The officer shines his bright-as-fuck flashlight on it, and I see him read New York across the top. "I'll be right back. Hang tight."

My nerves are shot as I impatiently wait. I'm sure he's pulling my driving record, and I know he'll find nothing. I don't get behind the wheel enough to have any violations. But speeding is a first for me. I can't wait to tell my sister.

"All right. Well, I need you to step out of the vehicle, because I'd like to do a sobriety test if you don't mind."

"Fine. I've had nothing to drink, though." I exit the truck, and he leads me to the back, where I see his vehicle. Across the side, it says *State Trooper*. The last thing I need is to go to jail.

He leads me to the side of the road, and the lights on top

of his car are blinding, so I squint. The expression on his face is hard as stone as he makes me do a sobriety test. After I touch my nose, follow his finger, and walk in a straight line, he concludes that I'm not intoxicated.

I'm eventually escorted back to the truck. "Do you know how to turn those high beams and wipers off?" he asks.

I shake my head.

"May I?"

"Please, be my guest," I say, opening the door.

He reaches in and flicks a switch, then turns the end of the blinker for the windshield wipers. "There ya go."

"Thanks. I'll have to remember that. I was more concerned with focusing on the road."

"I understand. Well, ma'am, after everything, I'm gonna give you a citation for speeding because it's dangerous to be drivin' that fast on these roads. One person crosses the line, and it's a head-on collision. Many don't walk away from things like that."

"Okay." I suck in a deep breath, glancing at the clock. The last thing I want to do is piss this guy off, but I'll be lying if I say I'm not growing impatient. As I glance in the rearview mirror, I can't see shit because of the ridiculous lights on top of the car.

Ten more minutes pass, and he finally returns. He spends another few minutes explaining my rights and how it's not an admission of guilt. "Not to be rude, but where do I sign?" I ask because I don't need every detail.

The officer glares at me and continues as if I said nothing. Then I'm told to sign on the dotted line at the bottom of the electronic device. He hands over my speeding ticket and driver's license, then tells me to be careful and to slow down. I give him a tight smile, then buckle.

Once he's in his car, I put my blinker on and guide the truck onto the straight road I've been driving since leaving the airport. Not wanting to get pulled over again, I follow the speed limit signs.

When the Welcome to Merryville mural comes into sight, an overwhelming amount of relief floods me. I made it, but I missed the ceremony.

Getting here was the easy part. Now comes everything else.

CHAPTER 30

JAKE

Hank stands next to me as the gigantic Christmas tree in the middle of the town square is lit with colorful lights. The crowd cheers, and everyone is grinning except me.

My father is on stage dressed in his full Santa garb, waving and pointing at different kids who are yelling for his attention. He's more popular than any celebrity, and I'm proud of my dad. He works hard and can put a smile on his face in a snap of a finger. Each year, he makes people's holidays special and brings joy wherever he goes. Goals, honestly.

The elves move him to his Christmas throne, where he'll allow people and pets to take photos with him. Mom is around somewhere, but I lost track of her. She typically dresses like Mrs. Claus and joins him for public events, but she's also judging the quilt contest that's held at the town hall, so she may be over there.

Hank stands beside me and laughs when the elementary kids sing about Christmas trees and Santa Claus. The smell of fried foods fills the air, and we're lucky it's in the upper forties. Some years, it's colder than this. Right now, though, it's nice, but I'm also glad I wore layers.

"I think I've had enough. Are you headin' to the bonfire, or are ya leavin' for the night?" Hank asks me.

"I'm not in the best mood, but I'm not missing out on our tradition. Plus, I promised Mawmaw that I'd do everything I normally do. And she'll find out if I ditch, so I might as well just go."

"Great. I brought an old friend," Hank says, flashing me the silver flask with his name engraved on the outside. With a smirk, he shoves it back into the inside pocket of his jacket.

"Another tradition of ours."

There are tons of food trucks, boutiques, and other local businesses selling goods at the festival. Usually, after the Christmas tree lighting, the town scatters to all the different areas. A live band plays in the gigantic circus tent, and the laughter echoes out. There are small carnival rides and games for the kids, too.

One of my favorite activities to celebrate the winter solstice is the large bonfire that's set up in a contained area on the opposite end. It's quiet and relaxing, and there are several long logs and stumps placed around it so people can enjoy the heat.

When Hank and I arrive, we're handed a sheet of paper with a pencil. Each year, we write out the things we're leaving behind and throw the page into the fire to solidify it and rid those things from our lives. I find a seat away from the small crowd.

"You didn't write anything yet?" Hank asks, wadding his up into a ball and tossing it into the flames. We watch the paper catch and then burn to ash. He hands me the flask, and I take a long pull from it, another tradition we've kept since we were teenagers.

"No. Feels like I could fill the page." I hand the booze back to him. "Shit, what's in there?"

"Fireball."

I make a face. "Coulda warned me. Also, I've been

thinkin' about that bet. To keep my word, I'm gonna give you my bike."

"Nah, man. I can't do that. Plus, I'm not convinced that girl wasn't in love with you. Have you tried reaching out to her?"

"Yeah. My text didn't send. I think she blocked my number. It's pretty much over."

He gives me the flask. "You keep that. Helps numb everything."

"Because it tastes awful." I chuckle. "But beggars can't be choosers, I guess." When I take another sip, I try to shake off the taste. "Next year, whiskey, okay? Cinnamon ain't my favorite."

"Noted."

We grow quiet, staring at the fire and watching different locals throw their papers into the flames. I hold my blank sheet in my other hand.

Across the way, I see my cousin Wendy with one of her friends and give her a wave. She returns the gesture and then goes back to chatting.

"When are ya gonna tell her?" I ask, noticing how Hank's demeanor changes when my cousin is around.

"Never," he says, and he doesn't have to explain himself. I know he's had a thing for her since high school. He's been sitting on the sidelines waiting for her to be single. Her last relationship failed six months ago, and he still hasn't asked her out.

I shake my head, leaning over to put my hands closer to the fire. "You should before she starts datin' someone else again. You're gonna miss your chance."

He grabs the flask and takes two gulps. "We're a fucking mess."

"I know," I mutter.

"How'd your drive to Dallas go yesterday?" he asks.

"Awful. The traffic downtown had me road ragin'. No way

I could ever live in a city like that. Made me more grateful to be home. But I'm exhausted."

"What was in the box?"

"Gold bars," I tell him. "I was shocked. Never seen nothin' like that in my life."

"Enough to save the farm?"

I sigh. "Sadly, no. Grandma told me to bring it home, so I did. It wasn't the answer we needed. I talked to Mom about fundraising, and she said no, that there's another way."

"I'm sorry."

"I've got two weeks to figure it out, or there will be a Manchester resort built five miles outside of town. Makes me sick thinking about it."

"Yeah. A lot of people are worried. This could happen to any of us. We'll stand together, and if it gets too bad, I'll move away," Hank admits.

"And that's where the problem lies. Locals start leaving and selling off businesses, they get bought up by big corporations, and then we're no better than any other commercialized city. There will be major chains of coffee shops and restaurants lining Main Street. Then the magic of Merryville disappears. Sad."

He nods. "It just feels like a big change is happening."

"Yeah, it's in the air."

"Shit," Hank suddenly whispers. "Don't look."

"Who is it?"

His mouth transforms into a firm line. "Lacy."

My eyes slam shut, and I shake my head, hoping she doesn't walk in our direction.

"Jake," she says. "Can we please talk?"

I turn and look up at her.

"I'll leave you two alone for a minute," Hank says, getting up. I glare at him, and he shrugs. If I could kick his ass right now, I would. When I get the chance to get him back, I will, without hesitation.

Lacy sits next to me on the log, and I stare at the fire. There are a thousand other people I wish were beside me other than her.

"I just want to talk to you," she finally says, her voice softening. "Can you at least look at me?"

I do, and I feel nothing. No love, but no hate, either. It's indifference. Like she's a stranger. She smiles, but I don't return the gesture.

"I'm sorry I was the one who told you about Claire," she offers.

My eyes move back to the flames.

"Yes, I wanted her gone," she continues.

"Why?" I glance at her. "Because you were jealous?"

"Yes," she says. "When I saw you with someone else, I realized I wanted you back."

"I'm not doing this, Lacy," I tell her. "Not here. Not ever. I promised myself that if you ever wanted me again, I wouldn't fall for it. And it's a promise I plan on keeping."

"People make mistakes," she says, but I'm not sure who she's trying to convince.

All of my life, I've been too forgiving, too willing to accept those who hurt me. Lacy and I broke up once before the engagement debacle. Then, after a month, she told me she had made a mistake. I took her back with open arms and pretended it was water under the bridge. She told me she was afraid of commitment. Two years later, I proposed when I shouldn't have. That one decision would have saved me a lot of heartache and disappointment. Then again, not picking Claire up while she was walking into Merryville would have, too. It's funny with some perspective how one decision can change a person's entire life.

She repeats herself as if I didn't hear her the first time. "You should forgive people for their mistakes. It's the right thing to do."

"Not mistakes like that." I take a swig from the flask.

"Would you forgive *her* if she came back?"

I think about the question. "I'm not sure. But it's not the same."

"That woman you love came here to destroy your entire family and many of the locals' livelihoods. With all of that, you still believe what I did is worse?"

I look around to see most people have left the area. There's a couple across the way making out and a few teenagers in the back that I'm pretty sure are passing a flask around, too.

Lacy scoots closer to me and places her palm on my face, forcing me to look at her. She moves close, and I'm so shocked at her boldness that I'm nearly frozen as she presses her lips against mine.

"No," I say, standing up. My gigantic shadow dances on the ground behind her, animated by the flames from the fire.

"I still love you," she urges, standing, too.

"You don't. The only reason you think that is because you're afraid I'll move on after seeing me happy with someone else. And I *have* moved on, Lacy. There was a time when I wanted to spend the rest of my life with you, a time when you were my world and you owned my heart. I loved you so damn much that I threw a party and got down on my knee and proposed. You laughed in my face and told me no in front of everyone. I'm tired of being the man people talk about in town, and that never happened until I met you. I see you for who you are. I wish you the absolute best. But that best doesn't include me."

"Jake," she whines.

"Just because I'm alone now doesn't mean I'm saving space for you. I'm not. And I'm not apologizing for that, either. Now, stop. You're embarrassing yourself. Please leave me alone. It's the last time I'll ask."

"Fine. The next time I see you, I'm going to pretend like you don't exist," she retorts.

"Please do," I say, and she gasps like I slapped her. Then she walks away, pretending to cry.

That might work on everyone else but not me. I saw no tears and never have when she pulled that trick out of the hat.

"Good riddance," I say, wiping my mouth on the back of my jacket, then I take a seat.

My paper is still blank, and I think about the word that I'll write on it. *Loneliness* is the only thing that comes to mind. I scribble it across the page, fold it into a paper airplane, and let it soar into the fire. The tip catches first, and then the wings. I watch as it burns to ash.

A cool breeze blows, and I let out a deep breath. My life has been a whirlwind of emotions.

Someone sits close to me on the log. If it's Lacy, I swear I'll make a scene, but as I turn, my mouth falls open.

CHAPTER 31

CLAIRE

When I pass the coffee-roasting building, I immediately notice all the vehicles. Many are parked on the curbs, and others are in the grass. The Christmas tree is already lit with colorful rainbow lights. I'm sad I missed it, but there is always next year. As I drive around the block, I see a line snaked around the tree. It takes me a minute to realize that's the line to take a picture with Santa. I leave the downtown area because it's packed. It seems like a long distance from the festivities, but it's nothing compared to a city block, plus I'm wearing proper footwear.

I park, grab my cell, then lock the truck. It takes me fifteen minutes to walk to the town square because it's farther away than I thought. If I were anywhere else, I'd have a small canister of pepper spray tucked in my hand, but not in Merryville. It's one of the safest towns in the nation, even with all the tourists traveling in and out each year. I'm not scared here, another reason why I love it so much.

As I round the corner and pass a food truck with extra-long corn dogs, I run into Hank.

His jaw drops. "Claire?"

I hold up my gloved hands. "Listen, I know you're

probably the last person on earth who wants to see me, but have you seen Jake?"

He grins widely. "Actually, yeah. I was just headin' to get a beer and then was gonna go back to where he was. Wanna join me?"

"Do you think he'll leave between now and then?"

"Nah," he says, chuckling. "He's not goin' anywhere. I'd guarantee it."

I let out a sigh. "Okay. But if he does..." I warn.

"Trust me, he won't."

We walk across the grass to the beer garden beside a circus tent. People are dancing inside and look like they're having the time of their lives. I've never experienced anything like this because my father refused to take us to carnivals as kids. They were beneath him. Of course, we went to all of the major theme parks and were treated like royalty, but the food was something we avoided. There's something special about buying an oversized piece of meat on a stick for six bucks.

"Did that sign say fried cheesecake?" I ask, walking past a truck with a big plastic slice of cheesecake attached to the roof.

"Yeah, and it's pretty good. Almost too much of a good thing, ya know? But if you're a cheesecake lover, you'll probably enjoy it. You want a beer?"

"Nah, I'm good. Thanks for asking."

He orders and pays the guy. Then we follow the sidewalk past the busy crowd of people.

"So why are you here?"

"I need to talk to Jake. I owe him an explanation. Also, I know he's pissed at me right now. I get it. I'm pissed at me, too."

Hank's brows rise. "I think he just misses you."

I swallow hard. "I miss him, too. I care about him a lot, and my conscience won't let me pretend like nothing happened between us. That would be a lie."

265

"I understand that. But I've got one question for ya, and no matter what, you have to answer honestly. No fibbing, *Claire Manchester*."

I huff. "Fine."

"Are you in love with him?"

I meet Hank's brown eyes, feeling my heart lurch forward. "Yes," I whisper. "It happened so fast, and he means a lot to me."

He snaps his fingers. "Well, damn. I guess I would've lost anyway."

"Lost what?"

Hank shakes his head. "I had this stupid bet with Jake that he couldn't make you fall in love with him."

My brows furrow. "So I was a game?"

"No, no, it wasn't like that. He pretty much told me to go fuck myself and refused to play. It was something we'd started as teenagers, and he'd bet his motorcycle that he could make any woman fall in love with him. Long story short, I was convinced you'd never go for a nice guy like him. Low-hanging fruit, ya know."

"Why would you think that?"

"Because you looked like a snob. Women like you typically go for the bad boys. I was also convinced that bike would be mine."

"Pardon my French, but you're an asshole."

He chuckles. "I know. Jake was going to give me his Harley, too. You know why?"

I shake my head.

"Because his word is his life," he says. "The man has integrity and loves hard, and he doesn't take advantage of people—or women." Hank doesn't realize his words are like a dagger to the heart.

He continues. "Jake's a good guy, Claire. He deserves to be happy and have someone reciprocate all the love he has to give. I don't like to see my best friend hurt. But there's no doubt he's not been the same since you left."

"I know. It's why I flew here to apologize and tell him the truth."

"Okay," Hank says, taking a sip of his beer. "I can respect that."

Laughter and music drift through the breeze, and I keep Hank's pace as we walk to the bonfire. It's stacked high, and when we enter the area, I'm handed a sheet of paper.

"You're supposed to scribble down what you'd like to leave behind and start the solstice without the dead weight. It's tradition," Hank tells me. I look at it, wondering what I'll put. "But this is where I leave you. If you keep walking straight, you'll find him at the front and to the left. You won't be able to miss him."

"Thank you," I say as he holds up his plastic cup and leaves.

From where I'm standing, I can hear the crackling of the wood as embers glitter above. I think about what I'd love to leave behind. The past. That's it. If I could bury it, I would. I'm sure my father would, too.

I write my word on the paper and fold it in half as I walk behind all the logs. A few people are making out, and a couple snuggles in a blanket two feet away. I understand why Jake is here, for the solitude.

As I carefully walk behind everyone, I spot Jake, and I see Lacy sitting next to him. My cheeks burn as she touches him and kisses him. At first, I'm devastated until he stands, creating space between them. I'm too far away to hear what he's saying, but based on his body language, he's not pleased.

Moments later, she says something else and then runs away, covering her face as she fake cries. When her back is to him, she drops her hands, and she's expressionless as if she's realized her manipulation didn't work. Jake returns to where he was sitting, staring at the flames.

He's so close, yet so far away. Right now, I could leave, and he'd never know the difference. Hank might tell him he ran into me, but it wouldn't matter. I feel as if I've already caused him enough pain, and the last thing I want to do is add to that. Then I remember my why and look down at the slip of paper in my hand and what I'm leaving behind me.

I take a few steps forward and sit down next to him.

My heart is beating so hard it might be lodged in my throat, but I push the fear of rejection aside.

At first, he doesn't notice. But when he turns to me, his jaw nearly touches the ground.

"Claire? What are you doin' here?"

I cross my feet at my ankles and stretch out my legs. "It's a very long story."

"I've got time," he says, moving his eyes from mine.

It doesn't take an optometrist to see the hurt I've caused. The light that burned bright is gone, and he seems like a hollowed-out version of himself. Guilt floods me, and I try to catch my breath by sucking in ragged air.

He looks over at me. "You good?"

Butterflies flutter in my tummy when he asks. "I will be," I whisper.

"Okay," he says, and the concern on his face isn't lost on me. I'd do anything to have him pull me against him and hold me in his arms. But I'll never be a Lacy; I'll never force myself on a man who doesn't want me. It's awkward as hell not to know where we stand, but I don't have the courage to ask, not yet.

"To answer your question on why I'm here, it's because I needed to have this conversation with you face to face. No more lies, Jake. No more secrets. We're past that, and I know you hate me, but—"

"I don't hate you."

"You should."

He shakes his head, picking up the flask from between his feet. "Want some?"

I take a big drink without asking what it is. I brace myself for whiskey, but my throat is nearly assaulted with cinnamon. I cough. "What is that?"

Jake chuckles. "Tastes like shit, doesn't it? This is Hank's idea of a good time."

I smile, and he glances over at me, then back at the fire. It's a start, at least. "His taste buds must be broken." But I take another swig, needing the liquid courage to work. I hand it back to Jake, and he puts his perfect lips to the top, but I force myself to look away. Emotions stream inside of me, and I try to find the right words, but everything still feels so wrong.

"So you drove here alone?" he asks.

This makes me laugh. "Yeah. Nearly ran out of gas again and got pulled over by a state trooper, but I'm here in one piece. Before the storm, too. I try not to make the same mistakes twice." There is more truth in that sentence than he understands.

"You were speeding?"

"And driving with my high beams and windshield wipers on. Swerving, too. The state trooper was convinced I was drunk, so I was given a sobriety test."

Jake tries to hold back laughter, but he fails and shakes his head. "Leave it to you."

"I know. But I refused to let anything stop me. I missed the tree-lighting ceremony, but I guess there's always next time."

He doesn't say anything, and his happiness fades quicker than I want. "I've missed you."

"I've missed you, too. And Tinsel," I say. "I thought about getting a cat after spending so much time with her."

"She's been meowing a lot since you've left. I think she got used to you."

I place my hand on my heart and swallow. I want to reach out and grab him and confess how fucking miserable I've been since I left, how I've done nothing but think about him, and how I finished that sad book and cried in the bathtub while drinking wine. But I don't. Not yet. The last thing I want to do is emotionally manipulate him. I don't want him to feel sorry for me, not when I've knowingly put myself in this position.

I'm used to fucking up and owning it and now is no different.

"When your father buys the farm, you think he'll immediately level it?" he asks, and it's a reminder of why I'm here.

"He probably would," I tell him truthfully and watch Jake's jaw clench. "But that's not happening."

He turns to me with confusion on his face. "It is, Claire."

I shake my head and stand, pulling an envelope from my back pocket and handing it to him.

He looks down at it and then back at me. "What is it?"

"Open it, please."

CHAPTER 32

JAKE

The envelope feels thick in my hand, and the angry part of my soul tells me to throw it in the fire and walk away because whatever is inside doesn't matter. But when I meet her sparkling blue eyes filled with hope and regret, I can't.

Claire's a woman who does things with intention. She wouldn't have flown from New York and driven this way with more weather rolling in without a particular reason. Not after what happened the first time she traveled here alone.

I'm fully aware that whatever is tucked inside this envelope will either help or destroy any potential of us ever having a relationship. With where we stand now, there is no in-between. That saddens me. I've never been one to have an all-or-nothing mentality, but with her, I have to.

Above all, I have to protect my heart.

I suck in a deep breath and turn my attention back to her. "Why did you block me?"

I don't flip open the flap; not yet, not until I get some of the answers I need. I don't care what it says and won't look until my questions are addressed.

"What?" Her cute button nose scrunches.

"I texted you, and it didn't go through. It said undelivered."

Her expression changes, and her perfect lips part. "Oh, I'm sorry. I received a lot of random calls because I think Dale leaked my number to retaliate against me. He's an asshole like that. So, to stop the hate, I changed my number. I would've texted you and told you, but I honestly thought I'd be the last person on earth you'd want to speak to. I wouldn't have been able to handle that, so I didn't try."

I almost smirk but hold it back, not allowing myself to grab on to a sliver of hope. Not yet, at least. "Okay. I'm sorry you had to go through that."

"No, please don't be. I'm used to changing my number every other year. It happens." She picks lint off her gloves, and I can tell she's nervous. "What did your text say?"

"It doesn't matter now." I glance down at her shoes, wishing we could go back in time to when we were comfortable around one another. I chuckle and point at her shoes. "Nice boots."

She beams. "Yeah. I got some like yours. Maybe I won't bust my ass or have to slide my way across a parking lot if it rains. They're comfortable and practical."

"Yeah, they are."

We grow quiet, and the silence takes over. There are so many unspoken words streaming between us. I want to know how she's been and if she's missed me as much as I've missed her, but I don't ask. It's not my business, not right now, not when everything between us is unsettled.

The wood cracks and pops, and the fire tenders add more limbs, causing the flames to rise slowly.

Claire clears her throat. "I've done a lot of soul-searching since I left. More than I think I ever have. I'm extremely sorry for lying and betraying your trust, Jake. It's something I never wanted to do."

"But you did," I mutter. "Are you sorry you lied or sorry you got caught?"

She shakes her head. "I'm sorry for hurting you and for lying. It's an apology I should've given you before I told you the truth."

"Tell me the truth. I want to hear it from the horse's mouth, Claire."

She draws in a deep breath. "Okay." She pauses for nearly a minute, then interlocks her fingers together and starts talking. "Initially, I was here for the tax auction that was taking place. My lawyer had been following the progress of the back taxes owed for years. When he got a special notification that the farm would potentially be sold the first week of December or January, I made a reservation at the inn. My dad's secretary is an idiot and booked the wrong location. And yes, I legitimately ran out of gas. None of that was fake. And I gave you one of my aliases, but it wasn't to deceive you. It's for my protection. Everyone knows the last name Manchester. The hotels and resorts are the first thing anyone thinks of. I didn't need anyone snooping on me or my life. If the wrong person finds me, I could be taken for ransom or hurt. So it's a rule when I travel: I'm Claire Chester."

I nod. "Okay."

"I was hesitant to let you help me because I knew about the farm already. I knew you were part of the family. My goal was to leave as soon as possible because I'd overstepped a boundary."

"You're right about that."

"I deserve that," she tells me. "I do. I deserve all of your frustration and anger. What I did was wrong. Staying with you while knowing I was there to buy the property should have never happened. But I didn't expect to fall in love with you in two weeks. Some will say that was my mistake. I don't regret it, though. I feel like I've known you all my life and that you knew me, the real me. I've never shared myself with anyone in the ways I shared myself with you. I've never felt comfortable enough. But Jake, you're different. You're not like anyone else. And I hurt you. That's not okay."

My eyes meet hers, and all I want to do is kiss her and taste the cinnamon alcohol on her lips.

"Once I realized what was happening, and after I met your adorable grandmother, I knew I couldn't go through with it. At that point, my father learned where I was and put the pieces together, and it all got out of control quickly. I fucked up big time. But I want you to know that I was never buying that property and taking it away from your family. I couldn't. I know it's easy for you and everyone else in this town and online to villainize me. I've read the posts. I spent an entire night scrolling and reading threads about me on Reddit. They hate me there. You'd think I kick puppies for shits and giggles."

I shake my head. "I know. I saw. Leave it to the internet to destroy a billionaire princess."

"Yeah, they're great at that. In case you're wondering, I don't kick puppies. I just have to take it, all of it, as per usual. It's why I keep to myself."

"I'm sorry," I whisper.

"Don't be. My problems aren't yours. Now, can you please open that envelope?"

I pull out a thin slip of paper. It's blank. Then I realize there's writing on the other side and flip it around to discover it's a receipt from the county.

At the bottom, I read: *All taxes paid with a credit balance of $100,000.*

"Claire, I can't accept this," I tell her, shaking my head, trying to return it to her as if that will make this all disappear.

"The money has already been transferred and put toward the account. You told me at the very beginning, when you allowed me to stay at your house that I could pay you whatever amount I wanted after my stay. Remember?" she reminds me.

"Yes."

She points to the receipt. "That amount doesn't fully cover it. I can't put a price on what I experienced with you."

My lips part as I get ready to protest, and she places her finger on my lips. Her touch nearly singes me, and I crave her so deeply it hurts. The hint of her perfume surrounds me, and I want to brush my scruff against the softness of her neck and smell her sweet skin, then run my fingers through her brown hair. But I don't. I keep my hands, lips, and thoughts to myself.

"You once told me that a person shouldn't look a gift horse in the mouth, and you had to explain what that meant. I added it to my Texas lexicon. And considering you taught me the meaning, I don't need to explain it to you." She glances at me with kind but sad eyes. "Please accept this. It's not charity. Just think of it as a rich, snobby girl overpaying for your hospitality for two weeks, okay?"

A small smile plays on my lips, and I shake my head. "Sure thing, Stubborn Susan."

"You're damn right. So it's settled, then." She lets out a relieved breath. "A woman who once fell in love with you also taught you about boundaries. And I won't be the one to walk all over yours. Being this close to you and not touching you is very difficult for me, and I know it's not easy for you."

"It's not," I say. It's harder than I think she knows.

"Your feelings are valid. Like I said before, I'll always, *always* regret hurting you, but I think what we both need right now is time. When and if you want to see me again, I'll be waiting for you, Jake Jolly." She sucks in a deep breath and writes something on her slip of paper. As she stands, she throws it in the fire. "Hopefully, I'll see you around town."

"You're not rushing back to New York on your daddy's private jet?"

She gives me a small laugh. "I don't fly private. Too much fanfare. And no, I'm not leaving anytime soon. I bought a house a few blocks from Main Street on Candy Cane Lane. I found magic here with you, and I want to lean into that more."

This news comes as a shock, and I'm not sure what to say. My expression probably says it all because I know no houses were on the market. And usually, when there are, they don't last long. "What? How?"

"I made an offer, and the owners couldn't refuse it. Take care of yourself, JJ." Claire waves and then walks away. I'm not able to take my eyes off her as she moves past the fire and fades into the crowd.

She's brave to show her face, with so many locals knowing what she did. But then again, if she's a Manchester, she's used to being treated that way, something I never wanted to do but something I'm guilty of, too. She's a good woman, compassionate, and not the villain the internet makes her out to be. It hurts my heart that she subjected herself to those vile things. I read them, knowing most of it wasn't true, but wondering if I was wrong about her. I wasn't, though.

The Claire I got to know is the real version of her. Not the act.

As I look down at the receipt, my hands shake. It's almost like I've won the lottery, like I'm one of the luckiest people in the world, even after everything I've been through. None of this feels real, and I'm shocked by the whirlwind of emotions. From finding out Mawmaw didn't have enough money to cover the taxes. To Lacy, weirdly begging me to take her back. To Claire moving to Merryville.

Am I living in the twilight zone? Is this some odd alternative reality that I've fallen into?

"Unbelievable," I whisper, almost tempted to pinch myself and make sure I'm not dreaming.

Being kind to Claire saved my family. She's a Christmas miracle.

I grin, thinking about all the highs and lows I've experienced. What has happened since December 1 is as odd as the stacks of solid gold bars on my grandmother's kitchen table.

CHAPTER 33

CLAIRE

Walking away from Jake is difficult, but I need to create space before I do something stupid and kiss him when he doesn't want it. Once again, I refuse to be a Lacy.

His lips looked soft, and I noticed his heated gaze. It felt like we were both struggling and this time around, I want to take things slow.

If he's willing to give me another chance, I won't mess it up again. I want to learn everything I can about him, and I'm happy to share anything about myself. There will be no secrets. That's a promise I'll make and keep.

I taste the cinnamon liquor still on my tongue and realize I'm thirsty. As I walk past the crowd, I see the cider stand. There's a giant plastic apple on top and a line that's at least thirty people deep. Since Ginger made it a point to mention it after she pumped my gas, I decide it's a must-try.

Going forward, I've decided I'll live my life for experiences, not because of expectations. No more hobbies that I hate. No more doing things I don't like because I want to fit in.

The line moves faster than I thought it would, but I decide to text my sister.

CLAIRE

I found him at the bonfire and gave him the receipt. He knows what I did.

EMMA

Aww. So did you two make up and kiss?

I laugh.

CLAIRE

No, that's not how this works. I didn't want to be pushy, so I walked away and gave him space. I've decided there's no rush on forever. Honestly, I don't expect him to immediately forgive me after what happened. We need time.

My phone rings as she calls me.

"I couldn't text anymore. My hands are full. I grabbed some Chinese food and a drink, so I'm chatting with you through my earbuds because if I drop my food, I might throw a fit. I'm hangry."

I snicker. "Whatever works for you. It's fine. What did you order?"

"Lo Mein. Egg rolls. Wontons. I feel like I got the whole menu. Anyway, I didn't call to chat about me and my dinner. What did he say? Did he seem happy to see you?"

"I don't remember everything, honestly. It was a whirlwind, and I couldn't believe I was sitting beside him. It didn't feel real." I keep my voice low, not wanting anyone to overhear. "He asked for the truth, so I told him and apologized. I don't know if he was happy to see me. Maybe? Maybe not. I guess time will tell." A few people grab their ciders, and the line moves some more. "Looks like he hasn't shaved since I left. And that sparkle in his eyes wasn't quite there. That's my fault, too. I know it is."

"You made it right, sis. That's all you can do. You should sleep well knowing that you made a difference. And stop blaming yourself so much. You put that man above a career that you've worked so hard for over the past decade. I'm sure he recognizes that, and if he doesn't, eventually he will."

"Standing up for what I believe in is really hard, but I'll do it again. Eventually, our father will forgive me, and if he doesn't, that's his problem, not mine. Jake's family won't have to suffer now, and that's all that matters."

"It's called having compassion, something a lot of people in our father's social class don't have," Emma says. "It's also something money can't buy."

"You're right about that. Hold on one second." I step up to the window and order a large apple cider. A minute later, I'm handed a gigantic cup with a thick cinnamon stick poking from the top. I wait to put the lid on top as the steam rises. It smells heavenly as I blow on it, but it's too damn hot to drink right now.

"I just got back to my place, and I'm gonna eat," Emma says.

"Great. I'll text you when I get home tonight. I've got one more thing to do."

"Awesome. I'm really proud of you. You deserve all the goodness in the world."

"Thank you, means a lot." I end the call and shove my phone into my back pocket.

As I walk farther through the crowd, I put the lid on my cider and take a sip. My mouth explodes with sweet cinnamon and apples as I listen to carolers dressed in full Victorian-style costumes. Once they finish their song list, I notice the line to see Santa is much shorter. I've got something on my Christmas list that I haven't asked for yet, so I step in line behind a mom and a little boy wearing an elf suit.

He looks adorable, and when his eyes meet mine, I give him a wink. Instead of returning the gesture, he sticks his tongue out. So I keep my attention pointed forward so I'm not tempted to do the same. He taps my leg and does it again. I cross my eyes at him, and he laughs.

The cider is so delicious I drink half of it while I wait, my gaze trailing over the festival. The people in the circus tent look like they're having a good time. A large group is doing line dances to "Cotton-Eyed Joe." That's something I've never done, so I open the notepad application on my phone and search for the note named "Southern Bucket List." Midway down is horseback riding and swimming in a pond. Then I see the one that says, "Take a picture with Santa," toward the bottom. It was added recently since I never had the opportunity as a child. Once I've finished my cider, I toss the cup in the trash. A teenager dressed as an elf asks me which photo package I'd like and then slides my card. A few minutes later, I'm led to an area that looks like Santa's workshop.

When I'm closer, Jake's dad notices me and immediately grins. He pats his lap, and I sit.

"Ho, ho, ho! Tell Santa what you want for Christmas," he says.

I lean in and whisper in his ear. "Forgiveness."

When he pulls away, he nods. "Consider it done," he tells me.

"Thank you," I say. "Thank you."

One of the elves snaps her fingers at me. The flash on the camera is so bright I can barely see after the photo is taken, but they still escort me away. When I push open the exit gate, I'm handed my picture. These elves are efficient as fuck.

As I walk away, I look down at the photo. A single tear runs down my cheek, knowing his parents don't hate me. I came here to undo my wrongdoings, and I hope I can accomplish that.

When I pass the cheesecake booth, I stop and order one. "No carbs" can kiss my ass. I take a bite and realize what Hank was talking about. It's sweet, but it's delicious.

Since I parked so far away, it gives me plenty of time to

think about my life and how angry my father is at me. Maybe one day he'll understand why I did what I did. Maybe one day he'll even forgive me. Until then, I'll live my life for me.

In the end, my father was right. I don't think I would've been happy running Manchester Holdings anyway. Maybe he understood that.

Carrying my half-eaten cheesecake on a stick, I make it to my truck. Cars are closely parked in front and behind me, and there isn't a scenario where I don't crash into one trying to leave. Instead of trying, since I know my limits, I grab my carry-on out of the back seat and head to my new home.

I laugh because here I am, walking down the road with a suitcase in tow, just like the first time I visited. But this time, it's not temporary.

When I turn onto the sidewalk of the neighborhood—I'll now be calling home—an overwhelming amount of happiness soars through me. I check the addresses, and when I'm standing in front of my new place, all I can do is smile.

"Home sweet home." I breathe in deeply, knowing this is where I'll live. No more New York.

White Christmas lights trim the roof and windows, lighting the entire yard. Every house on the street is decorated. It's a requirement for anyone who lives within city limits, something I adore about this place.

The two-story country home with red shutters and a green roof is festive, and I adore it already. I take the steps up the porch, loving the two tiny Christmas trees on both sides of the entryway. I punch in the key code, and the door unlocks. Once inside, I flick on the lights and am amazed by how spacious it is. Or maybe it seems like that because it's empty.

I stroll through the living room, kitchen, the main bedroom that's downstairs, and the gigantic bathroom. Then I make my way upstairs, where there are two more bedrooms, an upper den area, and a bathroom. To be honest, this is a lot of house for me, and I'll probably stay downstairs most of the time, but that's okay.

I'm in Merryville, and that's all that matters.

I wake up and stretch, feeling like a million pounds have been lifted from my chest. The house is empty, something I told my real estate agent I'd take care of when I was settled. Right now, all I have is a bed, a couch, and appliances.

Last night, the temperature dropped into the twenties. I turned on the furnace before I fell asleep, and I'm thankful because there isn't a chill in the room.

After I use the bathroom and brush my teeth, I go to the kitchen, where there's an espresso maker that's like Jake's. It was a requirement of mine. The only problem is there are no coffee beans, and I have no dishes. So I'm currently running with no caffeine.

When I glance out the front window, dark, angry clouds float above. I return to my room and grab my cell phone to check the forecast. There's a break for the next few hours, so if I get dressed and leave now, maybe I'll avoid getting wet.

I pull a pair of jeans and a sweater from my suitcase and grab my beanie with the fuzzy ball on the end. After getting ready, I wait ten minutes, then make the hike to my truck.

As I glance at my neighbor's house across the street, it's hard not to notice their pretty Christmas tree in the front window. I didn't have one in my penthouse, but I think that will change this season.

Christmas Day is in seventy-two hours, and I know the perfect place to get a tree. I'll add that to my list.

CHAPTER 34

JAKE

"**G**lad you took my advice and pulled the stick outa your ass," Hudson says when I walk past him. I've got a coffee in my gloved hand and wore an extra-thick coat since it's nearing the twenties.

I give him a grin, not ready to tell him what I'm smiling about yet. I'll share the news over lunch with him and Lucas, but until then, I've got a shift to get through. "What do you need me to do today?"

"Well, since you're in a better mood, why don't you help shoppers? Lucas is hungover, and I'd rather put him on precut duty so he can get over *his* attitude."

I nod and go to the front, where we keep the golf carts to drive customers around. The farm is so large we've found this to be the easiest way to travel quickly.

It's just past seven, and we've only been open for ten minutes, but the parking lot is already full. It's incredible to see so many last-minute shoppers driving all this way. Then again, it's also odd because I don't remember the last time we've been this busy.

A woman who reminds me of Mawmaw pulls up with her Cadillac's window down. "Hi, sweetie, are you JJ?"

"Yes, ma'am."

"Honey, I'd like for you to help me pick out a tree," she says, her Southern drawl thick.

"Great! Why don't you park and meet me right there?" I point in the direction of the parking area, and she quickly finds a spot.

I walk to the edge of the sidewalk. "You from around here?"

"No, just outside of Dallas."

My eyes widen. "That's kinda far, almost ten hours away."

"That's right," she says. "But I wanted to meet you after hearin' about you on the internet."

I shake my head. "Sorry, ma'am, I didn't get your name, but also, I'm not sure what you're referencin'."

"It's fine," she says, not explaining herself. "You can call me Mary Jo."

"Okay, Mary Jo." I shoot her a wink.

Before leaving, she asks a random person if they'll take a picture of the two of us together and hands them her cell phone. She's a foot and a half shorter than me, and I tower over her, but I pose for the camera.

"Thank you, dear. My granddaughters are gonna think I'm the coolest grandma now."

I laugh, even though I'm utterly confused. I've learned when people act delusional, sometimes it's better not to ask questions. It's also way too early in the morning for all of that.

"So would you like to handpick a tree, or do ya want a precut?"

"Let's cut one."

"Sounds good. I'll be right back to pick ya up." I slide the keys off a hook in the payment booth, then hop on the cart and pull it around for her. She climbs on, and then I drive her around the farm.

"How tall would you like it to be?"

"Lumberjack height." She winks.

All I can do is chuckle as she chooses a random one and pulls out her phone to record me standing next to it to prove it's the same height as me. Then I grab my saw from the back and start whittling away at it.

I can hear her talking as she holds it up. "Look. JJ is cuttin' my tree down for me. Now he's loadin' it up. And we're headin' back to go pay." She blows kisses at the camera as I wave, then I drop her off.

When I return, Hudson is standing by the payment shack, and down the sidewalk, there is a line of women that goes as far as the eye can see. As soon as I come into view, they scream.

"What is goin' on?" I ask him.

He holds out his hand. "They're all waitin' for you to chop their trees."

"What?" I say, alarm written all over my face. "Why? You know I can't possibly do that. That's too many people. I'd need to clone myself."

A smirk touches his lips. "Oh, you're gonna love this." Hudson turns his phone around, and there's a picture of Claire with her sister, who looks exactly like her. Under that picture, there's a long post she wrote to her *fifteen million* social media followers. I quickly scan over it.

See this woman right here? This is my older sister Claire, but her friends call her CeCe. There are a lot of rumors being said about this brave woman in the media right now. Many of you have messaged me awful things that I wouldn't say to any of my enemies. However, she deserves praise because she chose love. You see, she's gone through life dating pieces of shit and getting used by people, including my father. And then she met a lumberjack of a man who picked her up when she was stranded in the middle of nowhere in Texas. This man offered her a ride, a place to stay, and his heart.

Talk about a lumbersnack! And yes, I've seen pictures. He looks like a Hemsworth, and I'm told his brothers do, too.

Anyway, the details regarding Manchester Holdings and Jolly Christmas Tree Farm aren't important. There is no deal. My faithful followers know I don't involve myself in family business for a reason but leave my sister alone.

While she can be a Grinch in public, she's kind. And if you're in Texas, you all should go buy a tree from Jolly Christmas Tree Farm this season and put them on the map. If you're lucky, maybe you'll meet the infamous JJ. But back off, ladies. His heart is taken.

XO Emma

P.S. I might have to visit and have a sit on Santa's lap. Also, I heard his brothers are single.

I swallow hard, feeling a lump in my throat as I look into Hudson's eyes. "Can I disappear, please?"

He grins widely. "You were searching for a Christmas miracle to save the farm. Well, I think this is it."

I pull him to the side of the shack because there are over fifty pairs of eyes staring. Then I hand him the receipt I stuffed in my pocket this morning.

He takes it. "What's this?"

"I was going to tell you over lunch."

He carefully reads every word and then looks at me with wide eyes. "Paid in full? How? What did you do?" He searches my face, a smile not touching his lips.

"I didn't do anything," I admit. "It was Claire. She said she owed me for letting her stay at my cabin."

"What?" he yells, and I hear his voice bounce through the woods and echo.

The crowd goes quiet, and I peek around the side of the shack, then back at him. I don't know why I'm nervous. I never wanted this attention.

"Please explain," Hudson says.

"I saw her last night at the festival," I say. "She apologized and gave me that."

"And then what happened?"

"Then she left." I shrug.

He pinches the bridge of his nose. "Please tell me you at least told her how you feel and you didn't let her show up, pay off the family's debt, and then leave."

"No, I didn't mention that at all. It was a weird night, so excuse me for not pouring my heart out to her after I hadn't seen her for a week. I have time, though."

Hudson shakes his head. "I'm not following along."

"She bought a house in town." His mouth falls open, and he looks just as shocked as I felt when she told me. "I know," I say.

I hear hoots and hollers from the long line of women waiting for me. They grow louder, and I know I can't keep hiding. "We should probably go see what's goin' on out there," I suggest.

He nods, places his hand on my shoulder, and squeezes it before we round the building that was providing privacy. I stop in my tracks as I come face to face with Claire. She looks just as confused as I am. Whispers float through the crowd as I approach her, and some pull out their cell phones.

"What are they doing here, and why did they burst into cheers when they saw me?" she asks as if I have all the answers.

Considering there's a crowd forming, and I don't want to put on a show for anyone today, I grab her hand and lead her to the golf cart I just arrived on.

As we drive away together, they erupt into applause.

"Uh, can you pretty please tell me what's going on?"

I burst into laughter as we escape. Once we have some privacy, I stop driving and turn to her. "Your sister made a post online."

She places her face in her hands. "Do I want to know what she said?"

"Probably. Considering it was about you and me."

"Please tell me this is a joke."

When I shake my head, Claire pulls her phone from her pocket and unlocks it. She goes to her sister's social media profile and begins reading the same post I just speed read. Then she scrolls the comment section, and I notice her cheeks are rosy red. "I'm so sorry. I didn't know she was going to post this. I'll tell her to remove it immediately."

I smirk, finding it adorable that she's embarrassed. "It's fine. I noticed she called you CeCe. I dunno if that still works, considering."

"And I thought you did your research on me." She bumps her body against mine. "My middle name is Caitlyn, so it still works. Were all those women lined up for you?"

"Yeah, apparently so." I sigh, then meet her blue eyes.

"Guess that means you won't have any issue finding your person. It's like the *Lumberjack Bachelor*."

I burst into laughter. "Darlin', you jealous?"

She bites her bottom lip, not answering the question.

We sit in silence for a few seconds, then I ask, "Uh, so what are you doin' here? Didn't expect to run into you today. Not that I'm complainin'."

"I thought I'd get a Christmas tree for my house. Everyone in my neighborhood has these beautiful trees in their windows, and I've never purchased one before."

"Never?"

She shakes her head. "Nope. But I know a guy who's a lumberjack during tree-cutting season."

I lick my lips and nod, then press on the gas pedal of the cart and drive her through the rows. "When you see one you like, let me know."

Her eyes on me, she smiles. "Okay."

"The woman I helped before you told me she wanted one that was lumberjack size."

Claire snickers. "Don't blame her. That sounds great. What, six foot three?"

"Yeah." We pass my brother Lucas on a golf cart, and he looks at me, then Claire and his mouth falls open. I lift my fingers at him to wave.

He yells, "What? How!"

"Shut up! You're supposed to be taking care of precuts!" I yell as we make a turn onto another row. The trees are older and much taller. I park, and we get off the cart and take a stroll.

"I've missed you," I mutter. "Tinsel misses you."

She turns to me. "I've missed you both. But especially her."

I chuckle. "I'll let her know when I get home. Or maybe you can stop by sometime and tell her yourself."

"I'd like that." There's another long pause. "I hate this tension between us," she admits, brushing her gloved hand across the branches.

"I do, too. But I don't know what to say. I don't know how to act. All I want to do is kiss you and hold you and forgive you. But I'm really fucking afraid of being hurt again," I confess.

"I understand. This time around, I have no secrets. I don't want to rush. I want to know everything I can about you. Like, what's your favorite color? What did you want to be when you grew up? Your lucky number?"

I take a step forward. "Green. A lumberjack. Seven. Yours?"

"Red. CEO. Eighteen."

I laugh. "Somehow, none of those answers surprises me."

She grabs my hands and pulls me toward her. Then she looks up into my eyes. "I'm not going anywhere, Jake. I'm here for the long haul. But I won't be a Lacy. I won't chase you if you don't want me. I don't need an answer right now, but if there's no chance in hell for us, please respect me enough to let me know so I can move on and not have false hope."

My heart thumps forward, and my brows furrow. "CeCe, I don't want anyone else. Just you."

I place my fingers under her chin as I search her eyes. Then I slowly lean in and gently kiss her. Emotions overtake me, and I pull away, swallowing it down. She's breathless as her eyes flutter open.

"I finished that damn book," she says.

"Yeah? And?"

"I cried like a baby," she admits.

I wrap my arm around her. "I guess you aren't dead inside, then."

"Not anymore." She pokes her finger into my chest. "And it's all because of you. Now, maybe we should get this tree chopped, considering you have a fan club lined up to meet the infamous Jake Jolly. Just remember who your number one is, though."

"Right back atcha, babe." I shoot her a wink.

"I think this one would be perfect," she says, pointing at a tree that's the same height as me.

"You gonna need some help settin' this up at your house?" I ask, going to the cart and grabbing my saw and gloves to protect my hands.

"Nah, I got it," she confidently says.

I give her a look. "Love an independent woman."

"I don't expect you to drop everything for me during the busiest time of the year. I'll be fine. So, are you going to let me chop this tree down?"

Taking a step back, I look at her with a lifted brow, then grab a pair of extra gloves from the cart. "Abso-fucking-lutely."

She puts the gloves on, and I hand her the saw. "You'll use two hands at the base of the tree."

I guide her over to it and get down on my knees. She looks down at me, and I smile. I pat the ground, and she joins me.

"Like this?" she asks.

"Yeah, now go back and forth on it, and when it feels like the saw is getting caught, I'll help ya."

She laughs, putting her weight into it as the teeth of the blade cut against the bark. After a couple of minutes, she takes a breather.

"I thought this was supposed to be easy. I have so much more respect for lumberjacks." She wipes sweat off her brow, then returns to it.

When she's halfway through the base, I stand and add some weight to the tree. It cracks and then falls over. Claire stands, placing her boot on the bark and finishing the job.

I lift my hand, and she gives me a high five. "You kicked ass. Got a perfect cut."

"Thanks. Had a good teacher." She winks. "First time I've ever done that. Feels good."

"Might need to make it a tradition," I suggest.

"I'd like that a lot," she admits as I grab the tree and load it on the golf cart. Before I start the engine, I turn to her. "You sure I'm what you want in life? I'm not a billionaire. Just a Christmas tree farmer with a sassy cat."

"And that's what makes you so damn special."

CHAPTER 35

CLAIRE

Jake drives us back to the front of the farm, and I insist on paying. Hudson refuses and stands his ground. With them staring at me like I've lost my mind, I realize it's a lost cause.

"Fine," I say, tucking my card back into my pocket.

"Will you be joining us for Christmas?" Hudson asks.

I glance at Jake, and I nearly melt.

"The invitation still stands if you're not busy," he says.

It's hard for me to hold back a smile. "I'll have to check my calendar."

"Do that and let me know so I can let my parents know." Jake smirks. "Wanna drive up here so I can help load your tree?"

"Sure, I'll be right back." I suck in a deep breath and make my way to the truck. The line of women waiting for Jake is impressive. Shows me how extensive my sister's reach is.

I honestly can't believe she posted that last night after we spoke. I even texted her that I was going to bed, and she didn't mention it. I'll have to call her later.

When I arrived this morning, I found a parking spot that

would make it easy for me to drive straight out. I hop in, crank it, and the engine roars to life. When I arrive at the loading area, Jake's eyes widen.

I climb out, using the running board since it's so tall.

"You rented one of the largest trucks Ram makes."

"And? It drives like a dream. Already got a speeding ticket, too."

"Wait, are you serious?" Hudson asks.

"Yeah. A state trooper pulled me over and made me miss the Christmas tree lighting."

Hudson chuckles. "Ahh yeah. The troopers can be dicks. They never give anyone a break."

"He thought I was drunk and made me take a sobriety test," I explain.

A howl of laughter escapes Jake. Then I notice we're being watched by everyone who is waiting for him. His eyes meet mine.

"You good?" he asks and places his hand on my shoulder and squeezes.

"I am now," I whisper.

Jake loads the tree in the back for me, then opens my door. I step up and climb inside, then roll down the window. He leans against the truck. "Let me know about Christmas," he says.

I meet his eyes. "I'll be there."

"What are your plans today?"

"I'm not sure," I say. "I haven't fully decided yet. Want to get home before it starts raining."

"Whatever you do, have fun. If you struggle with that tree, call me?"

"I've got this," I say. I'm stalling because I'm not ready to leave yet, but I force myself to go.

He looks as if he wants to say something more but doesn't. And I understand why. I need to earn his trust again. It will take time for us to get back to where we were.

I drive away, and when I look in the rearview mirror, I feel happiness because it's not goodbye. This time, it's a new beginning.

Cars are parked on the side of the road and are stacked nearly to the farm's exit. I make my way back to town. It's crowded, and the sidewalks are full of people in heavy winter coats and mittens. Carolers are on each street corner singing. Magic fills the air, the magic of Merryville.

By some Christmas miracle, I find a place to park that's not too difficult to pull into, even though I have no idea how far forward I need to be. When I get out, I see the back of the vehicle is still in the street, so I climb in and pull forward. Eventually, I'll get this right.

I tuck my hands into my pockets and slide into the home goods store. Inside, it's full of Christmas decor, dishes, decorations, pretty much everything I need. A woman strolls from the back of the store and greets me with a grin.

"Hello! Lookin' for anything in particular?"

"I just moved into a house and have nothing but a couch and a bed. So I need everything." I look at the living room display with mantel decorations over the faux fireplace, a beautiful Christmas tree with snowflake ornaments and white lights, and a rug that's striped like a candy cane.

"That's exciting. Congratulations," she offers.

"Thanks." I turn and study the display. "Can I purchase this?"

The woman is confused. "Everything?"

"Yeah, I'd love to have my living room look exactly like this. It feels very cozy."

"The furniture, too?"

"Yes, please." I sit on the large leather recliner. Closing my eyes, I imagine myself in my house taking a nap, and then I turn and look at her over my shoulder. "Do you work on commission?"

"I do," she confirms.

"Great. I'd like that dining room setup, too," I tell her. She excuses herself to grab a pen and paper to write everything down.

The table is large enough for eight people and has a long red-and-white Christmas runner down the middle. Silverware is rolled into red napkins with gold reindeer embellishments. The chairs are carved from wood with high backs. I don't plan on having that many people over, but maybe I'll make friends or invite JJ's family for dinner. "Oh, I need dishes. Plates, pans, skillets, pretty much everything. Especially coffee mugs."

She leads me over to a wall with floor-to-ceiling shelves filled with individual items and sets. I point at some white ones with gold trim and smile. "Those will be perfect." I turn to her and read her nametag. "So, Magnolia, how difficult would it be to deliver this stuff to my place today?"

Her brows rise. "I think I could make it happen. But you'll be charged a rush delivery fee."

"Thank you. I'll be happy to pay whatever." I add a few more items to my list. Toward the back of the store, I come across some costumes for animals and see a tiny Santa hat that would look adorable on Tinsel. I grab it and take it to the counter.

Magnolia is busy tapping away on the computer and scanning barcodes from a binder. As she continues, I see two coffee mugs stacked on top of one another on a small table with other knickknacks. One says HIS, and the other says HERS. I grab the set and place it on the counter.

Thirty minutes later, Magnolia's eyes are wide.

"Ma'am…" She hesitates.

"You can call me CeCe," I say.

"CeCe." She clears her throat. "This is your total."

She turns the screen around, and I see it's close to seventeen thousand dollars.

"Great. Do you have the delivery fee added?"

She nods.

"Would you like anything for yourself?"

Her mouth slightly falls open. "You're serious?"

"Yeah. You've helped me tremendously. Whatever you want, add it to my total."

She walks over to the baby clothes with one-word sayings on the front and grabs two onesies.

"I'm expectin'," she admits.

"Oh, congrats! It's a congrats, right?"

She grows giddy with excitement. "Oh yeah. I've been tryin' for the last eight years, and it finally happened. I'm thrilled and excited. Nervous. But that's normal. Not sure what I'm havin' yet."

"Absolutely. I love buying gifts. Have you registered anywhere?" I grab an armful of baby items and carry them to the front for her.

"Not yet. But thank you. Thank you so much."

We return to the register, and I pull my card from my pocket. She asks for my driver's license and card and compares the names. Her eyes widen. "You're Claire Manchester."

"In the flesh," I say with a wink.

"I, uh, I, I…"

"My friends call me CeCe. Less formal and all that."

"You're royalty," she tells me.

"Trust me, I'm not. Need my address?"

She hands me a piece of paper and a pen. I write it down.

"I hope they're paying you a nice commission." I sign on the machine as she prints out my receipt.

"They are."

"I'm so glad you helped me. Thanks again! Oh, what time should I expect them to show up?"

"Probably right after lunch. We'll spend the rest of the morning packing everything for you."

"I'll make sure I'm home," I promise.

"You're a Christmas miracle. Thank you again for

everything," she offers as she walks me to the door. I give her another wave and make my way to the coffee shop on the corner. It's got large windows out front, and inside, I see a few people tapping away on their laptops. When I enter, the bell above the door dings, and I go to the counter.

"Black coffee," I say.

The woman behind the counter shakes her head. "That's a Grinch drink."

I furrow my brows. "So you won't make me a black coffee?"

"Babe, you gotta live a little. Try something else."

I laugh. "Surprise me, then."

"My favorite words," she says. "What size?"

Before I can answer, she holds up her hand. "Never mind. You look like the type of woman who wants it large."

She goes to the espresso machine and brews some shots, mixes different syrups inside, adds a splash of something, then rings me up. I read her nametag.

"What does BJ stand for?" I ask.

"Bristol Jolly."

I laugh and shake my head.

"Why is that funny? Upset it's not a weird blow job joke?"

"God, no. Are you related to Jake?" I sip my coffee, and caffeine and sugar explode in my mouth, but it's not too overwhelming and finishes light. "This is great."

"JJ? Yeah, he's my cousin. Wait, are you Claire?" she asks. "You're back in town?"

I guess everyone in Merryville knows who I am. I shrug with a grin and extend my hand, and she shakes it. "Nice to meet you. I didn't realize he had more cousins. And yeah, I officially moved here. Just bought a house on Candy Cane Lane."

"Couldn't have predicted that one." She's confident and doesn't seem to care about who I am, and I like that.

"Me either. Anyway, why weren't you at Moonshiners the night I met everyone?"

"I'm twenty. They don't like it when I sneak in, so I don't try anymore. They caught me using Wendy and Bella's licenses far too many times. They're my older sisters."

"I can see the resemblance." I take another sip. "This coffee is great. It's nice to meet you."

"You too. Need anything else?"

I glance around and see a shelf of coffee beans from the local roasters. I grab two bags, and she adds them to my total. I swipe my card and then make my way to the general store.

Call me spoiled, but I've never been grocery shopping. I've always had my food delivered each week.

When I walk in and see all the food and fruit and bread, I'm amazed. It's foreign to me, but I grab a cart and walk down every aisle with my coffee cup in tow.

I buy anything and everything. I take the basket across the street, and it clanks and shudders on the pavement. People stare, but I'm at the point in my life where I don't give a fuck. I'm happy because I'm in Merryville, and the man I've fallen head over heels with kissed me today. And that's all that matters.

After I pull into my driveway, I get out, and as soon as I glance at the tree in the back, sprinkles hit my cheeks. I look up at the angry sky. Part of me had hoped the forecast I read earlier was wrong.

Clearly, it isn't, so I pick up my pace.

After I drop the tailgate, I grab the stump of the tree and tug on it using all my weight. I inch it back, pulling it until it falls on the ground with a whoosh. The branches are tied tightly together, so at least I don't have to wrestle with it too much. Turning around, I grab it with both hands and drag it across the driveway and up the sidewalk. It's heavy, so I have to take a quick breather before I go up the steps. Tree needles mark the trail I took. When thunder rolls, I continue up the steps, then I realize the tree stand I bought hasn't been delivered yet. So I give up, leaving it until I have everything in place for it to be set up.

I unlock the door, then I rush to the truck and grab as many grocery bags as I can, sliding them up my arm. They dig into my skin, but it's either that or make five hundred trips, and considering it's now raining, I opt for the temporary pain.

My groceries need to be put up. I have a tree lying on my porch. And I have a house full of furniture and decorations being delivered after lunch.

I'm living, and for once, I feel normal. Something I've only dreamed of.

CHAPTER 36

JAKE

After work, I'm exhausted from entertaining people for ten hours straight. While it would be nice to go home, shower, and then lounge around and relax, I have an overwhelming urge to talk to Claire.

Seeing her this morning was a pleasant surprise. How it felt to kiss her has been on my mind since it happened. I'd love to meet her for dinner at the café, but she changed her number, and I never got her new one. But, since I'm so tired, I opt for my first option and just plan to talk to her tomorrow.

However, I have a feeling she won't be randomly buying another Christmas tree in the morning. So I'll have to go to her.

The next day at work is exactly like the one prior, except the line of women waiting is even longer. When Hudson sees me, he chuckles.

"It's not funny," I explain. "Do you know how many numbers I got yesterday?"

"Five?"

"Fifty," I tell him. "And they were all like, 'If you and Claire don't work out, call me.'"

He slaps his hand on his thigh and laughs harder.

"Dude, maybe you should be escorting them around," I say. "They actually have a chance with you."

"Nah, they don't," he says.

"I'll be happy to," Lucas says.

"Can you please let him?" I nearly beg Hudson.

"They came to see you, though. Customer satisfaction guaranteed."

"Right, but they're not cuttin' the trees. They're too busy watching me on my hands and knees doing it for them."

"And that's why I'm creating a new option. Precut. Cut yourself. Or have a Jolly personally cut your tree for you. The last one comes at a premium."

"I feel like I'm being pimped."

Hudson pats me on the shoulder. "That's a good way to think about it. Now, go get 'em, tiger."

As soon as I come into view, the crowd screams. I now understand what it feels like to be a celebrity or how Claire felt in her twenties when the paparazzi followed her. Knowing I can't do this every day of the season, I pull out my Uno reverse card.

"Ladies!" I whistle loudly, the one my mama used when we were kids. The last time I had to pull it out was to get Claire's attention when she was busy being a Stubborn Susan. "Hi!" I yell.

"We can't hear you," someone says from the back of the crowd. I walk over to the pay booth where Wendy is happily serving hot cocoa.

"Hey, you still got that megaphone back there?" I ask.

She nods. "One second." She bends down and reaches under the counter and grabs it, then hands it to me.

I move back in front of the crowd, press the wrong button, and it squeaks. Then I click the other one. "What about now?"

They erupt into applause. "Hi, good mornin'. I'm Jake. My friends call me JJ."

I hear several of them verbally swoon.

"We know who you are!" one woman screams from the back, and it only energizes everyone else.

"Thank you! Okay, so here's the deal. Y'all all know I'm only one man. And honestly, all this attention is kinda freakin' me out."

"Marry me!" someone yells.

I laugh nervously. "Example *A*."

Several ladies chuckle. "I'd like y'all to meet my very handsome but single brothers. Hudson, come on out here and meet everyone." I wait for him to step into view, then continue. "Ladies, this is my older brother Hudson. He's thirty-eight going on thirty-nine and is more of the serious type, but you'll know if he laughs at your jokes, it's actually funny."

I wait for him to break into a smile, but he doesn't.

"See? He's just showing you how broody he can be. He might have a hard exterior, but he's like M&M's, soft on the inside." I stop speaking before I rub his buttons a tad too hard.

"Now, my younger brother. This is Lucas." He walks out like he's on a mini runway and does a turn before coming and standing next to me. "He's thirty-two and likes to goof around. If you like a teddy bear of a guy, he's it. Everyone says he's like my twin. Honestly, think of them as extremes of my personality. Hudson is more of my serious side, and Lucas is more of my funny side. I just stand somewhere in the middle."

Most eyes are on them, and I let out a relieved breath. "The truth is, my heart is taken, and I'm only one man." The awws happen simultaneously.

"And I know you're here for a reason, and it ain't to say hi. So please, find a friend in the crowd and make a day out of cutting a beautiful tree. You probably have something in common, like you might like books." I raise my hand, and several raise theirs, too.

"Some of you may like brown-haired, green-eyed single men." The majority raise theirs. "And if that's you, one of these fine gentlemen will be happy to get on their knees for you"—I clear my throat, patting them on the back—"and cut your tree down. So if you're ready to get a choppin', feel free. I'll be right here and will be willing to chat with any of ya if you have questions that aren't about my relationship status."

Hudson shakes his head as Lucas bursts into laughter. Women surround them, and I move to the side and return the megaphone to Wendy.

"That went well," she says. "Hudson looked pissed."

"That's what he gets for tryin' to pimp me out." I shake my head. "If he thought I was gonna sit around and be worked to the bone when my woman is back in town, he's got me fucked up. That's not happenin'."

She knocks on the counter and howls with laughter. "Well, since your schedule has been cleared, whatcha plan on doin' for the rest of the day?"

I check the time. It's not even eight. "I'm gonna help them. I'm not a complete dick, but I'm leavin' here at five on the dot."

"Yeah? Gonna go see her?"

"You bet your ass."

After work, I shower, then I stop by the café and order food to go. Glenda immediately rushes over and pulls me to the side. "Did you know CeCe is back?"

I burst into laughter because she thinks she's telling me something I don't already know. "Who do you think this other bowl of chicken and dumplings is for?"

She pats my back. "Good. I was hoping that was the case. I'm throwing in some chocolate cake for you two to celebrate."

"Thank you," I tell her. "How much do I owe ya?"

"On the house." A few minutes later, she hands me a paper bag with her logo on the outside, and she tries to shoo me away. I give her a hug with a thank-you, then head to the flower shop. When I enter, the same woman who helped me before is behind the counter. She immediately perks up when she sees me. "Back again?"

"Yeah," I say. I know she probably saw the flowers I left on the sidewalk last week. "I need a Christmas dozen," I tell her. It's red and white roses mixed together with mistletoe sprigs throughout.

She returns with my order, and I happily pay. "Hope she gets them this time," she says.

"Me too," I say and climb into the truck. My heart rate ticks up at the thought of seeing my girl.

The truth is, I have no idea where Claire lives. I just remember she said Candy Cane Lane. So I turn onto North Pole and drive toward South Pole. Toward the middle of the neighborhood, I see the large Ram truck she rented parked crooked in the driveway. It makes me laugh as I find a place on the street. When I take to the sidewalk, I'm impressed by the lights on the house and the tree we cut down displayed in her window. I'm also impressed that she was able to get that tree in by herself, and it looks perfect.

As I get closer, I hear the fire alarms going off inside. I

pick up my pace and run up the steps. I frantically knock on the door. "Claire! Open up."

I move to the window and can see around the top of the tree. There's smoke inside, and she's in the kitchen waving an oven mitt around. She opens the oven and pulls out a tray of something. I tap hard on the window and capture her attention. When she finally sees me, she rushes over and opens the door. The alarms are still blaring. "Sorry! I didn't hear you. Oh, what's that?" She looks down at the food, and I hand her the flowers.

Then I rush inside her house and open the window in her kitchen. Christmas music is blaring, her fireplace is lit, and it's the perfect temperature. There's a bottle of wine on the counter and a half-drunk glass.

I turn off the oven and look down at the black crisps on the tray. "Chicken?"

"Cookies," she states, and I try not to burst into laughter.

The ingredients on the counter look familiar. "Gingerbread?"

She nods. "I wanted to start my own tradition. And I wanted to make enough to eat through Christmas. Also, flowers?"

"Yes, I thought you'd like them," I tell her.

"Love them, thank you. They're beautiful." She smells them and puts them in a vase.

"You are. It looks incredible in here," I tell her, noticing the rug resembling a giant peppermint, her gorgeous tree, and all the decorations on her mantel. "You did this?"

She chuckles, grabbing the pan of burned cookies and scraping them into the trash. She sets the pan on top of another one that looks the same. "I did, but I can't take credit. The home goods store had it all set up, and I loved it, so I had them deliver it to me. But I did decorate the tree on my own."

I cross my arms over my chest and smirk. "I'm impressed."

"What's in the bag?" She glances at it, grinning.

"Open it up," I tell her.

She pulls out the chocolate cake and two large bowls. When she peels the top off one, she inhales it and moans. "What is it? Smells incredible."

"Chicken and dumplings," I say. "One of my favorites when it's chilly outside."

Claire grabs two spoons, then hands me one. "Wanna eat in the living room?"

"Sure." I move to the kitchen and grab our food. I carefully set it on the table in front of her couch, and she plops beside me. We're close, almost too close, but I don't move. She dips her spoon in, pulls out a thick dumpling, and takes a bite. "Oh my, this should be illegal. Thanks for this. I was starving. It's like you knew."

"Glenda's treat. She gave us cake, too." I point at it.

"I saw her yesterday at dinner, and she asked if you were joinin' me. It hurt my heart to tell her no. Was pure disappointment."

I chuckle. "Yeah, I think she's a fan, which, she can get in line. It's been insane at work."

She gives me a sly grin. "I told my sister to remove your name and the farm name. She did, but I think the damage has already been done."

"Yeah, the internet is latching on to the story."

"I'm sorry," she offers.

I shake my head. "No more apologizing the rest of the night, okay?"

She moves her gaze back to her food. "Okay. I'll try."

I point to her fireplace. "Natural gas?"

A giggle releases from her. "No way I'm chopping wood in the winter."

"Aww, you're no fun," I joke. "Makes it easy, though."

"Yeah, but it's not quite the same as the wood burning and

the light fading throughout the night. Loved falling to sleep to that." She blushes and glances at me.

I find it cute that she's trying to avoid talking about us. It's hard, though. I get it. Anytime I'm around her, all I can think about is how I wish we were back at my house together.

"I met your cousin BJ yesterday." She laughs. "Refused to sell me a black coffee, told me it was a Grinch drink."

"Oh yeah, I haven't introduced you to all of my family yet. There are a lot more Jollys. Some of them are just much younger than us, so we don't hang out because of the age difference."

"She was hilarious and confident. I could tell she doesn't take shit from anyone," she says.

"Yep, that's pretty much her. Has been like that since she was a little kid, too."

Claire smiles. "I'm happy to be here. People have been nice to me. I almost feel like I belong."

"You do, CeCe. I wish you could see yourself the way I see you. Today, I told the women at the Christmas tree farm that my heart was already taken."

"Did you?" she whispers. "Why?"

"Because it's true."

She shakes her head. "I don't deserve it."

"Who said I was talkin' about you?" I lift a brow and smirk.

She bumps her shoulder into mine. "You're not?"

I place my palm on her cheek. "You know I am, darlin'. There ain't nobody I'd rather be with. You're here. Are you really staying?"

"I am. The first thirty-five years of my life I spent trying to prove myself to a world that didn't give a shit about me. The next thirty-five years, I want to prove to myself that I deserve to be happy. Merryville is the only place that's ever felt like home. My father didn't understand, and he may never. And that's okay."

"You do deserve to be happy, and you will be. I'm sorry to hear that about your dad. You're a good person, CeCe. I'm sure he recognizes that, and if he doesn't, he needs glasses."

"Noticed you were wearing yours." She lifts a brow. "I loved seeing Clark Kent rescue me tonight."

I smirk. "My eyes were dry."

"Uh-huh. I'm sure that's why you put them on." She doesn't sound convinced. "How did you know where I lived?"

"You told me the street, and I just drove until I saw your truck. Nice parking job."

She snickers. "I did what I could."

"Also, I don't have your number," I tell her.

"Oh shit. Let me rectify that." She grabs her phone and shoots me a text.

Mine buzzes, but I don't unlock it. "Thanks. So, want to join my family for Christmas? I know you told my brother you'd be there, but if you don't want to come, I'll understand."

"I'd love to."

"Great. My parents have asked me several times. It starts at six on Christmas night. I told them to chill out. Everyone is excited you're back," I admit, taking another bite.

"Are you?"

I place my hand on her thigh. "Yes. So fuckin' happy."

She sighs. "Thank you. I was hoping moving here wasn't a mistake."

"Sometimes mistakes are miracles," I tell her.

She lifts her glass of wine, and I tap mine against hers. "That I agree with."

We finish eating, dig into our cakes, and then I follow Claire to the kitchen. "We'll have to make cookies soon."

"I know it looks like a bomb exploded in here," she says, looking at the flour and sugar that are everywhere.

"And? It's your place, darlin'. You can do whatever you

309

want. It's perfectly you. But do you want me to help you clean up?"

She nods. I don't think she's ready for me to go, either. I just want another hour with her, but I also have to be up early for work.

"Oh, I got something for Tinsel," she tells me, rushing to her tree and pulling a miniature Santa hat from under it.

"She's going to hate this," I say, laughing and giving her a side hug.

"Just wait until I'm around before you put it on her. I need pictures and to see her reaction."

"That's a deal." Neither of us rushes to clean the counters, but when I yawn, I know it's time for me to go.

"You're exhausted," Claire says as she places the jar of cinnamon on her spice rack.

"I am. But it's fine. Just have to work tomorrow, and then I have the next three weeks off."

She gasps. "Really? I didn't realize. Can we hang out?"

"I'd love that," I admit.

When the kitchen is clean, I know there's no more stalling. Claire won't ask me to leave, but I don't want to wear out my welcome. I'm just grateful I got to spend time with her.

She leads me to the door and follows me onto the porch. Before I step off, I pull her close and brush my lips across hers. She grabs my shirt with tight fists, pouring her emotions into me, but I'm just as guilty. The kiss deepens as she gently slides her tongue against mine. Electricity soars through us, and when we're breathless, I pull away. When she meets my gaze, I smirk and point up at the mistletoe she hung. "Strategically placed."

"I'm just glad you noticed. Don't want any bad luck."

I shoot her a wink. "Night, CeCe."

"Good night. Thank you for the flowers and dinner. You're welcome to stop by anytime."

I blow her a kiss and walk to my truck with the biggest

fucking smile on my face. My girl is back because of me, and this time, I don't think I'll ever let her go. I want to carry her to bed and worship her until morning. But she mentioned wanting to take it slow. Let's see how long that lasts.

When I get in my truck, I unlock my phone and look at the text she sent me. It's a picture of her sitting on my dad's lap, and I hope she gets her Christmas wish.

CHAPTER 37

CLAIRE

It's officially Christmas Eve, and I can't remember the last time I felt this excited about the holiday season. This morning, there was a parade downtown with floats, golf carts, and the high school band. The grand finale was Santa on a sleigh throwing candy to the kids. I'd ordered a cup of coffee to go from Jake's cousin, then happily watched. When Jake's dad gave me a wink and a wave, it made my entire day.

Afterward, I went to the café, sat at one of the booths by the window and happily ate a large stack of red-and-green pancakes for breakfast. I wanted to text Jake to join, but I'm also trying to give him his space. I think we'll be okay and will work through the awkwardness. Once he kissed me last night, I knew we would.

When I make it back home, my phone dings.

I pick it up and see a text from Jake with a picture of him and his grandmother.

JAKE

> Mawmaw told me to invite you over! We're baking cookies and pies.

CLAIRE

Aww, really? I would love to.

JAKE

Want me to pick you up?

CLAIRE

I can drive! ;) Need anything from town?

JAKE

Just you…to get your ass over here.

How can one simple text cause butterflies to flutter?

I grab my coat and slide on my boots, then I head over to his grandmother's. The drive is pleasant, though I'm surprised there is so much traffic. There are lots of last-minute shoppers going in and out of the stores. However, everything will close in just a few hours, and the whole town will shut down on Christmas Day.

I turn into the farm and make the turn to his grandmother's. When I arrive, I see Jake's truck, and it makes me smile. I promised him I'd be here on Christmas, and I'm keeping my word on that. As I get out, the door swings open, and I see his mawmaw in the doorway, wearing a red-and-green-striped onesie. Jake comes to the door, and he's got one on, too. They both match right down to their Santa hats.

I can't hold back my laughter. "You two are adorable."

"So happy you joined us, sweetie!" His grandma gives me a wink.

Jake meets me on the sidewalk, placing an extra Santa hat on my head. Then he wraps his arm around my shoulders and leads me inside. "Glad you came," he whispers in my ear.

"Me too," I tell him.

We follow his grandma down the hall and enter the

kitchen. It smells like sugar, cinnamon, and bread. It causes my mouth to water even though I'm full.

"You two have been busy." I glance over the goodies they've already baked. There are a variety of cookies and four different pies.

"And to think, we're just gettin' started," Jake says, realizing how amazed I am by it all.

"Jakey told me you burned the hell out of some gingerbread cookies," his grandma says over her shoulder.

"Mawmaw!" He shakes his head. "You were supposed to keep that to yourself."

"I did," I admit. "It was so bad I had to throw the pans away. No one got hurt, though. Didn't even burn or cut a finger or have to call the fire department." I meet Jake's eyes, thankful he arrived when he did. Otherwise, the last one might've come to fruition.

Jake smirks. "A win is a win."

She snickers. "Honey, if you learn anything while livin' here, it's gonna be how to bake. Ever made a pie before?"

"I haven't. Totally willing to learn, though." I move to the sink, rolling up my sleeves to wash my hands. Jake offers me an apron.

"Oh, I forgot to mention we do this while drinking spiked eggnog," his grandma says, and my eyes widen as she pours and then hands me a glass.

"I knew I liked you," I tell her, taking a sip and then meeting her eyes.

"Might make hair grow on your chest," she warns me.

"So you two are currently trashed?" I look between her and Jake.

"No, that comes later," he admits. "But these pies ain't gonna bake themselves. Mawmaw has the cookies on lockdown. I'm on pie-bakin' duty."

I take a sip of eggnog, and we move to the end of the

breakfast nook, where there's flour, sugar, and salt all laid out. There are also several eggs. I see a machine plugged in. "What's that?"

"Food processor. Makes life easier," his grandma says as she rolls balls of cookie dough onto a tray, then squishes chocolate into the middle.

"Yep, takes out having to mix everything so much. Cuts down prep time." Jake stands close, his arm touching mine, and I can't stop staring at how adorable his ass looks in that onesie.

I look at him, impressed. "I didn't realize you knew how to bake everything."

"I've got all sorts of tricks up my sleeve," he says.

"Apparently." I take another drink of eggnog. "This is so good."

"It's our tradition," Jake explains. "We skip the parade, have a huge breakfast, and then start drinking and baking until the sun sets. Then we eat roast and potatoes and finish it off with a hot toddy. It's always just been the two of us because my brother is always busy, and Dad has to do the parade and then private parties. Lucas and Mom are occupied helping Dad. So me and Mawmaw started doing this years ago."

"Years? Sweetie, we've been doin' this since you turned twenty-one."

"That long?" he questions. "Damn. Well, that means fifteen years. Either way, I wouldn't miss it for the world."

"I wouldn't let ya," his mawmaw says with a wink, placing the cookies in the oven. "And you're now required to join us, too, Claire."

I snicker. "Oh, I wouldn't want to impose on your quality time."

She chuckles. "Honey, you're practically family now. *Our* tradition is *your* tradition. So you better be here next year with us. We eat breakfast at seven sharp, then start bakin' soon after. Learned a long time ago that if I didn't eat a big meal to start, I'd be jingle belled out before lunch."

"It's a secret, though. Can't tell anyone how much fun we have, or they'll all want to join us."

"I won't tell a soul," I say. "Thank you. Yes, I'll be here next year."

"That a promise?" Jake asks with a brow popped.

I bump him with my hip. "Yes, and you know I'm good at keeping them."

Jake rubs his hands together. "You are. Now, let's get started. We've got exactly fourteen minutes to get this pie crust prepped so we can use the oven next since we take turns."

He gives me the measurements, and I dump the flour, salt, and sugar into the plastic reservoir.

"Now pulse it," he says, moving to the fridge where he pulls cold butter out.

Once he dices the butter into tiny squares, he places it into the food processor with the powder mixture. "Do it some more."

I don't know what it is about him, but he has my pulse increasing with each stolen glance. When he walks over with a measuring cup of ice water, I'm confused. "This seems like a lot of steps."

He puts six tablespoons of ice water inside the mixture. "Now, do it again, but stop when you see little balls of dough."

"Jakey, you're such a good teacher," his grandmother compliments, refilling her eggnog.

"He is," I agree.

Once it's to the texture he wants, Jake dumps it out in front of me and pats it together, then splits it into half, moving one side in front of me. "Should look like a block of brie, a disk shape."

"Like this?" I ask, making sure it looks like his.

He nods. "Good... *job*."

I smirk, knowing what he was going to say good *girl*. Then he wraps the dough in plastic and puts it in the fridge.

"I thought we were making pies!" I say.

He pulls a stack of them out and sets them on the surface in front of me. "Oh, we are, but you should always replace the dough with new batches so you don't run out. The ones we just made need to sit for an hour."

"Oh." I meet his eyes, wishing I could kiss his lips, but I drink some eggnog instead.

"Ever had that before?" He lifts his chin, referring to the nog.

"No, but it's sweet and thick. The way I like it." I chew on my bottom lip, and he swallows hard.

"I like it thick, too," his grandma says, pulling us away from our intense eye contact. We both burst into laughter.

"That's great, Mawmaw." He shoots me a wink.

Once we flatten the dough with a rolling pin, Jake glances over at me. "What's your favorite pie?"

"Uh. I'm not sure," I answer truthfully. "Can count on my hands how many pies I've had in my life."

His mawmaw turns to me with her hand on her chest. "Bless your heart. Sweetie, we're gonna have to change that."

"You will," I agree, glancing back at Jake. "What about pumpkin?"

"We'll make several different ones, but make sure tomorrow at dinner you leave room for dessert so you can give me an official answer," he says.

I nod as he guides me through the recipes.

The rest of the day, the three of us laugh and drink. His grandma tells me embarrassing stories about Jake that I find endearing. I can't remember the last time I laughed so hard. And when the sun finally sets and we have enough pies and cookies to feed a small army, we sit at the table and eat pot roast. After we're full, and as his mawmaw takes a shower and gets ready for bed, the two of us clean up the kitchen. When Jake passes me, he places his thumb on my cheek and wipes. "Flour on your face."

My breath hitches as I look up at him. "Thank you for inviting me. I've had one of the best days of my life."

"It was Mawmaw's idea, but I agree. I love spending time with you."

It's as if we're suspended in time as I place my hand behind his neck and slide my lips across his. Jake takes a step forward, his knee spreading my legs apart as he presses me against the counter. Our tongues fight a war neither of us will win.

"Come home with me," he whispers in my ear, causing goose bumps to trail along my skin.

"You're sure that's not the alcohol talking?" I hold on to him for dear life.

He smiles against my lips. "Absolutely."

"I don't want you to regret crossing the line, not this time."

"I can't get enough of you, darlin'. I miss you. Tinsel misses you. Please," he whispers. "Don't make me beg."

His cock presses into my stomach.

"Yes," I say desperately, grabbing his cheeks and kissing him again.

The bathroom door opens, and Jake's eyes bolt open. He takes a step back and looks down at the tent in his onesie. "Shit," he says, allowing the counter to hide his thick cock. Moments later, his grandma enters the kitchen.

"Looks good in here." She glances between us, and I know my lips are swollen because Jake's are. "Good night, you two. Hope you've both been good this year. Maybe Santa will bring you what you want."

Jake looks at me, reaching out to grab my hand. "I've already got my Christmas wish."

I smile widely. "Me too."

She nods and lifts a brow. "You two lock up when you're done. See ya tomorrow. Also, try not to stay up too late?"

"Yes, Mawmaw," Jake tells her.

When she's out of sight, his mouth returns to mine. "Ready to get out of here?"

"Hell yes."

CHAPTER 38

JAKE

As soon as we walk inside my cabin, our hands and mouths are on one another. I've wanted Claire since the moment I saw her again, and now I'll finally have her alone without the fear of interruption. Or so I thought.

"Meow! Meow! Meow!" Tinsel trots up to us, her bell jingling and paws at Claire's leg, using her claws.

She breaks away from me and bends down. "Did you miss me?" Claire pets and then kisses her head. When I hear Tinsel purr, I can't help but chuckle. Claire looks up at me, smiling widely.

"She totally missed you," I say.

When Claire reaches to pet her again, Tinsel nips at her and then runs away. "I guess I deserved that."

When she stands, I place my hands on her hips, meeting her eyes. "I missed you, too. The thought of losing you forever nearly destroyed me."

"Me too. I was sick for a week. Couldn't eat. Sleep. Life didn't matter. First time I'd ever been lovesick."

I place my hands on her ass, kissing her slowly. She wraps her leg around me, and I pick her up and carry her to my bedroom. Lying her on the bed, she looks up at me.

"I risked it all for you, Jake." I take off her boots and slide down her pants until she's wearing nothing but her panties. A reindeer with a red nose is embroidered on the front, and I snicker.

"Cute."

"I was trying to be festive," she says, peeling off her shirt and unsnapping her bra. I'm still wearing my ridiculous adult onesie, but she seems to like it. She sits up, unsnapping the buttons on the front, and my cock flies out.

"Mm." She pops a brow, then opens her mouth and taps my tip against her hot tongue before sucking.

"Fuck," I groan out, loving the way she makes me feel. "I haven't…" I shake my head. "Not since you left."

She pulls away, looking up at me. "Me either. I thought I'd be broken forever."

I give her a small smile. "Me too."

"I want to feel you deep inside me, Jake." She strokes me a few times. "Please. I need you so bad."

There's no way I can deny this woman. I need her so bad it fucking hurts.

I peel off my clothes and slide my boxers down to the floor, then I climb on the bed, positioning myself between Claire's legs. It feels intimate, almost too intimate, as I slowly kiss her and slide into her. She's so wet as I push forward, her mouth falling open and a sigh releasing.

"Oh my God, it feels so good," she cries out. "I've missed you."

"Fuck, darlin', you feel like home," I say softly in her ear.

She scratches her nails down my back as I rock in and out of her, taking my time and loving her moans of pleasure. I want her to feel so fucking good.

"Yes, yes, yes," she hisses, digging the heels of her feet into my ass. I dip my head down and suck on one of her nipples before switching to the other.

Have I shifted to another dimension where Claire is mine?

She came back for me, for us. And I will never let this beautiful, caring woman slip through my fingers again. The emotions are almost too much as we moan together. It's intense and sensual, and I hold her tight.

"I love you," she whispers.

I push upward, looking into her eyes.

She continues, "You don't have to say it if you don't want to. It's early, and I know you're not supposed to say it too soon, but I can't keep living my life not telling people how I feel. I don't know how you did it, Jake, but I'm so in love with you it hurts."

I smash my lips against hers, kissing along her jaw and up to her neck until I meet her ear. "Fuck the rules, babe. I love you, too." I nibble on her lobe, my cock buried deep inside of her. "I've fallen for you hard. And I'm never letting you go again." I pump into her, and her back arches off the bed; I know she's close. Her entire body tenses under me as she rocks against my cock. "And one day, I'm gonna make you my wife, Claire."

I slow my pace as she moans. "Yes, yes. Please. The thought of spending forever with you...fuck," she hisses. She groans out, every muscle tight as she teeters on the edge.

"Come, darlin'." And then she does.

She squeezes me so tight I can't hold back my grunts. I slow my movements, gliding in and out of her, and my breaths grow ragged. She wraps her arms around my neck. "You're mine, Jake Jolly."

The orgasm takes hold of me, and a moment later, Claire is coming again. She screams my name. "Mine," she whispers.

We stay how we are for a few minutes, and I brush her hair back from her face. "You're gorgeous."

She smirks. "You are."

I place a kiss on her nose. "You're mine."

"Forever," she whispers, and it's a confirmation.

"Claire Manchester is in love with a lumberjack."

She kisses my chin. "I'm in love with a caring, funny, and sexy-as-hell man who has a huge cock."

I chuckle. "Yeah? Well, I'm in love with a beautiful Stubborn Susan who's also a very *good girl*."

"I've won the boyfriend lottery," she says, kissing me once more.

"Boyfriend?" I lift my brow.

"Unless…"

I place my finger on her lips. "I want it to be official, Claire. I want it to be forever. But we'll go slow."

"I don't want to rush forever," she whispers, her eyes hooded.

"Never."

The next morning, I open my eyes and find Claire sleeping soundly next to me, with Tinsel curled up next to her.

"I see how it is," I whisper, and Tinsel stretches a little farther. Then I glance back at Claire to discover she's awake.

"Good morning," she says, reaching for me, and I softly kiss her.

"Mornin'," I say. "Merry Christmas, darlin'."

She smiles. "Merry Christmas. I feel like I'm dreaming."

"Shall we see if Santa left any presents under the tree?"

She makes a face. "I hope you didn't get me anything, Jake. I didn't…"

I stop her with a kiss. "You are my gift, CeCe. I didn't get you much. It's just a little something. Meet me in the living room when you're up."

"Okay." She stretches, then notices Tinsel and finds a different way to put her feet on the floor so she doesn't disturb her.

I grab my glasses, then go to the kitchen and brew us both a cup of coffee. Outside, there's a buck in the distance, and I stand at the windows and watch the animal. He's regal, a monarch surveying his kingdom.

"Wow," she whispers, walking over to stand beside me.

I wrap my arm around her and kiss her forehead. "Made you a cup of coffee. It's on the counter."

"Ooh." She moves to the counter and grabs it, then comes back to me.

"His antlers are huge." She blows on the top before taking a sip. "Is that the same one that scared the shit out of me?"

I chuckle. "Very well could be. There's a herd of them that stays around here. It's safe, with lots of land, 'cause no one in my family hunts."

She's listening but is not quite awake yet. "Coffee is great."

"Ready for your gift?" I ask.

"Jake," she says, "I feel awful."

"You've done enough, CeCe." I grab the small box and hand it to her.

"Oh, it's heavy," Claire says. I hold her mug as she carefully unwraps it. Then she gasps. "The other snow globe! Thank you so much."

"I kept thinking about you only choosing one when it was clear you wanted both. Stupid rule, by the way. But if you look closely at the people inside, they kinda look like us," I say, pointing at them.

She shakes it, and the snow falls around the couple, who are happily holding hands. "They do," she says. "And they're clearly happy. Smiling. Almost as if he just told her something funny."

"Oh, almost forgot." I set down the coffee mugs, then pick up the tiny Christmas hat that Claire got for Tinsel. I click my tongue, and that old girl comes running to me. When she's close, I bend down and put the elastic on her head.

Tinsel shakes her head, trying to get it to fall off. It doesn't work. She jumps on the back of the couch, still fighting it. When she gives up the fight, she sits and glares forward, but neither of us removes it.

Claire snickers. "Oh my God, she hates it!"

"She looks cute, though."

I turn to Claire. "Are you happy? I want to make sure this, me, living in Merryville, is really what you want."

"Jake." She wraps her arms around my waist, and I dip down to kiss her. "I've fallen in love with you," she says. "Being near you feels safe. And I'm so attracted to you that I'd be okay with you walking around naked all day, every day. You're always on my mind. I'm not used to feeling this way about anyone because I've never experienced anything like this. When you look at me, I know you care. I know you want me. I know you'd protect me. I know you'd love me forever."

"I do love you," I say. "It's quick. All of this. But I've never clicked with someone so fast. It scares me because I'm so fucking afraid of losing you." I set the coffee mugs down on the table in front of the couch and move back to her, painting my lips against hers.

"I'm scared, too," she admits. "I don't want to live my life without you in it."

I laugh against her mouth, tugging her bottom lip between my teeth and sucking. "I've waited a lifetime for you."

"I'm never letting you go," she says. "Unless you decide you no longer want me."

I grab her hands. "That would never happen. My mama told me that when I find the person I'm supposed to spend forever with, I'd instantly know, and I do."

"I love you, Jake Jolly." She kisses me, her emotions pouring into me, and all I want is her.

"I love you, CeCe. I was serious about what I said last night."

She looks down at her left hand, which is bare of any jewelry. "I'll be waiting."

I wrap my arm around her waist and laugh. "Just tryin' out the girlfriend thing for now."

She nods. "And one day, I'll be your fiancée."

Hours later, we get dressed and drive to my parents' house. The front yard and driveway are full of vehicles. It looks like the whole crowd has already arrived.

"Are we late?" Claire unbuckles her seat belt and glances at me.

I shake my head. "No, we're ten minutes early. They're just punctual. Plus, anytime there is a lot of food around, people show up early."

"I'm somewhat nervous," she admits.

I chuckle. "Don't be, darlin'. They're very excited you're joining us. And if anyone tries to give you a hard time, Mawmaw will stop them in her tracks, trust me."

"Okay." She sighs. "I hope you're right. I'm just not used to being around a large family, I guess. It's always just been me and my sister."

"You'll get used to it." I lean over and kiss her cheek.

We walk into the garage and enter through the side door. I grab Claire's hand and pull her toward me, placing a soft kiss on her lips. "You good?"

"Yes," she whispers. The counters are full of pies and the buffet of food that we'll be eating tonight. We ate eggs and bacon for breakfast and skipped lunch to save room for supper.

As soon as we walk into the living room, I smile.

"There they are!" Mawmaw announces.

Heads turn, and everyone cheers when they see us.

"Finally! I guess now we can eat," Hudson says.

Colby wiggles off the couch and bolts toward me. I bend down and lift him in my arms. "Unckie!" He laughs.

"Did Santa bring you everything you wanted?"

He holds the toy in his hand. "Yes! I got this truck!"

"Sweet ride, buddy!"

"Who is that?" he asks as Claire grins at him.

"Oh, this is my girlfriend, Claire," I tell him.

"My friends call me CeCe, though," she says, and he turns his head and acts shy. Claire holds back laughter.

"She doesn't bite," I tell him. "And she's really nice. You would like her."

He looks at me. "Does she like dinosaurs?"

"You should ask her yourself."

Claire nods. "I love dinosaurs! My favorite is a stegosaurus! That's the one that's big with things on its back. It has four legs, but it could also walk on two, just like you!"

Colby looks impressed. "Wow. I like T. rex."

"Really? Did you know their teeth were so strong that they could crush cars?"

I love watching her with him, seeing her so excited to share facts about dinosaurs.

"Whoa!" he exclaims.

"And the head of a T. rex would have been as large as I am tall! Just his head alone!"

He looks her up and down and giggles.

"T. rex is the coolest," Claire says, holding out her hand, and Colby gives her a high five. He wiggles down from my arms, just like Tinsel does, and runs back to Hudson. He turns around and points at Claire as Hudson listens to him.

I wrap my arm around her and lean in to kiss her cheek. "You made his day."

We move farther into the living room and find some folding chairs off to the side. "Oh, don't let me be rude. This is my aunt Pamela and uncle Jerry, my dad's brother."

"Nice to meet you," Claire tells them, waving.

"Nice to meet you, too! We've heard so much about ya," my uncle says. "I assume you've already met the girls?"

"Yes sir, I have," Claire tells him, smiling at Wendy, Bella, and BJ.

"My dad's other brothers couldn't make it this year. They decided to go on a ski trip," I explain.

"And they're gonna have a lot of makin' up to do when they get back," Mawmaw adds.

She was pissed when they'd announced they were leaving for the month to spend the holidays in the Rockies. I don't blame them, though. I love the mountains.

"Can we please eat now?" BJ asks, and when Mawmaw stands, we all get up and enter the dining room.

I pull out Claire's chair for her, and she sits, then I slide in next to her.

"Can I sit by her?" Colby asks Hudson, who looks at Claire.

"I would love that," she tells Colby. Hudson puts a booster seat in the chair and helps Colby. Then he sits next to him.

I rest my hand on Claire's thigh, and she meets my gaze, smirking as Lucas and my cousins help carry the food to the table. "Wow," Claire whispers. "This looks incredible."

"Remember to save some room for dessert," Mawmaw tells her. "I still wanna know what your favorite pie is after you taste them all."

Lucas chuckles. "Y'all are gonna scare her away."

"Nah," I say. "CeCe ain't goin' anywhere."

"Taste them all?" CeCe gulps.

"Yes, sweetie," Mawmaw says with a wink.

We eat family style, with all the food in the middle. The sound of chatter and forks clanking against plates fills the room, along with smiles. I wrap my arm around my girl, and my heart is so fucking full I can't stop smiling. She's here with me, and she's mine.

After dinner, she eats a bite of every pie, and Mawmaw

forces her to choose. She decides on the chocolate one with the fluffy whipped cream topping. Then we play Monopoly until everyone's worn out and make our way back to the house.

Before we step off the porch, Claire grabs me and pulls me into a kiss. I look up and don't see any mistletoe. She laughs. "That one was just because."

I take her hand, guide her off the porch, and box her in against the truck with my arms as I slide my tongue into her mouth. We're insatiable for one another. When I pull away, she's breathless. "That one was just because," I repeat.

"Get a room!" Hudson yells.

"I've got a whole house," I tell him as Claire climbs into the truck and I shut the door.

When I climb inside, I glance over at her. "Want me to take you home?"

"With you," she clarifies, and I smirk as I crank the engine.

"My Little Miss Christmas Miracle."

"My Little Mr. Make Me Come Three Times in a Row."

I burst into laughter. "Tonight, we might have to make it four."

CHAPTER 39

CLAIRE

FIVE DAYS LATER

"You good?" I lean over and whisper into Jake's ear as the plane takes off.

"As long as you're with me, yes," he admits with his eyes closed as he breathes.

I told him that we could drive to New York if he'd prefer. My lawyer called me and said I had to return to the city immediately to review some paperwork my father sent him. He refused to give me any information.

Driving would've taken nearly three days to get there and three days back. Plus, driving in the snow wasn't something either of us wanted to do, so we decided to fly.

When the plane finally lands, we grab our bags, and I spot one of my drivers holding an iPad with my alias on it.

Jake gives me a look, lifting his brow at me with a sexy-as-fuck smirk. "After you, Claire Chester."

Seeing paparazzi by my car doesn't faze me, but Jake puts his arm around my shoulders, protecting me. They scream my name and his, and when we get in the car, he smiles at me.

"So you've dealt with that all of your life?"

I shrug as the car zooms off. "They stopped following me for a while because I wasn't enough of a train wreck. It was nice. However, they're milking our relationship at the moment."

Several articles have been printed about us online. You'd think we were a football player and a pop star with how much they've recently mentioned us.

"I'm not upset about it," Jake says. "Just shows the world that everyone can find love, even a Stubborn Susan."

I snicker. "I agree, but I don't like what they're saying," I tell him. The lies are what pisses me off the most because Jake wanted me when he thought I was a real estate agent who didn't know how to pump gas.

He leans in and mutters into my ear, "Who cares? We know our truth. And that's all that matters."

"Always so logical," I tell him, snuggling into his warmth.

"I don't want your money, Claire. Just your love. Wouldn't matter if you were broke."

"After I meet with my lawyer and see what my father is up to, I might be," I say.

Jake captures my mouth with his and rubs his nose with mine. "Doesn't matter to me."

It's how I know that the relationship we have is different. Jake doesn't care about my career, money, or what I can offer; he only wants me. That's it. I'm unsure what I did to deserve this man who's so willing to stand by me as I face my father's retribution.

An hour later, the car stops, and we're dropped off outside my penthouse. Jake interlocks his fingers with mine, and I let us inside and up the elevator. He smirks, watching the elevator climb the floors until we're nearly at the top.

"What's that expression for?" I ask when the doors slide

open. He shakes his head as I go to my door and unlock it. My penthouse is clean; all the food wrappers are gone, and it's spotless.

His mouth falls open as he walks to the wall of windows that overlooks the city. "Are you kiddin' me? This view is incredible."

I look at the golden lights and see where the ball will drop tomorrow. "It is. I'm jaded to it, though."

Jake's hand slides past my cheek and around my neck as his mouth devours mine.

"I have a confession to make…" I whisper.

"Yeah?" he says, tucking hair behind my ear, a gesture so simple but one I adore.

"I've always wanted to…" I swallow hard and look at the windows. I don't even have to say it.

"Fuck against them?" A devious smirk touches his perfect lips.

"Yes, at night," I admit. "I've never brought a man here. Not even those I dated."

He searches my face. "Never?"

"No. This was my refuge, my safe space."

Jake's strong arms wrap around me. "Will you give me a tour?"

I interlock my fingers with his. "I'd love to."

In each room we enter, Jake is amazed. The bathroom, my office, the kitchen. It's a state-of-the-art penthouse with a view of Times Square. I lead Jake to my bedroom, where an entire wall of windows looks out over the city, just like in the living room. "Beautiful," he says, but when I turn and look at him over my shoulder, he's staring at me, not the city.

He takes a step forward and turns his head. "Your snow globes." They're neatly displayed on a glass mirrored shelf. "You have so many." His eyes scan over them.

"That's why I have that rule of only buying one. I'm

having these shipped to Merryville, along with a few other things, too," I explain.

"What will you do with this place?"

"Keep it for us to visit. And my sister might move in and sell her place. She's planning to start traveling again and even mentioned visiting Merryville."

"That would be awesome. I'm sure she'd love it as much as you," he says.

I point out different areas of the city and landmarks. Manchester Holdings is close enough that I can walk if I'd like. That life already feels like a thing of the past.

I sigh.

"You good?" Jake asks, noticing me losing myself in my thoughts.

"I am," I tell him, lifting his hand and kissing his knuckles. "I've realized when I'm with you, I don't have nearly as many anxiety attacks."

He wraps me in his arms, and I inhale his scent, which reminds me of the fresh air and evergreens. I squeeze him. "Or maybe it's because you've been doin' things that make you happy and stopped forcing yourself to fit into a role you never belonged in," he suggests.

I chuckle.

"What did I say that was funny?" He smirks.

"Nothing, really. In the past, had someone told me I didn't belong in that role, I'd have become a nightmare. But when you say it…"

"I'm not sayin' that because you're not good enough. You don't belong because you're better than that life. You care about people. You've got a big heart. Doing what your father does has to be hard. He's sacrificed a lot. That's respectable. But when he's at the end of his life, can he say he was truly happy?" he asks.

"No," I confirm. "He was briefly happy when my mother

was alive, but I think he buried his soul with her. You're right. I'm nervous about the unknown."

"Darlin'," he whispers. "It's all going to work out. I'll help and support you however I can."

I stand up on my tiptoes and wrap my arms around him. "It will. Thank you."

The following day, I wake up next to Jake, naked. I lift the fluffy blankets and take a peek, then slide out of bed. But I take one last glance at him before I walk away.

He's built like a statue, carved in all the right places, with a personality that's to die for, and when he wears those black-framed glasses… Well, I can barely contain myself.

After I use the bathroom, I walk into my closet, which is the size of a room. The space is the only thing that's missing from my house in Merryville, but as I look at my wardrobe, there isn't anything I want to wear. Everything was designed and tailored specifically for me and my body, created to help me fit in with my social class. It's arranged from light to dark and by season.

I huff and hear a chuckle behind me. I turn to see Jake leaning against the doorframe, wearing a boyish grin, and of course, he's wearing those glasses that make me weak in the knees. I swallow hard, my gaze trailing from his lips to the package in his black joggers. I gasp. "You're…"

"Cat got your tongue?"

I move toward him, brushing my fingers down his abs and around his back as he leans down and kisses me.

"More like a lumberjack has it," I say.

"You're too pretty to look so sad," he tells me.

"I was just thinking about all these clothes and how I don't like them," I explain.

"Then don't wear them." He kisses my forehead. "It's your life. Make your own rules."

"But—"

He crushes his lips against mine. "You're in control, darlin'," he says once he pulls away. "Be comfortable in your skin. Be yourself. You have nothin' to prove to nobody. Just showin' up is enough."

"I love how you make it seem so easy."

"It *is* easy. Twenty years from now, you won't remember what you were wearin' when you walked into that lawyer's office. You'll remember what's said and how you felt. Guaranteed. The rest of it…trivial bullshit." He places his fingers under my chin and forces me to look into his green eyes. "If they're gonna talk, might as well give 'em somethin' to talk about," he says.

I nod. "You're right."

"Don't be a Stubborn Susan."

I squeeze him just a little tighter. "I don't think I would've been able to do this without you."

"Do what, exactly?"

"Live my life. I've been a human robot for too long, even down to my clothes. But I've got to go. I'm supposed to be there by eight. I'm his first appointment, and I want to get this over with." I grab a pair of slacks and a sweater, along with some of my favorite flats. Then I slide the clothes over my body as he watches.

"You sure you don't want me to join you?"

"Nah, some things I have to do alone. I'm happy to leave all this in the past and start the new year without the worry of what my father is going to do."

He grins. "Have faith."

I open my mouth, and he presses his finger against my lips. "Having faith means letting what will happen happen."

335

Instead of being driven to my lawyer's office, I choose to walk. The building is one block away from Manchester Holdings. As I step onto the busy street, I place my hands in my pockets. More people are in the city because of the New Year's Eve celebration tonight. This used to be one of my favorite times because of the excitement that fills nearly every block by my penthouse. Tourists come from all over the world to see that glittering ball fall from the sky, hoping the new year will deliver luck and prosperity.

I love a new beginning, but usually, with that comes a chapter closing.

The frigid air brushes against my cheeks, and I keep my head down. Within fifteen minutes, I'm entering the building, taking the elevator to the forty-third floor, and strutting down the hallway. Nelson's secretary greets me and asks me to sit, but I kindly tell her I'd prefer to stand.

In two minutes flat, Nelson gives me a firm handshake. He looks me over from head to toe but doesn't say shit. I think he knows better. Neither of us makes small talk as we walk down the hallway toward his office. The door clicks closed behind us, and I sit in front of his oak desk, a seat I've often occupied.

Corporate Claire activates; it's a version of me that no one likes. She's all business and doesn't care about pleasantries. Right now, I just want this to be over.

"Can we please get to it?" I finally say.

"Right," he tells me, pulling out a file folder and sliding it across the desk. "Your father sent this documentation and would like your signature as soon as possible."

I don't look down at the papers but stare at him. "And you'd advise me to sign this?"

He laughs, and I furrow my brows. "Claire, he's giving you the rest of your inheritance that your mother left for you."

"What? What are you talking about?" My voice doesn't sound like my own.

"I'm sorry, I couldn't tell you over the phone due to confidentiality. All business regarding this has to be done in person to protect the agreement's integrity."

I shake my head. "Explain."

"When you turned eighteen, you were given some of it. Your mother wanted you to have the rest when you married unless your father released it to you earlier."

"Why would he do this?"

Nelson shrugs. "I'm honestly not sure. I didn't get the details of the whys or hows, just that this was being done now. He's already signed everything to turn it over. We're just waiting on your signature."

He hands me a pen, and I hold it tight as I read over every word in the document. Then, when I get to the end of the page, I see a five with nine zeros behind it. "This can't be correct."

"It is," he tells me. "Congratulations. Ms. Claire Manchester, the billionaire."

My jaw nearly hits the floor as I sign my name across the dotted line on the bottom. There is no more *the daughter of a billionaire* after someone says my name. And I'm speechless. I already had more money than I knew what to do with, and I was worried my father had found a way to take it from me and leave me with nothing.

I never expected this and almost feel guilty for making him out to be the villain.

"You might want to contact your financial adviser when you leave," Nelson suggests, handing over the original copies and keeping the others I signed. "So how will you celebrate?" he asks.

"By opening a business." I stand up and realize I'm smiling.

"Really? Hotels and resorts, like your father?"

I shake my head. "Snow globes."

CHAPTER 40

JAKE

When Claire returns, she's elated. She's talking so fast I can barely understand the words coming out of her mouth as she shakes the packet of papers she's carrying.

I grab her cheeks and laugh. "Slow down, darlin'. I don't know what you're sayin'."

"My dad released the rest of my inheritance."

I make a face. "What? I don't—"

"My father released the last half of my inheritance early. I wasn't supposed to receive it until I was married, but I had no idea this existed."

"Why would he do that?" I ask, still not fully understanding.

"I think he knows," she whispers.

"Knows what?"

"That I've found the one."

I slide my fingers through her hair and crash my lips to hers. "God, I've missed you."

"I was gone for an hour."

"An hour too long," I tell her.

"Jake, I was given billions."

My mouth falls open. "B-b-b—"

"Billions, with an *S*," she confirms, then bursts out laughing. "I told my lawyer I was opening a snow globe store." She's giddy with excitement.

"You should. You could even design your own," I suggest.

She gasps. "Yes. Would you help me?"

"I'll help and support you with whatever you need."

Claire and I dress up in black tie outfits and eat dinner by candlelight at a beautiful Italian restaurant. It's nothing fancy, and the place only accepts cash, but it's perfect for us, intimate and quiet. We walk back to her penthouse, hand in hand, then turn on the TV to watch the events in Times Square. We have a perfect view of the ball, but we want tonight to be about us, about ringing in the new year together.

After the sun sets, there's a knock on the door. Claire gets up to answer it and squeals.

"Jake," she says, pushing the door shut, and I look over my shoulder at her sister. I stand to meet her officially. "This is Emma."

When I move closer, Emma looks me up and down with her mouth wide open. "You're taller than I thought." She squeezes my biceps. "And strong."

I laugh, holding out my hand, and she looks at it.

"You do have very large hands," she says, looking back at Claire, who's blushing. "Okay, so which of your brothers should I date?" Emma spins around. Her hair is in curls, and she's wearing a black, long-sleeve dress.

"Hmm," I say. "Do you like kids?"

"Love them," she gushes.

"What about the broody type with a broken past?" Claire asks.

"Check," Emma says, smirking.

"Wait, how old are you?" I look between her and Claire.

"Twenty-nine."

I suck air between my teeth. "Mmm. Hudson might be too old for you."

"Oh, that's your older brother, right? How old is he—forty?"

"No, but close."

"Perfect," she says, giving me a side hug. "Might have to swing on by, then."

"She would be a handful," I say to Claire, who nods.

"Yes, she would. However, you really should visit soon," Claire urges, hugging her again. "I've missed you."

"Missed you, too. So go ahead, spill it. Tell me what the big news is that I have to hear from your mouth before I go out tonight," Emma says.

Claire grabs the paperwork from the bar where she left it earlier and hands it to her sister. She scans over it, flips it to the last page, and her hand flies to her mouth. The papers fall to the ground, but luckily, the paper clip keeps them together.

"I had no idea," she whispers.

"I didn't, either," Claire says. "You probably have the same thing waiting for you."

She turns and looks at me. "Your older brother want to get hitched?"

The three of us break into fits of laughter. The thought is completely ridiculous.

"I think the reason our father didn't want us to know is because he wanted to make sure we were getting married for the right reasons."

She gasps. "Did you two elope? If you did, I'll be so pis—"

"No," Claire says, placing her hand on her shoulder. "Not yet."

Now I'm laughing, but I wrap my arm around her waist. "Don't tempt me with a good time."

"Oh my God. You two are as cute as the tabloids say," Emma gushes. "Please take a picture with me and let me post it on my socials."

"No," Claire snaps. "Do you know how many people already want to steal him from me because of you?"

Emma playfully raises her hand, and Claire slaps it. "Just kiddin'. I want that broody brother, though. I do love a chase," Emma tells her.

Claire asks her what her plans are tonight, and Emma talks about some swanky party she's attending. Celebrities and runway models will be in attendance.

"Call me if you need anything," Claire says. "And text me when you get home."

"Okay, okay. Can we at least have a glass of champagne before I go?" Emma asks, crossing the room in her high heels. They click across the marble floor.

I laugh.

"What?" Emma turns and looks at me.

"You two and your impractical footwear."

Emma playfully rolls her eyes as Claire passes out flutes to us. "I can run in these just like Beyoncé."

"Never underestimate the power of a woman in stilettos," Claire says, holding up her glass. "What are we celebrating? We have to toast to something."

I clear my throat. "To new beginnings."

"I love that," Claire says.

"I love you," I mutter, keeping my eyes locked on hers.

"Love you," she whispers back.

"Aww, you're so adorable together. Wait, wait, one second." Emma pulls her phone out of her pocket and takes a selfie with us, and in the background is a tiny golden ball that will drop in approximately three hours. "The internet will lose it over this pic."

"Please don't put anything too wild as the caption," Claire warns.

"Okay, we can finish our toast. To new beginnings," Emma says, and we all drink. Once our glasses are empty, Emma gives me and Claire hugs goodbye and announces she's leaving. "Can't be early, but don't want to be late, either."

Claire snickers and walks her to the door. "Don't forget to text me."

Emma groans. "I know, I know. I won't."

As I'm sitting on the couch, watching the footage from Times Square, Claire walks toward me. She sits in my lap, her mouth automatically gravitating to mine.

"I'm so lucky to have you," she whispers.

"No, darlin', I'm the lucky one."

Just as the kiss deepens, there's a knock on the door. She groans and gets up. "Emma probably forgot something."

But when she swings it open, she gasps.

I turn my head and see a tuxedoed man with salt-and-pepper hair. He has the same eyes as Claire and Emma.

This is her dad.

"Father," she says in that serious tone I've heard several times.

I sit up straighter, smoothing down my button-up shirt. For once, I'm glad I dressed up for the occasion, even though we are staying in. I think Claire's overwhelming need to have the best first impression comes from him.

"Claire, may I come in?" he asks.

She steps to the side, allowing him to enter. I stand, and he meets my eyes.

"I assume this is the young man that you're seeing?"

"Yes," she states calmly. "This is Jake Jolly."

"My friends call me JJ, sir," I offer, taking his hand, and he gives me a small smile. It's polite, a reaction I'm sure he doesn't give many people.

"I wanted to talk to you in person," he says.

Not wanting to be the reason they have no privacy, I grab my coat. "I'll be right back."

Claire nods. "Five minutes."

"Okay," I say, kissing her on the cheek, then I leave.

This is a conversation they need to have after everything that's happened today. I take the elevator down to the bottom floor and walk the block. There are people everywhere, many wearing the silly hats I saw on TV with a sponsor written across the front and light-up glasses, souvenirs people who have been standing out there all day received. I'm patient, but I don't think I could do it.

I check the time on my phone and set an alarm for five minutes. As I'm strolling down the sidewalk, I try to take in the tall buildings and the crispness in the air and realize just how loud it is. It's almost as if the streets themselves are humming.

When I return, Claire hugs her dad goodbye. He steps outside, and I follow him. I glance over my shoulder at Claire, and she looks at me like I've lost my mind. All I can do is shoot her a wink.

I step inside the elevator with Mr. Manchester. He warns, "If you hurt my daughter…"

"I won't," I tell him. "I'll protect her from anyone who tries to, though. You included." I'm not intimidated by him as we stare one another down. "Sir, I respect you a lot. And one day, I will marry Claire. But I want you to know that she cares about you deeply, and all she's ever wanted is your approval."

"I'm proud of her and the decisions she's made. My daughter deserves happiness, and I will always approve of that. It's all I've ever wanted for her." He looks me up and down. "And I can see why she chose you." He squeezes my shoulder. "Protect her like you said you will, and you'll have my approval, too."

I nod, and we exchange a firm handshake, an unspoken agreement. People say her father is intimidating, but I don't see it. Or maybe the Manchesters just don't intimidate me much.

He gets in his limo and drives off, and I head back to Claire's place. When I walk in, I'm happy to see her smiling.

"You good?" I ask.

She pulls me to her. "More than good. Would be even better if you could fuck me up against that window and knock that fantasy off my list."

"Your wish is my command."

I guide Claire across the living room and press her back against the cold glass, then rest my palms flat against it as I lean in and kiss her.

She squeals with excitement. "You have no idea how hot that was."

I place my finger on her lips, then nibble on her ear as my hand glides down her body. "I think I might need to taste you first."

"Yes." She releases a ragged sigh, antsy with anticipation, as I slide my hand up her dress, then drop to my knees and kiss up her thighs. "Pantyless again?"

"Was just waiting for you to notice." Her fingers thread through my hair as I look up at her.

I peel the material from her body, kissing every inch of her as I stand and carefully unhook her bra. My hand tweaks one nipple as my mouth captures the other. Pants escape her as she presses her back against the glass, fully succumbing to my touch.

"Fuck. I'm about to devour you like my last meal," I tell her.

With her fists, she grabs my shirt, pulling me against her. "Don't keep me waiting."

I turn her around first, pressing her pretty breasts against the cool glass. She hisses as I lean in and whisper into her ear. "This whole fuckin' city will know that tonight and forever, Claire Manchester is mine."

I kiss along her shoulders, down her spine, and spread her cheeks to eat her ass. She arches her back for me so I have better access to her clit. I dart my tongue into her tight cunt, tasting the precum that's already lingering. She's so fucking wet.

"Jake," she whispers, standing on her tiptoes as her body trembles. I slow my pace, wanting her to teeter on the edge. "JJ. Please."

"I love it when you use your manners like my *good girl*." I slide a finger inside of her ass and twirl my tongue against her clit.

Claire rides my tongue, coming two more times, and I love the taste of it.

And when she's close again, she stops me. "Fuck me, Jake. *Please.*"

"Only because you asked nicely."

Her guttural groans release from deep inside her throat as I slide down my slacks and impale her with my cock. Reaching around, I pinch her hard nipple. She takes all of me, pushing against me, creating more friction as she widens her legs and arches her back.

"Claire," I hiss, loving how we feel as one, together, never able to get enough. "I love you," I mutter, my eyes squeezing closed.

"I love you," she whispers. "I think I'm going to…"

Her body tightens around me, and I can't hold back any longer as my thumbs dig into her hips. I lose myself inside of her, slamming into her tight cunt until there's a puddle on the floor.

She looks down, moaning out, continuing to ride out her release. "You've made me squirt again."

"Yes, darlin'." I slide out of her and turn her around. We're both breathless. I press her back against the glass, and she wraps her arms around me.

"How was it?" I ask.

"Better than my wildest fantasy."

After we clean up, we lie naked on the couch, holding each other. We're yawning, but we force ourselves to stay up until midnight.

When there's one minute left, we turn the TV up a little louder, but we don't leave the couch. It's surreal to see the ball in the distance lowering in real time beyond the TV. "Auld Lang Syne" plays quietly in the background, and confetti rains down on the crowd. I place my hand on Claire's cheek and kiss her, knowing we're bringing love and laughter into the new year with us.

"Happy New Year, darlin'."

"Happy New Year, babycakes." She snickers. "I'm trying out pet names."

"Not that one, please." I chuckle, petting her hair. "You know, I think back to everything that's happened in the last month, and it feels like a dream," I mutter.

She rests her head back on my chest. "Yeah? It's been a lot," she says, then she props herself up to meet my eyes. "But I think I've realized something."

"What's that?" I steal a kiss and smirk.

"You're my favorite mistake."

I reach around, wiggling my fingers into her side as she laughs and tries to squirm away. "I love you, CeCe."

I open my arms, and she returns to me, allowing me to hold her tight. "Love you, JJ."

"Oh, what did you and your father talk about?"

She meets my eyes. "He told me he was proud of me for standing up to him."

"I'm proud of you, too," I say.

"What did you two talk about?"

"I told him if he hurt you, I had a shotgun shell with his name on it."

She gasps. "You didn't."

"Nah. I didn't. But he told me he loves you."

"Yes, he told me as much, too."

I squeeze her tight and kiss her forehead.

"Everything worked out better than I ever could've imagined," she says, releasing a contented sigh.

"I couldn't agree more."

EPILOGUE

JAKE

SEVEN MONTHS LATER

"Y ou didn't warn me that Texas would be so hot," Claire says, fanning herself after lunch. We walk back to her shop, and she unlocks the door, allowing me in. Since it's a holiday, a lot of the boutiques on Main Street are open, and Claire is making the best of it.

CeCe's Collectibles opened a few months ago and specializes in snow globes. The locals welcomed her business with open arms and have been supportive. No other outsider has been able to genuinely win over as many hearts as Claire has. She's even started volunteering in town and has become fast friends with my cousins.

I smile, carefully glancing over the new inventory that was delivered earlier this week. She moves to the counter and turns on a tabletop fan, where it's blowing full blast in her face. "You get used to it. July is the hottest time of the year. Okay, well, some people say August is, but I disagree."

She clicks the thermostat down several degrees.

"You're gonna freeze customers out," I tell her, giving her a hard time.

"No such thing," she says. "I want it fifty in here. Maybe it being like a freezer will encourage them to take a break out of the heat. Oh, what time do the fireworks start tonight?" she asks over her shoulder.

"At dark, so nine-ish," I tell her.

"Great. I'll probably stay here and finish unpacking the inventory. I want to be ready for Christmas in July. So, meet you on the lawn?"

I nod as she glances out the front windows of the business. The streets are full of tourists eating red-white-and-blue popsicles. Food trucks line the perimeter of the city square, and several locals have already saved their places on the grass with lawn chairs and blankets.

"These look incredible," I whisper, my eyes trailing over the different globes she designed. Most of them are based around Merryville and the Christmas tree farm, and she's sneakily added our special moments inside them, too. I've been helping her when I'm not busy on the farm, but it's not like she needs it. She's hired an entire crew of people who love her as a boss.

My phone buzzes in my pocket, and I pull it out to see it's Hudson. "Hey, I'll be back in fifteen minutes," I tell him once I answer. I took a quick break to have lunch with my sweetheart. Leaving is always the hardest part.

"Sounds good," he says, and the call ends.

Then I return my attention back to Claire. "Need anything else before I go?"

She shakes her head. "No, I don't think so. Text me when you come back this way, please?"

"Mm. I love it when you use your manners like a good girl."

She bites her lip, and it takes every ounce of strength I

have not to carry her to the back room and devour her for dessert. Hudson would probably curse me out, though.

I take four large steps, removing the space between us and capturing her lips. I grab her ass, pressing her against me. Claire moans and the only thing that breaks us apart is the bell ringing.

"Look at you two," BJ says, shaking her head. "You'd think you'd already be sick of each other, considering every time I see you, your tongues are sloshing together."

"It's not every time," Claire tells her.

"Okay, *almost* every time," BJ says. "Anyway, just making sure y'all are coming to my bonfire birthday party this weekend. I'm finally turnin' twenty-one!"

"You know we are," Claire says, turning to look at me. "Aren't we?"

I shrug. "I mean, I dunno. I might have to wash my hair."

My cousin rolls her eyes. "Okay, boomer."

"Excuse me? I'm a millennial," I tell her, pretending to be offended. "Sorry you didn't grow up in one of the coolest decades ever."

"Sure. I'm so sad."

Claire chuckles. "I was just thinking about some facts I learned about Gen Z."

"Share with the class," I say, crossing my arms and staring at BJ, who is unamused.

"I thought it was cute that you stopped by to ask instead of texting," Claire says. "Apparently, Gen Z is known for wanting to have conversations face to face more than online."

She licks her lips. "It's harder for someone to bullshit you. But I also just clocked out."

"Ahh," Claire says. "You sure you don't wanna quit the coffee shop and come work for me?"

BJ looks around. "Nah. I feel like I'd break a lot of things in here. Too much glass. If I get desperate, though, I'll think about it."

Claire snickers. "Anything you want for your birthday?"

"A million dollars?" She laughs and waves goodbye.

"She's a little shit," Claire says, moving to the storage room, and I follow behind her. Everything is neatly organized by size and type, and I beam with pride. "What?" she asks.

"I'm proud of you. Really proud. Look at all of this, babe. You did this on your own. Turned your ideas into reality. Some people really suck at execution, but not you." I pick up a globe and study it. It features a woman and a man kissing under mistletoe. Many of our special memories have been captured forever in this art.

"I remember this," I tell her, and she walks over.

"Yeah," she whispers.

"It was when you kissed me," I remind her.

"Because you were too much of a Southern gentleman to make a move!" She shakes her head.

"I would've…eventually."

"Aren't you glad I did?" Claire asks as I set the globe back on the shelf.

"I wonder if we'd be where we are today if you hadn't."

She fists my shirt, tugging me toward her. "I wonder what would've happened had you not insisted I get in your truck."

"We can go back even further than that. What if you would've actually stopped for fuel?"

She laughs. "While it's embarrassing, it's still my favorite mistake because it led me to you."

"Everything happens for a reason," I tell her, kissing her forehead. "I gotta leave and help Hudson on the farm."

"Okay, fine," she grumbles. "I just love your company and selfishly want to keep you to myself. Always."

"I know, darlin'. I can never get enough of you. Growing old together is gonna be fun." I shoot her a wink.

"Still waiting," she says, wiggling her left ring finger. I laugh, blow her a kiss, then leave. I climb in the truck and make my way to the farm.

Lately, my brother has been drowning himself in work, but it's getting harder on my parents to help take care of Colby. Grandma can't keep up with a three-year-old anymore. Claire even offered to help, but considering the shop isn't great for toddlers, everyone knows that won't work. In two years, my nephew will be in kindergarten, but until then, Hudson needs help.

I drive up to where my brother's sweating his ass off. When I get out of the truck, he ends the call and walks over to me.

"Remember the other day when I told you that I was going to search for a nanny?" He meets my eyes.

"Yeah, but I thought you were kidding."

He shoves his hands in his pockets and looks defeated. "I was, but I'm not anymore. Mom can't keep babysitting. Her and Dad's schedules are too hectic, and they can't lug Colby around. Of course, they're too nice to say anything, but the writing is on the wall."

"Hey, I'm happy to help you however I can. You ask, and I'll make it happen." It hurts my heart to see Hudson like this. He never complains about his situation and does the best he can for his son. But still, I notice how hard it's been for him the last two years, raising a baby as a single dad.

"I appreciate that, but it's no one's problem but my own. Something has to change, or I'm going to wear myself out."

I grab his shoulder and squeeze. "You don't have to do it alone, okay?"

"Thanks. Now, want to help me move all this shit?"

"Yeah." I look at the items that came from the storage shed that have to be moved because that's where the new building will go. Since the farm did so well this last season, Hudson had an incredible idea to build a shop where we could sell souvenirs on-site. Once this area is cleared, they'll start construction. They've told us it will take about six weeks to complete, which puts it finishing in the middle of August. We have no time to spare, and Hudson has been working his ass off to make it happen, but that responsibility comes with being the operational manager.

I move lawn equipment, extra saws, random axes, and metal chairs out of the building. When I head back, I hear Hudson screaming and shaking around.

"Is it on me?" He jumps and swats around.

"What? Tell me!"

"It was huge. Black." He brushes his arms and his back.

I let out a howl of laughter, searching him from head to toe. "No spider, dude."

He's heaving. "Fuck. Could've been a scorpion."

"I think you're fine. Just don't kill them. I've heard it's bad luck. Learned that when I was hikin' Big Bend one summer."

He glares at me. "Thank you for the random fact of the day. Seriously."

I chuckle. "You need to get laid, bro. You're wound up tighter than a ball of yarn."

"That's the last thing I need. With women comes trouble," he tells me. "I just want to be happy. Raise my boy. Live a quiet life." He huffs. "Why are you lookin' at me like that?"

"Because I said the same thing. Replace boy with cat."

Mr. Grumpy turns around and returns to the shed, carrying several boards over his shoulder. But when I pass him, I see the scorpion sitting on his shoulder. I point at it. "Hudson."

"Oh, shut up," he says. "I'm not falling for it."

"No, I swear." I step forward, quickly swiping it off and onto the ground. "Now you owe me."

His mouth falls open. "What the hell? Did you not see it on me the first time?"

"No! I swear it wasn't there. Must've been on those boards or something."

He drops them on the ground. "All right. I'm done for the day. I've had enough."

"I've got it," I tell him, looking in the doorway. There's not much left anyway.

"Thank you. I'm just not myself," he says, and I can tell he's not.

"Bad days happen. Go home. Get ready for tonight and all the fun we're gonna have." I grab several rakes, unsure why we have so many of them, and move them off to the side.

"Oh yeah. Tonight. Almost forgot about it." He chuckles. "Wouldn't miss it for the world."

"Thanks," I tell him, a smile meeting my lips. "We're gonna have a blast."

It takes me a few hours to clear everything out of the shed, and then I sand down the sign I'm repainting for the entrance. Now, since the farm isn't struggling, we've tried to spend the spring and summer doing maintenance and updates that have been put on the back burner. After I've cleared the chipped paint from one side, I call it a day.

Once I'm home, I take a shower and change into some nice shorts and a red polo, which is Claire's favorite color. Instead of taking the truck, I grab the keys to the bike. We've been taking it out more since the weather has been nice. Every Sunday, we cruise to the café for breakfast. I'll be sad when the temperatures start dropping because I love the way she holds on and presses against me.

I grab my helmet and then strap Claire's onto the back just in case she wants to ride home with me. As I crank the engine, I check my pocket to ensure I didn't forget anything, then make my way to town.

I'm amazed by how many people have arrived since earlier in the day. Most of the places on the lawn are taken. The sun is hanging lazily in the sky and should set within the next hour. I find Hank, Hudson, and Lucas, and they've set out a blanket and picnic basket for me and Claire. I open the top and see chocolate-covered strawberries and champagne. "Whose idea was this?"

Lucas and Hank glance over at Hudson.

"Damn, you're fancy," I tell him, knowing one day he's going to make someone happy. "Where's Colby?"

"Mom is feeding him cotton candy and popsicles, then they'll do some activities. Something about a fish pond and water guns. She said she'll return him to me when the fireworks start."

I snicker. "Once he's good and cranky from walking around and being overloaded with sugar."

"See what you have to look forward to?" Hudson smirks. "Love the little brat, though. Speaking of...here comes Claire."

"I'm gonna tell her you said that," I warn, and he shrugs. The two rib each other like siblings, but it's all in good fun. Hudson adores Claire, I guess because they're both grumpy.

When our gazes lock, I immediately smile, and so does she. In a crowd of people, all I see is her, the love of my life. She picks up her pace, and when we're close, she wraps her arms around me. Our lips slide together, and before I can deepen the kiss any further, Lucas groans.

"Get a room!" he protests. "I don't mind the kissing. It's the mouth sloshing that grosses me the fuck out."

Claire pulls away, her eyes wide as she stares into mine. "Do we mouth slosh? He's the second person who has said that today."

"No, they're just being dicks." I flip Lucas off. He pretends his hand is a fishing rod, casts a line, and then winds his middle finger upright. I roll my eyes.

"Oh, what's this?" Claire says. I drop to my knee, open the top, and pull out the strawberries and champagne.

I wanted to wait until the fireworks started, but I'm impatient. No, I have to do it right now. So I place my hand in my pocket and pull out the diamond ring. She covers her mouth and looks around. My brothers and best friend are grinning widely, and thankfully, one of them is recording the moment on his phone.

"Claire Caitlyn Chester Manchester. CeCe," I whisper her nickname.

She bursts into laughter as I grab her hand. I swallow hard, nervous as hell. My PTSD of what happened the last time I proposed hits me like a ton of bricks, but it's different with Claire. It's right. She's the one.

"You good?" I ask, and she nods, biting the corner of her lip. "You're my favorite person. You're beautiful. Smart. Caring and full of compassion, and though sometimes you're a Stubborn Susan, I can't imagine a future without you as my wife. I want to experience life with you and grow old together. I'll love you until the end of time, but I've just got one question. Will you be a good girl and marry me?"

EPILOGUE

CLAIRE

Butterflies erupt inside of me as soon as the question leaves his mouth. "Yes. Yes!"

I glance down at the ring he's holding, then wrap my arms around his neck, falling onto my knees in front of him, kissing him, telling him how much I love him and have always loved him. Too much emotion is pouring out of me, but I don't care. Being with this man has already been a dream, but now we have forever.

"Yes, JJ. I'll be honored to be your wife," I whisper in his ear, then I kiss him like tomorrow will never come. As he slides the ring on my finger, I study it and gasp, my bottom lip quivering. It's almost too much seeing it on my hand, sparkling.

"My mother's ring," I whisper, covering my mouth. He nods, wiping the tears streaming down my face and splashing onto my jeans. "You spoke to my father?" I ask.

He places his hand on my cheek. "Of course, darlin'. It's the Southern way."

"Thank you for this. It means so much." My emotions threaten to spill over.

"That makes me happy," he says against my lips.

The only thing that reminds me that we're in public and people are around are the awws. Then I hear a familiar voice in the crowd. When I turn, I see my sister Emma rushing toward me, and she's laughing. Her hair is down, and she's got on short shorts and a tank top. I push away from Jake and rush to her, pulling her into a tight hug.

"I missed it, didn't I?" She sticks out her bottom lip and looks at the ring.

"Wait, you knew?" We walk toward Jake and his brother, who are giving high fives to one another.

"Yes, if I wouldn't have gotten pulled over by the asshole state trooper, then maybe I'd have made it on time."

A howl of laughter escapes me. "He gave me a ticket, too. What a dick. I'm so excited you're here."

"Me too." She loops her arm in mine, and we join everyone.

"Jollys and Hank, this is my sister, Emma," I announce, and they each wave.

"This is Hank, Jake's best friend. Watch out. He likes to call us city slickers."

Emma laughs.

"This is Lucas, the youngest Jolly."

My sister's brow pops up as he walks over to her and takes her hand, giving her a kiss on the knuckles. "Nice to meet you." Lucas winks.

She turns to Jake. "You didn't tell me he's flirty."

I laugh and continue my introductions. "And this is Hudson, the oldest Jolly."

"Nice to meet you," Hudson says.

Emma smirks. And I know that look. "Pleasure is mine. Heard a lot about you," she offers.

"Ahh," Hudson says, glaring at Jake.

Unspoken words stream between them, and she turns to me. "Please tell me I didn't miss the fireworks show, too."

"Not yet," Jake says, giving her a hug. "How was your flight?"

"It was great." Emma pats his back. "So glad she's keeping you," she tells him.

"Me too," Jake confirms.

"So when's the wedding?" Emma asks.

I laugh. "We've been engaged for ten minutes and you expect me to have it planned already?"

Moments later, Colby runs over, bolts straight past Hudson and Jake, and runs to my arms.

"Hey, buddy," I tell him, seeing his lips are blue and sticky. "What did you have to eat?"

"Nothin'," he says.

Hudson walks over and tries to pick him up, but Colby shakes his head. "No."

Then Colby holds his arms out to Emma.

"But you don't even know me," she tells him.

"You look like CeCe." He points to me, and I chomp at his finger, making him squeal. He continues holding out his arms until she takes him. He lays his sticky face on her shirt.

"Okay, you're adorable," she remarks.

When I turn my head, I see Jake hugging his mother. "I forgot how much of a handful kids are. I think I'm officially old. He runs so fast," she huffs.

Hudson chuckles. "He does."

"Mom, this is Emma, Claire's sister," Jake says, giving the introduction.

"Hi, sweetie, so nice to meet you!" Jake's mother says. "I hope you'll join us for dinner one night."

"Oh gosh, I would love that. Yes, please," Emma says, still holding Colby.

I glance at Hudson, whose face is hard like stone. "Come on, cowboy, fireworks are about to start," Hudson says to Colby. "Gotta give Ms. Emma time to talk with her sister."

"No." Colby growls and puckers his lips, making his best mad face.

"It's fine," Emma says. "Unless you'd prefer I not."

Hudson's face softens. "No, I just don't want him to be a bother. He'll become your shadow."

"I don't mind," she confirms, then meets Colby's green eyes. "Are you a little bother?"

He grabs a piece of her hair and runs his sticky fingers through it. "No. I'm a good boy."

Jake chuckles and reaches forward to tickle him. "Tell her the truth! You're a handful."

"No! No, Unckie!" He screams loudly.

"Is that your favorite word?" Emma asks him.

"No." Then Colby's face cracks into a smirk. "You're pretty," he says.

She laughs. "Thank you. I like your shirt. And you're handsome."

"Like my daddy." He beams.

Emma meets Hudson's eyes, then she returns her attention back to Colby. "Yeah, just like your daddy."

The first firework soars into the sky right then, and the crowd erupts into applause. Jake and I settle on the blanket on the ground. Emma stays standing with Colby as Hudson stays close by them. Jake's brother says something to Emma, and I think I see her blush as she tucks her lips into her mouth.

"How long is your sister stayin' in town?" Jake asks, wrapping his arm around me as we continue watching the display. One after another, the fireworks shoot up and fall into glittery sparkles.

"You tell me. I didn't even know she was coming," I admit, smirking and glancing down at the ring on my finger.

"Ah, right. Forgot I invited her. I have no idea, either."

The crowd oohs and ahhs. I hear Colby laughing, Lucas and Hank chatting, and the sound of music drifts with the warm summer breeze.

"Are you happy?" Jake asks, his fingers brushing against my skin, causing goose bumps to form. That will never get old.

"God, yes," I assure him. He tries to kiss my cheek, and I turn my head, allowing our lips to collide. "And you?"

"Happiest man in the universe. You're everything I've ever wanted, CeCe. I have to pinch myself every day to make sure I'm not dreaming."

"Me too." I interlock my fingers with his.

The fireworks continue, and when the grand finale begins, Emma sits down next to me. "How long are you stayin'?"

"Maybe a month?" She looks at me like she's asking for my permission.

I meet her eyes, then glance at Hudson, who's wiping blue off Colby's face. "Sis, I have a feelin' a month won't be long enough."

She lowers her voice. "I overheard his mother say something about being unable to watch that adorable little boy next week."

"Yeah," I whisper. "He's been struggling with that."

Colby runs over to us and crawls into Jake's lap. "Oh, look who's finally choosing me," Jake says.

"Unkie JJ, look at my dinosaur." Colby pulls a toy out of his pocket and nearly pokes Jake in the eye with it.

I glance back and see Hudson shaking his head.

"What if I helped?" Emma grabs my hands. "You know I love kids. And I'm traveled out these days."

"Are you sick?" I lift my hand and put it on her forehead. "You don't feel warm."

Emma playfully pushes me away. "No. I'm just tired of not vacationing during my vacations. Sure, I've seen some beautiful places, but I'm always on the go, trying to capture the right shot. I just want to relax."

There was a time when Emma wanted to be a kindergarten teacher. At eighteen, she found her love for photography and traveling, then found an audience for her passions online. The rest is history. But she has been seeing the world for the last ten years with very few breaks.

"You can stay as long as you want," Jake offers, shooting Emma a wink. "It's not like CeCe's house is being used."

All I can do is laugh. "He's telling the truth. Now I just run home for a bathroom break if I have a lot of employees at work."

Emma chuckles. "You can still stop by and take a shit anytime you want."

I bump her shoulder. "I don't need your permission. But honestly, I'd be honored to have you stay there as long as you want. You should be careful, though."

"Why's that?"

"You might never want to leave."

After the fireworks show, I hug my sister goodbye and then text her my address and the code to get in. Then Jake leads me back to his motorcycle and hands me a helmet. He puts his on, and I bite my lip.

"Damn, you look good enough to eat," I mutter.

His cheeks squish against the helmet, and he smiles. "Funny. I was thinkin' the same about you."

After he cranks it and backs it up into the street, I hop on the back, wrapping my arms tightly around his waist. He doesn't live that far from town, and I enjoy riding with him, though we've only gone short distances. At each stop sign, he reaches back and places his strong hand on my thigh.

By the time we get home, I'm ready to rip off his clothes and ride him.

As he shuts down the engine on the bike, he removes his helmet. Then he gives me his hand, helping steady me as I place both feet on the ground and remove mine.

"Did I overhear your sister say she wants to help my brother?"

"Yeah." I laugh, running my fingers through my hair, trying to remove the tiny tangles from the wind.

"Did you tell her he was searchin' for a nanny?" he asks, grabbing my hand.

"I thought you said he was kidding."

"Apparently not, based on our conversation today."

I lift my eyebrow at him, wondering what this might mean. My sister is kind-spirited but also very eccentric, outgoing, and outspoken. "I don't think Hudson could handle her."

Jake laughs. "I'd agree with that."

As soon as we walk inside, Tinsel meows from the couch, too comfortable and lazy to greet us. Just as I'm about to speak, Jake presses my back against the door and nibbles on my neck. I love how he smells like man and sweat.

When his hard cock presses against me, I moan.

"I have a confession," I whisper. He sucks on my earlobe as I reach down and grab him.

"Shoot."

"I'd like to get married as soon as possible."

Jake smirks. "Don't tempt me with a good time, darlin'."

Did you enjoy *A Very Merry Mistake* and want more of Jake and Claire? Download this exclusive bonus scene that I wrote just for you!
https://bit.ly/avmmjjandcece

Need to know what happens between Hudson and Emma? *Continue reading the series in A Very Merry Nanny*
https://www.books2read.com/averymerrynanny

WHAT'S NEXT?

♥A VERY MERRY NANNY♥

A *Very Merry Nanny* is a single-dad contemporary romance with rom-com vibes. The hero is broody, and the heroine is pure joy. If you're searching for a small-town age gap, grumpy/sunshine romance set in a small Southern town, this book is for you! Each book in the *Very Merry Series* can be read as a standalone and ends with a sweet as gingerbread happily ever after.

https://www.books2read.com/averymerrynanny

WANT MORE LYRA?

The Valentine Series

Bless Your Heart
(enemies to lovers)

Spill the Sweet Tea
(second-chance)

Butter My Biscuit
(friends to lovers)

Smooth as Whiskey
(secret relationship/age gap)

Fixing to be Mine
(landlord/secret identity)

Hold Your Horses
(fake dating)

The Valentine Series is a Southern small-town interconnected stand alone series. The books can be read in any order and end with a happily ever after!

AUTHOR'S NOTE

I wasn't sure if I would write this book this year, and the more people I told about it, the more encouragement I got to do it. So, I did.

This is the longest book I've <u>ever</u> personally written in the history of my career. It's thicccccc, and I could've added more because I love Merryville, the characters, and even Tinsel.

Over the last few months, my friends would ask what I was working on, because I'd been quiet, and I'd tell them about *this* Christmas book. I'd go into detail about Jake Jolly (because I love a kitschy name) and how his family owns a Christmas tree farm that's failing. Their eyes instantly lit up with excitement. I felt like I had something special, and I still believe that. It's the magic of Merryville!

A Very Merry Mistake is a love letter to my readers. The nice guy does get the (good) girl. And sometimes mistakes are really miracles in disguise. I hope reading this feels like a warm snuggly blanket, a fluffy gray cat, and drinking a hot cup of coffee on an icy cold day...I hope it's a comfort to read.

ACKNOWLEDGMENTS

I'm going to *try* to keep this short and sweet!

A big thank you always goes out to my readers, who are always as excited as me about my books. You are the reason I get to keep doing this! I'm so appreciative. Thank you to my ARC reviewers for giving me so much grace and patience when I was working on little sleep. You're incredible and I'm so honored to have you all on my team!

A gigantic thank you to Erica Rogers for reading my *raw* words. Your reactions and comments were exactly what I needed. Thank you for loving Jake and Claire and my words. I'm honored and happy to have you in my corner and literary life.

A huge shout-out goes to Becca Mysoor for being *THE* Fairy Plot-Mother. Thank you, Becca, for chatting with me about this book when I felt stuck and reminding me to remember my WHY and WHO I am as an author. Talking it through with you got the cogs turning and helped me finish strong. I'm genuinely thankful for you and your time! (Without her, y'all would've gotten a completely different ending to this book. Maybe one day I'll share!)

The rest of the thanks go to my team for pulling through and helping make this book happen. It takes a village, y'all! Meg Latorre, thank you so much for everything you do. Without you, I wouldn't be able to juggle it all. Your excitement and encouragement give me life! I'm so grateful for your friendship!

Big thanks go to JS Cooper for pushing me to do this. When I had this idea and wasn't sure if I'd add it to my schedule, you gave me the encouragement I needed. I'm not sure this book would exist right now without that. 2024 is ours!

As always, I can't leave without thanking my editing team! Thanks go to Kiezha for working on my book instead of reading Iron Flame. I'm still sorry! Thanks, Rosa, for being my Fairy Proofmother! I've got all the fairy literary mamas in my life, and I feel like an author princess!

Last but not least, I'm always thankful for my hubby, Will (Deep Sky Dude), who makes me laugh, listens to me talk nonstop about my spicy Hallmark books, and reminds me to drink water when I've been working too hard. I love you and am so lucky to get to spend the rest of my life with you.

KEEP IN TOUCH

Want to become one of my VIP readers? Join my newsletter! It's where all the cool kids are, plus I'll keep you updated with what I'm currently working on. It's where I primarily share my ARC (advanced review copy) sign-ups, exclusive giveaways, and more. You'll get access to covers, teasers, and chapter reveals before anyone else!

Join the party:
lyraparish.com/newsletter

Let's be friends on social media:
TikTok 🤍 Instagram 🤍 Facebook

ABOUT LYRA PARISH

Lyra Parish is a hopeless romantic who is obsessed with writing spicy Hallmark-like romances. When she isn't immersed in fictional worlds, you can find her pretending to be a Vanlifer with her hubby. Lyra's a Virgo who loves coffee, the great outdoors, authentic people, and living her best life.

Made in the USA
Coppell, TX
30 December 2024

43714774R00225